DESPERATE
WARRIOR

DESPERATE
WARRIOR

DAYS OF WAR, DAYS OF PEACE
CHATO'S CHIRICAHUA APACHE LEGACY
VOLUME ONE

W. MICHAEL
FARMER

WILL ROGERS MEDALLION-WINNING AUTHOR
OF *THE ODYSSEY OF GERONIMO*

HAT CREEK

HAT CREEK

an imprint of
Roan & Weatherford Publishing Associates, LLC
Bentonville, Arkansas

Library of Congress Cataloging-in-Publication Data
Names: Farmer, W. Michael
Title: Desperate Warrior/W. Michael Farmer |
Days of War, Days of Peace: Chato's Chiricahua Legacy #1
Description:First Edition. | Bentonville: Hat Creek, 2023.
Identifiers: LCCN: 2023951092 | ISBN: ISBN: 978-1-63373-874-4 (hardcover) |
ISBN: 978-1-63373-875-1 (trade paperback) | ISBN: 978-1-63373-876-8 (eBook)
Subjects: FICTION/Indigenous | FICTION/Historical | FICTION/Westerns |
LC record available at: https://lccn.loc.gov/2023951092

Hat Creek trade paperback edition December, 2023

Cover Design & Interior Design by Casey W. Cowan
Cover art by Herman W. Hansen (1854-1924)
Apache Indians on Horseback, 1910, Watercolor on Paper
Editing by Amy Cowan

For Corky, my best friend and wife,
the wind beneath my wings

ACKNOWLEDGMENTS

THERE HAVE BEEN many friends and professionals who have supported me in this work, to whom I owe a special debt of gratitude for their help and many kindnesses.

Lynda Sánchez's encouragement and insights into Apache culture and their voices are a major point of reference in understanding the times and personalities covered in this work.

Audra Gerber provided excellent editorial support that contributed to this work's clarity.

Good friends, a rare and a true gift, Pat Fraley and Mike Alexander, supported me during numerous visits to New Mexico, allowing me time and a place from which to do research that otherwise would not have been possible.

The patience, encouragement, and support of my wife, Carolyn, through long days of research and writing made this work possible, and it is to her this work is dedicated.

The histories listed in Additional Reading that I found particularly helpful were those by Angie Debo; Eve Ball, Nora Henn, and Lynda Sánchez; Alicia Delgadillo and Miriam A. Perrett; Lynda Sánchez; Sherry Robinson; Edwin Sweeney; and Robert Utley.

TABLE of CONTENTS

CHARACTERS

APACHE

- **Ahnandia:** *Bedonkohe Apache. Warrior with Geronimo in 1886 surrender break away. Good friends with George Wratten. Married Tah-das-te, a messenger to White Eyes for Geronimo.*
- **Atelnietze:** *Chokonen Apache. Strong warrior and cousin to Naiche. Stayed in Mexico after Geronimo surrendered.*
- **Beshe:** *Chokonen Apache. Rode with Niache's band. Father of Haozinne. Lived to be 100 years old.*
- **Beneactinay:** *Chokonen Apache. Close friend of Tzoe. Only warrior killed during Chato's raid north in March 1883.*
- **Betzinez:** *Chihenne Apache, young cousin to Geronimo who served him as a novitiate until 1885 breakout.*
- **Big Dave:** *First Sergeant of White Mountain scouts who supported Chato in the attack on Chihuahua's camp after the 1885 Geronimo breakout.*
- **Bi-yah-neta:** *Chiricahua Apache. Taken on Geronimo's raid on Fort Apache Chiricahua. Married Perico in late 1885.*
- **Bonito:** *Chiricahua chief who led March 1883 raid that took Charlie McComas*
- **Bylas:** *White Mountain chief supporting Mestas at George Stevens sheep camp on Ash Flats.*

- **Cathla:** *Chokonen Apache leader in March 1883 raid north with Chato.*
- **Charley:** *Scout supporting Chato after 1885 breakout (also known as Askadodilges).*
- **Chato:** *Chief and feared warrior of Chokonen Apache band (c.1854—1934).*
  - **Chato's Family**
    - **Nalthchedah:** *First wife to Chato; Divorced Chato, married Dexter Loco about 1896.*
      - **Horace:** *Son of Chato and Nalthchedah (c. 1879—1888).*
    - **Ishchos:** *Second wife to Chato (c. 1847 – died in Mexico, date unknown).*
      - **Maud:** *Elder daughter of Chato and Ishchos (c. 1873—1902).*
      - **Bediscloye:** *Son of Chato and Ishchos (c. 1876—died in Mexico).*
      - **Naboka:** *Daughter of Chato and Ishchos (c. 1879—died in Mexico).*
    - **Helen:** *Third wife to Chato. Married at Fort Marion (c. 1872—died at Mescalero c.1944).*
      - **Maurice:** *Elder Son of Chato, mother was Helen, born Mount Vernon Barracks. (1891—1915) Married Lena Kaydahzinne.*
        - **Esther:** *Daughter of Maurice (1911—1912).*
        - **Alexander:** *Son of Maurice (1913—?).*
      - **Blake:** *Son of Chato and Helen, born Fort Sill (1894-1908).*
      - **Cyril:** *Son of Chato and Helen, born Fort Sill (c. 1897—1898).*
    - **Banatsi:** *Chato's widowed sister. Never remarried. Died at Mescalero (c. 1857 – died at Mescalero, date unknown).*
- **Chihuahua:** *sub-chief of Chokonen Apache, protégé of Cochise, primary leader of first group of Chiricahua shipped to Fort Marion in the spring of 1886.*
- **Chiva:** *White Mountain Apache married into Bedonkohe. Leader of small band at San Carlos.*
- **Colle:** *Chokonen Apache, member of Chihuahua's band in the breakout of 1885.*
- **Cooney:** *Scout and long-time friend of Chato.*
- **Daklugie:** *"Nephew" (second cousin) of Geronimo. Daklugie's mother Ishton was Geronimo's cousin, but he called her his "sister" and claimed Juh was his brother-in-law. Apache cattle herd manager. Eight years of study at Carlisle Indian Industrial School. Married Ramona Chihuahua.*
- **Dutchy:** *Scout supporting Chato for Lieutenant Britton Davis in 1885.*
- **Eclahheh:** *Chokonen Apache. Second wife of Naiche who he shot in the leg during the March 1886 surrender to General Crook.*

- **Fun:** *"Brother of Geronimo" (second cousin), a Britton Davis scout who intended to kill Davis and Chato in 1885.*
- **Geronimo:** Di-yen *(Shaman) and war leader whose chief was Naiche (c. 1823—1909).*
  - **Geronimo's Family**
    - **Chee-hash-kish:** *Wife to Geronimo.*
      - **Chappo:** *Son of Geronimo and Chee-hash-kish.*
      - **Dohn-say:** *Daughter of Geronimo and Chee-hash-kish. Married Mike Dahkeya, a Geronimo warrior.*
    - **She-gha:** *Wife to Geronimo.*
    - **Shtsha-she:** *Wife to Geronimo.*
    - **Zi-yeh:** *Wife to Geronimo.*
      - **Fenton:** *Son of Geronimo and Zi-yeh.*
      - **Eva:** *Daughter of Geronimo and Zi-yeh (Geronimo's last child).*
    - **Ih-tedda:** *Mescalero wife to Geronimo, taken in 1885, divorced in 1889.*
      - **Lenna:** *Daughter of Geronimo and Ih-tedda.*
      - **Robert:** *Son of Geronimo and Ih-tedda.*
- **Gil-lee:** *Chiricahua Apache camp leader in 1884.*
- **Gooday:** *Grandson of Loco and Mangas Coloradas. Sent to Carlisle as part of Fort Marion Children in 1886.*
- **Haozinne:** *Chokonen Apache and youngest wife of Naiche.*
- **Haskehagola:** *Chihenne Apache scout with General Crook 1883. Brother-in-law to Chato.*
- **Huera:** *Wife of Mangas. Best of the tulepai makers. Escaped from Mexican slavery after being taken captive when Victorio was defeated.*
- **Ishton:** *Bedonkohe Apache. Wife of Juh, "sister" of Geronimo, mother of Daklugie.*
- **Jacali:** *Nednhi Apache. Daughter of Juh. Wounded in leg during Rarámuri attack Jan. 1883.*
- **Juh:** *(pronounced "whoa") "Brother-in-law of Geronimo," Chief and di-yen of the Nednhi Apache.*
- **Jelikinne:** *Father-in-law (Zi-yeh's father) to Geronimo, leading warrior.*
- **Kayitah:** *Scout with Chato in 1885 search for Geronimo in Mexico and a warrior wounded in Aliso Creek fight.*
- **Kaytennae:** *Second in command to Nana and later leader of the Mimbreño Apache.*
- **Loco:** *Chief of the Chihenne Apache who preferred a path of peace.*

- **Mangas:** *Chihenne Apache chief, son of Mangas Coloradas, named Carl Mangas by the army.*
- **Martine:** *Scout with Chato in 1885 search for Geronimo in Mexico and later with Kayitah helped convince Geronimo-Naiche band to surrender to General Miles.*
- **Mestas:** *Former child captive of Geronimo. Didn't want to live with Apache. Geronimo traded him away. He was the Stevens ranch range boss at the Ash Flat Massacre.*
- **Nahdeyole:** *Chokonen Apache wife to Naiche. Divorced around 1892 or 1893.*
- **Naiche:** *Chief of Chokonen Apache, youngest son of Cochise, friend of Chato.*
- **Nana:** *Married to Geronimo's sister, Nah-dos-te, a war leader of the Chihenne Apache.*
- **Na-ni-Isoage:** *Apache scout with General Crook in 1883.*
- **Noch-ay-del-klinne:** *The Cibecue prophet who claimed he could raise the long dead great chiefs. He was killed when Colonel Carr tried to arrest him.*
- **Nolgee:** *Nednhi leader and most of his band killed while drunk by Mexican military at Janos.*
- **Perico:** *"Brother of Geronimo" (second cousin), Second Sergeant behind First Sergeant Chato in Britton Davis's scout command who intended to help Fun kill Davis and Chato.*
- **She-neah:** *Bedonkohe Apache di-yen killed in the attack and killing of Juan Mata Ortiz near Chocolate Pass.*
- **Shoie:** *Chokonen Apache. Scout who broke out with Geronimo in 1885.*
- **Sons-nah:** *Young Chiricahua woman beaten by drunk older husband, Was-i-tona.*
- **Tisnah:** *Bedonkohe Apache, brother to Fun, Perico, and Geronimo. Strong warrior.*
- **Toclanny:** *Major scout at Fort Apache and sergeant in the army at Mount Vernon Barracks.*
- **Tzoe:** *Cibecue Apache who guided General Crook to Chiricahua camps in the Sierra Madre.*
- **Tuzzone:** *Chokonen Apache. Scout supporting Captain Crawford after 1883 Chiricahua surrender.*
- **Ulzana:** *Segundo and brother to Chihuahua.*
- **Victorio:** *Great war chief and leader of the Chihenne Apache.*
- **Was-i-tona:** *Chiricahua Apache warrior who beat his wife Sons-nah and was punished with two weeks in the calaboose. His arrest gave impetus to the 1885 breakout.*
- **Yahnozah:** *Chokonen/Nednhi Apache. One of Geronimo's best warriors in 1886 break away*

- **Zele:** *Chokohen chief of a small band of Chiricahua living near Loco's People at San Carlos.*

FICTIONAL

- **Yellow Boy:** *Mescalero Apache. Retired tribal policeman. Legendary shot with Henry rifle.*

MEXICANS

- *Coronel* **Joaquin Terrazas:** *Premier Chihuahuan Indian fighter.*
- **Juan Mata Ortiz:** *Segundo to Joaquin Terrazas. Killed in 1882 near Galeana by Juh, Geronimo, and Chiricahua warriors in revenge for killing Victorio.*

SPECIALIZED NAMES

- **Blue Mountains:** *The name the Apache used for the Sierra Madre.*
- **Coyote:** *Clever but sometimes foolish character in Apache teaching stories.*
- **Owl-man Giant:** *Monster in Apache mythology.*
- **People:** *Capitalized when referring to a collective group as a whole, like the Apache.*
- **Power:** *Power is capitalized when referring to supernatural power.*

ANGLOS

- **Captain Emmett Crawford:** *San Carlos Indian Agent and with Captain Wirt Davis a chief of operations officer in Mexico for General Crook in 1885 charged with bringing in Geronimo's band.*
- **Captain Wirt Davis:** *With Emmett Crawford was a chief operations officer in Mexico for General Crook in 1885 and charged with bringing in Geronimo's band.*
- **Lieutenant Britton Davis:** *Commander of Fort Apache Chiricahua before 1885 breakout.*
- **Lieutenant James Lockett:** *Replaced Britton Davis as Fort Apache Reservation commander for the Chiricahua Apache.*
- **Lieutenant Marion P. Maus:** *Second in command to Captain Crawford, who after Crawford's murder by Mexican paramilitary Rarámuri negotiated Geronimo's March 1886 meeting with General Crook.*
- **General George Crook:** *Directed the war against Chiricahua from 1882 until 1886.*
- **General Nelson Appleton Miles:** *Replaced General Crook and made surrender terms to the Chiricahua that were never kept.*

- **John Clum:** *San Carlos Agent 1874-1877.*

- **Sam Bowman:** *Interpreter and Lieutenant Britton Davis's camp supporter in 1884/1885.*

- **Charlie McComas:** *Six-year-old white child taken during Chato-Bonito raid north of the border in March 1883.*

- **Lyman Hart:** *San Carlos Agent 1877-1879. Freed Geronimo and his war leaders from the guardhouse upon arrival at San Carlos in 1877.*

- **Albert Sterling:** *Chief of tribal police at San Carlos. He was killed during Loco breakout.*

- **Al Sieber:** *Chief of Scouts at San Carlos Reservation.*

- **Joseph C. Tiffany:** *Agent at San Carlos 1880–1882.*

- **Colonel Eugene Asa Carr:** *Commander at Fort Apache who arrested the prophet, Noch-ay-del-kinne, in 1881.*

APACHE WORDS

AND PHRASES

- *Ch'ik'eh doleel:* all right; let it be so
- *Di-yen:* medicine woman or man
- *Doo dat'éé da:* it's okay; it doesn't matter
- *Enjuh:* good
- *Googé:* whip-poor-will
- *Haheh:* a young girl's puberty ceremony
- *Isdzán:* woman
- *Ish-kay-neh:* boy
- *Ish-tia-neh:* woman
- *Iyah:* mesquite bean pods
- *Nadah:* Baked Agave
- *Nakai-yes:* Mexicans
- *Nakai-yi:* Mexican
- *Nant'an:* leader
- *Nant'an Lpah:* Gray leader
- *Nish'ii':* I see you
- *Pesh:* iron
- *Pesh-klitso:* metal or gold
- *Pesh-lickoyee:* nickel-plated or silver (literally "white iron")
- *Pindah-lickoyee:* White-eyed enemies
- *Rarámuri:* Mexican Indians also known as Tarahumara. Phenomenal distance runners.

- *Shiyé:* Son
- *Tobaho:* Tobacco
- *Tsach:* cradleboard
- *Tulepai:* (Lit. Gray water) Corn beer, also known as *tizwin*
- *Ugashé:* go

Reckoning of Time & Seasons
- *Harvest:* used in the context of time, means a year
- *Handwidth (against the sky):* about an hour
- *Season of Little Eagles:* early spring
- *Season of Many Leaves:* late spring, early summer
- *Season of Large Leaves:* midsummer
- *Season of Large Fruit:* late summer, early fall
- *Season of Earth is Reddish Brown:* late fall
- *Season of Ghost Face:* lifeless winter
- *Sun:* used in the context of time, means a day

Spanish
- *Ándale pues:* Go on now
- *Ataqué:* attack
- *Arroyo:* a small steep-sided waterway with a flat floor and usually dry except during heavy rain
- *Bosque:* brush and trees lining a waterway
- *Capitán:* Captain
- *Casa:* house
- *Hacendado:* wealthy landowner
- *Llano: open grassy plain,* dry prairie
- *Playa:* the flat sandy, salty, or mud-caked flat floor of a desert basin usually covered by shallow water during or after prolonged heavy rain
- *Que paso?:* What's happening?
- *Retirarse:* retreat
- *Rebozo:* shawl
- *Río Grande:* Great River
- *Segundo:* second in command
- *Teniente:* lieutenant

CHIRICAHUA APACHE BANDS

- *Bedonkohe:* Located in eastern central Arizona and western central New Mexico. Originally Geronimo's band as a young man. Eventually merged with Mimbreños and other bands.

- *Chokonen:* Located in southern Arizona. Band of Cochise and later his son Naiche.

- *Chihenne:* Also known as Warm Springs, Mimbres, or Mimbreños, Located in the Mimbreño Mountains of New Mexico. Band of Victorio, Loco, Nana, and Kaytennae.

- *Nednhi:* Located primarily in the mountains of Sonora and Chihuahua in northern Mexico. Band led by Juh.

INTRODUCTION

BEGINNING ABOUT 1877, the name of a warrior, *Pedes-klinje*—or as the Mexicans called him, *Chato* (meaning "flat nose")—appears often in the history of the Apache wars. Until 1883, he was known as a fierce, power-hungry, and belligerent fighter with no tolerance for those of his People who wanted peace with the White Eyes. He was often Geronimo's *segundo* (second in command) for many raids and battles after they escaped San Carlos Reservation in September 1881. In April 1882, he was a leader with Geronimo in forcing Loco's People at San Carlos to leave the reservation and join the other Chiricahua in Mexico. In March 1883, Chato and Bonito, with twenty-four of the best Chiricahua warriors, led a lightning raid out of Mexico's Sierra Madre Mountains and across southern New Mexico and Arizona. They killed anyone in their path, taking arms, ammunition, and supplies, and a little redheaded boy, Charlie McComas, after killing his father, Federal Judge H.C. McComas, and mother, Juniata, on the road between Silver City and Lordsburg.

In May 1883, General Crook led fifty cavalry troopers and nearly two hundred Apache scouts across the border on what Chato, Geronimo, and the other Chiricahua leaders believed was mission impossible––find Chiricahua camps in the Sierra Madre and bring the Chiricahua back to San Carlos. Crook's scouts found the hidden Apache camps in the Sierra Madre and destroyed Chato's camp before Crook could stop them. After talking with Crook, the Chiricahua agreed to return to the San Carlos Reservation. It was a high risk, near bloodless coup on Crook's part.

When he talked with General Crook in the Sierra Madre, Chato had an epiphany and change in attitude toward the army. The fact that Crook had found his camp, convinced the Mexican authorities to let him cross the border, and used the People as scouts against the Chiricahua convinced Chato that Crook had God-given power. Crook promised Chato that he would try to free Chato's beloved wife, Ishchos, and their two children, Bediscloye and Naboka, taken into Mexican slavery five months earlier. Chato, inspired and filled with hope, vowed to support Crook.

In the years that followed, Chato, desperate to free his wife and children from Mexican slavery, never failed to support General Crook or his officers. As a result of Chato's support for the Blue Coats, Geronimo, who had once called him his *segundo*, branded him a "traitor and liar." Chato, who became a leader among the Chiricahua wanting peace with the White Eyes, worked hard to find and return the Chiricahua led by Geronimo, the so-called "war faction," who had broken out of the Fort Apache Reservation in May 1885.

After Geronimo surrendered in September 1886, the army made its Apache scouts, including Chato and the Chiricahua who had stayed on the reservation (about 70 percent of the People), prisoners of war along with those who surrendered. All the Chiricahua were prisoners for the next twenty-seven years in one of the most shameful episodes in American history.

After the Chiricahua were freed in 1913, Chato, who never got his wife and children out of Mexican slavery, moved with most of the Chiricahua to the Mescalero Reservation. Chato's story is told in two books: Book 1, Desperate Warrior; and Book 2, Proud Outcast. Book 1, Desperate Warrior covers the years from 1877 to early 1886. In those years, Chato changed from a power-hungry, belligerent warrior to a hardworking and wise supporter of General Crook, desperate to get his wife and children out of Mexican slavery. Book 2, Proud Outcast covers the years from 1886 to 1934, when Chato survived betrayal by the army as a prisoner of war and proudly endured being treated as an outcast by some of his own People after they were freed.

Chato's story is taken from history, but its truth is told through fiction as imaginatively seen from the eyes of Chato, whom Lieutenant Britton Davis, his former commander, described in 1929 as "the finest man, red or white, I ever knew."

PROLOGUE

"CHATO, SOME OF your People say you're a traitor and a liar. You and Helen live up here at Apache Summit alone. When the men with picture boxes come to the reservation, you always wear the big silver medal the Great Father gave you many harvests ago. All these are threads blowing in the wind. I've known you for a few moons now, and you never speak about these things. Your lifeway doesn't fit any of the insults I hear thrown at you. I'd like to know. What's your story?"

Chato took a swallow of hot coffee from his speckled, enameled blue cup and frowning poked at the fire with a long yucca stalk, making sparks rise toward the myriad stars floating in the clear, startling blackness above them. He looked at his friend Yellow Boy, a Mescalero policeman, the legendary shot with his old Yellow Boy Henry rifle. "Ain't many who want to know my side of the story. You sure you do?"

Yellow Boy nodded, took a swallow of coffee from his cup, then said, "I've seen and killed bad men in my time. I know you ain't the bad man some of the Chiricahua say you are. You've kept your silence since I've known you. I want to make up my own mind. I want to know both sides. Tell me yours."

Chato gave the fire another poke and, laying aside his yucca stick, stood and gathered more wood to throw on the fire. Coyotes yipped their mournful songs as he tossed the wood on the flames. "All right. I tell you my story, but it takes many fires to tell. People who slur my name don't know or understand much about me. Are you willing to come here many times to hear all my story? I only tell it once, and that for you."

"Speak, and I will listen."

Chato stared at the flames and took another swallow of the black coffee, "Some of my People call me a traitor and liar. If Geronimo said it was so, then they believe it must be so. I wanted to be a great chief. He didn't like the way I went about it. I start my story with the first and only time Geronimo was captured. It was the beginning of ten harvests of war and peace. In that time, I realized the Blue Coats knew how to help us in ways we didn't yet know. Our People needed the White Eyes to show them the way. Three of those harvests, I led the scouts, some Chiricahua, to stop Geronimo's war and bring peace. It was in those days that Geronimo began calling me a traitor. He tried to have his brothers kill me when he left Fort Apache the last time."

Chato stared at the yellow and blue flames, took another swallow of coffee, then began the first of many storytelling times at his fire.

IN THE HARVEST the White Eyes call 1877, San Carlos Reservation Agent John Clum tricked and took captive Geronimo and five or six of his war leaders. He shackled them in chains at Ojo Caliente Reservation, where Victorio and Loco were chiefs for the Chihenne Apache People. Clum didn't put me and a few others he arrested in chains like he did Geronimo and his leaders. He knew we had been raiding too. He made clear to us that we were his prisoners. We also had to go to San Carlos with him.

Before returning to San Carlos, Clum talked Victorio and Loco into coming with him and moving their People to San Carlos. They were fools. Old Loco always wanted peace with the White Eyes. That's why we called him Loco. Victorio, a powerful war chief who accepted no nonsense from Apache or White Eyes, went to San Carlos because Clum convinced him it was a better place for his People. Clum and his Apache scouts lied when they told Victorio, Loco, and other Chihenne that San Carlos was a better place to live than Ojo Caliente. Victorio and Loco knew that the hundred Apache scouts and about one hundred fifty Blue Coats with him had come to make good what Clum had requested.

Other warriors and I walked three weeks in the heat and dust across what the White Eyes call the "Black Range" in western New Mexico and eastern Arizona as Clum's prisoners while Geronimo and the others in chains rode in a wagon under heavy guard. They never had a chance to run and hide. At San

Carlos, Clum told me I was free on the reservation if I agreed to stay inside the reservation boundary and do as I was told. I didn't want to live in the guardhouse like Geronimo. I gathered my People in a village on the Río Gila next to my friend the Chokonen chief, Naiche, youngest son of Cochise, who was close to my age, maybe a harvest or two younger.

Clum locked Geronimo and his leaders in the guardhouse. There, they waited for the sheriff from Tucson to claim them for a White Eye hanging ceremony. The sheriff never came, and Clum, angry with his great chiefs in the east over other reservation matters, quit and left San Carlos. The new agent, Lyman Hart, talked with Geronimo, saw no reason to keep him and his leaders locked up, and let them leave the guardhouse. They went to their wives' camp in Naiche's village. They lived in peace there for nearly two harvests.

The agents at San Carlos cheated us of our rations and made us live at places near the Río Gila where shaking sickness (malaria) came often to the People. I hated San Carlos. I was ready to leave like most others, but if only a few ran away at one time, the Blue Coats, using their good-for-nothing White Mountain scouts, would catch us before we reached the border. I despised those White Mountain scouts. One day, I vowed to the great god, *Ussen*, to repay them measure for measure for all they had done to us.

In three moons, soon after Geronimo was let out of the guardhouse, Victorio had his fill of San Carlos and left the reservation in a rage, stealing White Mountain horses and killing anyone who got in his way. Geronimo advised Naiche, who had asked him to serve as his counselor, not to follow Victorio and the Chihenne off the reservation. Naiche stayed at San Carlos. Since Geronimo's advice sounded good to me, I didn't follow the Chihenne out either.

Lyman Hart heard about the advice Geronimo had given Naiche. It so impressed Hart that he made Geronimo the *"capitán"* of the few Chihenne who had stayed at San Carlos. Geronimo suspected Lyman Hart wanted him to spy on the Chihenne if he took the job. He took the job but decided not to tell Hart everything he knew.

Nine or ten moons later, Geronimo believed he was responsible for a nephew's suicide during a *tizwin* drinking spree and decided it was time to leave the reservation for the land of the *Nakai-yes* (Mexico). He took a few of the People with him, mostly his relatives, and with the help of his brother-in-law, Juh, who had come to the reservation from the land of the *Nakai-yes*, left the reservation and joined Juh in his stronghold on a big flat-top mountain in Chihuahua about half a day's ride west of Casas Grandes.

Naiche didn't follow Geronimo out because he had promised his father, Cochise, that as a leader of the Chokonen Chiricahua, he would avoid war with the White Eyes for as long as he could. I was tempted to go out with Geronimo then but decided to wait with Naiche and see what happened to Geronimo and Juh.

Juh and Geronimo raided mostly in the land of the *Nakai-yes*. All the while, Juh tried to force the *Nakai-yes* in Chihuahua to make a treaty with him that gave them peace from his raids in return for rations when the Apache needed them. The treaty allowed him to raid in Sonora and sell what he stole in Chihuahua. He had done that for a long time. The *Nakai-yes* had other things in mind. They wanted to wipe Juh out and make slaves of his People.

Victorio started his war with the White Eyes four or five moons after Geronimo left the reservation. Juh and Geronimo rode with Victorio on a few raids later that harvest in the Season of Large Fruit, but most of the time, they stayed in the land of the *Nakai-yes*.

When General Willcox learned Juh and Geronimo were trying to negotiate a peace for themselves in Chihuahua, his representatives—Gordo, Ah-dis, who had ridden the raiding trail with Juh and were his friends, and *Teniente* Haskell who spoke for General Willcox—talked them into returning to San Carlos, where Haskell promised that the problems with the agents stealing rations from the Indians had been solved and that they would be left alone if they stayed on the reservation and didn't cause trouble.

Juh and Geronimo kept their promises about staying on the reservation and not causing any trouble, and Willcox kept his agents straight. As the Victorio War dragged on, Victorio began to have fewer victories in battles until, in the Season of Large Fruit, Victorio, nearly out of bullets, killed himself in a big battle with *Nakai-yi* military at Tres Castillos in Chihuahua. Juh and Geronimo were glad then that they had returned to the reservation and appeared to do everything they could to keep the peace, but appearances can be deceiving.

Nearly a harvest passed. I learned Geronimo planned to escape the reservation again. I decided to follow him. Geronimo was a *di-yen* (shaman) with many gifts, a man of great Power and war fighting skills. I knew he could teach me much about being a great chief, which I wanted more than anything else. I thought being a great chief would make it easier to settle the blood debt I had with certain White Eyes and the White Mountain scouts who killed my brother and father, José Mangas, brother of the great Mangas Coloradas. Those Blue Coats and White Mountains had to pay for what they did to my family. I had to make the Blue Coats pay, even if I had to smile at them before I sent them to their Happy Land, but I didn't have to smile for the White Mountain scouts. They knew I was an enemy. One day, I would come for them. Geronimo and Juh could teach us all how to live and survive in the land of the *Nakai-yes,* live strong and straight, take what we wanted when we wanted it, not live like a dog with his tail between his legs, trembling before being kicked and whipped like Loco, once a brave man, when the White Eyes were around.

FOUR HARVESTS AFTER Geronimo escaped the guardhouse, the Cibecue Apache prophet, Noch-ay-del-klinne, who claimed he could raise the great dead chiefs, was killed when *Coronel* Carr took him into custody. Some of the prophet's followers attacked Carr, killed Blue Coats, scouts, and White Eyes they found on the reservation and then disappeared. The San Carlos villages of all the bands, filled with desperation over the death of their prophet, fell into a restless calm. It was the kind of calm that comes before a big wind when crackling tension fills the still air before lighting arrows fly.

Blue Coats, so many that a man couldn't do his personal business without seeing cavalry hats passing above nearby brush, swarmed over San Carlos looking for those accused of attacking Carr. Leaders who had nothing to do with the prophet—Chihuahua, Juh, Geronimo, and others—worried that the Blue Coats intended to take them to the guardhouse or even to the little land in the big water far to the west called "Alcatraz." Fear of this happening grew in all the people. They thought, So many Blue Coats. Why are they here? We did nothing wrong. Still, experience says they plan to take our leaders away.

Juh, a *di-yen* and great war chief of the Nednhi Chiricahua, and Geronimo, now his *segundo* (second in command), back less than two harvests after voluntarily returning from their first reservation escape, feared the Blue Coats were there to arrest them. They had shed much blood raiding and making war in the land of the *Nakai-yes.* They asked Tiffany, the agency chief, if he expected their arrests. He told them no. Tiffany said the Blue Coats were only after those who had fought to free Noch-ay-del-klinne. Tiffany's face during his answer was plain and simple, without the smallest wrinkle of deceit. Juh and Geronimo knew he spoke the truth. They were glad to learn this and left the agency for their village believing the Blue Coats had not come for them.

Chiefs Bonito and George with their small bands, involved in the fight for the prophet, had surrendered, expecting to be sent away or put in the guardhouse, but the Blue Coats held them a few suns and then released them. A few suns later, the Blue Coats changed their minds and decided they wanted them back. Bonito and George were slow to surrender. Many more Blue Coats than normal came to take them prisoner on ration day. Bonito and George promised to surrender after their women had gathered their rations. But the Blue Coats refused to wait and rode for their villages.

Learning the Blue Coats were coming, Bonito and George rode on their fastest horses to our villages. Jerking their ponies to a stop and leaping from their saddles at the *wickiups* of our chiefs and leaders, they breathlessly babbled, almost shouting, "The Blue Coats have taken our women and children, and now they are coming here to murder your women and children. They'll put all the chiefs and leaders in chains and take us to a dark place."

When Geronimo heard this, the whites of his eyes turned red. His face trembled with rage. He snarled, shook his fists, stomped the dust, then yelled, "I knew the Blue Coats would do this! I knew it! I'll never go back to that stinking guardhouse. Let them kill me first."

Although Geronimo was like an outraged mother bear when he heard George and Bonito tell their story of the Blue Coats coming to their villages, Juh stayed calm. His glittering black eyes showed that he was ready to leave, but to decide what to do he called for an immediate council at our meeting place on the Río Gila.

THE PLACE WHERE we held our councils was deep in the *bosque* (brush and trees along a waterway) among big cottonwood and sycamore trees along the Río Gila. It was out of sight and hearing by White Eye agents and Blue Coats. Leaders, warriors, and chiefs quickly filled it. I sat near the front, my heart pounding in my ears like a pot drum.

Naiche, as chief of the Chokonen spoke first. He reminded the council of the Blue Coat trickery after they captured Mangas Coloradas, his grandfather, when he came in to talk peace. The Blue Coats had killed Mangas Coloradas, buried him, and then dug him up and cut off his head to boil in a big black pot for its skull. Faces in the council twisted in outrage as the men remembered the story.

Naiche recalled how his father, Cochise, had been betrayed after being called to a peace meeting at Apache Pass, where *Teniente* Bascom tried to take him prisoner. Cochise had escaped by slashing his way out of *Teniente* Bascom's tent. There followed ten bloody years of war as Naiche grew to manhood before Cochise made a treaty with One Arm Howard (General Otis Oliver Howard) for the Chiricahua Reservation land Cochise wanted and to use Cochise's friend, Tom Jeffords, as his agent. Cochise, his People, and Geronimo and Juh with their People lived in peace on his reservation until he rode the ghost pony two harvests later. Before he left for the Happy Land, he made his sons promise to avoid war with the White Eyes and Blue Coats. That was why Naiche had refused to leave with Geronimo the first time he left San Carlos and had remained silent at councils where there was much talk of leaving the reservation. Now their San Carlos agent made them live where there was shaking sickness. After George and Bonito came with their warning, he said that he needed to rethink what he must do.

George, so nervous he was shaking, stood and claimed the Blue Coats were coming to murder our women and children and to take those who lived to a dark place. Chihuahua sitting near me nodded and said, "He must know. He's related to a White Eye." A wave of angry looks and mutterings swept through the council.

Then Geronimo, still filled with rage, spoke of how Clum had captured him with a trick, dragged him to San Carlos, then kept him in the dark, stinking guardhouse for three moons. There, he waited for the White Eye sheriff to take him to Tucson for the White Eye hanging ceremony of dancing in the air, his neck tied to the end of a rope. Geronimo, his eyes red again with anger, said the Blue Coats had killed the prophet, stolen our rations, and forced us back out of the mountains where the water was sweet and the air good. Now they made us camp on land by the river where the water was bad, the air sour, and shaking sickness came.

Geronimo didn't talk long before Juh, his teeth clenched and arm muscles rippling, said for us to continue talking if we liked, but he was returning to Mexico that night. He gave us a choice: go with him or stay and wait for the Blue Coats to murder our women and children and take those who still lived to a dark place.

Naiche said the memory of Clum's trickery to bring Geronimo to San Carlos, the Blue Coat plan to kill women and children, the cheating agents, and being forced to live on shaking-sickness land made him realize he had done all he could to avoid war with the White Eyes and Blue Coats. He decided he and his People were leaving with Juh that night.

Geronimo said, "I ride with Juh. It's more manly to die on the warpath than to be killed in prison."

Jelikinne, short, no more than an old musket tall, powerfully built, and known as the bravest Nednhi fighter, said, "Geronimo, Juh, and Naiche speak true. I ride with them."

Other chiefs and leaders and I said we also were riding with them. Chihuahua and Nahilzay, reluctant to leave, made no commitment to follow the leaders until they thought they saw dust plumes made by Blue Coats and scouts riding for their villages. In fact, the Blue Coats and scouts never went there, but Chihuahua and Nahilzay didn't wait to be sure. They decided to follow Juh and Geronimo like everyone else—375 men, women, and children, all told—in this great escape from the reservation.

As I expected, Loco, Chiva, and Zele crossed their arms, shook their heads, then said they had promised the Blue Coats to stay at San Carlos. They kept their word. They were not leaving. I thought they were fools and cowards. They refused to face facts and live free to save the lives of their families.

DESPERATE
WARRIOR

ARIZONA, NEW MEXICO AND MEXICO

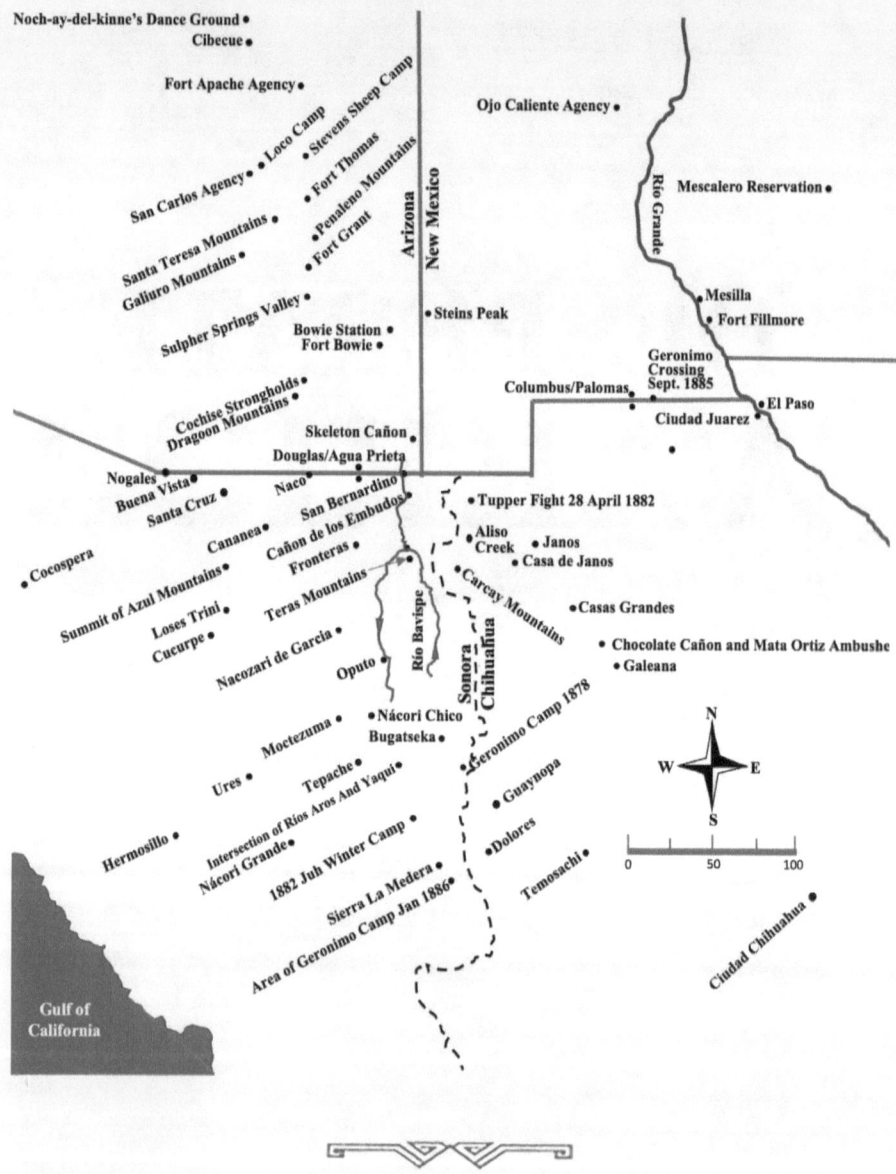

Approximate locations in the history of Chato and the Chiricahua Apache beginning at Ojo Caliente Reservation, New Mexico, in 1877 and ending in the summer of 1886, when Chato and his delegation left Fort Apache for Washington. Modern locations are provided for common reference.

ONE

ESCAPE TO JUH'S CAMP
IN MEXICO

AFTER THE COUNCIL, my warriors and I returned to my village in the dusk fading into black night. We went to our families and told our women to pack in a hurry. We were leaving for Mexico. Most of them believed it was for the best. They knew how hard life would be for us all in Mexico; still, they said little and made no complaints.

I had two wives. My first wife, Nalthchedah, a beautiful woman, hardworking, a good mother but full of self-pride, had my first son, who was then about two harvests old. He was a good child, whom the White Eyes later named Horace, at the place called "school."

My second wife was Ishchos, also a hardworking woman but ten harvests older than me. She was a good mother and an insightful woman whose wise council often kept me from making bad choices. I loved her, but Nalthchedah often spoke badly of her, telling me stories I knew were not true. Ishchos and I had three fine children: a girl of nine harvests, whom the White Eyes later named Maud and who rode the ghost pony at Fort Sill; a son, Bediscloye, of five harvests, who had much light behind his eyes; and a beautiful little daughter, Naboka, of three harvests and not long off the *tsach* (cradleboard). I lost both the youngest ones and Ishchos to *Nakai-yi* slavery not long after Loco was forced to lead his People to Juh's camp in the Blue Mountains, a story I'll you tell later.

I spoke privately with Nalthchedah and Ishchos by their fire in front of our *wickiup* while I sipped from a hot cup of their black coffee mixed with ground roasted piñon nuts, strong and good. I said to my family gathered around me, "I have been at council to discuss what to do when the Blue Coats come for us. The council decided it is too dangerous for us to stay at San Carlos. George says they will murder the women and children—I do not believe this, but it is possible. And they will take the leaders to a dark place—this I believe, but I'm not certain. We need to be ready to run by the rising of the moon."

Nalthchedah, with a frown making her face harsh and ugly, shook her head and said in a tone that sounded like a whining dog, "I won't go to the land of the *Nakai-yes* and risk the death of our son because you do not trust the White Eyes. You promised to keep us safe. This is not the way."

I wanted to reach across the fire and give her face the back of my hand, but now was not the time to beat a woman with no sense. She stood in the way of my learning from the great chief Juh and powerful *di-yen* and war leader, Geronimo. If I stayed, I would be known as a fool and maybe a coward throughout the camps. I had not been happy with Nalthchedah for a long time.

I clenched my teeth. "Either you go with me now, or we are divorced."

She looked away and shook her head. "I will not go."

"Then you will have many wickiups from which to choose here if the White Eyes don't kill you first. Tell your father to keep my bride gift."

She whined, "Chato, don't do this foolish and bad thing. It'll hurt all of us."

I pointed away from our *wickiup*. "Go! You are no longer a wife of mine."

Her face a mask of indifference, Nalthchedah stood, turned her back on me and disappeared into the *wickiup* to collect her things and our son.

Ishchos looked at me with the water of sorrow in her eyes. "We are packed and ready now, husband. Bonito's women told us what they expected to happen in their camp, and we knew the chiefs would choose to leave rather than endure Blue Coats putting them in chains. Nalthchedah has had time to think about what she is doing. I hate that you will lose your first son, but not your first wife. She thinks only of herself."

I shook my head in wonder. "Ishchos has much light behind her eyes. I'll ride my fastest pony. You take one to ride and one for the children. Use another to carry food and your camp tools. Anyone who needs the other ponies is free to use them."

Ishchos said, "My husband does a good thing. There are families who need them. Now go. Stay safe on this journey, husband. After we are in Mexico, I'll keep your bed warm now that Naboka is nearly weaned."

"Woman, I already hunger for you. Be ready for a long, hard run. We must beat the Blue Coats to the land of the *Nakai-yes* to escape San Carlos and live free in Juh's camp in Mexico."

WE LEFT OUR camps at San Carlos as a rising half-moon gave the People enough light to run by. Most of them had no horses. The leaders planned to take White Eye *rancho* horses for our families before we went far down the trails to the land of the *Nakai-yes*. It was cool, and the rains had stopped, the trails dry and the running easy. We were well provisioned, with rations issued to us earlier that day. Geronimo and I took the advance lead with a few respected warriors. Juh rode at the back of the long column with most of the other warriors to defend against attack from those any who chased us.

We followed the wagon road toward Camp Thomas and, after three hands against the horizon (about three hours), turned south and broke into four groups. I led one group, Juh, Naiche, and Bonito the others. In this way, we confused those trailing us by taking different trails. We regrouped south at Black Rock rather than head northeast for Eagle Creek and then pass through the Peloncillo Mountains south as we usually did. There were too many Blue Coats around the Eagle Creek trail looking for followers of the prophet who had attacked them when trying to free him for us to pass through there without being seen.

We took many horses and mules from nearby *ranchos* and killed all the White Eyes and Mexicans we found, taking their supplies, horses and mules, and guns and ammunition on our run south.

Soon we had all the women and children mounted and made much more distance than we had at first. It was still hard to find enough provisions for so many people, but we found enough to keep us from going hungry.

WE FOUGHT THE Blue Coats in two battles so our women and children could get around them and continue south. We crossed the border at Guadelupe Canyon with everyone mounted and with over five hundred head of horses and mules. This we did after losing a hundred head when scouts surprised us in the mountains the White Eyes called "Dragoons" while we were making meat in the old Cochise camps. Even with over three hundred and fifty people, including seventy men and twenty-two boys old enough to use weapons, we lost less than a handful fighting the Blue Coats before we crossed the border. One man was badly wounded but lived. A woman was killed, and two women and three children were taken in the fight in the Dragoons. We were very fortunate with our losses.

In the land of the *Nakai-yes,* Juh led us to his flat-top mountain stronghold west of Casas Grandes. On the way to Juh's stronghold, we crossed a trail that Juh, recognizing some of the horse tracks, said belonged to Nana and his People. Juh believed Nana would soon come to join us. With Juh's People and Nana's band, and including all the others who had come with him from San Carlos, Juh guessed that there would be about 450 people gathered in his camp. After the men and older boys who could use weapons rested for four days, we would need to begin hunting and raiding for cattle to feed so many people.

I was happy to hunt and raid and provide my family with meat, but I looked forward to resting for four days as Juh said we should, especially now that Ish-chos planned to wean Naboka. After weaning a child, women seemed especially eager for their men, but no more so than the men for their women.

TWO

IN THE SHADOW OF JUH'S STRONGHOLD

OUR PEOPLE CAMPED at the foot of Juh's flat-top mountain stronghold. Rather than our taking the long, winding climb to the stronghold at the top, Juh thought we would be safe at the bottom of his mountain with his People on the top watching for soldiers. Plenty of trees and brush provided wood for fires, and a small stream flowing down from springs on the mountain gave us water for cooking and bathing.

Dodging soldiers across Arizona and Sonora had required a long, hard run with little rest. We all needed rest once the women had their wickiups set up for their families under the trees by the stream. It was a very quiet first night of sleep for us at the foot of Juh's stronghold.

The next morning, I sat by the fire with Ishchos and the children, drinking coffee and listening to the crows passing above the trees and the twitter of bridled tits as they flocked from bush to bush, looking to make a quick morning meal of stirring insects. The sun, a red egg, rising above the distant mountains made the clouds spreading over them bright oranges, reds, and purples scattered against the sky's bird's-egg blue. Naboka left the side of Ishchos and toddled over to me to sit in my lap. Soft and warm, smelling of yucca flowers and prickly pear from the salve Ishchos had rubbed on her to prevent sunburn and skin rashes, she sat between my legs and leaned back warm and soft against my belly, playing with a smooth, round stone she had found that was just right for a sling. I thanked *Ussen* every day for my children and Ishchos. They filled my life with joy.

I felt like I had a battle wound in my chest from giving up the child I had with Nalthchedah when I divorced her. There was no other way to leave San Carlos with the other chiefs, and there was no question in my mind about leav-

8

W. MICHAEL FARMER

ing if I wanted to become a great chief. Living at San Carlos was too hard and too dangerous for the people. It was filled with enemies (Blue Coats and other bands), dust, shaking sickness, heat, and rattlesnakes.

While she played with my thumb, holding it with a good, strong grip, I decided to carve Naboka a doll. Her sister Maud was fast growing into a beautiful young girl. I didn't doubt that after her *Haheh* (puberty ceremony) her skill and beauty would bring a powerful warrior to our *wickiup* with a large bride gift. Our custom said for them to camp near us and help the wife's family as they were needed. Maud now helped her mother with the cooking and maintaining the fire. She and her brother, Bediscloye, who was about seven harvests, had been practicing with their slings in our camp at San Carlos. I decided to give them some instruction to increase their accuracy and the power of their throw they could practice here camping with Juh.

Ishchos handed me a gourd with a piece of beef, steamed dried mescal slices, and mesquite bread before feeding Maud and Bediscloye the same things that we ate. She gave Naboka a small gourd filled with a little meat and mesquite bread soaked in juice from the meat before she sat down to eat from her own gourd.

"Hmmph, woman. You must like the land of the *Nakai-yes.* Your bread and meat are very good." I glanced at Maud and Bediscloye, who with full cheeks nodded and reached for more.

Ishchos laughed. "It pleases me that my husband and children enjoy the good things we have and that the children know to use good manners at their mother's fire." She took bites of bread and beef from her gourd. "What does my husband plan for this day of rest?"

"I think Naboka is ready for a new doll. I'll make her one when I finish eating. Then I'll show Bediscloye and Maud how to improve their sling throws. They do well for their ages but must do better if they want to protect the camp when the men are gone."

"You're a good father to our children. You think often of protecting the People." She smiled and leaned toward me to speak in a low voice so the children wouldn't hear. "Naboka is now weaned and learns her lessons well for the everyday things she must do to look after herself. My body says I am ready to make my husband another child. Will you come to me when the children sleep?"

I smiled and nodded. "Woman, I've longed for you for many moons. Yes, I'm eager, like a young man for his woman. Tonight, we'll pleasure each other while we begin another child." I enjoyed the praise of my woman, warm and wise, who always gave me good advice, but I enjoyed her body even more next to mine and her sighs of contentment. This would be a good day.

I CARVED NABOKA'S little doll out of manzanita wood. It was good, dark hardwood, and I polished it smooth after I carved it because I knew she would put it in her mouth before Ishchos taught her better. I decided to wait on giving it to her until we were all together around the fire for our evening meal.

I found Maud and Bediscloye playing with the other children a little downstream from the camp wickiups. My heart swelled with pride when I saw them. Even at their young age, anyone could tell they were quick and strong and should be powerful people when they grew to adults. I called and motioned them to me, and they came running.

"I watched you practicing with your slings. You grow better since I first showed you how to use them, but you still have much work to do. Let's go to a quiet place, and I'll show you how to improve your accuracy and throwing power."

Even though she was more mature and taller than Bediscloye, Maud let him speak for them. "We were hoping you would do this for us, Father. I've already found a good place to practice alone up the mountain. Can we go there?"

I nodded and motioned for him to show the way as Maud, and I followed. He led us up an increasingly steep slope through tall grama grass and around cholla and junipers, following a faint game trail until we were high enough that we could look over the tops of the trees where our camp rested. We came to a bench about three paces wide and maybe a hundred long. It was part of the ground wrinkles going up the mountain like giant steps. Bediscloye was right. It was a good place to practice without being seen and listening to taunts from others who were better than them.

He pointed toward the crossed-stick target about thirty steps away, which he and Maud had put there earlier that day to use for their sling practice. I said, "You and Maud do well to practice by yourselves. While we stand back, let me watch you throw a stone or two at your target, and I'll tell you how to get more power in the stone from your sling."

He nodded, and Maud and I stood back so I could watch his way with his sling. He threw two stones, both a little high and wide to the left of where his target sticks crossed. I had him change his foot position, so he more nearly faced the target, slightly lengthened the strap length on one side of his sling, and then told him to flex his wrist more while he increased the turns on his windup by two or three more than he normally used.

I told him to throw again. This time, the pebble was much closer to the center of the crossed sticks and struck the earth behind it with a satisfying thump. He turned and grinned. "My father is a good teacher."

I smiled. "Keep practicing that way, and soon you can throw against warriors. Now let me watch Maud use her sling."

Bediscloye stepped back as Maud stepped to where he had stood. She was more polished in how she handled her sling than Bediscloye, and she was much more accurate. She nearly hit the stick's cross-point twice, but her stones lacked power when she threw them. I told her to take a couple more turns when she wound up to throw and to lengthen strap lengths by about a hand spread at a time until she got the power she wanted. She adjusted her sling, put another stone in the sling pouch, then wound up a couple of extra turns before she threw. She hit the stick's cross-point center with a sharp crack as the stick ends flew apart. I couldn't have done better with my rifle. I looked at them, shook my fist, then said, *"Enjuh!* Now practice that every day and soon you'll be ready to defend yourselves and take game. Just don't show off your skill until you have to. Others will try to make you look foolish if you do."

With solemn faces, they nodded they understood.

"Now practice. I have other things I need to do. I see you again at your mother's evening meal."

Maud smiled. "Yes, Father, we'll practice a long time and get much better. But now, I must leave soon to help Ishchos at her fire."

I nodded and waved my hand parallel to the ground, the all-is-good sign. I left them to check my horses, and Bediscloye looked for more target sticks.

WE HAD EATEN a fine evening meal of dried mescal slices steamed back to their original hot, baked goodness, mesquite bread, yucca tips, and beef chunks roasted on sticks angled over the orange and yellow flames that sizzled and popped from the dripping fat, its smell fanning the flames of our hunger. I had given Naboka the doll I carved for her and talked with Bediscloye and Maud about how their sling work would help make them powerful protectors of the People. Maud helped Ishchos clean up while Bediscloye listened to me tell the cut-the-tent story of Cochise escaping the Blue Coats. I was about Bediscloye's age when that ten years of war began and a young, experienced warrior developing a following when it ended. I had learned from the best—Mangas Coloradas, Cochise, Victorio, Chihuahua, and yes, Geronimo. I wanted to be like them, strong and powerful, respected by all the People, a great chief.

Cleanup done and stories finished, Ishchos and I sent our children to their blankets and sat by the fire, remembering the good times in our life together. When we heard the deep breathing of their sleep, we slipped from the fire and crossed the stream burbling near our *wickiup*. Earlier that day, Ishchos had found a grassy spot in the brush, where we spread a blanket. Eager to know my wife again after nearly four years apart on the blankets, I pulled her to me. She giggled and pulled away, whispering, "Wait, husband. I go to bathe in the creek first." Stirred to passion for her, I sighed, lay back, then stared at the twinkling myriad of little white lights scattered like seeds sown across the smooth obsidian-black sky.

I heard her pass, soft and quiet, along the little path to our hideaway and raised on one elbow to see her dark outline, as if by magic, appear at my feet. She slipped off her shift, and the grass made a little crunching sound as she stretched out beside me. "Husband, come to me. I am your woman, and you are my man. Let us enjoy each other and make another child while we still can."

I was eager for her and she for me as if we were back again during our first time together, but now we were experienced lovers riding long-denied waves of pleasure and no longer learning more of life's mysteries. Ishchos was my second wife, but she was and had always been first in my life, and our children were the fruits of our pleasure and life together. What more could any man ask of a woman who so filled his life with joy?

As the moon began falling toward the west, we folded our blanket and, crossing the little stream, returned to the dim coals and gray ash of our fire. We crept on to our *wickiup* blanket and in each other's arms listened to the peaceful sleep of Bediscloye, Maud, and Naboka as we drifted into our own.

THREE

COUNCILS WITH JUH

JUH SAID TO rest four suns after we made our camp, and then we would talk. On the fifth sun, Juh and his leaders came to our camp and gathered with us in council on a secluded grassy spot near the far side of the burbling steam from where we camped. Naiche spoke first. He asked Juh, with his experience making war and raiding in the land of the *Nakai-yes*, to become our leader if all agreed. No one said no to Juh being our leader. Tall and imposing, heavyset, muscular, his hair in a braid that reached to his knees, he stood and accepted our request.

Juh said, "I expect that soon Nana and his men come to us. I believe Nana accepts joining forces and helping plan where and when we raid. This will make our band even larger and more powerful." The men slapped the ground and shook their fists as they said with one voice, "*Ch'ik'eh doleel* (all right; let it be so)."

Waiting with crossed arms until the council was quiet again, Juh surprised us. He said, "In the next ten suns, I go to Casas Grandes to make a peace treaty with the local *Nakai-yi* military *jefe*, Joaquin Terrazas." He was the same *jefe* who had led the attack that killed Victorio and enslaved many women and children at Tres Castillos.

I thought, *This makes no sense. Any peace that Juh negotiates with Terrazas can't last. Nana, Victorio's segundo, has a powerful need to avenge Victorio. He's already led two moons of raids along the border, killing and burning everything in his path. Maybe Juh knows that Nana is willing to wait on his revenge. No treaties with Nakai-yes last very long. Who trusts Nakai-yes anyway? If Nana waited, we would get all the presents Terrazas offered Juh to make peace. Yes, Nana would wait and take all the gifts Terrazas had to offer before Nana killed him. Clever chief, this man Juh.*

Juh went on to say that if we agreed, he would ask Geronimo to be his *segundo* and, together with thirty chosen warriors, ride to the meeting with Terrazas. *Ch'ik'eh doleel, Geronimo wants me as his segundo on raids and war, so I go. Maybe if something happens to Juh, then I would be segundo for the entire band, and if something happened to Geronimo, then I'd be chief. Ha! Now I see a clear path to being chief over all the People.* But as I looked around the council, I saw others who were more likely choices for Geronimo's *segundo* than me—Naiche or Chihuahua, both chiefs with greater followings than I, maybe even Chihuahua's brother, Ulzana. *Patience, Chato, Coyote waits. Geronimo knows you're strong. He'll choose you.*

Juh said those who had horses or mules they wanted to trade for other things could come too, but they had to obey his rule that no more than half those wanting to trade entered Casas Grandes at a time. This told the *Nakai-yes* that if the Apache were given mescal and slaughtered when they were drunk, the Apache awaiting their turn to trade the next day would be ready for quick revenge. Hmmph, clever man, this chief Juh.

JUH STUTTERED BADLY when he was excited. To ensure the other side clearly understood the point of his words Geronimo often spoke for him. Terrazas studied them both and nodded with fixed, unblinking eyes and a frozen smile when Geronimo told him Juh's terms for peace. I think Juh surprised Terrazas by asking for the Carcay Mountains, where the People could gather desert food and live on the plains and valleys with grass on either side of the mountains for cattle. Juh also wanted help to learn how to grow crops.

Terrazas said through his wolfish grinning lips, *"Señores,* I have no authority to grant a request for land, especially for that large an area. I'll send the request to the governor of Chihuahua for approval. Soon we have his answer and approval. In the meantime, let us celebrate that you are here and that we are talking peace." He gave us presents, enough flour and sugar for all the band's families, fat cattle for meat, and cloth and other useful things for our women, but no cartridges for our rifles.

We were camped in the Río Casas Grandes *bosque* an easy ride (maybe half a hand against the horizon) from Casas Grandes. Terrazas kept coming to our camp and telling us that if we came into the town, he had fine mescal waiting to give us for our enjoyment while we discussed the details of a new reservation. Juh and Geronimo said no. They understood that Terrazas wanted to get us drunk and enslave or slaughter us. We also learned from friends in Casas Grandes of many soldiers arriving in camps near surrounding villages.

Nearly a moon passed while we waited for the governor's answer. We knew that, among the *Nakai-yes*, the greater the *jefe*, the slower the answer. Terrazas kept bringing us wagon loads of supplies and cattle every five or six suns, and we kept taking them. He even included a little mescal for Juh and his warriors, assuring us that there was a lot more in Casas Grandes if we wanted to come in for it. I could tell Juh and Geronimo's determination to stay out of Casas Grandes for mescal was weakening. They were near to going into Casas Grandes for the mescal when some friendly White Eye traders told them Terrazas was fast bringing up more soldiers to camps near Casas Grandes and that he planned to capture all the Apache and take them to sell as slaves in Ciudad Mexico. That opened the eyes of Juh and Geronimo. We slipped away the next day.

I stayed behind and watched the old camp with soldier glasses to learn what the *Nakai-yes* would do. I laughed at the look of surprise and disgust on Terrazas's face as he pounded his leg with his fist after he discovered we were gone, but he made no attempt to follow us. He knew better.

TO THROW TERRAZAS off our trail if he came after us, we moved north up past Kas-ki-yeh (Janos) and then made a loop turning west and, after a while, south to cross the Carcay Mountains, where we found Nana and his band. We had a good council with him and his warriors. His *segundo* was Kaytennae.

I had once wanted to be Nana's *segundo*. Nana was old, arthritic in his knees, and had a crippled foot. But, on a saddle with a good horse under him he was a terror, able to ride seventy or eighty miles a day and direct men in battle. I had expected that soon he would ride the ghost pony and leave the chieftainship to his *segundo*. By adding his band to mine, I would have one of the strongest bands among the Chiricahua. For a while, I camped and rode with Nana to show him how good a *segundo* I would be, but I learned he had already chosen Kaytennae—a good warrior but with the personality of a cur dog ready to bite at the first opportunity. I knew that someday I needed to teach that dog not to snap at Chato even if I had to catch and whip him in the dark.

Nana agreed to Juh's idea to support each other and to meet in a moon, where we camped at Juh's big flat-top mountain stronghold to discuss plans for raiding after the Season of Ghost Face.

JUH'S GREAT *TIPI* at his stronghold sat among tall pine trees that helped scatter the wind and provide shade. Near the beginning of Ghost Face, Juh and Nana sat around a fire in Juh's *tipi* with their leaders. They listened to ideas for raids beginning in the Season of Little Eagles after snow cleared the high passes.

Nana and his band arrived in Juh's stronghold the sun before their council with us. Before the council began, Kaytennae spoke with Geronimo a long time. I wanted to listen to Kaytennae, too, but when I signaled to ask if I should join them, Geronimo signed no. Now at the council, Geronimo sat near Juh, and Kaytennae near Nana. I should have sat next to Geronimo, but I had to sit next to Jelikinne and other leaders around the fire.

The wind passing through the tops of the pines sounded like water rushing over boulders in a mountain stream but seemed to stop when Geronimo rose to speak. The men looked at each other. Did Geronimo, the great *di-yen*, control the wind, too? He held the gaze of every warrior as he looked at each around the fire and began to speak.

"The Seasons of Little Eagles and Many Leaves come in two moons. Already the people at San Carlos are dying of hunger because the agents cheat them of their rations. It was a big reason why we left in the first place. Soon swarms of insects, heat and dust, and snakes come to strike them. Soon shaking sickness appears. How many of Loco's People will live through the long, hot days on the Río Gila?"

Juh and Nana stared at Geronimo and shook their heads. They had no answer.

Nana said, "Loco's People are our brothers. You, Loco, and I were born near the headwaters of the Gila. You know this. Loco has nearly four hundred people with him. Three hundred twenty-five are women and children, the rest warriors and *novitiates* capable of using guns to defend themselves. Many will die at San Carlos."

Geronimo nodded and said, "Yes, many will die. They will suffer from lack of food and grow weak. They will suffer from bad water and make many trips to the brush. They will suffer from the bites of many no-see-ems, insects almost too small to see, making them scratch and their skin burn as though touched by fire. The shaking sickness will kill many as they shake in the heat like the winter branches in the trees above us. Soldiers tried to camp there and could not. It was too hard. I believe they put Loco's People there to die."

Nana and Juh slowly nodded their heads. Kaytennae infuriated me as he sat looking around with crossed arms and a crooked little smile. Geronimo was doing his bidding. Where was he going with this?

"Loco belongs with his People. He is a Chihenne, and those who still live with him are the greatest number of the Chihenne. Why should he not join the fight with us? More *Nakai-yi* soldiers march toward our mountains every moon. We need more warriors to defend ourselves, or we will all become slaves. We need Loco to join us."

Nana said, "He has no guns or cartridges."

Juh, nodding toward Geronimo, said, "We have caches of weapons and ammunition he can use. We can raid for more before he comes."

Geronimo nodded and Nana nodded, saying, *"Ch'ik'eh doleel* (all right)."

I looked around the council, growing furious that Geronimo, after listening to Kaytennae, seemed to be suggesting that we attack San Carlos to help the Chihenne escape when their chief wouldn't fight. Our blood for their freedom when Loco wouldn't fight for their freedom—it was an outrage.

I spoke out of turn. I was so angry I couldn't help myself. "Loco is a woman!"

There was thunder in Nana's face when he turned toward me. "Loco has a scarred face and drooping eye because he fought a bear with only a knife. Loco is a man of great courage and a proud warrior we all respect."

All in the council except me shook their fists and said, "Ho!"

I wouldn't back up. "Loco sits idle in his lodge, drawing rations, while we do the fighting."

Nana snorted and spoke as if talking to a child, slowly, speaking every word clearly. "Each warrior decides for himself if he fights. Apache are free people. We have no forced armies as the *Nakai-yes* do. Forcing men to fight produces slaves, not warriors."

Again, the council said as one, "Ho!"

Nana looked from me to Geronimo, for I served Geronimo as his *segundo*. "Loco does the will of his band, and he believes more resistance will bear no fruit. Even the father of Naiche, the great Cochise, came to believe this. Loco has given his word not to leave San Carlos. He will not break this promise."

Geronimo nodded he understood, but I could tell from the way he narrowed his eyes that he wanted Loco in Mexico. He glanced at me and said to the council, "He could be forced to come."

Nana shook his head. "If he refuses, many will die. He has given his word."

"Always your People!" I said through clenched teeth.

"Always my People," Nana said softly in his raspy old man's voice.

I crossed my arms and sighed. "Nana wins by ambush and strategy. He doesn't fight face-to-face."

Nana nodded. "There is no greater compliment."

Juh watched this exchange in silence. Geronimo looked at him, nodded, then sat down as Juh stood, drawing everyone's attention.

"Chato is young, powerful, and has proven himself a strong warrior to lead the warriors and their families in his band. He needs to learn the wisdom of great leaders like Nana and Loco. Loco is a brave man. It takes courage for him to do as his People want and squat in the dust and misery of San Carlos. Geronimo is right. We need Loco and his warriors to help keep the *Nakai-yes* away from our camps. Nana is right. Loco has given his word to stay on his piece of the reservation. What to do? I say first let us ask Loco what he thinks now that he has lived at San Carlos for a while."

There were nods of agreement as the wind burbled through the tops of the pines.

"Let us send Bonito, a great warrior. He has relatives and family among the White Mountain People, and part of his band is still with Chiva on the reservation. Yes, send Bonito with no more than six warriors to speak with Loco to learn what he will do. If Loco does not want to come, then they should tell him that we will come to help him."

There were "hmmphs" and nods of agreement around the council. Even Nana was slowly nodding. Bonito looked around the council and nodded. *Juh is a wise chief. I will learn much from him.*

BONITO AND HIS warriors left the next sun for San Carlos. While they were gone, Geronimo and I with Chihuahua and Jelikinne and about forty warriors raided ranches and villages in the Sonoran foothills of the western Blue Mountains (Sierra Madre). Thirty harvests earlier, Sonoran military had wiped out Geronimo's family, and his thirst for revenge in Sonora was never satisfied. He killed many *Nakai-yes* in Sonora and took much loot.

Bonito returned from San Carlos in less than a moon. He told Juh's council that he had stayed in Loco's camp for a few days with three of the men who went with him—the others stayed with Chiva and Zele. He met with Loco and described what was said in our council. Loco told Bonito to forget him leaving San Carlos. He had given the White Eyes his word he would stay there. He would not leave. It was foolish to leave. Loco said again he was having none of it. There were others, like families of some of Nana's men and Victorio's wife, who wanted to leave then with Bonito, but he told them they would have to wait.

After hearing Bonito's report, the council chiefs asked him to return once more and tell Loco that a large band would come from the Blue Mountains in forty days and carry away his entire band and kill any who refused to leave. Bonito and his men left the next sun.

FOUR

THE ASH FLAT
MASSACRE

NEAR THE BEGINNING of the Season of Little Eagles, Bonito returned riding proud and defiant after his second council with Loco. Bonito reported that he had again asked Loco to leave San Carlos. Loco had answered as Nana said he would and as he told Bonito the first visit: "I gave my promise to the White Eyes to stay at San Carlos and will not break or dishonor my word."

Bonito said, "I told Loco that the camp of Juh wanted him and his People safe and would return in forty days to help them escape. Loco shook his head and said words to the effect, 'You had better stay away. The Chihenne don't need your help.'"

After the council heard Bonito's story, the warriors decided that Geronimo should lead about seventy of them to San Carlos to free Loco and his People and, if need be, force them to take the first steps to their freedom. Juh and Nana would stay at the stronghold with about thirty warriors to protect the 325 women and children, including fifteen teenage boys trained to use rifles.

Warriors going to San Carlos included about forty men on horses and thirty on foot. To keep the chances of our being seen small, we traveled when the light was low, crossing the border as two separate groups. I rode with Geronimo, Naiche, Jelikinne, Chihuahua, and Kaytennae at the front of the mounted warriors. We crossed the border between San Luis Pass and Guadalupe Canyon and followed the edge of the Peloncillo Mountains north to the San Simon Valley, which we crossed to meet the men running on foot at Doubtful Canyon, near the place the White Eyes called Steins Peak. We headed for the Río Gila, crossed it near the southern end of Ash Flat, then rode north across the great *llano* used for pasture by sheep and cattle ranchers whose *ranchos* were near Eagle Creek.

We were covering ground at a good pace but hadn't stopped to eat in nearly a sun, and even without my belly growling with hunger, I could tell all the men needed to stop, eat, and rest a while. An afternoon breeze brought the smell of sheep to us. I glanced toward Geronimo, who smiled and nodded toward me. We slowed our pace and moved forward, making as little noise as we could. Soon we heard the sheep and saw the smoke from several cooking fires. We stayed back in the brush and studied the camp, trying to learn how many men we might have to fight there if we raided the big flock for food. Geronimo and the other chiefs studied the wagons with their soldier glasses. Through mine, I counted nine *Nakai-yi* men and nearby three women working around covered wagons that they must have been using to carry supplies and for the women to work from when they fed the men and three children with them.

Maybe three hundred paces further down the creek, I saw three tents and recognized three or four White Mountain Apache men and their women around them. I knew these men from seeing them at San Carlos. One of them was Bylas, a White Mountain chief whose uncle had been killed in Victorio's revenge raid on the reservation against the White Mountains for their part in chasing the Chihenne when they left. It looked like the White Mountains were taking care of wether lambs—nasty, messy work I hoped never to do. Nine *Nakai-yes* and three or four White Mountain Apache who were well-armed could cause us serious losses if we attacked the camp and they fought back. Maybe we wait until dark and only take few sheep to satisfy our hunger and then pass on toward San Carlos.

Geronimo grinned as he studied the *Nakai-yi* man who was the *jefe* in charge of the others. Geronimo nudged his pony forward. We followed, keeping our silence, quiet as ghosts, as we approached the edge of the camp.

I heard the hammers on warriors' rifles clicking back to full cock and saw men looking around for possible cover, readying to attack or defend themselves. Like ghosts, we glided through the brush on the edge of their camp until Geronimo held up his hand for us to stop. We sat there, quiet and still, surveying the camp, trying to locate things we might want or need. The woman of the *Nakai-yi jefe* looked up from her cooking pot bubbling over her cooking fire, saw us in the still strong twilight, sitting on our horses like shadowy figures carved in stone. She covered her mouth with her hand for a moment and then called for the children to get under their wagon.

Geronimo called out in Spanish, "It is me, Mestas. It is me, Geronimo. I have many men, and they are hungry. We will not harm you. I am Geronimo, your *amigo*. Remember me?"

I saw Bylas step up close to Mestas—a big, young *Nakai-yi,* the range *jefe,* wearing a fancy shirt sewed with many symbols in colored thread—say something near his ear and then yell towards us, "You lie, Geronimo. You want to kill us. Always you are a liar."

It was like Bylas had said nothing at all as Geronimo said, "Mestas, we are hungry. Don't you remember how well I treated you when you lived with us. I gave you a pony and a bridle and saddle trimmed in silver. I let you go when you were not happy with us. Treat us like the visitors we are. I'm your friend."

Mestas stood thinking with crossed arms in the falling darkness. Bylas said something more and then, shaking his head, turned and walked away toward the tents. The *Nakai-yes* who worked for Mestas had gathered behind him to watch what might happen. At last, Mestas nodded and waved us into the camp. "Welcome, my old friend Geronimo. Come with your men and fill your bellies. We are glad to see and feed you."

Geronimo slowly walked his pony up to Mestas and, while the rest of us dismounted, said with a smile, "I see you, Mestas. You have grown into a big, strong *Nakai-yi* hombre. I don't much like the taste of sheep. A good pony is more to my liking. I see one over in that corral."

Even in the lowering light, I could see Mestas lose color in his face. *No, Geronimo. We just eat what they give us and leave. Don't make trouble that will run ahead of us and spoil our taking Loco and his People from San Carlos.*

Mestas, his face wrinkled into a frown, shook his head. "That fine pony is not mine. It belongs to Jimmie Stevens, young son of the man who owns the sheep, *señor* George Stevens. I just keep him out here to ride for Jimmie once in a while."

Geronimo grinned, reminding me of a cougar playing with a half-dead rabbit it was about to eat. He said, "The pony is not yours? *Doo dat'éé da* (it's okay; it doesn't matter)." He brought his rifle to his shoulder and, without even pausing to aim, shot the pony in the head from a good fifty paces away. Geronimo had always been a fearsome marksman. "Now we can have all the pony meat we want. Your women will cook for us?"

Mestas bowed his head, and I heard a low groan from deep in his chest as he realized he had made a bad mistake letting us into his camp. *"Sí, jefe,* they will cook whatever you ask. Take the sheep you want and the pony for your meal. We are glad to share what we have."

Geronimo nodded. *"Bueno, bueno."* He pointed his rifle toward the other men and told the warriors, "Find some rope and tie them together and sit them down by that wagon over there so they can't make any trouble for us." He turned back to Mestas. "Don't worry about your men. We're just being careful, so no one gets hurt. Who leads the White Mountains helping you?"

"His name is Bylas, nephew of the man with the same name who Victorio killed on his revenge raid against the White Mountains at San Carlos."

Geronimo nodded. "I used to live near the White Mountains. I think I know Bylas. He always had two or three bottles of whiskey around. Let's go over to his tent and see if he will give me a drink. I can always use a little swallow of whiskey."

My mind cringed. *No, Geronimo, don't get drunk. You don't think clearly when you drink whiskey.* I watched Mestas follow Geronimo as he walked his horse over to Bylas's tent and dismounted. Bylas stayed in his tent for a while before he came out. When Bylas finally threw back the tent flap and came out, he was a little wobbly. *He's probably drunk.* He talked with a Geronimo for a short time but always shook his head no after Geronimo spoke. Geronimo gestured toward the tent two or three times; still, Bylas shook his head. Geronimo led the horse and the men in the tents back with him, and he came to sit by the fire with the other leaders waiting for the women to finish cooking their meals. Bylas had a strong smell of White Eye whiskey on him.

Hmmph, he must have drunk all his whiskey before Geronimo could get it. Smart man, this Bylas.

Most of the warriors had taken sheep they wanted and were roasting their own meat. Some had taken meat from the pony and were roasting it on sticks angled over the cooking fires. The women also had a big pot of beans with chilies and a high stack of tortillas they shared out to the warriors.

While we waited for the women to finish cooking for us, Geronimo, Bylas, and his men, who included a young man, a son of one of the White Mountains, who with a scowl that seemed to be etched in his face, sat down in front of us. He watched Geronimo tell Bylas how thirsty for a little whiskey he was and ask if he was sure he didn't have a little hidden away that he could give him. Bylas shook his head each time and said, "No, the whiskey I had is all gone. I drank it all after I saw you coming."

The scowling young man said, "Why don't you leave Bylas alone? He's told you he doesn't have any whiskey. Give him some respect."

Geronimo turned to study the young man, and the slits of his eyes grew even more narrow. He turned the muzzle of his rifle toward the boy's belly and pulled the hammer back. I shook my head. *Don't do this, Geronimo. It's not right. You endanger our chances of saving Loco.*

The boy's eyes grew round, and he shook his head as Geronimo said, "This boy needs to learn manners. A boy doesn't speak for his elders. I don't believe he's a White Mountain. He's a Mexican. He's no Apache."

One of the White Mountains spoke up. "Hold! You are wrong. The boy's mother is of the 'black water' clan. He's full-blood White Mountain."

Geronimo seemed to snarl like a cur dog, "Bylas, you tell me what he is."

Bylas, still a little drunk but sobering up fast, said, "I know the boy's mother. He's a full-blood White Mountain."

The women brought us bowls of food, well prepared. It was good. Geronimo turned away from the boy and uncocked his rifle before laying it beside him. He had a good talk with Mestas while they ate. When he finished and wiped his hands on his legs, he said to Mestas, "Your wife does fine sewing on your shirt. I like it. Why don't you take it off and give it to me, so it doesn't get dirty?"

With trembling fingers, Mestas, his face etched in lines of sorrow, who now understood what was coming, unbuttoned the shirt as he looked at his wife and made the slightest motion with his head for her to leave. Geronimo took the shirt and, carefully folding it, motioned waiting warriors toward Mestas, his wife, and the other three women. "Take them and tie them with the others and kill them all."

Mestas's wife, who had her children sitting quietly under their wagon, screamed at them, "Run! Hide! Don't let them catch you!" The warriors dragged her, Mestas, and the other women to the men already tied together. Warriors chased the children and caught two, but the third one had disappeared.

Bylas, who was sitting close to me and Naiche, said, "Wait! Why do you want to kill these people after they fed you and you promised to harm no one?"

Naiche said, "Don't do this, Geronimo. You ought to pay the women for this meal. This isn't right."

I might be Geronimo's *segundo,* but I, too, thought, *This isn't right.* I understood why he hated the *Nakai-yes* with venom and passion in his spirit, but these people had let us into their camp and fed us.

I spoke up. "Naiche is right. Don't do this. Why would you kill these people when you promised them no harm? We would have lost many men if we had tried to attack this camp. Keep your word and let them go."

The roaring cry for blood and pain in Geronimo's face seemed to die, and he said nothing as he looked at the ground. But then Chihuahua said, "These people are *Nakai-yes,* and they are our enemies. Always the *Nakai-yes* have lied to us, tried to get us drunk and slaughter or enslave our People." I never again had any use for Chihuahua after he encouraged Geronimo to do what he wanted in the first place.

Geronimo said to the warriors, "Take them up that hill and kill them all. Make them suffer. Suffering makes their lives of value, and we take it."

One of the warriors said, "Even kill the little ones?"

Geronimo waved his arm toward the *Nakai-yes* being dragged up the hill away from the camp. "Kill them all. Let the little ones suffer like my children must have suffered when the *Nakai-yes* killed them. Yes, kill them all."

The warriors had knife and war axe–throwing contests, using the men as targets. Some throws were accurate, and the men died quickly. Others suffered through several throwing competitions. The women had their heads bashed in with rocks to save bullets. They threw the youngest child on the spines of a cactus; the other they stretched over a fire. The little ones screamed in agony a long time while Geronimo sat and nodded, saying often, "Yes, suffer little ones, suffer good, like my children must have." I knew how I would feel if the *Nakai-yes* had killed my sweet children like they had Geronimo's, but in my deepest parts, my Power said this was not right. For a long time afterward, I had bad dreams that were filled with the screams of those children. I promised myself then that regardless of what Geronimo thought, I would never take my vengeance against children.

Warriors searched through the wagons for things we might take. They found a new, loaded Winchester in Mestas's wagon and brought it to Geronimo. When he learned it must belong to Mestas, he walked a little way up the hill where the *Nakai-yes* were being killed. They hadn't gotten to Mestas yet. The *jefe* would be the last to go in this kind of execution, so he would carry the burden of the slaughter as he searched for the Happy Land. Geronimo had the warriors hold Mestas, who stood straight with his chin lifted in pride when he saw Geronimo with the rifle. Geronimo nodded and levered a cartridge into the chamber, took quick aim, then shot Mestas in his man parts. Mestas screamed in agony as the blood from his wound spread down his pants like a stampede of wild cattle. He was doubled over but still standing when Geronimo levered another cartridge into the chamber, motioned for the warriors to hold him up, then shot him in the heart. As he walked back to the fire, I heard him say, "See, Mestas, I am merciful. Now I take care of that lying Bylas."

Naiche, his face a thundercloud of anger, said to two nephews sitting near him, in a voice loud enough for Geronimo to hear, "Kill him if he says anything." Geronimo returned to the fire but said nothing. The screams from the two children had stopped, and the killing was done.

A warrior came to Geronimo. "We have done as you said, *Jefe.*"

Geronimo said, "Where is the third child? I saw only two suffer."

"Ah? Wait, we will find him."

Bylas's woman was standing nearby, her head bowed in sorrow. I saw her skirt moving and knew where the child must be hiding. She said, "Must the great Geronimo take the lives of children? This child is all that remains of the Mestas family. He is a good child. Please do not take him. Surely your thirst for vengeance is satisfied now. Let the boy live."

I wasn't the only one who saw her skirts move. A warrior moved up behind her, raised the edge of her skirt, reached under, then dragged the boy out into the open. "Here is the one we missed, Geronimo."

Geronimo nodded and said, "Kill him, too." My mind roared in outrage, as I thought of Bediscloye, who was near the same age as this boy. *No! This is not right. This has to stop.*

The mighty warrior Jelikinne, who had silently watched all that had happened, jerked the butt of his long blade spear out of the ground beside him, whirled to put the point against Geronimo's chest, then said, "I am a warrior, Geronimo. Always I have obeyed your orders. The people you have killed today are my People, but something—I think it is their god—has spared the little one's life. Do not harm him, or I will kill you." He turned and faced the entire band. "I will kill any man who harms the little boy. You are many. I am alone, but I will take many with me when I go."

The warriors stood ready to fight when Geronimo gave the word. I had decided that I would fight beside Jelikinne and moved to stand by his side, facing the warriors. Killing this child was not right. Killing any of the children was not right. My admiration of Geronimo was failing fast. His judgment seemed bad. I wondered if his Power had left him.

Naiche spoke up in the voice of the chief he was supposed to be. "This child will not be killed. Leave it alone, Geronimo, or you will die as Jelikinne says."

Geronimo held up his hands, palms out. "Naiche is chief. I obey Naiche. Let the boy go."

I thanked *Ussen* that many had not died fighting each other over the killing of *Nakai-yi* children. I never wanted to be in this kind of situation again.

To ensure the agents at San Carlos didn't know we were coming, we took Bylas and the White Mountain men with us and left the White Mountain women with a couple of warriors to watch them for a couple of suns but let them all go when their warnings would be too late.

FIVE

FREEING LOCO AND HIS PEOPLE

WE STOPPED IN a grove of junipers on the north ridges of the Gila Mountains and waited for Geronimo to consult his Power about the status of the raid and if it would be successful. He made a small fire, sang a song for each direction, and prayed to *Ussen*. His Power told him that all was going well on our way to San Carlos. *Ch'ik'eh doleel*. We moved on. South of the rough brown ridges north of the subagency close to the bluffs where Loco camped, we made a camp in the *bosque* trees and brush stinking of the black mud near the river and rested until the next sun.

As the setting sun turned the clouds from brilliant gold to orange and red and deep purple on their far edges, Bonito crossed the Río Gila and brought in Chiva's band of four men and thirty women and children anxious to leave San Carlos. With Chiva and his People in hand, we started for Loco's camp downriver.

Chihuahua took seven warriors and rode ahead to cut the telegraph lines as Nana had learned to do, using rawhide strings to tie the cut ends back together. With the wire ends connected by rawhide, no wire talk could get through, and it was very hard to find the break.

We came to where the Río San Carlos runs into the Río Gila near the bluffs where Loco had his village. We dismounted to wait while messengers were sent to tell Zele and Loco to make ready, that we had come for them and that their People must be ready to move at first light. Geronimo called Jelikinne, Naiche, and me to council with him.

Geronimo said, "Jelikinne, I ask that you go to Zele and tell him we're here to free him and his People from this place of suffering and to make his People ready to move at first light. From Bonito's story of their council meeting, I know Zele doesn't want to leave, but he'll go if we say so.

"For Loco, who has said he won't go with us and will stay here, he needs more persuasion. I ask two of my chiefs and best warriors—you, Naiche, and you, Chato—to take the message of our coming to Loco and his village. He will not want to go and will do or say just about anything to avoid leaving. Make him come, his People will follow him."

Naiche and I waved our hands parallel to the ground, the all-is-good sign, and headed for our horses. We followed the muddy swirling water of the Río Gila to the path up the bluffs to Loco's camp. The shadow on the moon (new moon), left the moon still visible with its low light in the night sky, and we could see it had passed its zenith by about a hand when we rode into Loco's camp, where orange coals from fires were turning black and gray after the elders had ended the evening telling the children stories.

Loco saw the tall and lean son of his old friend Cochise. He smiled, spreading his arms in welcome. "Naiche! It is good to see you, my son. I thought you were in the land of the *Nakai-yes* with Juh. Have you brought your People back to San Carlos?"

Before Naiche could reply, I stepped into the light, and Loco's face soured. "Chato? Chato comes with you, Naiche? I know how much he wants to be chief. Still, I know he rides often as *segundo* to Geronimo. Has Chato given up trying to become chief when the people don't want him that way?"

Lazy old Loco, who refuses to fight his way out from under the thumb of the White Eyes, who sits back and lets us do it for him. "Loco knows why we have come. Make yourself ready to lead your People away from this place of sorrows."

He looked at Naiche, but he was speaking to me. "I will not go! I promised the White Eyes I won't leave San Carlos. I won't break my word. No good for the People to run from here. The women have grown soft and dependent on the White Eyes. The men and boys can't even hunt. Weak, very weak have they grown here at San Carlos. I know life is very hard in the land of the *Nakai-yes*, very hard on the women and children, very hard on the men. We must stay here. No, I will not go, and neither will the People."

Naiche frowned at Loco. "Do you not get the shaking sickness here?"

"No, not so much. It is a good place where we camp."

"Don't the agents steal your rations?"

"Yes, sometimes, but we can do without them. We share. No one goes hungry here."

On a ridge up the Río San Carlos, a coyote yipped. I thought, Loco should be a coyote. He has an answer for everything.

Naiche shook his head, perplexed that Loco would want to stay here. He said, "The water is bad. It makes you sick."

Loco shrugged. "We have learned where the springs are nearby that give us good water."

"There are other Apache here who fight and attack you at every opportunity."

Loco smiled. "The Blue Coats and White Eyes see that they mind their own business. We don't fight often."

Naiche seemed to be pleading with Loco, who wouldn't give even a little in his argument. "There is little land here for you to farm. It doesn't grow much."

"What we cannot grow, the White Eyes and Blue Coats give us. We will not leave."

This back-and-forth between Naiche and Loco lit a fire in my gut that roared to rage the more they talked. I shoved my rifle against Loco's chest and cocked it, making him step back a little, but his eyes showed no fear. They should have. I was ready to kill him. I tried to speak evenly as if I was in control of myself, but all I could do was snarl, "If you refuse to leave, I will find you. I will send you to the Happy Place. Live for your People if not for yourself, or when light comes to the mountains, I will come here and kill you."

I turned and disappeared into the cool darkness lit only by the orange flickering flames on coals of dying family cooking fires. I heard Naiche's quiet padding behind me and felt my anger cooling. I had meant what I told Loco. I hoped he would lead rather than die. We needed him to lead his People and help us in the land of the *Nakai-yes*.

Naiche walked up beside me as we found our horses and left the camp. He said in a low voice as we felt our way down the trail to the river in the low light from the moon shadow, "Loco is a brave man. I hope he's not a foolish man. We need him to lead his People to get away from the Blue Coats without losing many of his People in fights with the Blue Coats following us."

I nodded. "We'll see. I hope he doesn't want to die, because if he does, I will surely kill him. There is no honor in staying at San Carlos."

GERONIMO WANTED US to cross the Gila at first light and begin moving Loco and his People up the Río Gila. I could see a weak glow behind the mountains toward the east. The sun was coming. A warrior tossed a pebble high in the air. We saw it along its entire arc, showing light was nearly with us, and knew it was time to go.

Warriors on foot formed a line between the camp and the agency buildings for the Chihenne two or three miles away. Those who were mounted began swimming their horses across the Gila. The men in the line and some on horseback began yelling:

"Come, brothers! Come, we take you away from here!"

"You suffer no more at San Carlos!"

"Take your things. Run up the Río Gila. Hurry!"

Geronimo was on his horse at the edge of the river, waving his rifle for the warriors to come on and yelling, "Take them all! No one be left in the camp. Shoot down anyone who refuses to go with us!"

The warriors ran into the village, pushing people from their wickiups and tearing them aside as they moved through the lodges.

I rode up to Loco's lodge. He was standing there deciding what to do, his women waiting behind him. I shoved the end of my rifle against his chest and cocked it. "Remember what I told you last night. Now move or die."

Loco looked at me, his scarred face with the drooping eye filled with disdain, but then he slowly nodded and turned to his women and told them to gather what they could carry and run. I motioned them toward the stream of people the warriors were leading forward and said, "Lead your People, Loco."

The stream of running people carrying what they could parted to let Loco get to the head of the line, where Geronimo, mounted on his pony, sat watching him. He gave the reins of a pony he led to Loco as he came up, and Loco swung up into the saddle in a smooth easy motion like a young man. Now Loco was easy to see and follow.

Geronimo nodded at Loco. "*Nish'ii'* (I see you), Loco. Now we go."

The people ran or walked in lengthening groups along the river. I rode in the back with other warriors to defend against any attacks. Chihuahua and his *segundo*, his brother Ulzana, waited with a few men in Loco's village. Hoping to draw the chief of tribal police, Albert Sterling, to the village, they fired a couple of booming shots, their thunder rolling up the valley of the Río San Carlos toward the agency. We pushed on upriver, but in half a hand against the horizon, there was a flurry of shots at the village and then a little later a few more.

Chihuahua, a big grin spread across his face, and his men came galloping up to join us. He said, "Hi yeh! I killed that sorry chief of police, Sterling, you know, the one who was always after us for making and drinking *tulepai* (corn beer), and his first sergeant, who showed up with more police. When the police saw Chihuahua kill the first sergeant, they tucked tail and ran for the agency. This should give us at least a full day's start without any harassment from the Blue Coats or the scouts."

I smiled and nodded. Chihuahua was a smart warrior. But my admiration for him was fading fast after he goaded Geronimo into killing those *Nakai-yes*, including their children, at Ash Flat.

Before the sun was halfway to the time of no shadows, Geronimo turned toward the ridges and canyons leading up to the *llano* plateau that held Ash Flat. As the people reached the top of the plateau, the sun began to hide behind the far mountains. We stopped near a spring and let them drink and rest. They were tired and weary. They had lost much of their strength and become soft squatting in the dust at San Carlos. That meant on foot they were much slower than our People in Mexico would be, a point Geronimo had missed in his planning. We were losing time, and the distance narrowed between the Blue Coats and scouts coming after us. It was a problem we had not counted on.

We stopped to rest again when the fingernail moon was at about the top of its arc before falling south and west. We were lucky the *llano* that we traveled over was well grazed, so the brush was grazed down making the ground easy to walk and run on. Geronimo sent out warriors to ranches and settlements to find horses and mules for people to ride after we crossed the Gila, after passing out of the Nantane Mountains at Eagle Creek, which we had followed out of the mountains. The People couldn't make any better time on horses and mules than on foot until we were out of the mountains. Then we had to make a strong run across the San Simon Valley, where many mounted Blue Coats looked for us. Only mounted might we beat the Blue Coats chasing us.

Geronimo sent another band of warriors to take sheep from the flock at Ash Flat, where Geronimo had killed Mestas and his herders. He told them they should be able to meet us at sunrise at the spring near the trail up the cliffs leading into Nantane Mountains and over to Eagle Creek.

THE RAIDERS DRIVING a few hundred sheep through the cliff shadows came just as Geronimo had said they should when we reached the spring. The hungry people, four or five hundred of them, who hadn't eaten in a day and a half, feasted, and we let them rest for two days while we decided the way south.

The council of leading warriors and chiefs, including Loco, met to decide how to get this large number south and safely in the land of the *Nakai-yes*. We knew Blue Coats and their San Carlos scouts would be after us like a pack of wolves soon. Following Geronimo's Power, we decided the trail south should be up and over the Nantane cliffs, down Eagle Creek, past Steins Peak, across the San Simon Valley, and into the Chiricahua Mountains, where we could avoid the Blue Coats as we slipped through Guadalupe Canyon into Mexico and into the Sierra San Luis not far south of the border.

As the warriors brought in more and more horses and mules from raids on ranches, the people were able to move faster. We followed the route we had decided on and stopped for spring water and rest at Steins Peak. At a nearby canyon, twelve warriors going to scout ranches for livestock and food for the people discovered scouts in front of a large band of Blue Coats looking for us. They set up an ambush in the canyon and attacked the scouts in a hot firefight. The Blue Coats, with nearly two hundred mounted soldiers, alerted by the gunfire, came charging into the canyon, only to be met by rifle fire from our warriors. Ha! The Blue Coats didn't stay long and withdrew.

I learned from one of the scouts as we sat talking at the trading post a couple of harvests later that the Blue Coat commander, Forsyth, claimed he had found all our warriors, fought us until we retreated, and then left himself. Ho! Such lies. We lost a warrior in that fight. Forsyth had lost maybe four soldiers. The People and the chiefs watched it all from about halfway up Steins Peak.

After the soldiers retreated, we made a hard night run across the San Simon Valley and into the Chiricahua Mountains as we had planned. We knew by using soldier glasses that we could see Fort Bowie and plumes of dust from soldiers leaving there. We decided to rest until the soldiers left the fort for our direction, but none came all day. We ran another night on the east side of the Chiricahua Mountains, recrossed the San Simon Valley to the southeast, then crossed the border using Guadalupe Canyon. In the Sierra San Luis, we made camp, at last able to rest in peace where the Blue Coats couldn't come. We stayed in that camp and rested all day. The People and the warriors needed it.

SIX

SIERRA ENMEDIO

IT WAS GOOD to rest where the Blue Coats couldn't come and where we believed there was little danger from *Nakai-yi* soldiers. Geronimo called a council in the shade of some junipers growing next to boulders that had rolled down the canyon sides to provide us convenient places to sit as the sun began its late-day march toward the western mountains. After we smoked, we discussed the best trail to Juh's stronghold.

Since he was leader, Geronimo spoke first. He told us, as we all knew, that Loco's People were weak and weary. Since we had been so successful escaping San Carlos and the Blue Coats chasing us, we need not hurry or stay on mountain trails moving to the Juh's stronghold. A good, easy trail for us to take was across the plains of Janos to the Sierra Enmedio, where there was a good spring providing plenty of water for the livestock, we could rest a few suns, and the women could bake mescal and dry some meat—and we could all celebrate a near-perfect raid to free Loco's People. Then, with the People rested, we could move south into the Sierra Carcay and on into the Sierra Madre and the safety of Juh's stronghold.

As Geronimo spoke, the shadows were growing long down the canyon, and coyotes were beginning to call to each other. In the falling light, I saw Naiche slowly shake his head. I felt the same way. Looking around, I saw other warriors, including Kaytennae, whose solemn faces among the others grinning and nodding said they also disagreed with what Geronimo was saying. Geronimo always seemed too eager for Mexican blood and too quick to let his guard down.

When Geronimo finished speaking, Naiche stood, turned to the men, crossed his arms, then spoke. "Geronimo has led us well. He is a powerful *di-yen* and war leader. He's right, the Blue Coats won't touch us here, but the *Nakai-yes* can and will. They grow stronger in Sonora and Chihuahua every moon and want to kill or make us all slaves. Before we left for San Carlos, the *Nakai-yi jefe*, Terrazas, tried many times to get Geronimo, Juh, and their warriors into Casas Grandes for some good whiskey. He wanted to get them drunk and enslave or slaughter our People while more *soldados* (soldiers) closed around and attacked us. We would have been wiped out, our names left only on the wind. But our trading friends told us what the *Nakai-yes* had planned, so we escaped them. They still search for us, ready to enslave or kill us all.

"Have we come running this far, escaping the Blue Coats, sometimes doing without food, sleep, water, and rest, to be taken by *Nakai-yi* soldiers and killed and enslaved? No! We did not! I say we must get the People to Juh's stronghold as fast as we can, and then they can rest, alive and breathing easy. We take a great risk of *Nakai-yi* attacks if we do not. This is all I have to say."

When Naiche finished, many heads nodded in agreement. I and Kaytennae stood to speak at the same time, and we stared at each other, neither willing to give way to the other. At last, Geronimo nodded in the direction of Kaytennae. "Kaytennae is the *segundo* of Nana, who waits for us with Juh. Kaytennae speaks first and then Chato."

Geronimo made me angry. I was his *segundo*, yet he chose to let Kaytennae speak before me. Perhaps it was because Kaytennae had convinced him to go to San Carlos to take Loco's People and gain many fresh warriors. Kaytennae's lips hovered near a smile as he glanced in my direction, nodded, and then spoke. My dislike for Kaytennae grew.

Kaytennae said, "I am Nana's *segundo*. Before we came to Juh's stronghold, we were attacked by *Nakai-yi* soldiers when we weren't expecting them. They killed several of our People, mostly women and children. They have *Rarámuri* scouts who are good trackers and fighters. I know Nana doesn't want to lose any more of his People, nor those of Loco. Even if Loco's People are weary, we should run to the protection of Juh and Nana, not walk. Walking risks being attacked and taken by the *Nakai-yes*. This we must avoid if we want to stay strong. I have no more to say."

Geronimo nodded, then raised his hand toward me. "Chato speaks."

I stood and faced the warriors. I was anxious to return to Ishchos and my three children. I was lonesome for them, needed to see and feel them in my arms. Naiche and Kaytennae were right. The risk of being attacked grew every sun as the *Nakai-yi* soldier numbers grew across Sonora and Chihuahua and their *jefes* grew more aggressive in trying to kill and enslave us.

"I have great respect for Geronimo's Power as a *di-yen* and his war leader skills. What we have been through since leaving San Carlos speaks to that, and we all see it. I am proud to serve as his *segundo*, and I will continue to do this as long as he wants me. A *segundo*'s first duty is to speak the truth to his leader. Now I speak truth to Geronimo. What Naiche and Kaytennae say is true. We risk much if we don't run back to Juh's stronghold, where Loco's People can be protected. The *Nakai-yi* soldier numbers grow, and they become more powerful by the day. If they catch us walking rather than running on the trail, many of the People will die. All that we have accomplished since leaving San Carlos will be of little value. I have said all I have to say."

Geronimo's forehead was furrowed, and his brows raised made him look surprised at the resistance to his proposal for taking the slow trail to Juh's stronghold. He seemed to waver in his judgment that we should first let Loco's People rest and recover from the hard run they had made on leaving San Carlos.

Geronimo said, "Our chiefs have spoken with wisdom. They are cautious, and they should be. Perhaps caution is the better trail."

Chihuahua stood and waited to speak. Geronimo paused and nodded toward him. "Our great chief, Chihuahua, is a mighty warrior. I ask him to speak to us."

Chihuahua said, "The other chiefs say we should be cautious and hurry to Juh's stronghold. They are men of wisdom and many battles. But here there is nothing to battle. And even if there were, Geronimo likes to say that we don't need to waste bullets on *Nakai-yes*. Rocks we throw will work just fine. Loco's People have been driven hard for nearly ten suns. They grew soft squatting in the dust at the reservation, waiting for their rations. They need rest, and we should take our time and let them regain their strength. I do not think there is any *Nakai-yi* threat nearby, and even if there is, our many warriors can handle it. What does our Chihenne chief Loco have to say? I have said all I will say."

I looked around at the warriors who were nodding and smiling and thought, *Fools! We risk many lives this way.*

Geronimo waved for Loco to speak after Chihuahua's invitation. Loco, old, with his drooping left eye, stood and looked around at all the warriors. He said, "Getting here from San Carlos without losing many of my People is hard to believe. You have saved us from the shaking sickness, heat, snakes, and lying agents. Truly, Geronimo, a mighty war leader and *di-yen*, is guided by *Ussen*. Now Geronimo says my People, who have been driven hard, sometimes without food or rest, for nearly ten suns, can walk the trail to Juh's stronghold, and Chihuahua says we can easily defeat any attack from *Nakai-yes*. I say my People need to rest and gain their strength to live in this land. I agree with Geronimo and Chihuahua. We need not hurry. Let us stop at the spring at Sierra Enmedio, rest for two or three suns, and then take the slow trail to Juh's stronghold so my People can make ready to live in this land. I have said all I have to say."

Looking around at the warriors, I saw that most were nodding their heads in agreement.

Geronimo looked over the group, and he, too, nodded. "Loco has spoken. We will not push hard for Juh's stronghold while Loco's People regain their strength. Tonight, we ride for the Sierra Enmedio."

Most of the men, agreeing, said, *"Ch'ik'eh doleel."*

THE RIDE ACROSS the Janos *llano* from the Sierra San Luis near the border southeast to Sierra Enmedio took most of the night. A great weight lifted from the shoulders of Loco's People knowing that the Blue Coats could no longer attack them and that the constant run, hide, and starve of the past ten suns was over. They rode slowly across the *llano*, careful to avoid the cholla, prickly pear, and mesquite easy to see in the brilliant, cold white light of a nearly full moon trailing across a shiny-black-cloth sky filled with myriad points of white light slowly turning around the north star that never moved and a great milk river of stars flowing past and outlining the Sierra Enmedio. The children were free to play, and they raced each other across the grama grass or hid in creosotes to surprise their friends running past. The young men in or near beginning their *novitiates* and the young women, some near marriage and others near their womanhood ceremonies, sang songs of happiness back and forth to each other while their parents joked and watched with amused looks as they remembered their younger days. It was a good time that night for us all.

In the early-morning light, we came to the dark, distant bump on the *llano* called Sierra Enmedio, a short stretch of low mountains with a good spring. This time of year, the spring overflowed its natural tank near the rocks clustered in bunches around the base of the mountain to provide a good place for watering the animals and making the grama grass and other plants growing there tall and green. The women and children found enough brush to make shelters up a draw up into the mountains for each family and wood for cooking fires. A few warriors rode a great arc around the north side of the Enmedio but found no traces of tracks that indicated soldiers from either side of the border were near us. We ate and then, in any shade from boulders or trees we could find in the bright, fiery sunlight, took naps and relaxed the rest of the day.

That night, enough wood was gathered for a great roaring fire, and we danced, some all night. Agave, tall and green and ready for harvest, grew in abundance on the sides of the mountain ridges. The next sun, women harvested some agave hearts, while the novitiate boys dug a pit and built a fire over rocks on the bottom, and the women and other boys brought the hearts to the pit edge. It took all that night to keep fire on the rocks to get them hot enough for the agave to bake. Early the next morning, the stones were too hot to handle. The boys laid the hearts in the pit and covered them with a thick layer of grass; then they covered the grass with dirt and rocks to hold the heat and water smoke in. It usually took a night and a day to bake the agave. When it was done, it came out of the pit soft and close to thick liquid and had to be spread out in thin sheets and dried before it could be carried. This meant we could probably leave in two or three days with enough of the good *nadah* (baked agave) to get us to Juh's camp without stopping to hunt and make ourselves fat on it while we waited for the rest to dry.

With the coming of the moon, big and bright, seeming to fill the low mountains with its light, we had another great fire, and again many danced all night. The next sun, the *nadah* should be ready to dry, and we would be ready to move on within a sun or two.

As the mescal cooked, I sat with the leaders near the end of the day, before the dancing began. We smoked, drank good strong coffee the warriors had taken on a ranch raid not long before we crossed the border, and talked of the trail we would follow and assembly points if we had to scatter. I had a bad feeling about this delay but didn't know why. Maybe my Power was trying to warn me, but I had felt no muscle tremors that usually came with a warning. I glanced at Naiche and Kaytennae as the talks went on. They sat with solemn faces, taking occasional sips from their cups sitting on the ground before them. We discussed the line of march for when we headed south. Geronimo, Loco, and the most feared warriors would ride behind the main group to protect from rear attacks, about half the warriors would ride on the sides of the main group, and Naiche, Kaytennae, and I with ten or twelve warriors would lead the group toward the next assembly point. We would leave as soon as the *nadah* was ready. We all loved its sweet taste, and I looked forward to getting a bite or two before we left.

Again, there were drums and songs by a big roaring fire as the dancers made a night of it. I was tired of dancing and wanted to sleep. I took my saddle, blankets, and rifle up to a place on the south side, away from the pounding of the drums, singing, and dancing. It was a little rock-covered hill a short distance from the camp. I was ready and anxious to get on the trail leading to Ishchos and our three children.

SEVEN

BLUE COATS
ATTACK

THE CAMP WAS quiet, light from the sun still behind the eastern sierras beginning to stretch over the *llano* and reach the side of the mountains across the valley
from Sierra Enmedio. Down below the little butte where I slept, two men, who
had danced all night, sat by a fire drinking coffee a woman poured them from an
old pot that she had somehow held on to through our week of running and fighting. A woman crawled out of her blankets and staggered toward some creosotes
that would give her a little privacy. To the south, coyotes yipped and called to each
other. I stretched and yawned and left my blanket to grow cold while I made water. Around the little mountains next to us, the Sierra Enmedio, its western side,
nearest where we camped, slept in deep, dark shadows. In the fast-changing gray
light, a young man, Gooday, appeared with two young women and his mother,
moving toward the boulders scattered around the pit used for baking mescal.

I was up high enough to see most of the pit and, even in the low light, saw
whisps of water smoke drifting up out of the grass and dirt covering the pit.
When the People pit-baked mescal, they placed agave leaves that stretched from
where the hearts cooked on the grass above the hot stones to reach up through
the top layer on the surface. By pulling an agave leaf and looking at how much it
had cooked, an experienced mescal pit baker could tell when the *nadah* would be
ready. Gooday was having a good time laughing and joking with the girls on the
way to pit. I watched them with a smile, remembering the days when I helped
women with a pit. It was hard work, but young men and women used the time
to get to know each other. The boys had a chance to decide how good the girls
working the pit might be as mates, and the girls a chance to see the personalities
of their future men in action.

Gooday and the women stopped near the pit, and a girl walked on to check it. I watched, hoping she'd signal the *nadah* was ready. She seemed to scan the leaves, saw one she liked, and walked to the opposite side of the pit to pull it. Just as she was reaching for it, the sharp, distinct crack from a rifle sent her flying forward to land facedown and unmoving on the dirt and rocks in the pit. A dark spot on her dress was quickly spreading. Gooday jerked his mother behind a boulder with him as the other girl disappeared in the boulders.

My sleep-clouded mind jerked into action. I ran for my weapons where I had spread my blanket. The People were up, confused, shaking the fog out of sleepy minds, groping to understand what was happening.

From boulders on a low ridge next to the cooking pit, rifle fire began to send a rain of lead down into the awakening camp. Warriors were up and firing toward the ridge while they herded the women and children to cover on the little boulder-covered butte where I had slept. Rifles on the ridge spewed bright pinpoints of yellow flame in the black shadows as I tried to find a target. I glanced to my left and saw a growing dust cloud out on the *llano* filled with black shadows and flashes of fire. I pointed at the growing dust cloud coming toward us and shouted, "Blue Coat cavalry!"

The warriors turned to fire in that direction. Geronimo yelled, "Wait, don't fire until you can't miss. They can't see us in the rocks and shadows."

As the riders raced toward the camp, they spread out in a long line, their pistols out, some already shooting, their bullets sounding like angry hornets whizzing over our heads but hitting nothing.

Blue Coats! In Mexico? What had changed?

Nodding, I thought, *If Geronimo lets the Blue Coats come close enough before signaling to shoot, we can wipe the charging riders in the first volley.* He waited until they were about a hundred paces from us and motioned us to fire. The men up in the rocks, excited by battle, didn't adjust for shooting downhill and shot over the tops of the soldiers' heads. The soldiers practically fell off their horses, dismounting and running for cover. I didn't see any of them hit, but men with deadly accurate trapdoor Springfield rifles, Sharps long guns, and Winchesters kept the Blue Coats pinned down until they began crawling backward, staying in the brush and shadows low to the ground, until they were out of range.

The firing slowed, the scouts up on the ridge only firing enough to keep us locked in place under cover. The Blue Coats sent scouts to take our animals near the watering place, and they got away with most of them. No more than maybe five or six warriors and maybe three women were killed in that first rain of death.

One old woman, her hair gray and straight, pulled back from her face wrinkled from years of hard work, Toclanny's mother, thought Toclanny was with the scouts. She climbed up to the top of the butte where we had taken refuge and stood waving her arms and calling for Toclanny to leave the scouts and help his mother. A single rifle shot hit her in the head and silenced her forever. I learned later that Toclanny was not with these scouts but with those in New Mexico.

Loco called out to the scouts to join our escape. "Brothers, help us! Come join our escape. You owe nothing to the Blue Coats. We are your family. If you're not with us, then go back to your families."

They answered with whining bullets ricocheting off the boulders around and near Loco and yells filled with scorn, wrapped in sarcasm:

"We're not your brothers, not your family—old fool."

"Why did you leave the reservation? Surrender now."

"We'll protect the People, but we'll hang you, you weak old woman. Give up!"

"Soon as we have you, then you'll be worse off, not safe in Mexico with the renegades."

"The Blue Coats are our brothers. We made our marks on their papers."

A ricochet whining off a boulder near Loco left a long bleeding trench across the meat on his left leg, but it didn't seem to do much damage as he kept urging the scouts to join us or go home.

The cavalry for the most part stayed back where our rifles wouldn't reach them. The scouts on the ridge near the mescal pit continued to keep us pinned down with their sniper fire that did us no damage, but most of the People didn't dare move for fear of exposing themselves to a deadly rifle shot. The scouts on the ridge yelled taunts at us to come get them if we could. I realized from their accents that they were Yavapais, and my anger burned hot. Yavapais had killed one of my uncles for no reason at San Carlos in the fighting when the prophet was killed.

The sun was maybe two hands away from the time of no shadows. I decided to go after those Yavapai scouts. I gathered a few warriors who, for one reason or the other, had no use for the Yavapai. Among the best of them were Kaytennae, a young Navajo whose name I never learned and who was with us because he wanted one of our women for a wife, and Fun—his Apache name, llt'i' bil'ik halii', which means "Smoke Comes Out," because he could load and fire his trapdoor carbine faster than most men could shoot with a lever gun like a Henry or Winchester. We stripped down to our breechcloths for action, threw bandoliers of cartridges across our chests, and asked She-neah, a *di-yen*, to pray for and bless us before we ran to get behind the Yavapai. This he did while turning each one of us to the four directions and as he sang and said we would be successful.

We ran fast and low through the tall grass, blooming yucca, and creosote bushes south toward the end of the Sierra Enmedio. When we were sure we couldn't be seen, we disappeared into a canyon east into the Sierra Enmedio. The canyon's bottom and sides were filled with juniper, and there was an animal path going up the northside that let us get to the top of a ridge to circle around behind those Yavapai scouts near the mescal pit.

We crept up close and hid behind smooth white boulders not more than two hundred paces away from the scouts, who were laughing and yelling insults and having a fine time keeping our People pinned down. I motioned for the men to pick their targets and stay low and out of sight. I sighted on the one I thought was their leader, and motioning them to fire, we rained lead and thunder down on them as they were doing to the People. I killed my man, the bullet tearing through his back and throwing him out of the rocks where he hid to land near the mescal pit. As soon as our bullets splattered in the rocks around them, making deadly whirring ricochets, the scouts hit the ground and rolled into cover trying to find where we were. Bullets from the warriors around the butte still pressed them from the front. They realized they had been flanked and were now in the center of a deadly crossfire. I watched the shots from our position with my soldier glasses and laughed as the Yavapai tried to hide from our bullets and ricochets. Those scouts were getting just what they deserved.

Soon they ran ducking from one cover to the next toward the Blue Coats who had charged us but then had to back up. With the rifle fire from the east silenced, the chiefs hurried the People away from the little butte where they had taken refuge and into a little canyon leading into the Sierra Enmedio not far from the butte. The canyon was filled with juniper, and the shade gave the People a place to rest and bind up wounds they covered with prickly pear pads growing scattered all around us. The women scraped off the pad needles and split them open to expose its juicy pulp, which made healing much faster.

The hot, brilliant sun was about halfway down its arc toward the western mountains when I and the other warriors found the People in the little canyon. From up on the canyon ridge, we could see the Blue Coats withdrawing and moving north. Naturally, they destroyed everything they could reach in our camp before leaving. After the Blue Coats disappeared, the People came out of the canyon and, in the long shadows, not having eaten since the evening of the day before, salvaged what little food was left. They would not eat the mescal because the girl had died on top of it, letting her ghost claim it all, so said She-neah. I thought that was a foolish idea but didn't argue with him. *Let the fools go hungry if they won't eat to keep from starving.*

Warriors gathered up those who had been killed and took them up the can-yon for burial in some cliffs in the southern wall. All told, there had been four-teen warriors and maybe six women and two or three children killed that sun. We wrapped the bodies in blankets, laid them on benches in the canyon cliffs, and covered them with piles of stones while, in despair, their women made low wails. Geronimo made a ceremony for the fallen to hurry them on their way to *Ussen* and the Happy Land.

No one had any idea why the Blue Coats had crossed the line dividing the Mexicans from the Americans, but we all wanted to find out. The chiefs, me among them, decided we had to leave that night for a rendezvous point in the Sierra Carcay foothills in case the Blue Coats came back for further attacks. No one knew when they might come. From the rendezvous, we could run to Juh's stronghold before the Blue Coats could rearm with ammunition from a mule supply packtrain that followed them. We believed Juh and Nana had probably learned in Janos or Casas Grandes why the Blue Coats were now crossing the border when they didn't before.

As it grew dark, some warriors followed the Blue Coat trail back to their camp and reported back that they had seen many soldiers and scouts. Other warriors were able to gather thirty to forty horses and mules the Blue Coats had over-looked. The Blue Coat herd was too well protected to get more mounts. Those who had lost their horses would have to walk until we could find more at a ranch.

THE NIGHT WAS turning cold when the People finished eating and gathered what was left of their personal belongings. It was time to move on to the ren-dezvous point. I helped the wounded mount and then the old ones and very young children, so they wouldn't slow us down.

As we had planned the evening before, Geronimo directed Naiche, Kayten-nae, me, and ten other warriors to lead the People south along the foothills of the Sierra Madre to the rendezvous place. He would stay in the rear with most of the warriors to protect against attack by the Blue Coats, and he put a few warriors on each wing of the line of march as a guard against unexpected attack from those directions.

Most of the People were on foot, weary and weak from dodging bullets in the heat of the day and from having little to eat. We in the lead slow-walked our horses. Even walking, some of the People were slower than others, and the line we led grew longer and more stretched out. The moon rose to the top of its arc and began to fall in the west. The line grew longer and longer. Word came from Geronimo to stop and let the people catch up and rest a while before we went on.

THERE WERE NO fires for the weary. The People didn't care as long as they could lie down, huddle together, and rest in the cold night air under the great milk river of stars. Naiche, Kaytennae, and I sat together off to one side with the other lead warriors wrapped in our blankets, looking like big stones scattered in the moon shadow of a tangled mesquite tree. We rolled *tobaho* (tobacco) in papers a warrior had taken during a raid on a ranch and smoked, feeling its good bite in our noses and watching it drift and spread away in the cold, still air as we exhaled.

We sat in silence for a while, each man bathing in his thoughts. Naiche glanced at me and then Kaytennae before he said, "Geronimo, Loco, and Chihuahua must now see our wisdom in wanting the People to run and not delay. Even if we had only stopped for a sun, we would still be far ahead of the Blue Coats after us and would not have suffered what we did this sun. I wonder what has changed for Blue Coats to cross the border after us?"

Kaytennae smiled, showing his white teeth in the darkness. "It doesn't make any difference."

Naiche frowned. "What do you mean?"

"I mean it doesn't make any difference whether it is on this side of the *Nakai-yes* or on the American side. We can kill them all anyway when the sun shines as long as Geronimo and the other old chiefs don't get in the way."

I said, "As long as the Blue Coats have scouts with them, they'll be hard to surprise or put down. Don't underestimate the Blue Coats. They're fighters even if they don't know the country. You know how well they fight. I blame our losses especially on Geronimo for listening to Chihuahua and Loco. He listens to himself too much—he didn't even have sentinels guarding the camp, he was so sure no enemy was near. One day, many will die because of his pride leading to bad judgment. Our work will be to keep from being killed before we can help when the attacks come. We need to be the attackers, not the defenders, if we want to live."

Naiche nodded. "Hmmph. Chato speaks true." Kaytennae just stared as if he hadn't thought about what to do against the Blue Coats if they were in Mexico. That was his big weakness. He didn't think far enough ahead and was too impulsive when he did act.

The rest of the time we waited, we talked of what we saw and did during the day's battle and how we could be stronger in the future.

We rested a couple of hands against the horizon and started south again.

EIGHT

ALISO CREEK

THE MOON WAS fast disappearing behind the dark, jagged outline of the mountains to the southwest. The People, still weary, moved slowly, the line of march stretching out longer and longer. Those of us in the lead, although walking our horses, kept up a steady pace and were far in front of the main band when we came to a big *arroyo* with a dry creek showing a few scattered pools of water between long stretches of sand and boulders. The *Nakai-yes* called it Aliso Creek. *Arroyos* coming from the western mountain foothills, also dry, fed the creek we followed.

The sun edged up behind the eastern mountains, casting a low but steadily brightening glow across the *llano*. As we came to cliffs running on the eastern side of the creek, maybe six hundred feet high by White Eye measure, casting great long shadows and defining part of the northern edge of the Sierra Huachinera, the trees along the *arroyo* grew bigger and more numerous than those out on the *llano*. We crossed the *arroyo* and took an easy trail that ran along the *arroyo's* western side. The trail crossed the entrances to two nearly parallel *arroyos* out of the western mountains that were not more than three or four hundred paces apart.

Something wasn't right. I heard no birds calling from the brush or trees, and I thought I heard a horse snort. There was a faint smell of coffee and smoke in the air. In the cliffside shadows, it was still too dark to see much. I nose pointed toward the west and frowned a question at Naiche and Kaytennae, who shook their heads and kept riding. The smells of smoke and coffee were undeniable, but they weren't interested in trying to find their sources, especially crawling around in the weak light in the cliff shadows. Perhaps they came from a *vaquero* camped up one of the *arroyos* or maybe Mexican soldiers and militia, which we wanted to avoid. We stayed quiet until we were well past the *arroyo* where we had smelled the coffee and smoke and near a low hill about a half mile away with a few trees on top. The hill was high enough that, with more light, we could see surrounding *llano* and, maybe by that time, the sources of what we had heard and smelled. I signed to Naiche and Kaytennae for us to ride to the top of the hill, and they nodded. We followed a shallow wash to trees on the back side of the hilltop, where we motioned for the warriors to dismount while we went to the top with our soldier glasses and sat down in the tall grama grass to study the scene.

The light was already much better than when we had crossed the *arroyos*. It didn't take long to find the object of our search. I heard Naiche mumble words of despair and Kaytennae make a low whistle. Our line of sight from the hill toward the east was limited by the cliffs on the east side of the creek. The cliffs made a sharp turn toward the east about a mile away from us and blocked any view of the line of march along the creek out on the *llano*. Hidden by the deep trench of the last *arroyo* we had passed were many *Nakai-yi* soldiers checking their rifles and ammunition. One of their *jefes*—all the fancy symbols on his uniform said he was the comandante—stood on the top of the *arroyo* bank, using his soldier glasses to study the direction from which the people must be coming even though we couldn't see them. It was obvious the *Nakai-yes* were planning an ambush, and it was clear he knew there was a larger group of Apache coming because they hadn't ambushed us, no doubt to avoid scaring away the larger band.

I felt my nerves tingle and my heart pound with a steady rhythm like I was running. I knew those signs. My body was making ready for a hard fight while my mind was trying to sort through what to do. We had to do something. If we did nothing, the *Nakai-yes* would slaughter many Chihenne women and children before Geronimo and the warriors behind them could come to help them.

I counted the soldiers beginning on the western end of the *arroyo*. When I finished, I said to Kaytennae and Naiche, "There are at least two hundred fifty *Nakai-yes* in the *arroyo*, and most have soldier uniforms and good rifles." Through clenched teeth, I said, "Why didn't the chiefs listen to us? Why? We tried to warn them, but they were blinded by their own false wisdom. Now many women and children will die despite anything we do. This is a bad day to die."

Naiche said, "If we try to ride around the *Nakai-yes* to warn the line of march, they won't shoot because that would warn them and make them scatter, but the comandante will send some men running forward to attack the line of march. We won't reach the People in time to defend them or for them to run from the attack. If we try to ride straight through the way we came in past all those rifles, we'll be killed, but maybe the sound of their gunfire would be loud enough to warn the others."

Kaytennae said, "If the sound of gunfire is all we need to warn them, then let's fire from here. Maybe those in front of the main band will hear it."

I shook my head. "As soon as we fire, the comandante will send some of his soldiers after us. We can hold them off, but snipers in that creek *arroyo* could easily hold us down. There's no place to hide on the sides of this hill. If we get on the back side of this hill, they'll come overtop or around from behind to take us. The comandante will still use the rest of his soldiers to run for the main band. We're half a hand's ride from the leaders of that band. By the time we can get to them, it'll be too late to warn anybody."

The *Nakai-yi comandante* moved his arms and motioned his men into position along the creek bank beyond where the cliffs made a sharp turn east. They were hiding and waiting in the *arroyo* parallel to the trail toward the main band. All those men were going to be shooting and charging, so they hit, at the same time from the side, the front part of the line of march, mostly women and children and a few men. My mouth felt dry. It was like watching someone I knew slowly slide over the edge of a high cliff and disappear to smash into the rocks below. There was nothing we could do to stop it.

I said, "Once the *Nakai-yes* finish here, they'll likely go on to Juh's camp and finish off our families. The men Juh and Nana have aren't enough to defend against a two-hundred-man army, although they'll have fewer after Geronimo and the others take their shots. These soldiers must be part of the Terrazas army that's been trying to kill us all ever since we escaped him last harvest in the Season of Earth Is Reddish Brown (late fall). We can't let this happen. Somehow we have to get into the fight and do what we can."

Naiche stared through his soldier glasses at the *Nakai-yi* soldiers arranging themselves in the creek bed parallel to the trail as far as he could see and said, "We made a bad mistake forcing Loco's People to come here. It will be remembered a long time around the evening story fires. When the *Nakai-yes* attack, mostly women and children will die. Those not killed will run and hide and come together later when the sun hides. Geronimo and the warriors in back will charge forward to fight the *Nakai-yes*, and maybe they can fight them off. What if the Blue Coats we fought yesterday come in behind Geronimo from the north—there were probably half again as many Blue Coats as *Nakai-yes* soldiers down there now when we attacked the Blue Coats near Steins Peak. The same soldiers weren't at the fight yesterday—those had Yavapai scouts. They'll go north until they find their mule train with ammunition, reload, get more soldiers from the band we fought at Steins Mountain, then come back. When they see we've left the Sierra Enmedio camp, they'll think they have us on the run and have a chance to catch and wipe us out. If the People are caught between many Blue Coats and the *Nakai-yes*, Geronimo and the warriors will be wiped out along with the rest. There is no use for us to go die with Geronimo and the chiefs who thought we were safe in the land south of the border.

"We can protect those who run and get away from the soldiers. They'll find each other after the sun leaves, and we can find them if we watch where they go. Tomorrow we'll head for Juh's camp. We'll need to move fast and take horses for those who got away. We have to get back to Juh and warn and protect our People. We can't stop the *Nakai-yes* from attacking the main band. Who knows? Maybe Geronimo's Power will save them, but we can't risk our People being attacked because we're killed in a hopeless fight protecting Loco's People."

Kaytennae and I stared at Naiche. This wasn't the Naiche we knew. This man spoke like a strong, tough chief, like a son of the great Cochise, not just a warrior who took directions from his leader.

Kaytennae slowly nodded. "I want to kill these hateful *Nakai-yes* and send them torn to pieces to their Happy Land, but Naiche speaks wise words. We can't let these *Nakai-yes* and maybe Blue Coats with them attack Juh's camp. I have a wife and my adopted son to care for. Chato has a fine wife and three young children. Naiche, you have three wives and two children in that camp. Can we leave all our women and children to be slaughtered or leave them without fathers and husbands because Geronimo and the others made bad mistakes guiding Loco's People in Mexico? I say no. Many in this march will die. I'm sick at heart about it, but we have to protect our families first. The *Nakai-yi* and American chiefs have agreed to fight us together. How else could the Blue Coats be here? We have to defend Juh's camp first."

I stared at the grass and shook my head. "This is not right, but there is nothing else we can do unless we want to die leaving our families at risk and hungry. I say we protect and defend those who run."

AS THE LIGHT grew brighter, dust from the line of march rose above the tall trees along the creek and hung in the cool morning air. Our soldier glasses showed *Nakai-yi* soldiers scrambling up out of the creek and charging the line of march from the side with long knives fixed on the end of their rifles. There were the sounds of a few distant pops, rifle fire, and the sight of a swell of men seeming to rise out of the *llano*, yelling as they ran toward the women and children.

The reaction of a few was quick. They ran like rabbits in all directions, some even south down the road we had followed. I followed the path of most of them who ran toward protective canyons of the western mountain foothills, which gave me an idea of where we could find them later. We could barely hear other women screaming to those behind them, "Go back! Go back!" But most were caught like a fawn in a neck noose, jumping and kicking in a frenzy to be free and all the time trapped and choking. The long knives wielded by the *Nakai-yi* soldiers stabbed and chopped them down like White Eye scythes laying low long green grass. Those who didn't run, and the knives missed, were killed by the distant pops from rifles growing more and frequent. I had never seen such killing of women and children or heard the faint distant screams of terror from our People. Naiche and Kaytennae stared and listened with me, transfixed by helpless anger at what we were seeing and hearing. Those screams and images filled my dreams for a lifetime.

Out of the dust and screams and pops of *Nakai-yi* rifle fire thundered Geronimo and the other leaders and warriors on their horses with their rifles turned on the *Nakai-yi* soldiers. The soldiers began spreading out. Some backed down into the protection of the creek *arroyo* and retreated toward where the cliffs turned east. The warriors screaming their war whoops and racing between the attacked women and children and the soldiers drove them past the first *arroyo* coming from the western foothills until the *Nakai-yi* comandante appeared out of the second *arroyo* with more men firing as fast as they could load their rifles. Geronimo and the warriors backed up and took cover with the women and children in the first *arroyo*. There was so much shooting, horses rearing and bucking, and people running that the smoke and dust made it hard to see what was happening around the *arroyos*.

Men and boys followed by a few women and children burst out of the smoke and dust cloud. Most ran for the canyons and foothills to the southwest, but two boys and a man who had been running with a small group of women and children ran toward our hill. *Nakai-yi* rifle fire was heavy around them, raising many little clouds of dust as the bullets pounded the earth near their feet, but none hit the runners.

One boy was much faster than the other boy and the man. He was soon far ahead. When the fast one ran over the top of the hill, he stopped to catch his wind. Disgust and anger flashed in his eyes as he looked around at chiefs who had weapons and plenty of cartridges but sat hidden and smoking in the grass on the top of the hill, watching the People die. I hated that look in the boy's eyes saying we were shameful cowards, and I wished we were in the fight, but we had to think of boys like this, others who had gotten away, and our families, whom we could protect, rather than struggle and die surrounded by Blue Coats and *Nakai-yi* soldiers.

The man soon made it to the top of the hill. He pointed off toward the southwest and said to the boy, "Your mother ran toward the mountains." The boy nodded and ran toward the canyon out of which came one of the *arroyos* from the foothills. The canyon was near a mountainside where we had earlier agreed to meet if people had to split up.

We turned our attention back to the fight down by the creek. Geronimo had led the People into the first *arroyo* feeding the creek, and the *Nakai-yi* comandante had his men in the next *arroyo*. From where we sat, we saw furious fighting between the *arroyos* and then long pauses while the comandante tried to decide what to do next. Several times, he had his men charge Geronimo and the People across the wide space between the *arroyos*, but they were driven back. I wondered if the warriors were running low on ammunition and believed they probably were. I learned later how an old woman had crawled out of cover in the *arroyo* to cut loose and drag a big bag of ammunition under a hail of bullets to the *arroyo* after the mule carrying it had been killed. I learned later how Fun had gripped the People's attention with his rapid-fire marksmanship and courage during the *Nakai-yi* soldier charges and how Geronimo and Chihuahua and others had distinguished themselves. It was a time of singing for heroes, a time of wailing for those who had died, and a time for me and my brothers to regret for choosing only to defend runaways against Blue Coats who never came.

When the sun was near to passing behind the western mountains, we went down the back side of our hill and mounted our ponies to ride for the rendezvous place in the foothills, prepared to defend it but not knowing how many were left to defend.

NINE

A LONG NIGHT'S JOURNEY TO THE SUN

THE NIGHT COVERED us like a heavy blanket as we rode toward the meeting place where those who had escaped the *Nakai-yi* attack waited. As we climbed up the *arroyo*, heading for the mountainside where we were to gather, I looked back over my shoulder. I saw flames and smoke around the stretch of *arroyo* where Geronimo and the other warriors had fought the *Nakai-yi* soldiers. They would have to leave the *arroyo* without a sound soon or be taken and killed by the *Nakai-yes*. It meant either leaving the babies, or strangling them, and carrying on someone's back those who were too badly wounded to walk. I looked away and shook my head in despair.

We heard the low wails from the mountainside meeting place before we found it. There was no guiding light, no fires to give the place away. Lying in the deep grass, were many wounded who suffered while making no sound. Others panted in their painful misery, and still others who had family killed in the initial *Nakai-yi* attack wept in sorrow. The People had no blankets to keep warm but covered themselves with grass or juniper needles under nearby trees and, staying close together, tried to stay warm in the cold darkness.

I looked among the suffering People for some I might know and could somehow help, although I had no supplies with me except a jug of water and a small bag of dry trail food. I found Tzoe and Kayitah, a more proven, older warrior than Tzoe. Kayitah, cousin to Martine, whose woman was my sister, lay with a wound in his calf covered by a prickly pear pad. Tzoe had split prickly pear pads tied to a wound on his lower thigh. Dry grass had been pulled over both men in an effort to keep them warm. Tzoe made no sound, but I heard deep breathing and saw that he clenched his teeth against the pain.

Tzoe was a young White Mountain man, a good warrior and part of my band before I left the reservation with Geronimo and the others. He had married two Chihenne women, cousins of mine, and the family had a child, a little girl. When I left the reservation with Geronimo, Tzoe's women insisted on staying with their People in Loco's camps at San Carlos. Since his White Mountain People were nearby, Tzoe chose not to run for Mexico with my men but stayed with his women. Tzoe was the kind of powerful warrior who made Geronimo want to come back for Loco and his People.

My sister Gotsi sat nearby, looking after both. I think Martine must have been with Geronimo and the other warriors fighting from the *arroyo*. I didn't see either of my cousins married to Tzoe or their child.

I squatted down by my sister, who nodded to acknowledge me, and whispered to her to avoid disturbing the others. "Ho, my sister. It has been a bad day, but at least you got away. Are the wounds of Kayitah and Tzoe bad? Are you hurt? How can I help you?"

"We need water. These men are very thirsty. By the time we got here, it was too dark to look for a spring or water in the *arroyo*."

I gave her my water, and she crawled across the bent-down grass and lifted each of their heads in turn to give them a couple of swallows. There was some left, and she lifted the canteen toward me. I waved my hand for her to drink, and she took a swallow. Returning to my side, she gave me the canteen.

I said, "I know where to get more. Drink the rest if you need it."

She shook her head. "Please get more first. I'm sure the men are still thirsty."

I nodded, "This I do. But first tell me of Tzoe and Kayitah and your husband, Martine. Are Tzoe's and Kayitah's wounds bad? What do you know of Martine? Where are Tzoe's wives and child?"

She puffed her cheeks and blew, looking off in the darkness toward the fires of the *Nakai-yes* and the fire around the stretch of *arroyo* where bits of the grass fire around our rifle pits still burned. Even at this distance, we could smell the smoke from the grass fire. "Martine was with the warriors on the flanks of the march. He asked Kayitah to stay up close to the front of the line and keep an eye out for me if there was any trouble from the front. Kayitah told me to run as soon as the *Nakai-yes* attacked us, and I did. He began returning their fire, but the bullets were thicker than falling hail from a black cloud. He was lucky his only wound is in his calf. I ran back to help him up, and we headed for cover in an *arroyo* that led up into the mountains.

"Tzoe was firing fast as a man could with his trapdoor rifle when his women and child were killed, and he took a bullet through his lower thigh and fell. Kay-itah saw him hit and told me to run on while he aimed for the yelling *Nakai-yi* soldier with a long knife on the end of his rifle, running to stab Tzoe. Tzoe man-aged to draw his revolver and shoot the soldier about the same time Kayitah's bullet hit. Kayitah ran up and grabbed Tzoe, who didn't want to leave his family, but Kayitah dragged him into the *arroyo*, telling him his family was gone and there was nothing they could do. I helped both men as we staggered and crawled up the *arroyo* that led into the foothills. We heard Geronimo and the warriors come, and the shooting and war whoops picked up as the *Nakai-yes* fell back in the dust and smoke. They tried to stay in the first *arroyo* they came to, but their officers kept backing up, so they retreated to the next one, and Geronimo and the warriors took the first over while the women and children dug holes in the banks for cover.

"Finally, late in the day, we found this place where others had come. I bound Tzoe's and Kayitah's wounds with prickly pear pads and, with the cold night coming, covered them with grass."

I nodded in pride at the strength and bravery of my sister. "You are a fine woman for Martine and for all of us. Stay here. I'll bring you more water." I crept away and found the little spring where I remembered finding it before. Rubbing the cold water on my face felt like a slap of a *di-yen* trying to awaken me from a bad vision, but when I opened my eyes, the day past and its night were still there. I filled the jug and returned to give it to her.

Naiche, Kaytennae, and the warriors with us had also helped and brought water to those who needed it. When we had done what we could, we found a place just below the camp where we could keep an eye on the trail we had fol-lowed and watch the grass fire around the *arroyo* battle site about three miles away burn itself out. The night, clear and cold, lighted by the milk river of stars surrounded by myriad scattered points of brilliant light across the obsidi-an-black sky, glowed bright and beautiful. Coyotes yipped and called all around us but grew silent when a couple of wolves called them out.

Looking out across the valley to the place where the battle was fought, we saw a second set of fires about a mile north and east of the *arroyo* Geronimo and the warriors had held with the surviving women and children. We wondered if the comandante had reinforcements coming to help him. *Nakai-yi* cavalry re-inforcements had come soon after the time of shortest shadows and had made a half-hearted charge toward the *arroyo* before being driven back and had not reappeared in the fighting the rest of the day; otherwise, we saw no soldier

replacements coming for those he had lost in the fighting, and our People had
wounded and killed many.

MY SHORT SNATCHES of sleep that night were filled with visions and voices
of the slaughter the day before. I awoke just before dawn, the darkest time of the
night, and saw the flares of a few fires just starting in the *Nakai-yi* soldier camp. As
the sun behind the eastern mountains began to fill the *llano* with light, I looked to
where the second set of campfires were and, using my soldier glasses, studied its
men just becoming visible around the fires. I had to stare at it a while before the
light was good enough for me to realize that it was a Blue Coat camp.

I cringed to think, It must be true. The Blue Coats and *Nakai-yi* soldiers are
joining forces. Our concern about this had been right, but the Blue Coats had
come too late to get in yesterday's battle. As I studied the camp, I counted the
soldiers and realized the ones we had fought two days earlier must have joined
forces with those we had fought at Steins Mountain. There were five or six
times as many soldiers before my eyes as those who had attacked us at Sierra
Enmedio. If they had come earlier last sun, everyone in that *arroyo* battle would
have been wiped out. I no longer had any doubts that Naiche, Kaytennae, and I
had made the right decision not to get involved in the *arroyo* battle. Now we had
to get these people and *arroyo* survivors back to Juh and decide how to attack
this new Blue Coat–*Nakai-yi* army.

Without a word, Naiche and Kaytennae studied the Blue Coat camp too,
glanced at me nodding, and then continued to watch, as did I. The *Nakai-yi*
comandante and a *segundo* rode over to the edge of the Blue Coat camp and
stopped. Blue Coat officers rode out to meet them. The Blue Coat comandante
and his *segundo* at the head of the column rode up to the *Nakai-yi* comandante
and made the touch-the-forehead-with-the-edge-of-his-hand sign of respect,
which the comandante returned. The Blue Coat *segundo* translated between the
two comandantes. There was much talk and arm waving back and forth.

The talking and arm waving came to pause, and then the *Nakai-yi* comandante motioned for them to follow him and led the Blue Coats around the space
where the *Nakai-yi* soldiers first attacked the women and children and then between the two *arroyos* where most of the day's fighting had taken place. There
were bodies everywhere, mostly Chihenne women and children at the site of
the first attack. Between the *arroyos* were many soldier bodies.

The Blue Coats rode into the *Nakai-yi comandante* camp. We saw that the co-mandante had taken maybe thirty women and children prisoners, which the Blue Coats and their scouts visited. It looked like there was some bargaining for them by the Blue Coats, but no prisoners were moved between camps, so the *Nakai-yes* must have kept the prisoners—soon, I was sure, to be sold as slaves. The Blue Coats brought five or six mule loads of supplies over to the *Nakai-yi* camp and left them, and the Blue Coat *di-yens* helped wounded *Nakai-yi* soldiers.

Midway to the time of shortest shadows, the Blue Coats left the *Nakai-yi* comandante camp and rode east past where the cliffs turned east. We mounted the wounded on what horses we had and led the survivors down an *arroyo* that would take us south toward Carretas and the trail toward Bugatseka, where Juh and Nana waited for us with our families. I wondered why the Blue Coats were going east. The *Nakai-yi* comandante probably wanted to refit and get more troops before they headed south in search of Juh's camp. That delay would give us time to reach Juh and plan how we would face the *Nakai-yes* and Blue Coats. We needed to understand what they were planning, but none of us had any idea how to do that.

WE HAD MOVED in the *arroyo* for more than a hand against the horizon when we found Geronimo, Loco, and Chihuahua leading their warriors to the meeting place. We were all happy to see each other and gathered in the shade of some tall brush, where Geronimo told us of the day-long battle with the *Na-kai-yi* soldiers. He described how Fun had become the hero of the day with his bravery against the *Nakai-yes* charging the *arroyo* again and again. He told how they had nearly run out of ammunition when an old woman ran out to where a mule carrying a big bag of cartridges had been killed, cut the bag loose, then dragged it toward the *arroyo* under heavy fire until Fun and Chihuahua helped pull her and the bag down into the *arroyo*.

I could tell from their smiles and bright eyes how proud the People were to hear these stories, but as I looked around and counted the women, children, and warriors, I felt like I had eaten bad meat. Nearly half Loco's People were missing, killed, or taken into slavery. We had taken forty warriors from San Carlos but had lost twenty in the two days of attacks and fighting—all because Loco's People were tired, and our "great" leader let them rest. My admiration for Geronimo as a great war leader was fast shrinking like a leaking water bladder going dry. None of us in the advance guard, who never fired a shot while others fought and died, had anything to say, and when Geronimo looked in our direction, he never acknowledged or seemed to see us, like we weren't there. We, too, had made a mistake by staying away from the fight, thinking the Blue Coats were coming sooner than they did.

With the People's spirits raised, Geronimo sent warriors out to raid ranches for mules, horses, and cattle. Most of the wounds were minor, but the wounded moved slowly. They needed to ride, and most had not eaten in over two days.

Late that sun, we reached a place with a good spring we called Bent-ci-iye (plentiful pine trees) about a slow three-hour ride past the springs of Carretas. The trail up a wide *arroyo* had been easy, but the weary, starving people sat down to rest, unmoving in the late shadows of the day. Soon the warriors Geronimo had sent out returned with horses and cattle. The warriors butchered the meat while the women made cooking fires. The juices from the meat dripped into the fire, making smoke with a smell that drove the people near crazy with hunger, but they had the discipline to wait until the women said the food was ready and served it.

TEN

RETURN
TO BUGATSEKA

THERE WERE MANY sighs of quiet pleasure as the cooked beef filled hungry bellies. The People, after a long day of fighting Blue Coats, a night of walking across the *llano*, and then a cold, freezing night of fighting *Nakai-yes* or hiding on a mountainside, needed rest. Geronimo stayed for two days at Bent-ci-iye, waiting for their strength to return before heading up into the mountains to Bugatseka, where Juh and Nana camped. While others rested, those wounded were tended by *di-yen*s, and Geronimo made medicine to help them. Kayitah's and Tzoe's wounds seemed a little better but were so painful they couldn't walk or ride any distance. Martine let his wife, who had healing Power, continue to look after them with Geronimo watching.

The first rest day, I rubbed down my pony with grass I found in the open spaces, hobbled him, then left him to graze with the camp's other ponies under the watchful eyes of some boys not quite ready for their *novitiates* to begin. I sat on my blanket back in the shadows of some tall pines and cleaned and oiled my rifle and revolver. I knew that, for me to survive, my weapons needed to function perfectly in the coming days.

As the shadows grew long toward the eastern mountains, I saw Kaytennae sitting in the shadow of a big juniper, talking with many hand gestures for emphasis, to Geronimo. I couldn't understand why the old man listened when Kaytennae's words to him, and especially to the council, had gotten us all in trouble, wiped away half of Loco's band, and gotten some of our own good warriors killed. Kaytennae was a brave warrior, but his ideas brought us nothing but trouble. My liking for him grew less the more I was around him.

After Kaytennae left and headed for the horse herd, Geronimo motioned to me and called, "Ho, Chato. Come speak with me a while. Let us smoke to the four directions."

I nodded, set aside my weapons, then walked through the long shadows to his blanket. To smoke to the four directions meant he had serious business to discuss. He motioned for me to sit to his left, a place of honor, while he took *tobaho* from a beaded pouch he carried in a vest pocket and rolled a cigarette for us to smoke, which he lighted by snapping a match against his thumbnail like I had learned to do while watching White Eyes.

After our smoke, Geronimo stared into the growing darkness among the pines for a while and then said, "Every man has to make his own decision about when and where to fight, no matter where he is or when. You're a brave man and have shown your courage and skill in many battles. I know you're never afraid to fight. Yet you and the advance guard at Aliso Creek didn't help us when the *Nakai-yes* attacked. I don't understand. Tell me. I don't blame you for not fighting, I only want to know why."

I looked first at Geronimo and then up into the nearby trees lighted in gold from the falling sun. I said, "I'll answer your question if you'll answer mine."

He raised his brows and nodded as if to say, "Yes?"

"Why do you think the Blue Coats came into Mexico when their chiefs say they cannot cross the border? Have the *Nakai-yes* and Blue Coats agreed to fight us together with no concern for the border location? If this is true, then we must worry about our People in Juh and Nana camps, like those at Bugatseka, being attacked."

Geronimo shrugged his shoulders and shook his head. "I don't believe there is a war pact between the *Nakai-yes* and the Blue Coats to fight us. We were so close to the border at Sierra Enmedio they probably thought they could disobey their *jefe*, take us prisoner, then go back across the border without making him angry. They left the night we crossed the *llano* to Aliso Creek. There's no danger from Blue Coats or *Nakai-yes* to our People at Bugatseka."

I watched children playing while they hid among the trees and shook my head. "Yesterday morning, the *Nakai-yi* soldiers let Mangas and then us pass so as not to warn the others. This we realized looking back from our hill a long rifle shot away. We didn't warn those in front of the march because we couldn't get around the *Nakai-yi* soldiers in time. We didn't shoot a warning because even the sound of gunfire wouldn't carry that far, but the *Nakai-yes* could certainly hear it and come after us. We had no chance at all if we rode back through or around the *Nakai-yi* soldiers to warn the front of the line. I counted two hundred and fifty *Nakai-yi* soldiers just before they attacked the front of the line of march, which by then was stretched out a couple of miles.

"When the *Nakai-yi* attack came, your rush forward with the warriors saved many, but many also ran west, wounded or not, for the meeting place on the mountainside. We nearly went down to the fight where you were, but Naic-he asked what would happen if the Blue Coats returned. Then we would all be caught between two big armies and wiped out—not enough warriors, not enough ammunition to defend ourselves after the Enmedio fight. The *Nakai-yes* and Blue Coats would probably go on to Bugatseka and wipe out the rest of our People. We decided to protect our families at Bugatseka with Juh and Nana in case the Blue Coats came back rather than risk being killed in a fight from which we had been freed."

Geronimo nodded. "Hmmph. You made a wise move, but for nothing since the Blue Coats didn't come back."

I stared at him and shook my head. "The Blue Coats did come back."

"No! Where were they?"

"They came when the light was nearly gone, about the time you were leaving the grass fire and smoke around the *arroyo*. They camped about a mile away to the west, out on the *llano* next to the big *arroyo*. We saw all this using our soldier glasses from where the survivors camped."

His face seemed carved in stone as he stared toward the last light of day. "Then you did the right thing staying back to protect the survivors and your families in Bugatseka. My Power could have warned me about the Blue Coats but did not. It was silent all yesterday. I don't know why. Tell no one of this. We will speak again."

I said, *"Ch'ik'eh doleel,"* and walked back to find my blanket and weapons while there was still enough light in the shadows of the trees. When I looked back, Geronimo was gone.

THE NEXT DAY, Geronimo, working with Martine's wife to heal the wounds of Kayitah and Tzoe, said their wounds would get worse if they walked or rode any distance. She suggested building them a hidden *wickiup* near a spring, leaving them food, then letting them return to Bugatseka when their wounds were not too painful for travel. Tzoe and Kayitah and Geronimo all looked relieved when they heard this. Geronimo wanted to leave the next sun. Martine agreed to let his wife stay with the scouts, act as their *di-yen*, and help get them back to Bugatseka when they could travel. If she got them back to Bugatseka alive, the recognition of her Power would grow, and so would the gifts for her services— although that wasn't the reason she stayed, but maybe the reason Martine let her stay. The women put up two wickiups, one for the men and one for Martine's wife. They left enough drying meat from the slaughtered cattle to get her and the two men through a moon of healing and back to Bugatseka.

Next sun, as new light began falling over the western mountains and hills, Geronimo led the People up the dim trail that stayed on the ridgeline nearly all the way to Bugatseka. My last memory of that camp was the dim outline of Martine's wife, her hands on her waist, standing near the unseen wickiups, watching us leave. The first night we stopped, Geronimo sent a man with more food for the three we had left behind and instructions to stay and help as much as he could, but he came back early the next morning and said they were gone. We learned later, he never went to the camp of Tzoe and Kayitah. They stayed there until they returned to us but never saw the man with the supplies.

TWO SUNS AFTER we left Tzoe, Kayitah, and Martine's wife, lead scouts from our march found Juh and Nana's camp in Bugatseka near the time of short-est shadows. They told Juh and Nana we were near to give the women time to prepare a big welcome for their returning men and Loco's People.

A few others and I led the People out of the trees across the big, grassy meadow in front of the camp where the horses grazed. The women and children in camp had formed two long lines for us to pass through, where they raised their hands in welcome, some waving pieces of bright cloth and all the women ululating in joy at the return of their men and in welcome of our Chihenne brothers and their families to their new camp.

I saw Ishchos and the children near the head of the line, and my heart leapt with the joy and pleasure of seeing my family again. I wanted to stop my pony and gather them in my arms, but a man must show no emotion for his family until they have some privacy. Still, I looked in Ishchos's direction and smiled. She saw me and, with a shining face, pointed, yelling, "Chato comes! Chato comes!"

We led the People toward the center of the village, where Juh's great tipis stood. We stopped and waited for Geronimo to come forward as Juh stepped out of his *tipi*, followed by his sons and wives, and stood waiting with crossed arms. Soon Geronimo and Loco, followed by Chihuahua and Kaytennae, Naic-he, Mangas, and me, rode up. Geronimo threw a leg over his saddle and slipped off his pony, walked up to Juh and nearby Nana, then said, "Juh! Nana! Great leaders of the Nednhi and Chihenne, your warriors have returned, bringing with them Loco's People from San Carlos."

Juh, who was a big, tall man, full bodied, looking fat but all muscle, gazed between Geronimo, Loco, and the chiefs behind them to see the large group standing behind us. He smiled and said, "We welcome the great Chihenne chief, Loco, and his People. Let us have a feast when the sun disappears. Let Loco's People take shelter with us, and our People will give them what they need. We will help them make their lodges next sun. Loco and your People, we welcome you to our camp. Come meet old friends and new ones and refresh yourselves."

Loco's People, who had lost everything during the attack at Aliso Creek, were welcomed with great joy by the People in the camp. It made no difference whether the families knew each other or not; food and shelter, even cloth and clothes were shared. The feast Juh called for seemed to appear out of the air, and it was a great celebration for the arrival of the People. It was a happy time and the biggest gathering of Chiricahua and Chihenne together since the time of Mangas Coloradas and Cochise.

MY FAMILY AND I were alone at last. I sat down in front of the little fire in front of Ishchos's *wickiup*. My son of seven harvests, Bediscloye, stepped up to me, his face serious, and stood straight and tall like he imagined a man should and said as he had seen men do, "I have protected your lodge, Father. I am happy you have returned."

I replied as he expected, "I thank you, my son. Well done. Soon you must show me what you have learned while I was gone."

My oldest child, Maud, about ten harvests, and youngest, Naboka, about four harvests, came to me to take them in my arms and hug them as they threw their arms around my shoulders.

Maud said, "We have waited with our mother a long time to see you, Father. Welcome back to your family's lodge."

I smiled. "My daughters are a pleasure to my eyes. Their welcome, I have waited a long time to hear."

I released my daughters, who wore happy smiles, and stood. Ishchos, her eyes shining, said, "My husband has returned. Now I am whole again. Our lodge and your family have longed for your coming and prayed to *Ussen* that you stay safe." She stepped up to me and wrapped her arms around me to press her body close as I held her. She smelled of crushed cactus flowers, yucca soap, and good things to eat she made around the fire. My heart gave thanks to *Ussen* for her as our children stood there grinning.

"My woman and children make me feel great joy, and I thank *Ussen* for them."

ELEVEN

CASAS GRANDES

GERONIMO SAT AND talked with Juh every sun. I was not invited to sit with them, but neither was anyone else. I wondered if they talked about the *Nakai-yes* and Blue Coats joining forces to wipe us out. Nana and Kaytennae sat with Loco often, and they talked long into the night. It made hot coals of anger burn in my gut every time I saw them together, knowing that I should have been the one talking with Nana and Loco. I should have been Nana's *segundo*, but Kaytennae had been chosen. It was bad for a man of little leadership to serve as a *segundo* for a leader like Nana. Loco's heartbreak over the *Nakai-yi* attack at Aliso Creek showed in the dimming light of his eyes. What made things worse for Loco was that his beautiful daughter had been taken captive.

On the fourth day after our return, lead warriors gathered at Juh's place of council in the shade of tall pines amid shafts of sunlight making small golden pools on the reddish-green needles. It was our first council since returning to Bugatseka. While we waited on Juh and Geronimo to join us, we talked of when the *Nakai-yes*, and maybe the Blue Coats with them, might be planning to attack us and how we might get the first blow in the coming fight.

Juh, tall and heavy, stepped from his big *tipi* near the center of the lodges, carrying the geometric-patterned blanket on which he used to sit. In a few paces, he joined Geronimo already heading toward the council. Nana, Kaytennae, and Loco sat at the back of the council and kept their silence.

Juh stuttered when he was excited. He often had Geronimo speak for him, so there was no misunderstanding what he wanted. This day, in front of his own men, Juh spoke for himself. He held out his arms, his big muscles swelling with power, and he spoke in a commanding, booming voice as he first addressed us.

"Brothers brought here from the reservation. We are glad you came to us and want to stay far away from the White Eyes and Blue Coats. I know the trail was long, and your fights with *Nakai-yes* and Blue Coats were hard. But you are here! You have lived through a hard journey. You are always welcome in the camp of Juh. Others have returned from a good raid in Sonora with cattle and much loot from the ranches there. Now I tell you what my *segundo* and I have decided. We tell you what we plan. It is your choice whether you stay or follow us."

The listening men, their ears cocked forward from one side, were as still as hunting cats waiting for a deer. Even the breeze and birds were still. I felt a muscle tremble in my upper arm, a signal of danger close by, a warning from my Power.

Juh looked at each man before he continued. He seemed to linger when he looked at me as though he might speak, but he continued on studying other faces before he said, "Many *Nakai-yi* soldiers now camp close to the mountains in northern Chihuahua. My men who live in *Nakai-yi* villages say more are coming. They plan to wipe us out. My *segundo* tells me the Blue Coats and *Nakai-yes* may be planning to fight us together. This I have not heard from my men but will learn if it is so before another moon. Regardless of whether the Blue Coats join with the *Nakai-yes* to fight us, the *Nakai-yi* soldiers are many and their presence fences how and where we can raid and move across the mountains and deserts. It is time for us to consider a lasting peace with the *Nakai-yes*. I have good agreements with the *alcaldes* in Janos and Casas Grandes. If we do not attack them, they will let us trade freely with their men who have supplies, and when we need food, they will give it to us. We'll have no need to take it. I think we can trust these men if they agree to give us land in return for not raiding their homes or killing them. What have the warriors to say to this?"

Warriors looked at each other and frowned. What was Juh saying? There was no more war or raiding? Out across the meadow where the livestock grazed, I saw the shadow of Buzzard sailing like a great black cloud on the ground. I wondered, Is Buzzard coming to feed on our bones? Geronimo told me in another time and place that Juh had tried peace before but that the *Nakai-yes* had just wanted to kill us.

Naiche stood up on the other side of the council warriors from me. He crossed his arms and spoke in a tone of respect, but his words formed a question we were all thinking. "What does Geronimo, the great *di-yen*, think of a lasting peace with the *Nakai-yes*?"

Geronimo, squatting near where Juh stood, stood up straight as he answered

Naiche. "I don't know what the *Nakai-yes* will say to Juh's terms for peace. He believes that there are enough of us now that they will want peace. After all the fighting and running we've been through returning from San Carlos, I need a drink of good whiskey. While the *Nakai-yes* talk and think about Juh's peace terms, we can drink all we want. I plan to drink plenty."

Naiche made a thin-lipped smile. "I could use a drink of whiskey myself." There were nods and a low rumble of talk among the warriors. "When does Juh plan to leave for Casas Grandes?"

Juh said, "We'll go quietly so the *Nakai-yes* don't call their soldiers, fearing we come for war and raiding. We'll move east two days and camp on the Río San Miguel maybe two hands' ride from Casas Grandes. Those who want to do business in the village and drink its good whiskey will make another camp maybe two fingers' (half an hour) ride away. There we talk with the *Nakai-yes* about my peace terms. After we talk, they'll want to council with the gran *jefes* in their villages grande about my terms—they always do that—and we will take turns trading, no more than half of us in a sun, going into Casas Grandes to drink and trade. When the *Nakai-yes* know there are many warriors who can come after them if they try to kill those who are drunk, they will not do to us what they did to Nolgee four harvests ago."

The men looked at each other and then Juh and Geronimo, nodding they approved, and slapped the ground in agreement, saying, *"Ch'ik'eh doleel."*

Juh said, "We go to Río San Miguel in two suns. Have your women make ready. We leave when the sun comes."

The council broke up with little groups of warriors off speaking among themselves. I walked back to Ishchos's *wickiup* thinking I didn't like this move. If we wanted to drink whiskey, it was too dangerous to trust the *Nakai-yes*, even with half the warriors sober. What I saw at the council told me that Geronimo was more interested in getting a drink of whiskey than talking about peace terms for the People. That was foolish.

I LAY IN the blankets with Ishchos as we listened to the call of night birds and the movement of little night animals in the brush and under the trees. Our passion and pleasure had been great while our children played with others in the night after our evening meal. They knew not to enter the *wickiup* when the door blanket was down.

Ishchos, lying in the crook of my arm with her head on my chest, said, "Will we stay in the first camp on the San Miguel or the one closer to Casas Grandes?"

"Make your *wickiup* at the first camp. I'll go with the leaders to the second camp when Juh discusses terms with *Nakai-yes*, but that won't last more than a day. The *Nakai-yes* from Casas Grandes will want to discuss Juh's peace terms in council with the *jefes* in the village grande to the east. That'll give Geronimo and those who want whiskey time to drink plenty before they have to make an agreement. Drinking now is foolish. We can't trust the *Nakai-yes* not to try to kill us when we're drunk.

"I'll do some trading using horses and mules I have and then return to the first camp with you and the children. All the time we are there, be ready to leave for the mountains in a hurry. My Power tells me this is a dangerous move, but Geronimo wants his whiskey."

Her hand moved lightly on my chest, and she sighed. "My man is a wise and powerful warrior. The children and I will be ready for trouble, ready to run for the mountains when you tell us.

"Soon the children will want their blankets. Naboka is weaned. Let us try again to make another child."

I smiled at the pleasure and great help this good woman gave me. "If that's your desire, my woman, then it's my desire too."

"Yes, I much desire it so."

WE FOLLOWED THE narrow winding trails across the mountain ridges, through deep winding canyons mostly in shadows, some so narrow that when you looked up you could see stars well into the morning time. At last we rode down the green-and-brown east sides of the mountains west of Casas Grandes. We first camped hidden in the *bosque* near Río San Miguel about two hands against the horizon's easy ride from Casas Grandes and southeast of Colonia Juárez and Las Tinajas. The *llano* along the *río* gave the livestock we brought for trade good grazing and let us fatten them and rest them for a better trade in Casas Grandes. The trees, saplings, and brush growing along the Río San Miguel gave the women good poles and limbs to make shelters, and the *río* provided good water with which to cook and wash. I could tell Ishchos was happy there, as were most of the other women who stayed at the first camp.

The next day, Geronimo led about thirty families, mostly those with men who wanted to drink and trade in Casas Grandes, up the *río* and made camp facing a thick *bosque* about half a hand's easy ride from the *Nakai-yes* village. Juh sent two women who knew and were known by the merchants into the village to tell the *alcalde* that we would meet with the *alcalde* and soldier *jefe* to discuss peace terms in two suns, two fingers' easy ride south of Casas Grandes on the river trail when the sun was halfway to the time of no shadows. The women returned and told Juh and Geronimo that the *alcalde* had agreed to the time and place of the meeting.

THE *NAKAI-YES* FROM Casas Grandes came riding down the dusty road running by the willows draped in streaming veils of light-green leaves, tall ancient cottonwoods, sycamores with peeling strips of dark brown bark, and weeds and flowers scattered along the Río San Miguel. In the lead were the *alcalde* and a soldier *jefe*, behind them three of the traders with much to trade in the village. The traders were followed by soldiers in two columns of ten riding two abreast in perfect high-stepping rhythm. The *alcalde* rode a big black stallion, its saddle and bridle covered in silver conchos that caught and reflected sun like mirrors. He carried no weapons—guns or even a sheathed knife and managed the reins with one hand while resting the other on his upper thigh. His hair was as white as the big, high clouds above us and that on his face neatly trimmed, although for an Apache, any facial hair was ugly. The whiteness of his face hair made his black eyes stand out and seem to throw darts impossible to dodge when he stared at someone.

The soldier *jefe* wore a blue-gray coat with what looked like cloth braids in three rows of fancy curls and circles, and there were ornaments on it made of narrow shiny cloth from which medallions of many shapes and sizes hung. His pants were the same color as his coat but had a red strip down the side. Gold trim lay in two directions across his cap, which had no brim but a little black shiny piece in front that helped keep the sun out of his eyes. He was a proud and arrogant man in his prime. A big bush of hair grew at the end of his nose, which, like the *alcalde*, he kept carefully trimmed but also pointed and curled at the ends like ram's horns. His horse, a big black, stepped with precision. There was no silver on the bridle and saddle of finest quality leather. Now I know where to look when I want to take a good saddle and bridle, but I didn't think the big horse would do well in the mountains.

The soldier *jefe* also carried no weapons except for the long knife that hung at his side, jangling against his leg. The traders behind the *jefe* and *alcalde* wore the clothes we always saw them in, open vests with little golden chains hanging from their pockets, white shirts, and black pants. They also appeared to have no weapons. The soldiers were well mounted, and all wore the same kinds of blue-gray clothes as their *jefe*, but the edges of their coats and pants were trimmed in red, and they wore a black shiny-leather harness that they could hang weapons from. They had high shiny boots and hats with a black piece in the front, like their *jefe*. Mounted on the front of the hat was a stick with a ball of red material that stuck up above the top. Each had his long knife hanging and jingling from his side. We could have wiped them out in an instant, and I wished later that we had.

The *alcalde* and soldier *jefe* led their men up to Juh and Geronimo sitting on their horses in the middle of the road with their war leaders spread out behind them. Each leader made the all-is-good sign with the flats of their palms swinging out from their bellies, parallel to the road.

Geronimo, who spoke very good Spanish, said, "We're glad the *alcalde* and the *jefe*, *Coronel* Terrazas, speaks with our leader Juh about his terms for peace. Come join us in the shade of trees nearby, where we can sit in council. Juh sometimes stutters. He wants our words clearly understood and asks that I speak as his representative."

Looking at the thin man with the carefully groomed hair under his nose, I thought, *So that is Terrazas. I know the name. He led the soldiers who wiped out Victorio. He's the one who wanted Juh and Geronimo to move to a reservation at Ojinaga while trying to get them drunk and murder or enslave them. He's the one who got Nolgee drunk and murdered him and most of his band. This peace is a sham. He wants to murder us like he did Nolgee's band. Geronimo and Juh must know this. This is a very dangerous game they play.*

The *alcalde* glanced at Terrazas, who nodded and then smiled and motioned for Geronimo to show the way. Soon we sat in the shade of big trees near the *río*, the leaders on both sides facing each other and their men scattered behind them. As Juh's *di-yen* and *segundo*, Geronimo led the smoking of cigarettes to the four directions and made a prayer to *Ussen* that we might all live together in peace. When the cigarettes were finished, the *alcalde* and Geronimo spoke of the old, hard days of war and how peace was better, and this was what both sides wanted. Terrazas sat grinning and staring like a rattlesnake with his hands folded in his lap. The *alcalde* thanked Juh for asking for peace terms and asked what those terms were. The sun was nearly to the time of no shadows, and the remnants of the cool morning breeze coming from the mountains had stopped. The soldiers and Terrazas in their fine clothes began to leak water down their faces. The warriors sat with faces masking their thoughts, but their eyes studied every move the soldiers made. There was a stillness in the air. Not even birds called as the two sides eyed each other.

Geronimo, answering the *alcalde's* request for peace terms, said, "We welcome the *alcalde* and *Coronel* Terrazas for this time to talk peace after a long time of war. Our chief, Juh, says for peace that you give us the Carcay Mountains and nearby land—few of your People live there—but the mountains and land have food, like mescal cactus, the Apache cook and eat. It is where we can raise livestock and our women can farm. Trade with us in Chihuahua villages, and when times are hard, give us food to eat so there is no need for us to take it in raids on your People so our families don't starve. Do this and Juh's People won't make war or raid the People of Chihuahua."

The *alcalde* nodded at Terrazas, who had been studying the face of Geronimo as he spoke. Terrazas said, "We hear the peace terms of the great chief, Juh. They sound acceptable to me as soldier and to the *alcalde* and his traders here with us, but the big chief, the governor of Chihuahua, must agree to them for the peace to apply everywhere in Chihuahua." As the soldier chief spoke, I watched his eyes, saw the laughter behind them, and knew he was lying. Geronimo must have seen this too, but he sat there and nodded. The soldier *jefe* went on. "But while we wait, let us be brothers. All the war we have fought with Juh is gone. Either side takes no revenge. Come, let us be brothers and fight no more. Come, trade in Casas Grandes. We share our mescal with you while you trade and we wait for the governor's approval, which ought to come in less than a moon. While we trade and drink, let us be true friends. What do you say?"

Geronimo spoke to Juh in Apache, translating what the *jefe* had said, although Juh had understood every word. When the translating was done, Juh made the all-is-good sign and said, *"Ch'ik'eh doleel!"* as did most of the warriors in the council, but I said nothing. I knew it was just a matter of time before the *Nakai-yes* would try to get many of the People drunk and kill or enslave them. I planned to trade my animals the next sun and then stay in camp with Ishchos and the children, ready to leave when the *Nakai-yes* attacked us.

TWELVE

"TRUE FRIENDS"

AFTER THE COUNCIL with the *alcalde* and Terrazas, I rode back to the first camp, where most of the People had stayed. It was calm and peaceful riding by the *río*. The *río* had a low singing burble and glinted in many places like a thousand mirrors. Crows chattered from the tops of tall sycamores, and bushtit flocks lifted from the brush in small gray clouds that swirled over the *río* and back again. In a hand against the horizon, I returned to our peaceful camp by the *río*, near good grass on the *llano* for the livestock and with easy access to the *río*. Boys nearing their *novitiates* kept the livestock from wandering too far from the camp and watched for *Nakai-yes* who might become raiders. I saw my children playing with others along the *río* and knew Ishchos was out with other women looking for mescal and mesquite with bean pods that could be harvested later when the time was right.

I sat down in the shade of cottonwoods near our shelter, intending to rest a little before choosing the stock I wanted to trade for supplies Ishchos needed for the next three moons and ammunition I wanted in Casas Grandes. It was very comfortable in the shade, and I slumped back against the big cottonwood behind me, listening to the slow-flowing *río* sing its peaceful song.

My mind kept returning to the question of how the *Nakai-yes* would try to get us drunk and then slaughter or enslave everyone they could. Keeping half the warriors in camp while the other half went to the village was a smart move, but *Nakai-yi* soldier *jefes* were clever too. They would find a way to attack the people in town.

MY EYES SNAPPED open in the warm breath of a dusk breeze. Naboka saw I was awake and ran from where she had been watching to tell Ishchos, who nodded and looked over to wave me to the fire. She was cooking meat on sticks, boiling plants in a pot, and baking mesquite bread in an iron pot sitting on the edge of the fire with coals on its iron top. She sent Naboka to call the older children, and I staggered up and walked to the *río*, kneeled, then drank from my cupped hands and splashed water on my face.

As usual, the meal my woman made was a very good one. The children gobbled it down, and the two youngest ran off to take their places around a big fire where an elder would tell them stories from the long-ago times about Child of the Water and the monsters he faced, stories about why we have our customs and ways of living, and maybe a Coyote story. Maud, my oldest child, helped her mother clean up around the cooking fire, and then she, too, ran to hear the storytellers.

After Maud left, Ishchos said, "Tell me, husband, what did the *Nakai-yes* say about Juh's peace terms? Was it a good council, or do you still worry they will betray us?"

"The *alcalde* and the soldier *jefe* thought the peace terms were acceptable, but for them to work everywhere in Chihuahua, their big chief in the City of Mules (Ciudad Chihuahua) must approve them. This we knew would happen. It's happened before when they wanted to get us drunk and kill us all, but we slipped away in time. They invited us to come into Casas Grandes to trade, and since they want to be our brothers, they will give us all the mescal we want to drink. Juh and Geronimo agreed. With about half the people in the camp near the village, Juh and Geronimo plan to take their families into Casas Grandes tomorrow while those left in the camp will wait until the next day. That way, if the soldiers want to attack us while we're drunk, they know at least half of us will come after them, and they'll leave us alone. This has let us trade freely before, but one mistake and we'll ride the ghost pony."

"Will you trade your horses and mules tomorrow? If we go early, we should be safe. Can I and the children go with you?"

"My woman is wise. I, too, think it will be at least three days before the soldiers attack after trying to get us drunk. Next sun is the best time to go. You and the children come with me. Decide what supplies you need, and I'll get more ammunition. Maybe I'll get a bottle of their mescal and bring it back here to drink." I smiled and stretched to see the children at the storyteller's fire before saying, "The children will be at the storyteller's fire for a while." I saw her eyes brighten and a smile begin. "Do you want to try again to make another baby?"

A bright smile filled her face as she laughed that fine throaty laugh of hers, and she said, "My man knows my thoughts and my heart." She stood and took my hand. "Come into my *wickiup*, husband."

WE RODE INTO Casas Grandes two hands before the time of no shadows. Already there were many of our People walking the dusty streets, some with loot taken in raids to trade, others with horses and mules they wanted to trade for things they wanted inside the trading places. Most of the men already had a bottle of mescal but hadn't yet uncorked it. People seemed to show extra care that they weren't drunk before they traded anything. I stopped with my string of ponies and mules and waited for Ishchos and the two girls to go inside a traders place we had often visited. He didn't always give the best prices for what we had, but he always kept his word and spoke straight when we argued price. I pulled my moccasin out of a stirrup and lowered my hand to Bediscloye for him to take while he slid his foot into the empty stirrup and scrambled up behind me.

We led my horses and mules down dusty streets to a trader's corral on the north side of the village. A couple of wranglers, an old White Eye with much hair under his nose and on his chin, and a much younger one who could not yet grow hair on his face, sitting on either side of a big gate, grinned as we rode up, and I said, "We trade?"

They nodded and said, *"Sí, señor.* Do you want other animals or things from a trading post?"

"Trading post."

They climbed down from the fence, opened the gate to let my horses and mules in, then took the rope I handed them to keep them together until they looked them over in the swirling dust raised by the other horses and mules trotting back and forth to avoid the wranglers and the new animals.

Bediscloye and I stood outside the rough gate and watched the wranglers as they looked over my horses and mules, brands, and how well they had been taken care of. They used wooden sticks tipped with pointed, black, smooth tips to make marks on paper. These they gave to me when they came to the fence. The older man said, "Those are good-looking animals, and we give you a fair price since the brand from northern Whites Eyes *ranchos* ain't clear. This here paper you can use anywhere along the stores on that street over yonder to make trades."

I looked at the paper, saw the marks, and, not knowing what the marks meant, folded it, slid it into an upper vest pocket, and said, "Trade no good, I come back."

The men smiled and nodded. The older one said, "Get some mescal and have a drink on us. Just tell the trader we said so."

I grinned and said, "This I do." I lifted Bediscloye up behind my saddle, and we rode back to the trading place where Ishchos and the two girls had stopped. Their ponies were still tied to a hitching post near the water trough in front of the building. I heard Ishchos laughing inside the dark doorway of a big, white adobe building among many on that side of the road. I went inside with Bediscloye to find his mother talking with Chee-hash-kish, Geronimo's beautiful woman and mother of two of his children, about cloth for clothes, a big fold of canvas to help cover our *wickiup*, and three or four heavy new blankets she had bargained for that were piled on a smooth table in front of the trader. There were also a couple of bottles of mescal standing by the stack of blankets. The trader was an old man with thin, gray hair cut short on top of his head, a big pile of white hair on his chin, and light twinkling in his eyes. He was friendly and laughed easily. I had known and traded with him since my first raids in Sonora.

Ishchos and Chee-hash-kish saw me and made motions to come inside. The street was fast getting hot and the cool gloom lighted with lanterns high on the walls and posts and light coming through the door. The good smells of spices, fresh blankets, mescal, and gun oil made me glad we had come.

I said, "*Nish'ii'*, Chee-hash-kish. It is a good day to trade. Where is our brother Geronimo?"

She laughed and said, "He's a few doors down the street with a bottle of mescal, looking for more cartridges for his long rifle and the short gun he wears. He was looking for you earlier but couldn't find you. I was looking for new blankets and a big iron pot for baking bread when Ishchos and the girls came in the door. We've missed you. You should stay in the camp nearby with the other chiefs, so you don't have to ride so far to come here. Geronimo says it is safe."

"Hmmph. I will talk further about this with Geronimo. My Power warns me to be careful. His Power must know more than mine."

"His Power is strong. Speak with him and move closer to the second camp so you have more time to drink, and Ishchos and the children can enjoy the good times in this *Nakai-yi* village."

I gave the all-is-good sign, and Ishchos said, "I told the trader you had horses and mules to trade and would be back soon. The pile of blankets, canvas, and other things, I think, are good for us."

I smiled at her and gave the trader the marked paper the old wrangler had given me at the corral.

The trader looked at the paper and then said, "It is good to see my old amigo, Chato, and his family. The paper says you have much credit for trading. I give your children sweets and your wife mescal for your drinking time. We have a drink together before you leave, eh?" I smiled and nodded. "Now what else can my trading post provide you?" He held up the paper and said, "There is much you can have against this paper."

"Hmmph. Then I want ten boxes of .45 cartridges."

He looked on the shelf where he kept ammunition and said, "Sorry, but I only have four boxes left. If you want to wait, more comes in three or four days."

"Go ahead and give me four now, and I come back to get the rest when they come."

"Good! Come back for the bullets in four days. They should be in by then. Maybe Ishchos needs a few new knives? I have several kinds, all very sharp. Maybe you could use a new revolver and holster or even a fine new hat? Maybe sacks of good coffee? There is plenty of trading room for all that on this paper."

We looked at the trading post loot for a time, haggled, then bought more. The trader helped Ishchos wrap our things in the canvas she bought and mount it on a good pack mule we had tied outside with the horses. As we rode out of the village, some of the men were sitting on the boardwalks, their backs against buildings, and passed out. Others were having a good time staggering in the street and tossing empty bottles for others to catch. Traders leaned in their doorways, watching what the men were doing and grinning.

We saw Geronimo and Chee-hash-kish sitting together, each with a nearly empty bottle of mescal. Chee-hash-kish looked sleepy and Geronimo barely able to sit up. He saw us and waved us over.

He said, "Chato! I look for you all day. Be sure you get your mescal. The *Nakai-yes* give it away. Have a good time."

I nodded and glanced up to see nearly all the traders were watching us.

"I spent most of the time trading with Gonzalez. He gave us some bottles of mescal, but I wait to get back to our first camp to drink it and then have a good time."

"Why go back to first camp? Drink it here so your family doesn't have to ride so far. Make a camp with us. We'll have a good time. Don't you want to have a good time, Chato?"

I grinned. "Yes, I want to have a good time, but I remember your stories about what happened to Nolgee. I won't let that happen to me and my family."

Geronimo looked at his feet and then raised his head to me with a silly grin. "Yes, Nolgee used poor judgment. We made the *Nakai-yes* pay for what they did to us, but no one from Casas Grandes harmed Nolgee. We're careful. Juh waits in the second village. His turn is tomorrow. I see you in a sun or two, and we talk. Bring your family and come stay with the other chiefs in the second camp. You'll be fine."

"Maybe so. Now we go back to first camp. I see you maybe tomorrow when the mescal doesn't cloud your thinking."

Geronimo raised his bottle. "In the next sun or two. *Ch'ik'eh doleel.*"

I made the all-is-good sign, and we rode off toward first camp. When we passed the second camp, we could see the adults wandering around with bottles in their hands, but most people were not drunk. I hope it stays that way.

THIRTEEN

THE TRAP

FOUR SUNS PASSED. More people from first camp decided to go on into the second camp. They wanted to get their share of giveaway mescal and to trade for loot with livestock or other things, like baskets. After meeting with Terrazas about where our land would be, and drinking a bottle of mescal, Geronimo told me to come to his *wickiup* on the sixth day after we came to Casas Grandes. He wanted to speak of where we would raid in Sonora in the Seasons of Large Leaves and Large Fruit (summer and early fall). The sixth day was one when he didn't drink. His mind was clear when he was sober. It's a good time to plan raids.

There were many more people in the second camp on the sixth day than usual. I thought this strange and asked a young man, Haozous, who had just become a warrior, why more people hadn't gone into the village. He shrugged his shoulders. "Last sun, traders in the village started acting strange and distant, like they were afraid of us or that we were coming after them. They made many jokes, but there was much trembling. Many of the warriors think that maybe the *Nakai-yes* are planning to attack us. But I don't know."

I thanked him. My fears about *Nakai-yi* soldiers attacking us grew as I weaved through the cluster of camp lodges to the *wickiup* of Chee-hash-kish. As I expected, it was near the middle of the camp, close to Juh's big wickiups.

Geronimo and I sat by the ring of fire stones Chee-hash-kish used for cooking in front of her *wickiup*. We had smoked and were talking about places to raid in Sonora. I suggested we also consider places in Chihuahua, but Geronimo said we would be under a peace treaty with the Chihuahuans by then and needed time to see what they would do with it. We heard wagons coming down the *río* trail, and the camp became quiet as everyone tried to look past the trees and brush in the *bosque* to see the wagons. Geronimo and I looked at each other when, as if by command, the once-quiet camp suddenly roared with life as two heavily loaded wagons pulled into the camp. After they stopped, the People, filled with curiosity, gathered around them. A driver wearing a *gran sombrero blanco*, with little tassels around the brim edge, stood up in the seat space for the driver's legs in front, spread wide his arms, then yelled, *"Amigos!* Casas Grandes and its *jefes* are happy you are here to trade with us. They send you presents, a wagon load of corn to use as you want, and a wagon load of mescal for all to share."

Geronimo grinned and smacked his lips. "That is a lot mescal, and they know the women will use the corn to make *tulapai*. The *Nakai-yes* must have received word from their gran *jefe* that he approves the peace terms and are already making big presents to us. *Enjuh*. We talk and then I think it's safe to drink some of that fine mescal."

I wasn't so sure. Maybe the *Nakai-yi jefe* planned to get the entire camp drunk and then attack it with many soldiers, which we all knew he had camped around other villages nearby. Besides, the day before, the *Nakai-yes* in the village had acted differently, their faces worried and distant as though the peace was about to end. I said, "But what if this is another *Nakai-yi* trick to get us drunk and kill us all?"

Geronimo shook his head. "My Power tells me nothing about this. I think it's all right. Come, let us finish our Sonora plans and then have a little mescal, eh?"

I nodded, and we each took a bottle off the wagon. We returned to the fire ring of stones to finish planning who to raid and when and how many warriors the raids would take. Word got back to those trading and drinking in Casas Grandes about the camp presents, and they were soon back to get their share off the wagons. Women made a floor of poles to keep the sacks of corn away from ground water, and they covered them with canvas, so they wouldn't get wet from morning and sky water before *tizwin* making began.

As the falling sun began painting the thin clouds with purples, reds, oranges, and gold, Geronimo and I finished our talk and uncorked our mescal bottles. Nearly everyone, except the children, was drunk. Those who hadn't passed out sang happy songs and played nonsense games. It was time to join them. I planned to have a few swallows of mescal with the other chiefs and then ride back to my family. Drinking now was against my better judgment, but if Geronimo's Power had not warned him by now, I thought it must be all right to drink.

THERE WERE NO fights over mescal or anything else that night. There was plenty to go around, and we were all happy, singing and dancing. I drank half my bottle and decided that I would return to Ishchos and the children at first light. I was still nervous, and I wasn't the only one—the mother of Hao-zous talked her family into leaving at sundown, and Geronimo's young cousin, Betzinez, and his mother and sister made their camp away from the big camp, worried about the intentions of the *Nakai-yi jefe*. I too decided to sleep away from the main camp and, with the help of the cold white light from a setting half-moon, found a good place hidden in the brush. The ground was covered with dry leaves a couple of bowshots down the *río* from the camp, and as drunk as I was, I'd fallen asleep in my blanket's warmth on those soft leaves by the time I stretched out.

The sharp crack of a *Nakai-yi* rifle jerked me awake. I sat up wondering if it had been in a dream, but suddenly a volley came in a rush like the whir of fluttering birds scattering out of the brush. No dream. I looked toward the village and saw scattered flashes of light followed by the snap and pop of rifles off to the northwest. In the camp, people staggered up, trying to grasp what was happening. I heard screams and low, dull thumps as women and men were hit by the bullets filling the air. Juh bellowed, "Follow me! Run to the hill across the road. Run!" Dark figures ran across the road. There were occasional flashes from rifles in the camp and more yelling and screaming. I grabbed my rifle and blanket and ran for the hill.

The ricochet and whine of bullets filled the air, a few raising little dark geysers of dust as they zipped around or landed in front of me when I crossed the road. I kept low to the ground and ran for the place on the hill where Juh and the other chiefs led men who shot toward rifle flashes in the trees below us and across the river. Women and children huddled together in their blankets on the back side of the hill but not nearly as many as I knew had been in the camp. There were a few in the families of my band, and several of their warriors were firing as the circle of fire from rifles surrounding the camp grew smaller and smaller.

A lull came in the firing. I heard Geronimo say, "Chappo! Take my rifle. Cover me. I have to get down there and get your mother." Chappo ran up and took the rifle, and Geronimo ran bent over down the hill toward the road. Dark figures of soldiers suddenly arose from the brush on the far side of the road and charged up the hill, firing as they ran, blocking Geronimo's path.

At first, we didn't shoot, fearful we'd hit Geronimo, but Juh yelled, "Shoot!

Shoot! Geronimo's Power will protect him." The roar from our guns was deafening, and the soldiers below us fell like green grass before a sharp knife. We fired again, and there were no more soldiers charging up the hill.

Geronimo reappeared as if by magic, he was a *di-yen* after all, and called, "Chappo, bring me my rifle." I heard him say to Juh, "It's no good. I can't get down there. Too many soldiers. The *Nakai-yes* have thirty or forty women and children and maybe ten men herded together and tying each one so they can't move. I'll have to buy or trade her back."

Dawn was past, and the light was fast growing stronger and brighter. We saw soldiers down in our camp, taking our things in the wickiups and tying the prisoners and loading them in three wagons like logs of firewood before hauling them off toward Casas Grandes. With my soldier glasses, I could see at least ten bodies scattered around the camp.

As the sun floated up over the mountains, Terrazas and his *segundo*, Mata Ortiz, were studying our hill while their subchiefs sent their organized soldiers, I assumed, to attack us. *Ch'ik'eh doleel,* I thought, *we'll kill many that way.*

Juh motioned his leaders to a council below the top of the hill, out of sight of the soldiers. He was furious and stuttered, "This... snake Terr... Terr... Terrazas... who... who... who attacks us... is treacherous. I kill every soldier snake I see. His *segundo*, Mata Ortiz, one day I burn. Now they make their soldiers ready and think how to come after us. I'll use my Power against them, so they think we are here no more. Take the People and move over yonder behind that next hill to the west behind us and wait until I come."

The chiefs and warriors gathered up the women and children and ran with them down the back side of the hill and across the valley to the next hill. We avoided leaving an obvious trail by dodging and weaving and stepping as much as we could on stones and bare places among yucca and cholla cactus and thickets of mesquite without bending or breaking grass or brush. It was an easy run, and we rested in a shady place on a small *arroyo* on the back side of the second hill. It was quiet, just the occasional Jeet! Jeet! of a canyon wren and buzz and whir of grasshoppers and bees.

I crawled up the back side of our hill and, lying flat at the top, used my soldier glasses to study the first hill. Juh was walking back and forth along the top of the hill. He had marked himself with golden pollen in special symbol shapes I didn't understand, and it appeared that he sang as he walked and scattered more pollen in front of his path. I watched while the sun rose another hand above the horizon. Suddenly, Juh held his arms straight out from his sides, tilted his head back, then howled like a wolf. Then, with his arms still out, he seemed to float a quarter of the way down the hill, toward the hill from where I watched. He paused by a cholla and howled again. He did this twice more, the last time at the bottom of the hill, and walked up the hill directly to where I lay. When he reached me, he stopped and said, "The *Nakai-yes* can no longer see us. Now we go back to first camp and wait four days for others to escape and return to us. Then we go south to my stronghold at Guaynopa."

JUH WAS A *di-yen* of great power. The ceremony he performed on top of the hill made Terrazas and Mata Ortiz take their soldiers and return to Casas Grandes. We ran around the hills between us and the first camp, following *arroyos*, and reached the camp in less than two hands. I was relieved to find Ishchos and the children without harm, but her eyes told me she had been worried when I didn't return the night before. Geronimo told his daughter Dohn-say and his other two wives, She-gha and Shtsha-she, that Chee-hash-kish had been taken into slavery by the attacking *Nakai-yes*. After she heard Geronimo's story, Dohn-say hung her head and disappeared with She-gha and Shtsha-she into the family *wickiup*. Their cries and wails soon joined others heard throughout the camp.

Juh called the men to a council. He said he had no Power then to go after the captives, that we would wait the customary four suns for them to find their way back and then move south to his Guaynopa stronghold, from where we would raid during the Seasons of Large Leaves and Large Fruit. Then it would be time to take revenge for Aliso Creek and this attack. The *Nakai-yes* must be made to pay for the disasters they had piled on us.

In the days that followed, Chappo and Dohn-say urged Geronimo to take men and free Chee-hash-kish. But he told them the risk was too high; too many soldiers holding her made it an impossible rescue raid. They would have to be patient and free her through trade of *Nakai-yi* captives or buy her back, and he would do this as soon as *Ussen* let him.

Hearing this, I thought, This is not the Geronimo I once knew. He grows too cautious as he ages. He'll never get Chee-hash-kish back. Why didn't *Ussen* warn him of the *Nakai-yi* attack? Has he lost his Power?

FOURTEEN

GUAYNOPA

THE TRAIL TO Juh's stronghold, Guaynopa, southwest of Casas Grandes, led through deep canyons, some carrying slow-moving rivers, others dry as the desert. We passed around high mountains and crossed ridges via steep switchbacks, reaching their tops covered in scattered, dark-green junipers. Near the ridge-tops grew groves of tall, straight pines that would have made arrows for Owl-man Giant in our Child of the Water stories. In a straight line across a *llano*, the trail would have been a long, hard day's ride, but tracking through canyons and crossing ridges and mountains took three suns to reach Guaynopa. Most of that distance was covered on foot, except for the very old and the very young, who rode horses. In the mountains, we were faster on foot than on horses.

Guaynopa was high on a flat-top mountain covered with junipers and near the edge of a great canyon. There were two big springs and plenty of wood and brush to make shelters for the many People who had come. Within a sun after we arrived, the women had their wickiups and fire circles in place, and the men were hunting deer. Soon there was plenty of meat in camp, and the women and children were finding a good store of mescal hearts, yucca, and sotol; ripening juniper berries, prickly pear fruit, berries, and mesquite and paloverde pods; and onions, potatoes, and spinach. Instead of being drunk nearly all the time, the People began to eat much better than they had when we camped near Casas Grandes.

Juh and Geronimo talked for three or four suns, called a council, then told the leaders they had decided to raid west into Sonora and the People who wanted to travel with them should be ready to move to a new camp in Sonora in three or four days. After seeing Juh's Power in making us disappear from the soldiers at Casas Grandes and knowing Geronimo was still listening to his own Power, we all wanted to press on with them.

IN FOUR SUNS, we moved west until we made camp in a hidden place on top of a mountain near the Río Yaqui about three hands' ride north of Sahuaripa. It was a long trip crossing many canyons. After the women had made shelters and the men hunted, Juh and Geronimo sent out scouts to look over places we wanted to raid near Sahuaripa to the southeast or Tepache to the northwest. Chiefs and warriors argued over which direction to raid first, knowing that both places had provisions and loot we needed and wanted.

The scouts from both directions returned in three or four suns to say that soldiers were camped in or near the villages. It was a risky time to attack either place. Juh and Geronimo talked and argued for a day about what to do, couldn't agree, and then called a council.

The night before the council met, Ishchos had a fine meal made from desert greens, cactus fruit, and venison she had gathered and prepared while we were at Guaynopa. As we ate, Bediscloye told me how he had learned a new sighting trick with his bow that had improved his arrow accuracy, and because of it, he had begun to win arrows in shooting contests even with older boys. I asked what his trick was, but he laughed and wouldn't tell me, knowing I'd soon learn it when I watched him shoot. Naboka was quiet, pretending to feed her doll, and after the doll refused her offerings, she ate them, making sounds like she really enjoyed them. Maud sat quietly helping her mother near the cooking pot with meat sizzling in a pan.

After we finished eating, Ishchos cleaned up around the fire, told Naboka and Bediscloye they could go play night games with their friends, then sent Maud to go where they had collected wood earlier and bring back enough to maintain the fire for the evening and to cook the morning meal.

After the children left, it was quiet near our *wickiup*. I sat with a gourd of coffee boiled with crushed, roasted piñon nuts and studied the fire's blue and yellow flames and listened to its snaps and pops. I was trying to think of the value of raiding north or south when *soldados* were in either direction. Maybe we needed to raid farther west or even return to Chihuahua with Juh's strongholds and more villages. Ishchos looked up at me from a basket she was working on. "Who will you raid with, husband?"

I raised an eyebrow. "What do you mean? I'll lead my warriors for the most fruitful places and where the chiefs say is best to go."

She smiled and shook her head. "I was chopping wood for the fire near where Geronimo and Juh talked yesterday while you were off hunting. Their voices were louder than usual when men talk, and they were arguing. Geronimo wants to go as far west as maybe the village Ures. He says there are many pack-trains on the roads west and big *ranchos* loaded with livestock south of Ures. Juh believes raiding to the west is too risky, opening our camps up to attack by *Rarámuri* soldiers from around Temósachi, Yepómera, and Namiquipa. He wants to return east and raid from strongholds in Chihuahua. He knows even women and children can defend those strongholds if the men are gone, and Chihuahuan soldiers don't like to fight in the mountains."

I crossed my arms and shook my head. I knew women's gossip was often close to the truth, but it also led to trouble. She saw me frowning and laughed.

"Let me finish before you judge me just a silly, gossiping woman."

I waved my hand for her to continue while she poured me more coffee.

"I finished my wood cutting long before the time of shortest shadows, and they were still arguing. I sent Maud to bring some more wood for the evening fire from where I'd chopped it in the early sun. She came back with the wood and wanted to know why the chiefs were arguing. They must have been talking all through the sun's path across the sky. Where do you think we'll go?"

I shrugged. "I think we'll decide during tonight's council. Be patient. I'll tell you when I know."

She smiled and nodded.

THE WARRIORS GATHERED around a big fire for the council. As usual, we first smoked to the four directions, and then Geronimo stood to speak. When all was quiet, he said, "Juh and I have talked and argued about what to do in view of the information the scouts brought back from Sahuaripa and Tepache. They say that *Nakai-yi soldados* have come to the villages and are ready to fight us. I say let them come. I say we can kill those sorry warriors with rocks and not waste our ammunition. We can take their rifles and ammunition to use against them. It won't be hard to raid in Sonora."

Many men agreed and slapped the ground, saying, *"Ch'ik'eh doleel."*

Geronimo, his eyes shining in the firelight, continued. "There is much west for the taking. Juh says no. We take too much risk of the *soldados*, especially the *Rarámuri* fighting for the *Nakai-yes*, finding our camps and killing and enslaving our women and children while we're gone. Juh says his strongholds in the east are easy to defend, even by women and children. I say that is true, but the soldiers in Sonora are fewer. The *Rarámuri* are more interested in running all the time than fighting us."

Geronimo paused and looked at the warriors and chiefs who were looking at each other, some frowning, others smiling. The points of light in the soft black sky and the milk river that swung in a great arc from northwest to southeast glimmered brightly. Wolf called to his brothers, and a few answered. The fire, burning down, snapped and crackled.

Chihuahua, always impatient to resolve things, called from where he stood near the back, "So what will it be? Do we go east or west?"

Geronimo nodded. "East and west. Juh and I have decided to each take those who want to go with us. Those who go with me will raid to the west. We'll camp on a flat-top mountain across the Río Yaqui, but we'll be so well hidden *soldados* will never find us. Those who go with Juh will raid to the east and camp in his strongholds. Every man must decide what is best for him and his family. Who goes with me?"

A rustle of men shifting position and some sighing rippled through the group. Again came a long silence until Chihuahua said, "My family and I go with Geronimo. I ask my warriors to come with me, but they, too, must make their own best choices."

"Hmmphs" scattered through the men, a few nodding in agreement. Kaytennae, his face shining in the firelight, stood and said, "My family and I go with Geronimo. I want my warriors and their families to come with me and follow Geronimo leading us, but that also is their decision to make." Again, I saw nods and heard "hmmphs" of agreement.

Having been a *segundo* for Geronimo, I knew the People expected me to follow him. Geronimo had been a good leader, and I learned much from him, but in the last two moons, my respect for him had dimmed, and that for Juh had increased. Juh was a powerful *di-yen*. I had seen his Power when we disappeared from the *soldados* at Casas Grandes. Geronimo let his thirst for whiskey lead him and his followers into dangerous situations. Juh liked whiskey but rarely made decisions based on his thirst for it. I decided not to risk my family with Geronimo's judgment. It would be much safer for my family in Juh's strongholds in Chihuahua, even if there were more soldiers to fight.

First Loco and then Nana stood and said they thought their People would be safer in Juh's strongholds. They would go with Juh back to Chihuahua.

Tall, thin Naiche stood in the light, and all eyes turned to him. He said, "In the last two moons, the *Nakai-yi* soldiers and their Blue Coat friends have attacked us three times. We have lost many women and children and warriors. I believe I owe the *Nakai-yi soldados* and their People in Chihuahua revenge, and our People need time to heal from their attacks. Geronimo has been my counselor at San Carlos, and a good one, but I choose to follow Juh."

Bonito appeared out of the edge of the firelight circle. "I agree with Naiche. My People and I follow Juh."

Geronimo raised his hand toward me. "Chato, you are the last chief to choose. You have been my *segundo* many times. Which direction do you choose?"

I stepped into the circle of light and surveyed the men's faces before I looked at Geronimo. "Geronimo is a great *di-yen* with much power. A war leader who is more clever than even Coyote. I have been honored to serve as his *segundo* on many raids. Now I am asked to choose between Geronimo and Juh. Juh is a great chief who has dealt and fought with the *Nakai-yes* for many harvests. He has made powerful war against them and then lived peacefully with them. In the last moon, I saw his great Power when he made us disappear from before the eyes of *Nakai-yi* soldier chiefs at Casas Grandes. Geronimo will have many successful raids in Sonora west of the Río Yaqui. There are also many villages and *ranchos* in Chihuahua ready for the taking when we need to raid, and as Naiche has said, we owe *Nakai-yi soldados* and their People revenge for what was done to us in the last two moons. I follow Juh."

I will never forget the mixture of surprise, disappointment, and a little anger in the look on Geronimo's face when I chose to follow Juh back toward the east. My Power told me then that any friendship I had in the past with Geronimo would be forever limited. He somehow believed that by my choosing to follow Juh, I had betrayed him. That was not so. I was choosing the best thing for my family. Besides, he had Kaytennae, the *segundo* he wanted and who had convinced him that we needed to bring Loco and his People from San Carlos to our band in Mexico. It was a fool's trail that had wiped out half of Loco's People in Chihuahua. Kaytennae was not a good *segundo*. He made too many quick judgments and never thought about the consequences of what he did. I didn't think much of Kaytennae. My dislike for him was growing like a weed in the *bosque*.

Geronimo looked at the council and said, *"Ch'ik'eh doleel.* We go our separate ways, but soon enough, we will see each other again."

FIFTEEN

SUNS OF FIRE
AND BLOOD

JUH LED THE People back east to the safety of Guaynopa. After the band split, there were over five hundred of the People with us, and Geronimo, with Chihuahua's and Kaytennae's People following his lead, had about eighty. This meant that Geronimo had thirty men and boys old enough to handle weapons and that Juh, with Nana's, Loco's, Naiche's, and my People, had nearly three times as many warriors and experienced leaders. Juh held another council with the chiefs and leaders the sun after we arrived at Guaynopa, this after the women had settled back into the camp they had abandoned less than a moon earlier.

At the council under tall pines and a sky brilliant blue with thin white clouds streaking toward the east, we smoked and listened to Juh's prayer to *Ussen* for council wisdom. After his prayer, standing in shade scattered with shafts of light filtering through tall branches, Juh spoke easily with no sign of a stutter. "It is good to have five chiefs and their bands together for raiding. I ask them to tell us what they want to do and where they want to raid. Loco and Nana, speak first for the Chihenne."

Loco stood with crossed arms, his face marked by his famous sagging-eye battle scar. He looked over the council and then turned to Juh. "My People, especially my young men and warriors, not used to a warrior's life in the land of the *Nakai-yes*, need rest. I think the Chihenne will wait a while before joining the great chief Juh in his raids." Frowns on the faces of a few of Loco and Nana's Chihenne warriors said they weren't happy with Loco's decision until old Nana stood with his crippled foot and arthritic joints. Nana said he agreed with Loco, and the frowns disappeared. All Chihenne, who had come with Juh, agreed to wait a time before joining the raids.

Juh said, "I honor the wisdom of my brothers Loco and Nana. Let their warriors hunt and supply the camp with meat while others raid for stock and avenge the wrongs suffered at the hands of the *soldados*. What will Naiche and his warriors do?"

Naiche, tall and thin, stood and, with the somber bearing of a chief, said, "My warriors and I will follow Juh on these raids and make war against the *Nakai-yi soldados*."

Juh nodded. *"Enjuh.* Our strength against enemies will be great with Naiche and his warriors. What does the great warrior and chief, Chato, choose?"

I stood, looked over the assembly, and then spoke directly to Juh. "I, Chato, and my warriors follow the great *di-yen* and chief, Juh. Lead us. We have a debt we must pay for *soldado* attacks at Casas Grandes and at Aliso Creek. Blood will flow. Life will be smooth again."

The warriors slapped the ground in front of them, yelling, *"Enjuh! Enjuh!"*

OUR FIRST RAIDS were around Tarachi to gain fresh horses for our saddles and beef for our women's fires. *Vaqueros*, village men, and young boys who could use arms tried to stop us. We killed four and took two *vaqueros* prisoner. We tested their strength with fire that night and found they were too weak to live long. They went to the Happy Land screaming in their pain quicker than I wanted, but we had our satisfaction with them for opposing us.

Taking the stock to Guaynopa, we rested a couple of suns and then moved west and a little south across many mountains and canyons to a fertile green valley holding a *gran rancho, El Rancho* Carrizal, with many fat cattle. We watched the place with soldier glasses to learn the daily customs followed at the *hacienda*. After we learned when and where its men and women moved, took meals, and slept, Juh made his attack plans.

We were camped in a thick stand of junipers in a saddle between the top of the ridge behind the *hacienda* and a higher sierra behind us. As the purple and oranges in the high clouds disappeared into bright points of light in the black night and, up on the sierra, Wolf called his brothers, we gathered with Juh and stood around a small fire to smoke to the four directions oak-leaf cigarettes made with good White Eye *tobaho* we had taken in the last raid. Juh made his prayer to *Ussen* for help in making good plans and then, with a yucca stalk, drew the outline of the *hacienda* features in smooth dust next to the little fire.

He said, "I have watched this *hacienda* for a long time. *Soldados* go there many times for cattle to feed the army, and there are many women, maybe slaves, maybe wives of *vaqueros*, there who take care of them. Now I say they must go somewhere else for their cattle. Maybe they go hungry, as we have been when *soldados* take away our food. Next sun, we take the cattle and burn the *hacienda*. We drive the cattle north back to Guaynopa first, following the canyons east at the village of Río Chico. When the *Nakai-yi soldados* learn we are killing *vaqueros* and farmers and driving away their cattle, they will come for us. We must be vigilant. I think when the fight comes, we'll win."

Then with a yucca stalk he drew in the dust and flickering yellow firelight, casting deep ridges of shadows on his face, how the men should attack and burn the *hacienda* and the *vaquero casa* behind it. He drew how ten of the warriors would drive the cattle from the grass-covered *llano* south of the *hacienda* along the *río* road that ran by the *hacienda* and then north toward the villages of Río Chico and Onavas before turning east through the canyons toward Guaynopa. Those who stayed behind to burn the *hacienda* would catch up with the cattle and help drive them up the *río* until we reached Río Chico.

Juh looked at Naiche and me with narrowed eyes and a grim smile. "You've talked of revenge for Aliso Creek. There are many women who serve the *hacendado*. I think one has a child. These women are yours to do with as you please. It will be your revenge for what the *Nakai-yes* did to your women and children at Aliso Creek."

Naiche and I grinned and nodded. With just a few handpicked warriors, our revenge could be sweet.

IT WAS NEAR dawn, the skylight becoming a soft gray off on the eastern horizon and the stars disappearing, when we eased down from the top of the ridge and along the edge of a big brush-filled *arroyo* that grew wider and shallow as it neared the *río* and then turned toward the *hacienda*. The *hacienda* was east of the *río* on a large bench about a bowshot wide. The *rancho hacienda* was a big *casa* and the *vaquero casa* set back in the trees near the large corrals where cattle and horses were kept about a bowshot from the *hacienda*. Naiche and I, with four of our best warriors, moved down and waited in the trees facing the *hacienda* doors. Other warriors slid into cover in the trees around the *vaquero casa*, and still others went to the corrals and prepared to release the stock there. Juh and four warriors with bows and long arrows ready to carry fire found cover between the *casa* where the *vaqueros* lived and the *hacienda*. We waited in the shadows for the gray light of dawn.

I had done attacks such as this one many times in my life as a warrior and chief, but it still made my heart race with a fast beat. I pulled the hammer back to cock my rifle and nodded at Naiche, who also pulled the hammer back on his rifle. Juh and the men with the bows and fire arrows were behind a boulder in a low place south of the *hacienda*. I saw sparks fly and light from a sudden flame in a small fire behind the boulder. The sun was coming, and so was fire. The warriors held the pitch on their arrows in the fire's little flames, and as the pitch caught, the spot where the fire burned grew brighter, showing the warriors kneeling in its shadows. The arrows were quick on the bows and to their strings, drawn to full extension and released, creating fiery arcs in the low light and shadow of the rising sun. Another two flaming arrows sped after the first two, and then another two. All thumped into the roof of the *hacienda*. Flames caught and spread.

Yells and screams of *"Incendio! Incendio!"* flew from desperate voices inside. The front doors were flung open, with smoke billowing out into the cold night air and making an orange glow from the fire blazing inside. Two women and a child in clothes they wore in their beds ran heaving and coughing out into the clear air, where long arrows flew into their hearts. They had only the strength to grasp the shafts in stunned surprise and stagger backward to land flat on their backs in the billowing smoke. An old man with a great bush of hair under his nose ran out the door, stumbled to his hands and knees over the bodies, saw the open eyes and the arrows growing like trees in the middle of the women's chests, then opened his mouth and drew a deep breath to scream a warning, when an arrow struck him in the mouth and, with blood flowing from his mouth and nose, he made a sick stomach-gurgling sound we could hear even above the roar of the flames before he dropped to his knees and fell over on his side.

I heard boards on the corral gates being thrown to one side and the livestock, thinking they were free, come rumbling through the gate opening, but warriors were already herding them across the *río* and on to the wagon road heading north. More fire arrows arced into the *hacienda* and *vaquero casa*, which quickly became a pitch-torch-like roaring fire. More women in their nightclothes ran screaming through the front and side doors of the *hacienda*, followed by soldiers carrying their uniforms, boots, and guns. Now rifles began to thunder as Naiche, our men, and I shot them down and then turned our rifles on the *vaqueros* who came from the *casa* behind the *hacienda*.

The fires on the *vaquero casa* and the *hacienda* were roaring, and every *Nakai-yi*, men and women, even a child, rode their ghost pony. We watched and listened for life signs but saw or heard none. It had been a good morning's work. We gathered and mounted our horses and followed the river road, driving the stock toward Río Chico.

We rode up the *río* toward the village Río Chico and came to another *río* from the east that ran into the one we followed north. Juh sent ten warriors with the cattle and horses up this *río* toward Guaynopa, while the rest of us rode fast up the road toward Onavas to keep the attention of the *soldados* away from the cattle we had taken. We did well. At Onavas, we killed two *vaqueros* on the road, then hiding, ambushed ten *soldados* headed for Onavas. Further down the road we killed three and wounded three more before they managed to reach the safety of the village houses.

We moved south near Río Chico and, up in the hills, made safe places from where we could take cover and battle any *soldados* coming after us. In two or three days, *soldados* came just as Juh said they would. We attacked them and killed eight *soldados* before we moved south. The comandante of the soldiers stayed on our trail and wouldn't go away. We had several battles with them, but neither side seemed to gain on the other.

After two days of move-fight-move, we came to a big village, and the *soldados* were not far behind us. We hadn't lost them, and we were nearly out of ammunition. On the east side of the village, we rested at the mouth of a canyon with high walls as far as we could see. The warriors told Juh that we needed to disappear from the *soldados*, that we didn't have enough ammunition for another fight, and that we should leave and fight another day.

Juh shook his head and said, "You come with me, and I show you how to wipe out these *soldados* without firing another bullet."

The men looked at each other like Juh was crazy but nodded they would follow him, saying, "Show us!"

We rode east through the winding canyon with steep, high walls leading out of the village. It was hard on our horses, but Juh didn't care. We could always take what we needed from the *rancho*s near the village. But the *soldados* had to take care of their horses because their army bought them, and it made the animals valuable. This canyon was wearing the horses out. Soon they would have to stop and rest. Perhaps, I thought, Juh intends to wear out their horses in this canyon and then just disappear. I was wrong.

We came to the end of the canyon, where a string of sierras we would have to climb over blocked further passage. Juh rode slowly until he found what he was looking for and dismounted, leaving his pony to graze on the brush at the edge of a high ridge that ran up into the mountains. There was a dim, zigzag path up the side of the ridge, and he motioned for us to follow it and make a clear path. He led us up the path as it weaved back and forth in places, moving on a slant and then on a vertical before making another slow climb. Near the top, the path ran parallel to the top of the mountain.

Juh told the men to roll a line of boulders parallel to the trail and then move to its end, where it led over the mountain. It was hard work wrestling, prizing up, and rolling the boulders in place, and there was little water for us to drink, but we finished just as we saw the column of *soldados* coming down the canyon. Juh told us to hide and wait for the *soldados* to come off the path we had left for them to follow. When they reached where we were, we were to attack them, drive them back along the trail so they bunched up parallel to our boulders, and then roll the boulders down on them.

Far below, the comandante and his men had found our horses grazing, had dismounted from their own mounts, and were carefully looking over the ground in case we might surprise them. First one man and then another found the trail we had taken up the mountain. They pointed it out to their comandante, who used his soldier glasses to stare at the trail up the mountain a good while before shaking his fist in victory and ordering them to go after us. They hobbled their horses to graze with ours, took more ammunition off their pack animals, then confidently marched up the trail toward the top.

Juh took a place where he could watch the *soldados* progress up the mountain before signaling his men when to attack and when for others to roll the boulders. The *soldados* came slowly and breathing like they had just run half a day in the desert. They finally gained the part of the trail parallel and close to the top and slowed to catch their wind. Juh signaled us. We came yelling our war cries and running from our hiding places in the brush of a beginning *arroyo* and from behind rocks to attack the *soldados*. We were on them before they could raise their rifles. I'll never forget the surprised look on one of the *soldados* who thrust at me with the long knife on the end of his rifle as I dodged his knife, grabbed him by his shirt, then threw him bouncing and tumbling down the steep mountainside. With nowhere to run and few places to take cover, most of the column froze in place, unable to do much with so little room to maneuver against the action in front of them. The column leaders under assault began backing into the men behind them, giving orders to *"Retirarse! Retirarse!"* Juh gave to the signal to roll the boulders down on the column. As soon as we heard the boulders start to roll, we who were face-to-face with the column leaders ran back and away from the tumbling boulders crashing through the brush and crushing and knocking the *soldados* screaming in pain and yelling in fear down the mountain to be hit by brush and other boulders dislodged by the first wave.

A few *soldados* at the end of the column saw what was coming and got out of the way in time to save their lives. Others who were crushed or badly injured lay scattered up and down the trail as the great cloud of dust the landslide had created slowly rolled down the mountain, growing thin as the dust settled. Juh led us back down the side of the mountain, taking weapons and ammunition from the dead and dying and cutting throats of those who lingered.

When we got to the bottom of the canyon, *soldados* left to guard their horses had disappeared. The light was going fast. We found water and food on the *soldado* packhorses and spread our blankets in among the junipers to eat and rest and share stories of the great victory we had just won without firing a shot.

Truly, Juh was a great war chief and *di-yen*.

SIXTEEN

CHOCOLATE PASS

THE SEASONS OF Large Leaves and Large Fruit were filled with many raids and long rides across the steep canyons and mountains. Naiche and I split with Juh when he decided against his earlier words to continue to raid in Sonora and stay out of Chihuahua. We moved our camp north and a little east along the Río Aros and much closer to Bugatseka. Loco and his People joined our camp. Naiche and I continued to lead raids, but the Chihenne still weren't ready to fight and raid.

After Juh rolled boulders down on the *soldados* pursuing us, the *soldados* were reluctant to follow any Apache into the sierras. Late in the Season of Large Fruit, we moved our camp to the northern rim of the "Great Canyon" while our women gathered and prepared the fall harvest of mescal, mesquite and paloverde pods, acorns and walnuts, piñon nuts, juniper berries, dried cactus fruit, and many different kinds of roots for medicine and stewpots. With all the food and meat we had collected and dried, we would eat well through the Season of Ghost Face.

Ishchos and I spent much time in the blankets, but still no child grew in her belly. As our children grew older and learned the lessons that they needed to act as those who were grown, our family grew closer. Bediscloye's accuracy with his little bow and arrow approached that of nearly any man. Maud was beginning to show features of what a fine-looking woman she would become. Naboka was growing stronger and learning fast. I made her several dolls that she played with and showed she had been born with the knowledge for being a good mother. I was very happy with my family and wanted to give them anything they needed or that I found for gifts.

As the Season of Earth Is Reddish Brown approached, we drummed on big, dried cowhides and danced far into the nights. Then, one night when there was a break in the dancing and drumming, we heard distant drums and, looking south across the maw of the great canyon, saw flickering yellow firelight. With my soldier glasses, I saw shadowy figures dancing around a great fire. It was too far to recognize anyone, but by the way they danced and from the Mountain Spirit costumes worn by a few, I knew they were Apache.

Early the next morning, Naiche sent one of his best runners across the canyon to the other camp to learn who was in the other camp. The runner returned late that night weary and covered with dirt, dust, and dry salt from body water and all the climbing he had done on the narrow trails to the north and south rims of the great canyon.

Naiche, Loco, Nana, and I welcomed him and waited to hear what he had learned until after he drank coffee and ate something from the stewpot of Naiche's young wife, Haozinne. When he finished eating and rubbed his hands on his legs, he looked at us staring at him and waiting for him to speak. He laughed and then said, "Geronimo!" We all laughed. It was good to know that the great war leader and *di-yen* was nearby. The runner said, "Geronimo asked that I tell you he is longing to see you and hopes you will come and have a big dance and maybe camp with his People." After we heard this news, we talked more and decided to ask Geronimo to bring his People to the north rim and dance with us where our camp had plenty of wood, water, and food.

Again, Naiche sent another runner to Geronimo's camp, and he soon flashed by mirror his answer: "We come."

Two suns passed before we saw Geronimo leading his People down the steep zigzag path, across the rough canyon floor filled with boulders and slabs of stone that had over many harvests fallen from the cliffs. With the horses on the trail and women carrying big heavy loads of things for their fires and wickiups, Geronimo's band moved slowly but surely down, into, and across the big canyon and climbed the narrow path up to our camp.

We had a reunion filled with much gift giving, laughing and smiling, feasting, and dancing. Many stories were told of what happened during raids or battles. Our women helped the women in Geronimo's band set up their wickiups and made extra meals so they could rest a little after dancing until the night-sky lights grew dim.

A few suns after Geronimo joined his camp with ours, Juh and his People came wandering into our camp, and again there were many good times with feasts and dancing and telling stories. After four days of celebrating, the chiefs and warriors held a council as the sun was painting the high western clouds purples, reds, gold, and orange. We wanted to decide how we should pass the coming season before we made our fires to drive away the Ghost Face cold. There were suggestions for more raiding in Sonora, but nearly every leader and warrior believed it was time for payback for the attacks at Aliso Creek and Casas Grandes led by the *Nakai-yi jefe soldado*, Joaquin Terrazas, and his *segundo*, Juan Mata Ortiz.

There was much talking back and forth by the leaders and some warriors who were bitter that we hadn't already struck Casas Grandes traders in revenge for what had been done to us when we went there to peacefully trade and drink the mescal that they gave us. After listening to the talk and arguing back and forth, Juh raised his hands toward the glimmering night sky and stood. After the council grew quiet, he spoke.

"Brothers, I am convinced that the traders in Casas Grandes did nothing in the attack on us." Many of the warriors shook their heads, disagreeing with him. "Revenge must go to Terrazas and Ortiz. They wanted to get us drunk in Casas Grandes and slaughter all of us down to the last baby. Failing that, they took our families into slavery. Your chiefs have all lost family to them. Terrazas is a gran *jefe* for the Chihuahuan *soldados*. He travels often, and where he stays during any one sun is unknown. But his *segundo*, Mata Ortiz, I know commands *soldados* and a *rancho* for horses in the village of Galeana, south of Casas Grandes. Geronimo and I have attacked freight and other wagon trains traveling through Chocolate Pass between Casas Grandes and Galeana. We know the country well and the best places for ambush. I have a plan to wipe out Mata Ortiz and his *soldados*. Let us make a camp in the mountains outside of Galeana and take our revenge as it's given to us."

Heads nodded, the ground was slapped, then all yelled, "Hey ho heh! Hey ho heh! We go! Lead us!"

Juh held up his hands again, and it grew quiet in the darkness lying over us like a blanket, and in the nearby hills, Coyote sang his evening tune. "I will do this only if the other chiefs agree."

I would go, I knew Geronimo couldn't wait to go, and I thought Naiche and Chihuahua and Kaytennae would, too, but I didn't know about Nana and Loco. I was ready to step forward and commit to going to Galeana when Nana pushed himself up from the big stone on which he sat and looked around the myriad faces studying his. "Every warrior here must make his own decision about what is best for him to do for his family. I know not what Loco will do. I was Victo-rio's *segundo* when he was nearly out of ammunition and trying to stay out of the way of the Blue Coats until he could get more. Terrazas and Ortiz followed us to Tres Castillos and wiped out Victorio and his warriors and took many of our women and children into slavery. Kaytennae also knows this very well. He found Victorio had stabbed himself in the heart after there were no more bullets in his weapons. Victorio sent me out to find more ammunition. It is the only reason I didn't die at Tres Castillos. Two, nearly three, harvests later, these two tried to enslave us again or kill us all at Casas Grandes. They must pay. I go with Juh to take Mata Ortiz."

Again, there was much fist shaking and whooping from warriors in the council. The other leaders and chiefs, each asked individually, all said they also would go to Galeana under Juh's leadership and follow his plan.

WE TOOK A slow, leisurely ride through the mountains to where we camped overlooking Galeana. On the way, we stopped twice for big dances, one for celebrating and one for choosing and preparing boys who wanted to begin their novitiate. Bediscloye begged to begin his novitiate, but I told him that he was too young, to keep practicing his bow-and-arrow skills and other things a warrior needed to know, that his day would come soon enough, and that all warriors need to learn and know patience. This was a good chance for him to learn a patience lesson. He was a good boy and listened to what I told him. After thinking about it, he told me that he understood me and would patiently wait for his time. In fact, the chiefs and war leaders learned we had a number of boys who would make good *novitiates*, and we looked forward to training them while making Galeana soldiers and Ortiz pay for what they had done to the People.

We found a good camping place just below a ridge of the mountains on the edge of the *llano* and about a hand against the horizon's hard ride (ten miles) from Galeana. Galeana was easy to see with soldier glasses when we stood on top of the ridge above our camp and ensured the women and children could see the revenge we took for the People's honor.

The day after we made camp, Geronimo and Juh rode down out of the mountains near sundown to ride the wagon road that led to Chocolate Pass and where they would place warriors for an attack on the *soldados* and Mata Ortiz. The next day, Juh called a meeting of all the chiefs, war leaders, and warriors to hear his plan. We sat in the shade of cliffs, smoked, and waited for Juh with his hands raised toward the sky to finish his prayer to *Ussen*. Soon he folded his arms in front of him and looked at each chief and war leader.

Juh said, "After the last sun, Geronimo and I rode the wagon trail through Chocolate Pass. It was as I remembered it when I fixed my plan in my mind. Near where the pass begins, there is a long *arroyo* filled with brush running along beside the trail. It's a good place to hide men for an ambush. Farther up is a low place so well screened from the road that men on horseback can sit there and not be seen."

I smiled, and so did Juh and Geronimo when they heard numerous "hmmphs" and saw nods of insight from the gathered warriors.

"I plan for a large number of warriors to hide in the *arroyo* and have them wait to attack the *Nakai-yes* when they ride by. Geronimo and I will wait with warriors on their horses in the low place. When the *soldados* come thundering up the pass trail, we'll ride out to attack them. They'll turn to charge back to Galeana, but when they get near the *arroyo*, men hidden there will rise, firing out of the brush. The *soldados* will be caught between warriors after them on horses and those in the *arroyo*. Many *Nakai-yes* will die that day."

Again came many hmmphs and nods of approval. There was a significant piece of the plan missing. I had to ask and called out, "What will make the *soldados* come down the trail?"

Juh's grin showed nearly all his teeth. He said, "Mata Ortiz and several other ranchers have nice horse herds on *rancho* land in front of Galeana and by the *río* that runs nearby. Three or four warriors will take some horses to make the *soldados* think it was just a raid by a few Apache they can soon run down and overcome. They won't have any thought of an ambush and real fight that awaits them."

We all laughed and shouted, *"Enjuh!"* Decoys were not used very often in the way we fought, but when we did use them, they were very successful.

SEVENTEEN

THE CHOCOLATE PASS
FIGHT

I WAS AMONG the three men Juh and Geronimo picked to act as decoys. The next sun, before the dawn was gone, Juh and Geronimo put the men in place to await the decoys drawing the *soldados* out of Galeana. We rode up to the edge of a pasture, saw a few horses grazing, then took them. I know a *vaquero* at a nearby barn yelled and fired his *pistola* a couple of times when he saw us. Whooping and yelling, we charged up the wagon road to Chocolate Pass, driving the *Nakai-yi* ponies before us. We waited most of that sun, but no *soldados* came. They must have decided those horses weren't worth fighting for. After we left for our camp, I thought, If these people won't fight for their own stock, then we ought to come more often.

The next sun, the decoys went to Galeana again while the other warriors prepared for the ambush. We thought perhaps we hadn't taken enough ponies or gotten close enough to the village to bring the *soldados* out. This time, we were more daring than before and began at the barn where the *vaquero* had seen us the day before and found a herd of horses twice the number that we had taken before, these in a pasture on the east side of the wagon road leading to Chocolate Pass. Still, no *soldados* chased after us. Perhaps, truly, they were afraid of us.

That night, the war leaders talked with Juh and Geronimo and were uncertain what to do next to draw the *Nakai-yes* out of Galeana. Old Nana took his walking stick and made marks in the dust that looked a little like the marks the White Eyes and *Nakai-yes* made for tracks on paper to record their words.

Nana said, "This is the way Mata Ortiz marks his cattle and horses with a hot iron to show they belong to him. His *rancho* is over by the *río* on the west side of the wagon road. Tomorrow, Chato, you and the other two look for animals with this mark in pastures along the *río*. When you find them, make sure someone sees you and begin driving them down the wagon road as if you were thinking of nothing else except getting away with them. When Mata Ortiz learns you've left with his stock, he'll gather up his soldiers and come after you. Then we'll have what we planned."

The third time we tried, we finally pulled Mata Ortiz out of Galeana. We had nearly thirty horses carrying his mark, and before we reached the *arroyo* where the first group of warriors hid, we could see the dust on the road from Galeana and knew that at last the *Nakai-yes* were coming hard after us.

We rode just far enough ahead that as Juan Mata Ortiz and his soldiers thundered past the *arroyo* where the first group of warriors hid, they would believe we could be caught. By this time, we were in a hard run with our horses and flew by the horse-mounted warriors who had waited for us to pass and a little more before riding up on the wagon road to confront Ortiz and the *soldados*.

Seeing the Apache waiting calmly for them in the middle of the road, Ortiz, who was leading the charge, jerked his horse to a sliding halt, threw up an arm, then made a circling motion pointing back to Galeana, the signal to turn back. The *soldados* were good horsemen. They managed to stop without running into each other and, seeing Ortiz's retreat signal, turned and followed him back toward Galeana with the mounted Apache firing at them while hot on their heels. Like a newly appearing, twisting desert wind, Chihuahua, in charge of the men in the *arroyo*, leaped up and, running to the middle of the road, began levering and firing his rifle into the *soldados* charging toward him. Again, Ortiz jerked his horse to a stop as bullets from both directions began hitting the dust around him. He pulled his *pistola* and fired a few return shots, but we were too far for him to hit anyone. We had him. I hoped we wouldn't kill him before we caught him. In the time it takes to suck wind, he waved his arm again and led his soldiers west off the road toward a lone, cone-shaped hill rising about thirty paces in height above the *llano* and a long rifle shot away.

Geronimo, leading the mounted men and surprised at the unanticipated move, lost no time chasing them until he saw them ride to the top of the lone hill, dismount, then desperately begin making a circular wall of stones, from behind which they could shoot. Ortiz used two or three snipers to keep us off the hill while the rest of the *soldados* piled up rocks.

The warriors in the *arroyo* came running. Those on horses dismounted, turned their animals over to *novitiates* who had followed them from the rear, and were careful to stay out of the range of Ortiz's snipers. I followed Geronimo with Chihuahua, Nana, and Kaytennae to the lone tree at the bottom of the hill. Kaytennae and I, among the best shots in the band, kept up a covering fire as the *Nakai-yi* rock wall grew higher.

Geronimo and Chihuahua talked to Bonito and the warriors a short time before they encircled the hill, zigzagging to avoid sniper bullets, and began crawling up it from all directions while rolling rocks in front of them as cover for their heads. Kaytennae and I and one or two others kept the *soldados* low behind their wall of rocks with our sniper fire.

In about a hand above the horizon, the warriors were near the wall the *Nakai-yes* had put up for cover and the gunfire beat a fast drum. Behind Bonito and his warriors, where he was supposed to be and without a weapon, the great warrior and *di-yen*, She-neah, followed. He said that before we began Juh's plan, his Power had predicted victory for us but had also told him that if he went into the battle, he would be killed. Nevertheless, he followed Bonito, and, near the top of the hill, a *Nakai-yi* bullet hit him in the forehead, and he was on the ghost pony before he even knew he had left us. Bonito saw She-neah fall. The death of the great man so angered Bonito that he screamed his war cry and was up and running to jump over the wall, followed by the warriors behind him, slashing and chopping at the *soldados* who tried to fight back using their rifles as clubs and their short guns. One *soldado* threw down his rifle, vaulted onto a horse, jumped their stone wall, then rode down the hill headed for Galeana as fast as the horse could carry him. Kaytennae and I turned our rifles toward the horse and rider, but Geronimo yelled, "Let him go! He'll bring back more *Nakai-yes* for us to kill."

The fighting on top of the hill soon ended. We had lost She-neah, whose Power had told him he would die if he joined the attack, and one other warrior. We killed every *Nakai-yi* except the one we let get away and the one Nana and Juh wanted most of all—Juan Mata Ortiz.

Ortiz was a worthy enemy. Nana and Juh spoke to him, and the last words I heard Juh say to him were, "Show us your strength, Juan Mata Ortiz." Juh had the warriors dig a pit, fill it with the crackling dry brush scattered around the hill then, when it was full, tie Ortiz spread eagled across the top of it. The warriors made a torch and a small fire to light it. Ortiz could see what they were doing, but his eyes never showed fear. After the torch was lighted, Juh handed it to Nana, who nodded his thanks and walked to stand on the edge of the pit between Ortiz's feet.

I don't remember exactly what Nana said to Ortiz, but it was something like, "This is for Victorio. I hope you are strong," and then he thrust the flaming torch into the brush between Ortiz's legs and stepped back as flames roared to life. Ortiz jerked against the ropes and pegs that had him tied over the conflagration as his clothes caught fire. He tilted his head back, his mouth open in a voiceless scream, but never made a sound as his flesh popped and sizzled, sending fat into the flames and stinking black smoke high into the air as his body quickly turned to black char.

Nana turned to Juh. "That was a good death. Ortiz was a worthy enemy."

THE *NOVITIATES* CAME bringing the warrior's horses. Juh and Geronimo spoke a short time, and then Geronimo told the warriors we would ride back to the wagon road and then toward Galeana. He said that if his Power was with them, more *soldados* would come, and we would wipe them out too while fighting from our horses. Up on the road, we saw in the distance coming from Galeana a large dust cloud formed by many riders in a hard run. I glanced at the hill, where the last of Juan Mata Ortiz made a fast-rising column of black smoke, and smiled, thinking, This is a good day to die. Hey Ho!

We rode down the road a short distance and then spread out in a long line to await the *soldados* from Galeana. I watched them through my soldier glasses. Most were young, well mounted, and led by men in middle age, their jacket chests covered with symbols of past glory made from multicolor ribbons. When the *Nakai-yi* leaders saw our line, they stopped maybe a long rifle shot away and ordered their *soldados* to spread out in a line. I thought they were about to charge us, but after some notes on the brass flute they call "bugle," the *soldados* dismounted and, like rats digging a hole in the brush to avoid a rattlesnake, began in a big hurry digging a trench from which they could fight while others stood behind them with their rifles ready.

We sat on our ponies and watched the Galeana *soldados* dig and prepare for a fight the rest of that sun. As the late-afternoon clouds blazed with yellow, orange, red, and purple and the earth grew cool, I saw a great cloud of buzzards circling low over the hill where we had burned Mata Ortiz and killed his *soldados*. Geronimo raised his arm and pointed for the distant mountains to the southwest. We walked our horses away in the fading light.

EIGHTEEN

GHOST FACE
DISASTER

AFTER BURNING MATA Ortiz and watching the *soldados* dig their trench for
nothing, we returned to our camp but didn't dance in a victory celebration. We
had lost the great warrior and *di-yen*, She-neah. It was not a time to dance.

Geronimo and Juh led us back to Bugatseka. After a few suns, they decided to split again. About two hundred of the People, including thirty warriors,
stayed with Geronimo and Chihuahua; the rest stayed with Juh and included
Naiche, Nana, Loco, Bonito, Jelikinne, Kaytennae, and me. About 350 of the
People followed Juh south to camp in the rough Río Aros country. I learned
later that Geronimo's band had much success during this time raiding and were
undisturbed during Ghost Face, preparing for raids in Sonora beginning in the
Season of Little Eagles.

Juh first camped at Guaynopa, but after a few small raids, he became uneasy
about being attacked by *Nakai-yi soldados* who might be determined enough to
avenge Mata Ortiz during Ghost Face. We moved a long sun's ride into the rough
country west of Guaynopa and camped in a large *arroyo* between forks of a branch
of what the *Nakai-yes* called the Río Sátachi. A nice little stream of water, enough
for our camp and our horses, burbled over rocks down one side of the *arroyo*,
which was well hidden and out of the worst of the wind. Juh told the warriors
not to raid in Chihuahua so the *soldados* wouldn't get stirred up and come after us.

Soon after we moved to Juh's new camp, a raiding party near Sahuaripa
came upon a fat *Nakai-yi* leading four burros loaded with little jugs of good quality mescal. When the *Nakai-yi* saw the Apache coming, he dropped the burro
lead rope and rode like the wind toward Sahuaripa. The warriors were so happy
to get the mescal that they laughed and let him escape.

For the next moon, we drank the little jugs of mescal in Juh's camp. The firewater warmed our guts and lungs. It was so good we even gave our women a few sips to help keep them warm.

One night as my family and I sat around the fire while we ate and told funny stories about the work we'd done that day, Bediscloye showed me arrows he had made and, giggling, Naboka showed me the new doll he had carved for her. Both the arrows and the doll were fine work coming from someone not much past seven harvests. Bediscloye had been gifted with great talent from *Ussen*. Maud's beauty continued to shine and grow. I saw some of the novitiate boys watching her carefully as she helped Ishchos around the fire, chopped wood, or worked cloth and leather to make clothes and good moccasins with the tough leather soles of bull elk hide. Despite her laughter and pleasant face with our children, Ishchos had sad eyes.

After Maud helped Ishchos clean up around the fire and Bediscloye had returned with an armful of firewood, I talked a little more with the children while their blankets warmed, wrapped over hot rocks. When their beds were ready, Ishchos and I covered them in their blankets and then sat alone together by the fire. I was close to the last swallows of the good mescal from my jug before my share was all gone. I decided Ishchos and I would finish what was left, but she said that, as a warrior, I should drink it all, and I didn't argue with her. There wasn't enough left to make me drunk but would give me deep sleep.

As I brought the jug to my lips, I said, "I see your sad eyes tonight. What troubles you?"

She stared for a while at the blue and yellow flames slowly turning the oak and juniper firewood into orange, glowing coals. "We have been in the blankets many times trying to make another child grow in my belly. I want to give you another child, but none comes. Maybe *Ussen* tells me there are no more children for us. I'm very sad if that is what *Ussen* wants."

I swallowed the last drops of mescal from the jug. "I know you still have your moon times and are careful around me when you do. You can still have babies. Come to me under the blankets, and tonight I give you one. *Ussen* always wants more children." I stood and held my hand out. "Come." She took it with a smile brighter than the morning sun and happy eyes.

WHEN WE FINALLY slept, she in the crook of my arm, I dreamed we were drifting as though floating in the bank shadows of a deep, warm pool in a *río*. A roar, like that of a great waterfall, filled my ears. I began to struggle against the current that unexpectedly had us and was picking up speed. I heard screams and yells and a thunder like running horses. I struggled to get us to the *río*'s bank... and then there were loud shots and bullets passing through the *wickiup*. Ishchos had crawled past me toward the children, yelling as Naboka began to scream in fright, "Quiet. Stay down, stay down. It's an attack."

I yelled at Ishchos, "Hide in the *arroyo* brush. If they find you, don't fight them. Wherever you go, I'll find you. Just stay alive."

She yelled back, "Go, husband! We live."

I grabbed my rifle and bandoliers, threw a blanket over my shoulders, then ran out the door just as a horse thundered by, its rider carrying a torch in one hand and his rifle in the other. I snapped my rifle up without aiming and fired. My bullet hit his arm with the torch and sent the torch tumbling through the black air on to a tall, dry bush that instantly burst into a roaring fire.

A torch was thrown at a *tipi* belonging to Juh, and it flamed up with a roaring whoosh. In its light, I saw Juh's youngest son, Daklugie, on his knees, talking to his mother. Lying there as still as she was, I knew she'd been shot.

Men on horses were riding through the camp, firing and yelling, and I saw a woman and a child running for the brush shot and killed. Men on foot were running through the wickiups, gathering up captive women and children, herding them into an area where men covered them with rifles, but they weren't being abused.

I realized as I ran for cover that the *soldados* charging back and forth through our camp were *Nakai-yi* villagers. Some wore uniforms, but most wore sandals and blankets fixed loosely around them and had brightly colored head scarves tied around long, jet-black hair—*Rarámuri*, our worst enemies in Mexico. Juh had been right to worry that the *Nakai-yes* might use them. They were good fighters. I saw the gray light of dawn rising behind the mountains and knew then we were in for a long, hard fight. I prayed to *Ussen* to protect my family.

A rider charged toward me. He fired his single-shot trapdoor rifle, and I felt the big bullet rip through my shirt as I took aim. My bullet didn't miss as he rolled backward off his horse. Our warriors were careful with their ammunition but still poured deadly fire into those charging through the camp. Juh's *tipi* roared up in flames, and I saw many bodies around it. Most of our warriors took cover along the bank of the little stream while there was a pause in the fighting as the *Nakai-yi* comandante regrouped his men. Juh called for us to be ready for the next charge.

I looked over the camp as the sun brought light to our disaster and tried to find my family. I saw only a few women and children on the far side of the camp from where the *Nakai-yes* first attacked. Dead *Nakai-yi* horses and *Rarámuri* lying flat on the sand or held fast in thorn brush, their black eyes open but lifeless, were scattered across the camp. The women and children taken prisoners had been moved back among the *Nakai-yi* supplies and our horses they had captured.

A sudden shrill, burbling whistle and a *jefe* yelling, "Ataque! Ataque!" brought the next charge. I killed at least three in that charge but emptied my first bandolier of bullets. Our warriors stayed under cover in the brush along the bank of the little stream down the big *arroyo*, giving them a good position from which to fight. I don't think we lost any warrior in that charge or the one following it, but the stink of death in the morning mists was everywhere. The third charge ended as the sun began changing from a big red egg on the horizon to a bright yellow ball bringing warmth and bright light. We waited for less than half a hand, but all was quiet. Juh motioned us across the little stream to the other bank and then ran down the edge of the *arroyo* toward a wide trail that packtrains often followed toward Sahuaripa. We set up our ambush near the trail and waited.

Soon the *Nakai-yi jefe* appeared at the head of their column looking pleased and smiling. Just seeing his face made me want to kill him. My heart screamed, Where is my family? Have you killed them? You blood-thirsty dog. I waited, trembling with anger and anticipation, on Juh's command to fire. Juh waited until he saw the end of the line in front of the prisoners and livestock nearing our first man. It was a long shot, but Juh raised his rifle, took aim, then fired, knocking the rider off his horse. It was as if time stopped for an instant as the sound of the shot came back from the hills, and then the warriors screaming their defiance poured bullets into the column as men dove from their horses to find cover in the brush around boulders and along banks where water still flowed.

As the bullets whined, ricocheted off boulders, and whistled through the brush, I crept up through the weeds and brush to where I could see the captives. My guts trembling in fear, I hoped Ishchos and the children weren't there. My hopes died when, out toward the edge of the captive group, I saw Naboka sitting in her mother's lap and Bediscloye beside her as if standing guard. They were smudged and dirty and looked as if they had rolled in the ashes from a fire. Naboka had streaks through the dust on her face where she had cried, but there were none on Bediscloye, who looked around with his best lower-jaw-protruding fierce look, ready to defend his mother and sister. A feeling like someone jabbing me in the chest with hot iron made clear that Maud was not with them. Had she been killed or left behind by the *Nakai-yes* because she was dying? Had she escaped? Where was she hiding? I could only hope to find her somewhere near the main battle.

The ammunition in my second bandolier was fast disappearing. We were all nearly out of ammunition. Near the time of no shadows, Juh, recognizing we couldn't overpower the *Rarámuri*, pulled back and moved back to our broken camp to support the women and children who survived and to collect much-needed ammunition from dead or dying *soldados*.

The *Nakai-yes* had burned most of the camp, leaving it a smoking ruin. Many of the surviving women and children kept close together and hid in the brush high up the *arroyo*. When they saw their men returning from a second fight, they rushed out of the thickets and juniper groves and ran down by the bank of the little stream flowing back to their camp. Maud! I saw her running near Naiche's wives, Nahdeyole and Eclahheh, and their two children four or five years younger than Maud. During their captivity later at the White Eye school, they were named Dorothy and Paul. Maud saw me waving my arms over my head, and she waved back in the same way as she charged through the dry, broken grass and brush.

I swept her up in my arms as she ran to me, gasping and panting, "Father... Father, I live, but my mother and brother and sister have been taken by the *Nakai-yes*. Can we get them back?"

I sat her down on her feet and kneeled, so my head was about even with hers. "I'll do everything I can to set them free and bring them back to us. The *Rarámuri* have them while they march back to Namiquipa. First, we must collect all the ammunition we can from the dead *soldados* and recover what we have cached and bind up the wounds of the People who still live. I'll talk to Naiche and Eclahheh, his first wife, and ask if you can stay with them while I work and try to find Ishchos and your brother and sister. You don't mind living with them for a little while, do you?"

She threw her arms around my neck and said through the eye water streaming through the dust on her face, "I want to be with you, Father." She snuffed back the eye water and looked at me with red eyes. "Eclahheh has always been friends with Mother. She was good to me while we hid in the brush. I like her. I'll stay and help her until I can be with you again."

CHATO: DESPERATE WARRIOR   107

I was very proud of my brave girl child as I walked with her through the destroyed camp, stopping to take bandoliers or bags of bullets off dead *Rarámuri*.
Naiche, who had lost close relatives in the *Nakai-yi* attack, stood with crossed
arms, staring at Juh, who sat nearby, his head in his hands, his long hair tangled,
with dry weed bits hanging in it. I started to speak with Naiche, but he shook his
head and nose pointed where we could speak privately.

He watched Juh over my shoulder as he spoke. "Do you know where Juh was
when we were attacked?"

I shook my head. "No. Wasn't he in his *tipi* asleep?"

Naiche shook his head. "He was passed out drunk from three days of non-
stop drinking and staying drunk on the mescal we took a moon ago." Naiche
clenched his teeth. "Three days without stopping to ever sober up. We all had
our share of that mescal but drank it slow. But he took for his share a lot more
than us and couldn't put it down. Now his wife, Geronimo's sister, his baby,
and his son-in-law—all killed. His daughter, shot in the leg, will never walk
or run right like she should, if at all. The miserable *Rarámuri* scalped twelve
of our People for *Nakai-yi* money. All but four of his warriors are gone. We
lost two in that last fight. Now we must live on food we've cached to get
through Ghost Face. He's not my chief anymore. Many feel that way now. I go
to Geronimo's camp when the People can travel. I have not yet talked to the
other leaders and chiefs. Will you join Geronimo and Chihuahua with me?"

I felt bad that I was hungover when the attack came and could imagine how
Juh must feel if he was still drunk and barely able to fight. I didn't want Naiche
to know that I was barely able to defend the camp against the *Rarámuri* and
Nakai-yes. I shook my head and said, "Juh, the great leader of the People, is no
more. Our People will shun him. I join Geronimo and Chihuahua. I've lost my
wife and two children—only Maud remains. I have to get my wife and children
back. Will you let her help your wives at your fire and look after your children
while I try to free the rest of my family?"

Naiche nodded. "Maud is a fine child. She will make a good woman. Of course,
she is welcome to live with us. You come too. You have no chance of freeing Ishchos and the children until we know where the *Nakai-yes* plan to hold them. They
sell their captives in the City of Mules (Ciudad Chihuahua), and that's likely where
they'll be kept until the Season of Little Eagles when the slave traders come. I too
have relatives with the captives, and Geronimo's woman Shtsha-she and her child
also were taken. When Geronimo learns what happened here, he'll lead us to take
them back. Those taken at Casas Grandes have to be freed, too."

I crossed my arms as I listened and studied the toes of my moccasins, knowing that Naiche spoke with a clear eye. I nodded and said, "Naiche is generous and wise. Lead. I follow you to Geronimo's camp and listen to his advice."

NINETEEN

GERONIMO READIES FOR RAIDS IN THE SEASON OF LITTLE EAGLES

TIMES WERE HARD after the *Rarámuri* attack. We camped above the burned camp and buried our fallen People in the cliffs around us. We lived off cached food and slept in brush wickiups. Maud helped Naiche's wives gather supplies from food caches and from what had escaped *Nakai-yi* fires. With other women and children, they also collected rifles and pistols, managing to save a little ammunition, and cached them in a nearby cave. Naiche, the surviving warriors, and I hunted and took horses and mules from nearby *rancho*s to rebuild our herd.

The first day after the attack, chiefs Nana, Bonito, and Loco and leaders like Kaytennae and me talked with the men. We all agreed that returning to Geronimo's camp at Bugatseka was the best thing to do. Naiche and I told Juh, who sat off by himself, grieving and despondent over the loss of Ishton, their baby, and his son-in-law and the wounding of his daughter. He nodded agreement. We asked if he would come with us. He nosed pointed toward his three sons sitting near where their sister rested. "Hmmph. We come."

The wounded were tended and had healed enough that, within half a moon, they could walk—even Juh's daughter Jacali—with the help of a stick and without support for the long walk or ride through the mountains in cold, whistling winds and occasional snow. But we had recovered and taken enough horses to mount the wounded and pack food and supplies, when we left for Geronimo's camp. We followed the trails north in the mountains and the river canyons. We knew, and I suspect that he knew it as well, Juh would never have his leadership power again. We treated him with respect as chief and didn't oppose him in the leader's position behind the women and children on the march to Geronimo's camp.

THE RIDE TO Geronimo's camp took five suns across rough country. When we appeared in the tall pines at the edge of his camp, the People saw us and ran to welcome us with happy faces until they saw ours and realized we had come through bad times. Geronimo walked among us, welcoming the men and their wives and looking for his sister, who was Juh's first wife, and one of his own wives and a child. His face fell when he didn't see his sister or wife and child among Juh's sons and Jacali, with her wounded leg. When he looked at Juh, Juh looked down from his pony and slowly shook his head. Sorrow filled Geronimo's face as he turned and walked back to the little fire in front of his family's shelter.

The camp's women brought us food and helped our women set up shelters. The camp's men and boys helped with the livestock while Juh, the chiefs, and the leaders sat with Geronimo. After we smoked, Geronimo said, "I ask Chief Juh to us tell what happened to his band."

Juh looked around the circle and then at Geronimo, his eyes narrowed and his mouth set in a grim line. Juh's normal booming voice came low and raspy. "A good season of raiding followed after we wiped out Mata Ortiz at Chocolate Pass. After Geronimo and Chihuahua camped here at Bugatseka and raided west into Sonora, we raided in southern Sonora. I didn't want to fire up the Chihuahuans more after Chocolate Pass by raiding in Chihuahua. Even so, I knew their *soldados* would come after us and that they believed we would go to Guaynopa. They knew that the only way they could find Guaynopa was if they used *Rarámuri* scouts and militia and promised them money for our scalps to track us. I decided to move our Ghost Face camp to a big *arroyo* a long day's ride across the mountains west instead of staying at Guaynopa. I thought they would find the camp at Guaynopa empty and have no idea where we were. Then they would go back to their villages. The big *arroyo* camp was in a good place with much game, water, and plenty of firewood." He looked around at us, and we all nodded agreement.

The sun was disappearing behind the near mountains, and the clouds tinged with dark orange were turning blood red. How appropriate, I thought as I watched them sweep high over the mountain ridges.

"The morning the *Rarámuri* came, it was about a hand before dawn and very cold. I had slave boys watching with the sentries. The *Rarámuri* scouts saw them, recognized they were *Nakai-yes*, and tried to get the boys to come join them. But the boys ran for my *tipi* and entered screaming we were under attack.

I was out of the *tipi*, covered by my blanket, with my rifle and a bandolier of ammunition in time to shoot a rider charging through the camp with a torch. I yelled for my sons to take their mother and sisters to cover down by the banks of the little creek trickling down the side of the *arroyo* beside the camp."

I don't remember seeing or hearing much of Juh during that first attack.

Juh said, "I gathered the men for a unified front against the attack. We fought from the banks in the little *arroyo* stream. The *Nakai-yes* had many more men than we did. We tried to drive them out of the camp three times, but their numbers seemed to grow. They were good fighters. We killed many, but not enough to force them out of our camp."

Juh looked around at us, and we were all nodding and sighing agreement.

"We were running low on ammunition, and I decided our best chance for a successful attack was to attack the column leaders when they rode down the big *arroyo* toward the Río Aros. While we waited, hidden in ambush along the trail down the *arroyo*, they scalped twelve of our People, including men, women, and children. They took nearly everything of value in the camp and then burned every shelter and all our supplies.

"They killed Ishton early in the attack when she had our baby in her arms, ready to run out the *tipi* door. The same bullet that passed through our baby went through her too. Ishton fell with the baby in her arms, took my dead son-in-law's rifle and ammunition, and wouldn't let my sons help her. She fought to her last breath, but she didn't last long in the hail of bullets flying through the *tipi*. Jacali was badly wounded in the leg, but my strong sons got her to cover and escaped harm.

"Our ambush attack on the leaders of the column was less than a rifle shot from our camp. But no matter how much we shot, the *Rarámuri* still stood their ground. Two of my best warriors were killed in that fight. We couldn't make them free the prisoners, and we had to give up. I was a failure as a battle leader."

Grief as near eye water as I'd ever seen on a man filled the face of Juh. "My first wife, our baby, and your sister were killed. Your wife and child were taken too. Many in my camp have ridden the ghost pony. *Ussen* has left me. I can no longer lead the People. You are a *di-yen* of great Power. You must become leader. I have said all I have to say."

There were no surprised looks on the face of anyone. We had all reached the same conclusion that Geronimo must be leader, even if he wouldn't call himself chief. Geronimo crossed his arms and looked around the circle. He saw everyone seemed to accept Juh no longer being chief. Geronimo said, "Juh is a great warrior. Even if he chooses to no longer stay as chief, one day he might again lead his People."

A voice from the warriors crowded around us said, "Lead us, Geronimo."

He stared at the far wall of a nearby *wickiup* until he finally said, "I will lead but not be chief. Others, like Naiche, should be chief. Now I must think on what we do when the Season of Little Eagles brings the good raiding seasons."

THE DAYS THAT followed were quiet and peaceful, the sun warm, and breezes gentle. Maud and I were welcomed at Naiche's fire, and we slept there. Ishchos and the children filled my dreams, and I awoke a few times covered in body water even in the cold night air as I dreamed of laughing *Rarámuri* with spear points held against their chests. Each time my eyes opened, I knew I had to find them and get them back, even if I had to do it alone.

Maud had played with Naiche's children, Paul and Dorothy, and knew them well before our camp was attacked. Now living with them, they were even closer as friends, but Maud was more like a big sister and left off play to do many chores helping their mothers.

Naiche and I sat by the fire when the sun fell behind the mountains and smoked and talked often about how our war with the White Eyes and *Nakai-yes* might end. There were not enough of us to fight for a long time, but we agreed it would be a long time before we were all wiped out. We talked about what to do to replace all the ammunition we'd used in the Chocolate Pass fight and the fight with the *Rarámuri*. The obvious answer was to raid for more ammunition, but the questions of how, where, and when were left floating, argued, and unresolved in the cold, smoky air.

A few days later, our questions were answered. Geronimo sent his wife She-gah to ask me to come to his fire. I was cleaning my rifle when she came and, nodding I understood, set aside the barrel ramrod, cloth patches, and gun oil to follow her back to the fire in front of Geronimo's family *wickiup*. He saw me coming and waved me to sit down by him to his left. "Hi-yeh, Chato. Welcome to my fire."

As I was sitting down, I saw Bonito passing by the randomly scattered wickiups, headed for Geronimo's fire. Geronimo waved him to sit to his right. Bonito smiled and came around the fire to join us. Geronimo drew a *tobaho* pouch and an oak leaf from a vest pocket to roll a cigarette, lighted it with a wood splinter from the fire, and we smoked to the four directions. After Geronimo finished the smoke, he tossed the last bit in the fire. We were ready to discuss serious business.

It was near the time of shortest shadows, and that day, the Ghost Face sun was exceptionally warm and the air still, tree shadows barely moving. Geronimo held his hands palms out as if to feel the heat from the fire. He said, "The sun and wind seem to think this is the Season of Little Eagles, but clouds and snow come soon. It is good to have our brothers back with us. We help you all we can. Is there anything you need?"

Bonito looked at his crossed legs and shook his head. "You know I lost my wife and child in the *Rarámuri* attack. Your women take turns giving me meals at their fires, and I can lay my blanket by the fire of any *wickiup*. The wound in my spirit begins to heal. I will take another woman as soon as *Ussen* moves me."

I said, "Ishchos, my woman, and two youngest children were taken captive like your wife Shtsha-she and daughter. My dreams and thoughts are filled with them. I must find them and get them back. Perhaps you will guide me in how to do this or even join me in my search."

Geronimo's eyes glittered as he spoke. "Yes, we will get them back. The *Nakai-yes* know where they are. I have to get Chee-hash-kish and Shtsha-she and our child back. We have to take our own captives to trade for them. We will take captives and trade for them after our raids have taken enough to make us ready for the next Ghost Face. Will you support my way, Chato, or will you try it on your own?"

I wanted to leave Bugatseka that day, find Ishchos and the children, and free them, killing anyone who stood in my way. But I knew Geronimo spoke wise words, and I knew my best chance of freeing my family unharmed was his way. His fire was warm on my hands and face. I nodded. "I follow Geronimo."

He smiled. *"Ch'ik'eh doleel."* Then he began speaking of raids that needed to be made for supplies, how the women needed cloth, axes, and good iron pots for cooking. At last, he got around to the reason he'd asked Bonito and me to his fire.

"All the warriors are very low on cartridges. We used many in the Chocolate Pass fight and later in raids during the Season of Earth Is Reddish Brown, and then you used many during the attack on Juh's camp. We have the best rifles. They shoot many times and have good range, but they can't be used without cartridges."

The wind pushing through the tops of the pines seemed to whisper, Geronimo speaks true. Bonito and I nodded we understood.

Geronimo turned to me and said, "Chato, you and Bonito are smart, fierce warriors. Our band needs you to find us more cartridges. Will you do this?"

I looked at Bonito and said, "I cannot speak for Bonito, but I will do what I can. What you ask, I will do."

Bonito stuck out his lower lip and said, "Yes, I, too, will do as you ask. Chato and I will be as brothers in this. Tell us your plan."

Geronimo said, *"Ch'ik'eh doleel!* I want you to lead a fast raid north across the border. It must be like a lightning strike, so fast the Blue Coats will not even be sure you were there. They will think you are just marauders slipping out of San Carlos. Get in and get out, pronto. Take only the best, most experienced warriors with you so inexperience doesn't slow you down. I think maybe twenty-five men are enough, but use your judgment who is best to go. Kill all *Nakai-yes* and White Eyes you come across so they tell nothing to those who come after you. Go to mines and other White Eye camps. Strike those with mule packtrains and wagon trains. Ranches stock much ammunition. Take it. If you can raid a trading post, do it. Any livestock worth keeping, take it. Maybe you can send someone to San Carlos to learn what the Blue Coats are up to and other news. Leave for the land of the *Nakai-yes* when the Blue Coat numbers become too many for you to move without a fight or you risk being caught."

Already feeling excitement of the coming raid, I said, "What will Geronimo do?"

"I and Chihuahua will lead the rest on raids west into Sonora. With your People here, we will soon need more food supplies. Also take food if you can, but your main goal is cartridges."

"When will we leave?"

"I think the time will be right in about a moon, but *Ussen* tells me. During the next two or three suns, you and Bonito choose who you want with you. We'll all leave at the same time and camp the first night on the banks of the Río Bavispe. Next day, you go north. Chihuahua and I go west and south, maybe as far as Ures. There are many packtrains on the trails to Ures. Come back when you think you have enough cartridges or there are too many Blue Coats. Now let us smoke to success."

I saw Bonito's eyes shining with excitement, and I'm sure mine were too for the first time since Chocolate Pass and the end of Juan Mata Ortiz. I was already thinking of who we should ask to ride with us.

TWENTY

A HARD LOSS

BONITO AND I began comparing names of warriors we thought were good choices for our raid. We agreed on nearly everyone, and those we didn't agree on weren't asked to join us. We talked to every warrior in the camp, and all were eager to join us. Besides Bonito and me, the best-known warriors going on this raid were Naiche, Cathla, Shoie, Dutchy, Mangas, Atelnietze, and Beneactinay.

Beneactinay's best friend, Tzoe, had been my brother-in-law. (I thought of my cousins who married him as my sisters.) My sisters were killed at Aliso Creek along with a little daughter, and he was badly wounded. But he had the strength and courage to survive in the mountains together with Kayitah, who was also wounded, and Martine's woman who looked after them while they recovered from their wounds. Through their strength and courage, Loco's survivors weren't slowed in trying to reach Juh's stronghold. Tzoe, Kayitah, and Martine's wife showed up at the stronghold a month later, having made it through the wilderness and finding the stronghold without help. Beneactinay suggested that Tzoe, now recognized as a warrior of Power, come with us, and we agreed.

Two of the young men not yet warriors, Gooday and Haozous, wanted to come as *novitiates*. Mangas, their uncle, thought they should come. I hesitated to take any *novitiates*, but these two had proved themselves very capable at Aliso Creek and Chocolate Pass. Bonito and I agreed they would be welcome with us.

Our men sharpened their knives, cleaned and oiled their rifles and revolvers, and cleaned, fletched, and mounted sharp, impossible-to-remove arrowheads filed from iron barrel bands on their arrows. It was important to be clean before we rode our raiding ponies, so we bathed and washed our hair, used a sweat lodge several times, and joined our women often in their blankets. Wives pounded and ground dried meat mixed with many kinds of berries and nuts and bits of cooked mescal for sacks of food to live on when we couldn't stop to cook. My wife and two children were not with us, but Maud learned from the older women how to make me trail food. A moon after the beginning of the Season of Little Eagles, when the warm winds came, we were ready.

GERONIMO LED US down the steep, narrow trails from Bugatseka to the banks of the Río Bavispe, where we crossed out of sight south of the village of Huachinera. Washed and sweated clean, with our weapons oiled and sharp and our spirits high, we stopped to camp for the night in a stand of dark-green pines by a small burbling stream in a canyon in the El Tigré Mountains foothills on the west side of the *río*. We let the *novitiates* for both raids cook together for us all. I had to admit and the warriors agreed that their meal was good and that they acted like they knew all the trail customs of raiding and war as if they were already warriors. I was glad to have them with us. They would be useful as the raids took supplies and livestock and unavoidably drew blood.

I awoke to the *Jeet! Jeet!* of a canyon wren complaining about our invasion of its territory and the strong smell of good coffee and the fat dripping from meat on sticks angled over the fires. The cold morning air made my skin prickle as I crawled out of my blanket to find a place to make water. A round golden glow beginning to rise above the dark eastern mountains was turning the horizon sky above the mountains dark blue and making stars disappear as they raced for cover in the velvety blackness overhead. The water in the little stream by the camp was ice cold and shocked my sleepy lethargy awake as I plunged my head into it.

As we ate, Bonito and I talked with Geronimo and Chihuahua. Geronimo suggested, and we agreed, to go northwest over the mountains and head for the mining and ranching country at Cananea, where there should be stock and a good supply of ammunition for the taking to get us on our lightning arrow strike across the border. Bonito and I had discussed this in our first talks at Bugatseka and agreed then it was a smart thing to do.

We gathered our warriors and told them what we planned. It would be a trip of several days across rugged mountains and through deep canyons, but they were eager for action after a long Season of Ghost Face and wanted revenge against the *Nakai-yes* for the disaster that had befallen Juh and his People. We saddled our horses and told our brothers we would see them again soon at Bugatseka and then rode up the canyon from where we camped to a trail across the foothills and mountains.

We came to Cananea ranching country late on the fifth day after leaving our camp in the canyon near Huachinera. It had been a hard trail for our animals, and they needed rest. After crossing the *llano* northeast of Cananea, we camped in a wide and deep *arroyo* with a trickle of water running down to the *llano* out of the foothills of the Cuitaca Mountains. From there, we could rest and study the range to the northeast across the Río San Pedro and the ugly, stinking pit mines at Cananea to the south. The warriors rested, staying out of sight, while Bonito and I found a high hill from which to study the land with our soldier glasses.

Small herds of horses and cattle wandered near the Río San Pedro, grazing on the grama grass just turning green. *Vaqueros* and a few American cowboys were scattered across the range with their own little herds of livestock. We saw three men, who, judging from their hats, were two *Nakai-yes* and an American, driving a herd of ten nice horses toward Cananea, and we could see rifles on their saddles. We knew that, as they approached Cananea, they wouldn't expect trouble and that was the best place to take them. I sent four warriors and the two *novitiates* down to the river to set up an ambush two hands' ride from Cananea, where the *río* branched, one branch coming from the mountains and the main *río* running on toward Cananea.

The warriors were skillful and the ambush easy. The *Nakai-yes* and American were taken as they passed a grove of mesquite on the river trail. The *novitiates* then ran out and drove the horses before they could scatter up a nearby *arroyo* lined on each side by mesquite just beginning to turn green. The warriors, who had hidden behind large green creosote bushes along trail, shot the riders at close range. Two riders slumped from their horses but held fast to the reins. The third rider, still mounted, was killed, hit in the head, his hat gone. The warriors calmly grabbed the reins of the white-eyed horses startled by the gunfire but held in check by their riders holding the reins in their death grips. The warriors took the revolvers, ammunition, and a thing the White Eyes called "watch" from the vest of the American.

Not far from the *río* ambush, horses could be seen freely grazing on the *llano*. While the *novitiates* drove the horses just taken back to our camp up the big *arroyo*, the warriors rode out on the *llano* and drove the even-larger herd of grazing horses back toward the *arroyo* where we had camped. It had been an easy sun's raid. Now we had to travel fast before word was out that we were near.

THE SUN BLAZING in golden brightness floated over the eastern mountain horizon to light the dawn over the *llano* as we left our camp with our herd of newly taken horses running easy and relaxed before us. We came upon a camp of White Eyes just ready to saddle their horses near the border. We thundered through them like a sharp blade through green grass and killed two, but the other three managed to swing up on their horses and head for protection in a nearby village. Even so, we managed to add two horses and two mules to our herd and took two revolvers and ammunition from the White Eyes we killed.

We crossed the border and headed for the mines and other camps around the place the White Eyes called "Tombstone." Just before the sun began hiding in the west, we decided to raid a camp on the Río San Pedro. The men cutting and charring wood (they called the charred wood "charcoal") for making hot fires ought to have guns and ammunition we wanted.

Warrior arrows killed three men sitting around a fire, ready for a night meal after a sun cutting trees and burning the wood in the *río bosque*, but we found no cartridges or weapons on them—I thought while watching the attack, *Foolish men not arming themselves like that deserve to die.* A fourth man ran toward a tent a bowshot down the river on a little hill near a horse corral. He tried to hide, but we had seen him and knew he was nearby. We crawled up to the corral and, in the lengthening shadows, looked for him in the brush but didn't see him. If he had not been wearing weapons, then we knew his weapons and ammunition had to be in that tent, and now he probably was in the tent waiting for us to come taste his bullets.

I called out to him in the *Nakai-yi* tongue. "Come out of the tent. Give us your weapons and ammunition, and we won't harm you. Come out!" Nothing stirred. We knew he had to be in the tent. Mangas called to him in the White Eye tongue. "Save yourself. Give us your weapons and ammunition. We won't harm you. Come out of the tent or die."

Still, there was no response from the tent. The warriors were ready. I gave the signal, and they each fired two or three times into the tent, filling it with holes and making the door flaps dance, breaking one or two tie ropes to make the sides sag in and the entire tent shake and tremble like a wounded, dying man. After the smoke cleared, there was still no movement, no sound.

Beneactinay and Tzoe kneeled in the sandy dust behind corral fence posts. They intently studied the tent for signs of life as the shadows grew longer and the setting sun painted the high, thin eastern clouds blazing oranges and deep blood reds. Beneactinay and Tzoe looked at me, and I motioned them forward with a nose point toward the tent. Either the man was dead, or he had managed to leave unseen.

Beneactinay and Tzoe slipped between the corral fence poles and ran bent over and running and dodging from side-to-side up the hill toward the tent, Beneactinay a handful of steps in front of Tzoe. The crack and flame from a rifle in the brush downslope and a little behind the bullet-riddled tent jerked our attention from the tent to the brush and then to Beneactinay's body, now flopped forward and stretched out in a little low cloud of dust, while Tzoe was rolling toward cover and crabbing back into the shadows.

In all the years I had raided and made war, I never knew such a mixture of feelings, feeling sick like after eating bad meat and mixing that with rage. Three or four warriors silently slipped into the brush, attempting to take Beneactinay's killer, but he had disappeared in the dark gloom. We soon heard a horse racing through the brush on the other side of the *río*. It was too dark and too late to catch him.

Tzoe ran to his friend. I knew he was hoping against hope Beneactinay hadn't been killed. In the dusk, I saw Tzoe kneel by Beneactinay's body, gently roll it over, speak a few words, and then bow his head with a sigh we all heard. Beneactinay rode the ghost pony. Tzoe wanted to bury the body and do a ceremony to urge *Ussen* to hurry and accept Beneactinay as he came riding to the Happy Place. But I knew the man who got away would soon return with Blue Coats and Apache scouts who would know how to follow us, or many angry men with good guns would come from the nearby village. We headed for what the White Eyes called the "Whetstone Mountains." I left a scout to watch what the White Eyes did.

Our trail toward the Whetstones passed a camp of two American cowboys riding with a *Nakai-yi vaquero*. They soon rode their ghost ponies, and we picked up more cartridges and some good ponies, rifles, and revolvers. As we rode on, scouts we had sent out returned to tell us a fourteen-mule pack-train with four men was headed for Fort Huachuca down the trail from the village called Benson. We cut the talking wire running to Fort Huachuca and tied it back together with rawhide as I had seen Chihuahua do. Then we took the packtrain. It was quick and easy, especially at night with bows and arrows. The White Eyes weren't aware we were anywhere close until it was too late. They also were quick to ride ghost ponies.

We led the packtrain back down the road and then up an *arroyo* we cleared of tracks and signs as we headed for a spring up the slopes in a canyon where we could hide our herd of horses and mules and rest. We had no fires and ate the trail food our women had fixed for us while wrapped in our blankets.

Most of the men were snoring in the cold desert air when the moon began dropping into the mountains to the southwest. The scout I had left to watch the charred-wood camp left his pony with the *novitiates* watching our horses and guarding the camp. He came to Bonito and me, sleeping lightly, and squatted down in front of us. We were quick to sense he was there and signaled with a nod for him to speak. Tzoe raised up in his blanket and cocked his head to one side, stretching to hear what the scout had to say.

The scout looked at me and then Bonito, puffed his cheeks, then shook his head. "The Blue Coats came to the camp about three hands after you left. White Eyes from the village came riding while the Blue Coats were looking over the ground, and the man who brought them spoke many words. The men from the village were very angry. They kicked Beneactinay's body, and some of the soldiers recognized him as one of the scouts who had left San Carlos with Geronimo. Then...." The scout stared off into the darkness, his breath making a cloud for a couple of breaths. "Then one of the men pulled a big knife, squatted down by Beneactinay, grabbed his hair, stretched his neck out, then took off his head and threw it in a sack another held for him."

I heard Tzoe groan as if hit by slung stone and fall back on his blanket.

TWENTY-ONE
TZOE'S MEDICINE SPEAKS

WE LEFT THE Whetstone Mountains in the cold breath of morning, facing the gold outline of mountains to the east. The valley of the Río San Pedro lay under a thick green blanket of new grass, and our horse and mule herd was easy to push to another big *arroyo* with enough water trickling down one side out of the Dragoon Mountains to satisfy them. We had well over a hundred horses and mules, and it took half of the warriors to keep them in a tight herd.

After we rested, we pushed on north toward the Winchester Mountains. Near their foothills, we passed a ranch but saw no cowboys or *vaqueros* and no livestock. A scout told us two men worked in a corral attaching *pesh* (iron) to their horses' hooves, but they had seen no one else. I had not seen how White Eyes shaped and pegged *pesh* to the feet of their horses and neither had Naiche and three or four other warriors. We decided that if we could get close enough without being seen, we would watch the men work and maybe learn something before sending them off on their ghost ponies and taking their weapons and ammunition. It was a fool's thought.

We left the other warriors with Bonito to drive our new herd of horses toward the Peloncillo Mountains across the valleys scattered with swaths of new green grass, mesquite, cholla cactus almost white with spines, yucca sending tall stems crowned with buds ready to bloom high up toward the sun, and dark-green creosote bushes. We rode up close to the corral without a sound to watch the corral horses have *pesh* put on their hooves.

Two men worked the horses. One roped and pulled a horse out of a group stamping and snorting on the far side of the corral to bring it to a man with his shirt off and wearing a leather apron with pockets that held tools and nails for the *pesh* he fastened to each hoof after trimming and shaping it. He had a hot fire going on top of a pile of stones under a shed near the other side of the corral. He used the fire to heat an already-shaped *pesh* piece, one of several sizes for him to hammer into the best fit for a particular horse's hoof. Most of the *pesh* he had usually fit the hoof without need of additional shaping. The man nailing the *pesh* to the horses' feet was big, and his arm muscles rippled with strength as he lifted a horse's leg to place it between or on his own legs while he nailed the *pesh* on its hoof. I liked this work, liked to watch a skilled man at it, and I thought, Maybe someday I'll try it if I live to return to the reservation.

The sun was halfway down its arc toward the western horizon, and there lay a peaceful stillness in the hot air. As we watched the man work, a horsefly drew blood on the back leg of one of our horses. It snorted and kicked against a creosote to drive the horsefly off. That made enough sound to draw the attention of the man putting iron on the horse's hooves. When he saw us, he dropped his tools and, quicker than a rattlesnake, snatched up a rifle leaning against the corral fence to snap off a shot toward us. I remember watching him throw the rifle to his shoulder and then instant darkness, as if someone had jerked a sack over my head.

MY EYES FLUTTERED open to see the concerned face of Naiche staring at mine, and he was dabbing the left side of my throbbing head with a wet cloth. He smiled when he saw my eyes. "So you don't ride the ghost pony after all, Chato? You had us worried you were leaving us."

I shook my head, trying to drive the fog and confusion from my mind. "How long have I been wandering in the land of darkness?"

"About half a hand."

"What happened?"

Naiche grinned. "We were watching the man put *pesh* on the horses' hooves when one of the horses snorted and kicked a bush. The man looked up, saw us, grabbed his rifle, then shot. The bullet just grazed your head, but it was enough to knock you off your horse. We grabbed you up and headed to a place where we could hide and defend ourselves. About the time the man with the *pesh* horseshoes shot you, the ones with the horse herd galloped by toward the Peloncillo Mountains. He lost interest in killing us while he took some shots at them, but he hit neither man nor horse as far as I could tell."

Naiche, who had helped treat bullet wounds since he was a small boy, gently felt the bloody place in my hair where the bullet had passed. "Hmmph. *Doo dat'éé da*. The bullet just cut a little of your scalp. Nothing is broken. You are very lucky, my brother."

"I believe you, but my head pounds like a pot drum filled with water. Tie the pulp from a prickly pear over the wound so it doesn't rot and make me lose my mind. Then we join Bonito in the Peloncillo."

He nodded, grinning, and held up pieces of prickly pear pads that had already been scraped clean of thorns and had been split to get the pulp. He and Tzoe, who had hovered close by watching my every move, bandaged me with prickly pear pulp and white juice over the wound.

I drank a little water, staggered up with my head still thumping, then, after a little walking, knew I was ready to ride. We raced for the meeting place with Bonito and the horse herd.

WHEN THE MOON was at the top of its arc toward the south, we found Bonito where we expected in a box canyon with a spring and big natural tank that kept the horses watered and with enough nearby grass and brush for them to graze. Naiche, Bonito, and I smoked and talked a long while about how to find out what was happening at San Carlos. Geronimo made sure we understood and agreed to do this before we left our camp on the Bavispe. We decided the best thing to do was send two of our best warriors, Cathla and Dutchy, to visit one of the few interpreters at San Carlos we trusted, Hermenegildo Grijalva, and ask what he knew. Naiche was a chief who covered all his bets. He told Cathla and Dutchy to ask Grijalva if he would speak for us in the future if we had to surrender. They ate, saddled their ponies, then said they would find us in a few suns.

We rested and slept all the following day. My head wound had stopped throbbing, and I rested but didn't sleep well. My life in dreams was filled with visions of Ishchos and our children and my reaching out for them while some dark spirit kept them just out of my reach. Somehow, I had to get them back, get them out of *Nakai-yi* slavery. I was strong. I knew I had the strength, but I didn't know how. To be tied with bands that couldn't be seen and unable to act was enough to make any man fearful and angry.

As the falling sun was spreading orange and red light on the high clouds and purple over the canyons, we filled our bellies, gathered our herd, then rode north to meet Dutchy and Cathla and learn what Grijalva had told them.

WE RODE HARD north all night. The morning shadows on the eastern hills were disappearing when we found Cathla and Dutchy resting at big pool of clear water, Ash Spring. While the men rested and ate their trail food, Bonito, Naiche, and I smoked to the four directions and talked with our scouts.

Dutchy looked eager with his news, and I nodded toward him to speak first. He said, "Grijalva says big changes happening. *Nant'an Lpah* has returned. He speaks with all the chiefs, hears their complaints, then promises to fix them. He has already sent most of the agents who cheated us away, and now Blue Coats are the agents. *Tenientes* Gatewood and Davis are now chiefs of scouts. Captain Crawford is the agent for San Carlos. They are fair and keep things straight on the reservation."

Hearing this, I thought, Good, maybe one day we can return, maybe the Blue Coats can help us get our People out of slavery in Mexico.

Cathla said, "*Nant'an Lpah* is planning some kind of big soldier move. He is at the iron wagon stopping place at Willcox village. The iron wagons bring many supplies, and they organize big packtrains. Scouts are told they will be gone more than a moon. No one speaks or seems to know what the nant'an does."

I glanced up and saw Tzoe with his head cocked toward us, listening to all that was said. Always, Tzoe was curious, and our talk wasn't private. I didn't care if he listened.

Naiche looked from Dutchy to Cathla and back to Dutchy and leaned back on one elbow. "Did Grijalva say he will speak for us if we surrender?"

Dutchy nodded. "Yes, he said he is glad to help us when we surrender." He grinned and laughed. "That is, he said, if we ever decide to surrender."

Bonito, Naiche, and I decided we had heard good news, but we wondered what *Nant'an Lpah* was planning. It sounded big. We would need to be careful.

After two hands of rest, we rode northwest up the San Simeon Valley toward the ranches near Ash Flat and Eagle Creek, where we ought to find good herds of horses and many chances for taking revolvers, rifles, and ammunition from the *ranchos*. We rode hard all that sun and found a box canyon in the foothills near Ash Flat with water and grass, where it would be easy to hold our herd of horses and mules while the warriors ate and slept. They had been riding hard for most of a night and sun. They needed rest and the *novitiates* to fix them a hot meal.

Most of the sun, I had a sense of bad fortune coming to us. I told Bonito, and he agreed, that I would climb on the ridge above our canyon and watch for a while to make certain no one had been following us. I took my blanket, soldier glasses, and rifle. I found a good place in the pines on the ridge overlooking Ash Flat. I smoked and made myself comfortable watching the *llano*. I used my soldier glasses to watch the trail we had covered late that sun and saw no sign of anyone. As the light was dying, I slumped down drowsy and comfortable into my bed of pine needles. A voice next to my ear said, "Don't shoot, Chato. It's only me, Tzoe." I jerked up, cocking my rifle, fast looking around the brush and deepening shadows. I spotted the man and blew with relief. It was Tzoe! He shook his head and waved his hands palms out in front of him, saying, "Don't shoot! Don't shoot!"

I relaxed and laughed. "It takes a very good warrior to get that close without my hearing him. What do you want?"

Tzoe said, "I need to speak with you in private."

I nodded and motioned to a pine-needle pile next to me. It was getting cool, and, wrapping his blanket around him, he sat down next to me. We smoked to the four directions. Twisting the last bit of the cigarette out in my fingers as darkness spread its blanket over us, I said, "Speak. I listen."

Tzoe, quiet, gathered his thoughts as the tree peepers began to sing. He said, "If you look over toward San Carlos, you can see a few fires the People have lit. Their light pulls at my heart. It has been nearly a harvest since Geronimo brought us to Juh from San Carlos. On the way, the *Nakai-yi* soldiers killed my women—your sisters—and my child, and they nearly killed me. The wound where I was shot is still raw. Three moons ago, *Rarámuri* attacked Juh's camp and took many into slavery, including your woman and two of your children. They even took a wife and child of Geronimo, and I know Naiche lost family. Juh is finished as a leader and chief. No one will follow him again as he wanders the Blue Mountains. Now, here in the north country, we raid like lightning arrows looking for weapons and bullets for our summer raids. Just four suns ago, my great friend and warrior rode the ghost pony, and I am sick with grief for him."

In the low light from the full moon rising over the eastern mountains, I saw wet streaks on Tzoe's cheeks. I understood his sorrow. I had lost many good friends and brothers fighting the Americans and *Nakai-yes*. Although your body carries no wound, your spirit bleeds for those for whom you cared about.

I watched him closely as he continued. "Since my friend has ridden the ghost pony, I have prayed often to *Ussen* about how to understand all the misery we have endured during the last harvest. *Ussen* has spoken to me. He says there is no life for me in these raids and war. I must return to my People, the White Mountains, at San Carlos and help them. Will you let me go? Will you let me leave this raid and return to my People? I want war no more."

Bonito and I wanted Beneactinay and his friend Tzoe on this raid. But Beneactinay had ridden the ghost pony, and now his friend and my former brother-in-law, for whom I had much respect, said *Ussen* had told him to return to San Carlos to look after his People. Here, high in the pines, we could see faraway points of light, fires, at San Carlos and the tree peepers singing to us, but there was a kind of stillness with their songs, and my heart sighed. It was as he said. We had lost many and much loot during the last harvest. We needed to save ourselves, get our families back, live peacefully with the Blue Coats and White Eyes, and find a way to support ourselves without wars and raids. I knew in my deepest center this was true.

I said to Tzoe, "Who am I to argue with or say no to *Ussen*. You know some will say you should stay. Whatever Bonito says, I will abide. Is this fair for you?"

I saw his head nod. "Yes, it is fair."

"*Ch'ik'eh doleel.* Then let us, with the rising of the sun, speak with Bonito. Now rest, my brother. Soon I think you'll know the Power of *Ussen*'s message to you."

TWENTY-TWO

THE TAKING OF
CHARLIE McCOMAS

BONITO MOTIONED ME, with Tzoe not far behind, over to his fire. The *novitiates* had made four small fires and were cooking meat pushed on sticks hung over the fires at an angle that sent mouthwatering smells up in smoke, which drifted through the junipers and cholla scattered through the camp. Bonito held his hand out for us to join him, me on his left side and Tzoe on his right.

Bonito said, "Ho, Chato. Since you send us no warning, you saw no one?"

"No, no one to see. I watched the *llano* until the moon rode high, but none came. Tzoe came to sit with me, and we talked a long time. He tells me his medicine wants him to return to San Carlos and look after his White Mountain People. His good friend at the White Eye wood-burning camp on the Río San Pedro and his two wives and child at Aliso Creek all now ride the ghost pony. There is no one left for him in the land of the *Nakai-yes*. *Ussen* tells him his service should be to his People at San Carlos."

Bonito's dark, penetrating eyes, eyes that looked into a man and saw his thoughts written on his face, studied Tzoe as he listened to me, nodding he understood my words. When I finished speaking, he puffed his cheeks and blew, looked around the camp, then called to the men, "Ho! Brothers, come join us. We need your thoughts."

The band gathered around Bonito's fire, casting side glances at Tzoe and me.

Bonito said, "I ask Chato to tell you what he told me about a talk he had with Tzoe."

As I spoke, the men listened, unmoving and silent. Birds whistled and called out of the brush. A flock of crows from the big trees down by the Río Gila flew over us, squawking, and a scorpion ran from the fire stone near my foot. I told the men what Tzoe had said to me and that I had told him I would agree with whatever Bonito wanted to do. Tzoe listened with the rest of the warriors and looked at peace while cocking his ear toward me to hear my every word and looking out over the hills rolling down toward San Carlos.

I finished. Bonito looked around the group and said, "Brothers, should we let Tzoe leave us?"

Naiche, who had been listening with his arms crossed and facing the golden light rising above the Nantane Mountains, nodded and said without moving, "Tzoe's medicine says he should return to his family at San Carlos? He should go." There was a rumble of agreement among the men, but others were silent and shook their heads.

Kaytennae was one who shook his head. He said, "Tzoe should not leave us, regardless of what his medicine tells him. We have all lost friends and family during the last two harvests. Why should that change anyone's need to support the band? Tzoe has lost the will to fight. He wants to let the Blue Coats and White Eye agents tell him when he can make personal business visits to the brush. Chato is leader of this raid. He should have told Tzoe no when they talked. Now he, like the weak leader he is, passes the responsibility for leading to Bonito."

I felt my hand tighten around the handle of my knife. If Kaytennae wanted to question my ability to lead this raid, then let him raise the question and prove he is stronger than the steel in my hand. We stared at each other until I saw Bonito look at both of us and wave his hand parallel to the ground in a signal for us to forget any hint of fighting over what was said.

Bonito looked at the men and seemed to sigh. "I agree with Naiche. Who are we to argue with *Ussen*? If *Ussen* tells Tzoe to return to his People and serve them at San Carlos, then he should go." Nearly all the warriors nodded and said, *"Doo dat'éé da."* Bonito motioned to Yahnozah, one of the *novitiates* listening outside the circle of warriors. When the boy came, Bonito told him to find a good pony, a saddle and bridle, a lever rifle, and two days of supplies for Tzoe to carry as he rode to his family at San Carlos.

Tzoe stood as several of the men came up to him and told him they thought he was doing the right thing and knew *Ussen* would ride with him. He nodded and said, "*Ussen* guide your paths. Be in Power and listen to him." Kaytennae had walked away with most of the others. *Someday, Kaytennae, you and I will straighten out your insults and bad manners.*

BONITO AND I decided to break the men into two groups. He went west down the Río Gila to take travelers and raid ranches and mines for weapons and ammunition. I took my group with the livestock and rode southeast from the Gila, looking for more livestock, freighters, and travelers. We planned to meet at a spring in the Burro Mountains about halfway between the villages of Silver City and Lordsburg and then swing southwest the next sun to look for freighters along the road and stock on the *llano* around ranches.

Bonito and I had some success before we met two days later in the Burros. His warriors had attacked a mining camp and came away with a good load of ammunition and new lever rifles and, the next day, wiped out five at a stagecoach station. My men attacked a village that didn't have many to defend it and, later that day, took more livestock and moved on to the Burros, where we rested until Bonito and his men came in.

We were in a war with the Blue Coats and White Eyes, and we were far from the safety of the border and land of the *Nakai-yes*. We decided to push southwest until we could get into the Animas or Guadalupe Mountains and follow well-known trails across the border. The Blue Coats we had expected to come after us with many soldiers hadn't appeared. This we couldn't understand. We thought they must be planning some sort of ambush, so we kept scouts out in front and to the sides of us as we moved the livestock.

IT WAS THE time of no shadows the next day, and we had seen no one to attack or stock to take. We were on what the White Eyes called the "Thompson Canyon Road," which wound through the Burros between the villages of Silver City and Lordsburg. Naiche and Atelnietze led the scouts at the front. The sun was warm, the road smooth, and the pace easy but eating up the miles. I was dozing a little, when the crack of a rifle around a bend in the trail jerked me awake. I shook the clouds from my mind as we charged forward around the bend in time to see a wounded man, a nice-looking White Eye woman, and a small child, a redheaded boy about the age of my son, Bediscloye, with him trying to get the buggy racing away from the warriors, but this was an easy game. They didn't have a chance of escape.

A few more shots were fired toward the buggy before the man gave his woman the reins and, yelling something at her, jumped out of the wagon as she slapped the lines against the horse's back and screamed, "Hi yah! Get up! Hi yah! The man rolled into the trail's edge brush to kneeling on one knee. He threw his lever rifle to a shirt already red with his blood and started firing at the warriors to keep them back while she got away. He was filled with rage and Power, yelling as he fired, "Get out of here, you Apache bastards! Leave us alone, damn you!"

I and my warriors brought him down, and a shot from one of the warriors hit the buggy's horse, causing him to stumble in the traces and collapse to a stop in the middle of the road. The woman jumped from the buggy and, reaching up for her son, yelled, "Come to Mama, Charlie!" The child stood up and, holding on to the seat and watching her, his eyes wide with surprise, reached for her, when a warrior rode up behind her and smashed her head with the butt of his rifle stock. She staggered forward and slumped into the wagon, her hands still groping for the child. The warrior tossed his rifle into his other hand, dismounted, then cracked her head two or three more times with the barrel of his pistol until she was still. The little one she had called "Charlie" stared at her, his mouth frozen open to scream, but no sound came out. The warrior who had killed his mother snatched him out of the buggy and put him on the ground. Others had run up to cut the horse's harness free and strip the man and woman of their clothes, their money, their jewelry, and the box in which they carried their things behind the buggy seat.

The White Eyes had left a basket of food under a tree where they must have been eating when they first saw the warriors. Bonito and I ate from the basket, watching the warrior take their loot. The food was good but, like most White Eye food, too bland for my taste. Naiche took the blanket they had used to sit on while they ate and covered the man. No one carved him up so he would be ugly with no man parts in the Happy Land. He had fought bravely and died well, trying to protect his family. We respected him for that.

The two warriors who had taken what was on the wagon were arguing over who should get the boy. The one who had killed the woman claimed the rights to the boy. But the one who had stopped the wagon by shooting the horse, when the horse should have been his, now claimed the boy as his reward. Their argument became heated, and as hands began wrapping around knife handles, before I could interfere, Bonito rode up and said, "No! I take the boy. Maybe later we decide who he belongs to. Hand him up to me."

I watched all this with a sad heart and thought for a moment, I ought to take the boy to raise with Bediscloye. But I remembered I no longer had Bediscloye. He had been taken from me by the *Nakai-yes* along with Ishchos and Naboka. I might never get them back. It felt like a war club hammered on my chest when I saw the child being taken. I knew I couldn't take him even as a brother for my own son. I vowed that one sun the *Nakai-yes* would pay for this. I promised myself again that I must do everything in my power to get Ishchos, Naboka, and Bediscloye back.

Bonito used a lariat to tie the child next to his belly so he wouldn't fall if we had to make a hard ride. His movement was like one in a dream, but he had his eyes open, staring off as far as he could see. I had seen children like this before when they saw their parents killed in front of them. He would either come out of his dream or die. When we returned to the camp at Bugatseka, the child was taken in by Naiche and his wife Nahdeyole. The boy seemed to like her very much, but he talked little and made few sounds. Nahdeyole and Naiche thought he was weak-minded.

We rode a trail south following the Animas Mountains foothills. It was not as well hidden as the trails through other canyons and across other mountains, but we could ride and herd our livestock at a faster pace to cover more distance that sun, which brought us closer to the border if we had to run with the Blue Coats chasing us.

TWENTY-THREE

RETURN
TO BUGATSEKA

THE DUST FROM our herd of livestock crossing the *llano* made us easy to spot. We rode all day after taking the boy and, with a bright moon for light, all through the night. We found a water tank at the entrance to a canyon leading into the northern end of the Animas Mountains, and there we made camp. With enough water and brush, it was a good spot to pen up the livestock. We were about half a hard day's ride from the border.

The stars were disappearing in the early dawn light, but long shadows from the mountains kept the valley dark when we stopped. After eating, I took Dutchy, Shoie, Naiche, and Atelnietze with me to backtrack north toward the Burro Mountains. We stayed out of sight and looked for any Blue Coats who might be on our trail. I knew killing the White Eye and his woman and taking their young son would surely stir up the Blue Coats and White Eye villages to fury and that they would come thundering after us. We needed to be in the land of the *Nakai-yes* soon to escape them with our herd in hand.

When we lost riding hidden in the shadows as the sun reached midmorning, we raced for the hills between the Animas and Playa valleys. From those hills, we could see west toward where we had been the last sun and the approaches to the valley from the east where Blue Coats on scout might come. We scanned the horizon in both directions for a hand until the time of no shadows and saw nothing except a single freight wagon piled high and pulled by four mules headed up a ranch road into the Animas Mountains. Two men were on the driver's seat, one driving, the other with a rifle across his knees.

We raced down from our hill and around the foothills to the road, pulled our ponies into big boulder shadows at the edge of the trail, and waited until the wagon was in easy range when it rounded a curve and passed a thicket of mesquite. We all waited with our rifles up and sighted until the wagon appeared. When the driver filled my sights, I fired, and so did the others, our bullets knocking the men off the wagon. Both were wounded but still mobile enough to scramble behind some boulders on the other side of the road from us.

The unexpected thunder from five rifles firing at the same time startled the mules into charging up the road straight for us. They were beginning to tire when they reached us and were easy to catch. Stopping them, Dutchy and Shoie cut them out of their harness while Naiche and Atelnietze thew the canvas cover off the supplies to discover boxes of ammunition, cans of food, sacks of grain and the roots the White Eyes called potatoes, and twelve bottles of whiskey. We forgot about finishing off the driver and his helper and loaded up the mules with the ammunition, supplies, and eleven bottles of whiskey. The other bottle we opened and passed around, although I didn't drink any. Then we rode back to the canyon the way we had come. *Ussen* was with us. No Blue Coats were coming, and we had a big load of ammunition, provisions, and whiskey to drink while we rested.

As much as I wanted a good, strong drink when we returned to our camp in the Animas Mountains, I didn't touch it. I intended to stay sober until I got my warriors and loot safely back to Bugatseka and then somehow my family back. I vowed to never again be like I was in Juh's camp when the *Rarámuri* came.

Before he got drunk, I made it a point to talk with Bonito, about the trail we should take back into the land of *Nakai-yes*. He agreed the easiest trail was through San Luis Pass, not much more than a wide *arroyo* passing out of the foothills into the wash and *llano* that led to Sierra Enmedio. It was the same trail we had used the harvest before to take Loco's people into the land of the *Nakai-yes*. I told him I would check it the next sun to ensure we weren't ambushed by Blue Coats or White Eyes.

THE NEXT MORNING, while the men slept off their drunks and their pounding heads got better, I arose early, when the sun was just a golden glow on the far blue horizon, and rode for San Luis Pass trail leading down across the border. The air was cold, my pony and I blowing steam in the dark early-morning air like a couple of iron wagons as we slipped by the light-green mesquites and tall yuccas ready to turn their white blossoms toward the rising sun.

The sun was about a hand above the horizon when I neared the border and rode for a hilltop where I could see the pass tank with my soldier glasses. I was nearly where I could see the tank when I smelled smoke and thought I heard mules and saw a thin plume rising from a spot near the eastern edge of the *playa*.

I tied my pony down in a draw and crept up to the top of the hill. From behind a big creosote, I looked down toward the plume and felt my guts squeeze. Almost directly below me, not more than a long rifle shot away, were cooking fires and a herd of horses. My soldier glasses showed Blue Coat chiefs and packers drinking coffee by a fire and at least twenty Apache scouts around three other fires. Birds were calling from the brush as the sun rose to drive the shadows away, and the men appeared calm and relaxed. I was certain from their relaxed morning that they didn't know we were not far away. Nearby the water tank, newly green brush kept the men and their livestock well supplied with all they needed to stay for a while and keep watch on the trail. It didn't look like the Blue Coats and their scouts were leaving anytime soon. I slipped back down the hill to the wash where I'd tied my pony. I held him close and by the nose to avoid him smelling and trying to nicker to the mules and horses that he was there. Fortunately for both of us, he didn't try to signal the soldier horses. I mounted and raced for our camp.

I TOLD BONITO and the other chiefs what I had seen and what I believed we needed to do. We decided the best way to get to Sierra Enmedio and avoid the soldiers at San Luis Pass was to take a low northern pass east through the mountains and then ride hard directly for Antelope Springs on the border. From Antelope Springs, it was a straight trail to Sierra Enmedio and the good spring there for the livestock. We would be in open country, easy to spot, but we decided we could cover the distance to Sierra Enmedio from the northeast side of the Animas in less than a day, and if we traveled at night, the animals could move faster and not need water as often. It was a gamble. None of us liked to travel at night, but I was willing to take the chance, and so were Bonito and Naiche. The sun was low on the horizon when we ate and made ready to travel.

The path we took across the northern end of the Animas Mountains followed shallow canyons that, twisting and turning, led out onto the east-side *llano* with very little climbing. Out on the *llano*, a three-quarter moon gave us enough light to drive the livestock hard for the border, stopping long enough to let them drink at a big tank near Antelope Springs before riding on, almost on a straight line across the *llano* to Sierra Enmedio.

The sun was driving away the stars when we reached the springs at Sierra Enmedio. I asked Cathla and Dutchy to eat, get some rest, and then ride on to Bugatseka and tell the People that we were coming, to get ready for much celebration, and that I expected it would take us four or five suns. Good warriors that they were, Cathla and Dutchy ate, filled their canteens, reloaded their bandoliers, then left that day after only a short nap.

GERONIMO AND CHIHUAHUA arrived at Bugatseka two or three days after my warriors and livestock. He and his warriors had been very successful too. They had eighty warriors and had started out on foot. After they crossed the Río Moctezuma, they had taken a few cattle but not much else. Geronimo and Chihuahua changed strategy and took enough horses to mount the men and attack every ranch and village in their path. They rode hard, picking up stock, weapons, and ammunition as they pushed southwest of Ures. On their return to Bugatseka, they had a big herd (it made ours look small) and had taken a pack-train with a big load of blankets, provisions, and whiskey. Geronimo was very happy about the whiskey, and he and his warriors got drunk while the *novitiates* kept watch over the camp. I shuddered and shook my head when I heard the story. Juh's camp had been destroyed because we had been drinking and had not stayed ready to defend it. I thought, Will we ever learn?

The day after Geronimo arrived, we met in council and learned the raids for both bands had been very successful. We had new weapons, a good stockpile of ammunition, provisions, and many head of livestock. We had made contact with Hermenegildo Grijalva, who had agreed to act as our White Eye contact when we wanted to bargain for returning to the reservation. We had taken a captive who could be used to help get our families back, and we had killed many White Eyes and *Nakai-yes* in our path.

Soon after the council, fifteen warriors rode west to Oputo on the south-flowing Río Bavispe and took a large herd of cattle (some say there were a hundred head) and drove them through the mountains to Bugatseka, where they were butchered the same day. Two or three days later, while the meat was being prepared and dried, a fire sparked into the grass in the surrounding meadow. We put it out quickly with no harm done to anyone, except that the fire had made a great column of smoke that could be seen from far away. Mexican soldiers would see it and know where to march to find us. We wasted no time moving to a new camp up on a ridge where we could watch the old camp and sent out scouts to watch for *Nakai-yi* soldiers marching toward the area of the fire. We expected them to approach that camp the next sun about midday.

The battle with the *Nakai-yi* soldiers next day lasted over half a sun before they retreated and marched away with their wounded.

The chiefs met again in council and decided to send out two raiding parties. The first, twenty warriors under Chihuahua and his brother Ulzana, would ride west into Sonora for more livestock. The other, with thirty warriors that Geronimo, Naiche, Bonito, Kaytennae, Zele, Jelikinne, and I led, would ride east into Chihuahua, looking for captives to trade for our families taken into slavery when the *Nakai-yes* tried to kill or enslave us all at Casas Grandes and later had attacked Juh's camp. At last, I thought, it's far past the moons when we should have done this. I pray to *Ussen* that many captives are delivered into our hands and Ishchos and the children are soon with me again.

TWENTY-FOUR

GERONIMO'S VISION

LED BY GERONIMO, we rode east and a little south through the Blue Mountains following the same trail we used to Galeana, where we had taken our revenge on Juan Mata Ortiz near Chocolate Pass. Coming down out of the mountains, we passed quietly across the main road south of Galeana. Walking on our heels so we left nothing but round holes in the dust, we laughed at how the feeble-minded *Nakai-yes* would think the tracks had to belong to some animal they had never seen before.

We rode east through the feather-leafed, dark forest-green creosotes, mesquite thickets turning a light green, and yuccas with tall stalks filled with white blooms. We watched for those in villages we might take captive to use for trading for our People. But the land and the *Nakai-yes* were poor and didn't offer us much to take that we might use to bargain for our own People. After a while, Geronimo turned north until we reached the wagon road and the iron road nearby that ran close to the village of Carmen. We followed the road until we were near the village, where we saw six women, one of them carrying a nursing-age baby, accompanied by two young soldiers.

The soldiers, strolling along with their long rifles resting balanced on their shoulders, were relaxed and smoking. They didn't realize we had materialized out of the brush until a woman saw us and threw up her hand to cover her mouth. The soldiers moved to jerk their rifles off their shoulders, at the same time looking for attackers, but they were struck down by long arrows with barbed-iron points and their throats cut before any of the women could scream or wail.

The women in terror, too frightened to even scream, froze motionless. Geronimo, who had spoken the *Nakai-yi* tongue since he had been off his *tsach*, held up his hands palms out, making little fluttering, calming motions, and said, "Don't be afraid. You won't be harmed. We need captives to trade for our People taken at Casas Grandes nearly a harvest ago. Soon you are free."

He pointed toward an old woman, maybe the oldest, "Do you speak *español?*" She nodded, and I saw no fear in her eyes. Geronimo tilted his chin up as if pointing up the road and said, *"Bueno.* You follow the road to the stopping place for iron wagons near the village and tell the *jefe* there that Geronimo comes to Casas Grandes with his captives and ready to trade for his People in half a moon. *Comprende?"* She nodded but stayed in her place until Geronimo waved her away, saying, *"Ándale pues* (go on now)." She pulled her *rebozo* up around her shoulders in the cool evening air, the light fast leaving, turned, then followed the dusty road toward the stopping place for the iron wagons.

In the distance, we saw lights beginning to fill the dusk around the stopping place. I was filled with relief. Soon I hoped I would have my family back again.

WE HAD A few cattle taken from ranches along the road to feed ourselves. We camped behind a ridge, and warriors took turns watching the wagon road for captives for the next two suns but saw none worth taking. Other warriors looked for more livestock to take. On the third night in that camp, the *novitiates* fixed the warriors a meal of beef cooked on sticks over the fires and steamed mescal slices that had been baked and dried.

Betzinez, a cousin of Geronimo's, serving as his novitiate, had just handed him his meat on a stick, and Geronimo, his knife ready to cut a piece, suddenly stared off into the darkness, his mouth open in his craggy face frozen in disbelief. His knife fell from his hand, and he called out, "Men, our People whom we left at our camp are now in the hands of Blue Coats! What shall we do?"

We all stared at him in disbelief. How could this be? We didn't doubt his Power. We all knew he must have seen something in his vision, but Blue Coats in our camp in the Blue Mountains? It couldn't be.

Naiche sprang up and, shaking his fist, broke the silence. "We must return now, tonight. We must go."

I, too, stood and said, "Yes! We must go. Now!" "Hmmphs" of agreement and nodding heads rippled through the seated men. We scrambled to load our horses and gather the cattle we had taken. They would be driven into the mountains to Bugatseka by a group of warriors while the rest of us headed for our camps as fast as we could. We rode our horses while we were on the *llano,* crossing to the mountains west of Galeana, and the women captives rode behind warriors. But on reaching the mountain trails, we dismounted and ran on foot because, in the mountains, it is faster to run on foot rather than ride. We left the horses for the men driving the cattle to bring. We told the women they would have to run too. They were soft and slow and had a hard time keeping up. When we reached our Bugatseka camp, they were more than a sun behind us.

We were fortunate the moon was nearly full and spread bright, white light on our path through the mountains. Geronimo sent scouts to the camp we'd left in Bugatseka. They found it deserted along with the ashes and stink of burned wickiups, tipis, and personal things, including our winter food supply. It was hard to look on the charred skeletons of tipis and wickiups where we once slept and made our homes. I couldn't understand how *Nant'an Lpah* and his scouts had found us. Someone, I thought, knew where we were and showed him.

Nant'an Lpah made his camp in a place of tall pines on the edge of a tall grass meadow at the bottom of a high, steep ridge. We climbed the ridge and, in the bright darkness, looked down on the camp below in shadows from the falling moon.

The open meadow, which we could easily see, had many sticks stuck in the ground with ribbons of white cloth tied to them. The women who had already surrendered, and were living in the camp, had put the sticks up to show us the Blue Coats didn't want to fight. We understood that. But how did the Blue Coats find us, and what exactly did they want? We saw they also had made log barricades from which to fight behind.

Near the top of the ridge were many tall trees and shelves of stone sticking out from the side facing the camp. Geronimo told us to be ready and pick spots behind trees on the ridgetop and on the ledges down from the top where we could shoot from cover if a battle came. It was maybe three hands before dawn. We sat back and rested, some even sleeping.

When the sun began sending golden shafts of light down through the trees, the Blue Coat scouts saw us watching the camp from high above them. They grabbed their rifles and disappeared into the shadow of the trees or behind their barricades. Our women walked out into the meadow and yelled loud enough for us to understand that *Nant'an Lpah* only wanted peace.

Geronimo, Naiche, Kaytennae, Jelikinne, and I talked for a while about trying to wipe out the Blue Coats but knew if we started shooting, many of our People would die. We decided to call four scouts up to talk to us and tell us what had happened and what they thought the nant'an planned to do. Maybe then we could decide what to do. One of our men with a powerful voice yelled down to the camp to send four scouts up to talk to us and promised they would not be harmed.

Four men began climbing up the ridge. I watched them with my soldier glasses. So that's how *Nant'an Lpah* found us, I thought when I saw Tzoe leading them. I was tempted to shoot him then, but I decided to wait until after we talked. Traitors deserve to die, but I wanted to hear from his own lips what had happened. Another of my brothers-in-law, Haskehagola (Angry, He Starts Fights), Dastine, and Na-ni-Isoage followed. When they got to the top of the ridge, we took each one to a little fire where there were four or five warriors. Tzoe went with Geronimo, and Haskehagola went to my fire. Dastine, who was related to Jelikinne, went with him to his fire. Na-ni-Isoage joined Naiche.

At my fire, we smoked a cigarette to the four directions. I said to Haskehagola, "Why is *Nant'an Lpah* here? Speak. We will listen."

Haskehagola said, "*Nant'an Lpah* comes with almost two hundred scouts, some are even Chiricahua, to bring you back to San Carlos, but in a good way. Some of the scouts led by Sieber were far ahead of *Nant'an Lpah*. They found your camp and attacked it before *Nant'an Lpah* could tell them to stop. He says the attack was an accident. He never meant it to happen."

I squinted at Haskehagola, wondering if I should believe him or kill him, but we had already given the scouts safe passage to come talk to us. Warriors sitting with us stared at the scout and waited for more. The air was cool, and with no breeze, the smoke from our fire lifted straight up. So near war, so near peace. What should it be? Maybe *Nant'an Lpah* can find our families and get them away from the *Nakai-yes*. "Why should we return to San Carlos—to cheating agents, heat, snakes, and land of shaking sickness?"

"*Nant'an Lpah* spoke to all the chiefs he could find to learn about the hard times on the reservations. He sent away the cheating agents and made things right. He wants to talk with you and make things right for you when you come back to San Carlos. He doesn't want to fight you, but if he does fight, he says he will follow you anywhere in the land of the Americans or the *Nakai-yes* and wipe you out if it takes fifty harvests."

The warriors sitting around us shifted around in the pine needles. Their faces grew hard as they crossed their arms and leaned in listening, not to miss a word. A breeze stirred the tops of the tall trees, and shafts of sunlight pooled on warriors and the ground around them.

I said, "How did *Nant'an Lpah* find us. Did Tzoe show him where our camps were?"

Haskehagola shrugged his shoulders and shook his head. "I don't know. No one does. *Nant'an Lpah* was already planning this raid and forming five pack-trains, each with seventy mules, before *Teniente* Davis caught Tzoe at San Carlos. Tzoe is a powerful warrior and a good scout. Maybe he led the raid here, maybe he didn't. What do you think? Will you come back with us or not?"

"Hmmph. I talk with the other chiefs and Geronimo. Maybe we talk with *Nant'an Lpah*. Then we decide what we do. I know Loco didn't want to come to our camps in the first place, and most of the women with us think this life is too hard. They are tired of running."

I looked at the other warriors sitting around the fire with us. "What would you ask of Haskehagola? Speak. He will answer." They looked at each other, then at me, and shook their heads, saying nothing.

I said, *"Doo dat'éé da.* You tell us straight words. You go now. We will talk among ourselves and decide what we will do."

Haskehagola left our fire and waited a short time for the other scouts to join him at the beginning of the path down the ridge side. I stood with him, and we spoke of family. I told him how Ishchos and the children had been taken by *Nakai-yi* soldiers at Casas Grandes and that I had been out with Geronimo and other warriors east of Galeana, looking to take captives we could use to exchange for her and other family members when the Blue Coats came.

Haskehagola shook his head, crossed his arms, then stared off into the trees. "I hope you find them, Chato. Nalthchedah and your son Horace still live alone. She has taken no other man. A man needs a good woman if you return to San Carlos."

Haskehagola's words stung my ears. I thought only of getting Ishchos and the children back, but if I couldn't, maybe Nalthchedah would want to live with me on the reservation. This deserved some thought.

Soon the other scouts returned from their fires, and the four began climbing down from the ridgetop. Geronimo, chiefs, and war leaders sat together with the warriors and talked about what we should do. The leaders decided to talk with *Nant'an Lpah* face-to-face and that the warriors should do what they thought was best for them. By mid-falling sun, they had nearly all drifted into *Nant'an Lpah's* camp to be with their families. Geronimo, chiefs, and leaders studied the camp, trying to decide how to talk with *Nant'an Lpah* without being shot to pieces if they approached him.

NAICHE WAS WATCHING the camp when he saw *Nant'an Lpah* walk out on a hill covered with tall grass at the end of the camp meadow. *Nant'an Lpah* was hunting birds with his long gun that had two barrels and shot many little bullets when it fired. We saw that he was headed away from his camp, and we might be able to get on the downhill side, hide in the tall grass, then talk with him without being seen or shot by his soldiers.

Nant'an Lpah drifted down the hill out of sight of this camp. We hid in the tall grass, waiting for him to come our way. He had taken several birds, stuffing them in a sack he carried over his shoulder, when he walked by and nearly stepped on me. I rose out of the grass faster than a striking snake and snatched the double-barreled gun out of his hands, and Naiche took his sack of birds.

I growled at him, "You been shooting at us."

He smiled, but before he could answer, the interpreter Mickey Free had seen us rise out of the earth and snatch away his gun and birds. Mickey thought we were about to kill the nant'an and came running down the hill, leaping through the grass toward us, waving his hands with palms out and fingers spread so we saw that he wasn't armed, and yelling in Apache, "No shoot! No shoot!"

We all stood there staring at the nant'an until Mickey Free ran up to us. He arrived breathing hard but immediately made introductions. Introductions finished, *Nant'an Lpah* smiled and said, "I wasn't shooting at you. No one in the wilderness ever sees Apache." We all grinned. Then, pointing down the hill to big trees beside a small stream, he said, "It's hot in this sun. Let's all go down by the creek and sit there in the shade of a big tree to keep cool while we talk."

Mickey Free asked Geronimo if he would do that, but Geronimo just stared off down the canyon. When he asked me, I nodded agreement, and so did all the others. We moved down toward the creek with Geronimo following. *Nant'an Lpah* was right. There in the shade with the little stream murmuring over the rocks, it was much cooler, more comfortable, and easier to talk. We sat in a circle and talked, asking *Nant'an Lpah* why he came and telling him why we left San Carlos. As the shadows grew long and the sun in golden glow was sliding behind the mountains, we stopped talking and agreed to talk more in *Nant'an Lpah*'s camp the next day. I gave him his big gun back and Naiche his birds, and we all began to climb the hill to his camp.

TWENTY-FIVE

DECISIONS

NANT'AN LPAH TOLD Geronimo, Jelikinne, Naiche, and me that we could talk further with him if we joined him at his morning meal, and this we agreed to do. The night before, when the chiefs and leaders came into camp, there had been a big dance. Even a few of the Western Apache danced with us. The morning came with mists floating over the meadow and the camp slow to rise. The Jeet! Jeet! of a canyon wren sounded sharp and clear. Packers were feeding and watering their mules, and wranglers and soldiers were taking care of the soldier mounts. Women were laughing and talking with each other all over camp as they cooked their morning meal. They sounded happy. I wished Ishchos and the children were here. I might feel happy too.

Geronimo, Jelikinne, Naiche, and I sat near *Nant'an Lpah*'s cooking fire and drank strong, black coffee his cook gave us while he made the morning meal. *Nant'an Lpah* finished making tracks on paper and came out of his big tent to welcome us and tell the cook he and his guests were ready to eat. The cook gave us our morning meal on big, shiny army metal pans. We sat in the grass to eat while *Nant'an Lpah* sat on a stool.

Geronimo was convinced *Nant'an Lpah* had Power only given by *Ussen*. Without such Power, a man couldn't have found and invaded our sanctuary. Geronimo believed the *Nant'an* could command the sun, the moon, everything. I believed that he was a strong warrior and that he had been lucky we weren't in our camp when the scouts attacked or there would have been much blood spilled on both sides. Our resistance to returning to San Carlos was very low. Most of the women wanted to go back to the reservation, and most of the men were tired of running.

As we ate his bread, beef, and beans with chilies, *Nant'an Lpah* repeated what he had said under the trees the day before. "We have come to look for you and take you back with us, not to fight but to join you as friends." He looked over at Geronimo and said, "You need to surrender and return to San Carlos or fight it out now. If you do not, I'll chase you all until you're wiped out if it takes fifty harvests. I'm not going to take your arms from you if you return because I'm not afraid of you."

Geronimo stared at him. "*Ussen* makes the nant'an a great warrior. I go to any reservation he says. He will be my father. I will do as he says, but my People are scattered across many canyons, and I will need to leave today to begin looking for them."

The rest of us said the same thing. *Nant'an Lpah* nodded and made the all-is-good sign with a wave of his hand parallel to the ground.

We asked *Nant'an Lpah* when he would leave Bugatseka for San Carlos. He said his food stores were limited, and he would probably have to start in four or five suns. To ensure no one would go hungry on the trip back, he said that the scouts must hunt every day and that we should now make meat with the cattle we had taken. Our women and young men got busy.

GERONIMO, KAYTENNAE, NAICHE, and I left the camp to look for our scattered People, but they were very hard to find and wouldn't believe our smoke signals to come in. They thought scouts made the smoke to trick them into surrendering. After two days of searching, with little success for any of us, Geronimo asked that I go back to *Nant'an Lpah* and ask for four more days to find and return with our People.

When I returned to *Nant'an Lpah*'s camp, the sun had just floated above the mountains, sending golden shafts through the trees, and from many cooking fires, long shafts of gray smoke as straight as lodge-pole pine rose up through the trees. The slaughter of our cattle was finished, and meat had been laid out to dry on every bush and boulder. Young boys and girls watched it to keep birds and small animals away from it. I found *Nant'an Lpah* at his tent, having a morning meal with Loco. *Nant'an Lpah* motioned for me to come join them. I had been riding since before dawn and was hungry. The cook gave me a pan of bread and meat after I sat down with them. Loco eyed me with dislike, since I had threatened to kill him at San Carlos, but he said nothing.

Nant'an Lpah said, "Have you and the others found your People?"

"They are very scattered. The chiefs and leaders don't want to leave until they have all their People in hand. Geronimo asks that you wait four more suns before you leave. We still haven't found Chihuahua and Juh and the band of warriors looking after a herd of ponies and mules near the Río Aros."

Loco frowned, and *Nant'an Lpah* said, "I can wait a little longer, but in four days, we have to go, or your People will be very hungry on the trail. I can't have that. I've punished many agents already for making your People go hungry. I won't be one of them. Tell Geronimo I have to leave in four suns."

"I tell him. Maybe we talk more together before I return to Geronimo?"

"If you want. I talk with Loco this morning. You come when he leaves."

"I come."

I TOOK MESSAGES to the families of Geronimo, Kaytennae, and Naiche and told them we would return soon, and they should be ready to leave for San Carlos as soon as we found the rest of our bands. The sun was two hands from the time of no shadows when I returned to *Nant'an Lpah*'s tent. I didn't see Loco anywhere nearby. As I approached, *Nant'an Lpah* came out with Mickey Free, who pointed to the trees near where the leaders had first talked with him, and said, "*Nant'an Lpah* asks if you want to talk where it is cool and no one else listens?"

I nodded and followed them down the hill to the shady places. We sat down, and I made a cigarette, smoked to the four directions, then gave it to *Nant'an Lpah*, who smoked and passed it to Mickey Free, who smoked and returned it to me.

Speaking through Mickey Free, *Nant'an Lpah* said, "I know you are a brave and strong chief. Speak and I will listen."

I gathered my thoughts as a light breeze rippled through the tall hillside grass, bees buzzed to flowering weeds, and the little stream ran, singing a little song over the rocks. "I know only a few suns are left before our People must stay on land the White Eyes and Blue Coats say is theirs. Too many White Eyes and too few Chiricahua. We kill a hundred of your soldiers for every warrior of ours you kill, and if we had ammunition without limit, still the White Eyes are too many and we too few. Our hiding places in these mountains no longer secrets. Our own People wear red bandanas on their heads and fight and track us wherever we go. Blue Coats and *Nakai-yi* soldiers fight together against us.

Blue Coats cross the line dividing the land of the White Eyes from that of the *Nakai-yes* to chase and fight us, and the *Nakai-yes* let them."

Nant'an Lpah sat listening and staring at the ground in front of him, nodding often as I spoke.

"Through Juh, great chief of the Nednhi, we tried to make peace with the *Nakai-yes* in Chihuahua and asked for land and rations to help us settle in what they call the Carcay Mountains. They gave us rations and much mescal while we waited for their big chiefs to say that they would let us have the land we had asked for. The *Nakai-yes* kept wanting us to all come into Casas Grandes and drink all we wanted, but Juh had seen this trick before and would only let half the People drink mescal in a sun. Then we grew careless, and the *Nakai-yi* soldiers attacked us when we were not sober. They killed some of the People and took many of our women and children to the slave market in Ciudad Chihuahua. I have a wife and two children taken. Geronimo has two wives and a child taken. Naiche and Chihuahua have family taken. When you came to Bugatseka, Geronimo was leading us across the Chihuahua *llano* toward the east. We were looking for People we could capture and trade for our own families."

Nant'an Lpah said, "The women and baby who reached our camp two days after you came?"

"Yes. We planned to take many more before Geronimo saw Blue Coats in his vision in our camps. Now we have no captives to trade for our families. You are a great chief with much Power. I think now I must help the Blue Coats and White Eyes for my People's survival. I speak straight on this. I will be true to what I say. I ask you, then, to make the *Nakai-yes* return my family, my wife and two young children. I much want and need them back. You help me? I be your best soldier."

Nant'an Lpah crossed his arms and looked up into the trees and sighed. "I know you have the courage and mind to be a mighty soldier, the best of scouts. I need such men to help your People on the reservation. Yes, I will do all I can to get your family back from the Chihuahuans."

He stuck out his hand like the White Eyes do, and I grabbed it and gave it two strong pumps as I had learned to do during my first stay at San Carlos. *"Ch'ik'eh doleel, Nant'an Lpah.* I be your best soldier. Now I leave to give Geronimo and the other chiefs your words."

He smiled. "Tell them to hurry. We have to leave in three or four suns. Our supplies fast disappear with so many people here."

IT TOOK A day for me find Geronimo, Kaytennae, and Naiche, who had found Chihuahua. He was also looking for the rest of his People and Juh, who refused to return to San Carlos and said he would try again to make an agreement with the *Nakai-yes* to stay in Chihuahua. They had also found many of my People as well as their own, but there were still many missing. When I told them he was running out of supplies, and what Crook had said about waiting, Geronimo said we should go quickly back to *Nant'an Lpah*'s camp with about 116 we had found.

We returned to the camp in a day and talked again with *Nant'an Lpah* in a council. Geronimo told him we wanted to look for the rest of our People. We asked that he go on and let us continue to gather our People and meet him at the border. He thought about this while pulling on the long gray hair growing from his face and chin. He finally sighed and agreed we should stay and gather all our People but said, "Don't be late. Once I reach the border, the People I have must go on to San Carlos. If you're late, you'll have to make it to San Carlos on your own without army soldiers protecting you from civilians."

We all waved our hands parallel to the ground, making an it-is-good sign, and said we believed we could be there before he left Silver Springs at San Bernardino for San Carlos.

TWENTY-SIX

RETURN TO SAN CARLOS

FROM A HIGH ridge, we chiefs, leaders, and Geronimo stayed behind using our soldier glasses to watch *Nant'an Lpah* lead the long line of our People who had surrendered back to San Carlos. We knew they would take a trail over to the east side of the Blue Mountains, where they would turn and run north toward Carretas at the western edge of the Chihuahuan *llano*. From the springs at Carretas, they would pass Aliso Creek, where *Nakai-yi* soldiers tried to wipe out Loco's People, and then on to Sierra Enmedio and across the pass in the San Luis Mountains to the springs at San Bernardino, where *Nant'an Lpah* had soldiers to meet the People and protect them while they ran to San Carlos.

We continued to search for our missing people for suns past the time when we said we would meet *Nant'an Lpah* at San Bernardino Springs and join with our People the Blue Coats escorted to San Carlos. Geronimo held a council. We decided that as long as we were still south of the border, we ought to raid the *Nakai-yes*, with whom we were still at war, for all the livestock we could take with us when we returned to San Carlos.

On a raid near Nácori Chico in Sonora during the Season of Large Leaves, a *vaquero* made a lucky long shot at Jelikinne as he was climbing up some rocks, hit him in the head, then killed him. Losing him was a shock. We all prayed that *Ussen* let Jelikinne's ghost pony carry him fast to the Happy Land.

Late in the Season of Large Fruit, Chihuahua and Naiche decided they had enough livestock and had found all their People they were going to find. They returned to San Carlos. Geronimo, despite what he had told *Nant'an Lpah*, still argued with his spirit about the wisdom of returning to San Carlos. He sent his son Chappo with Naiche and told him to see for himself the way things were at San Carlos and then report back to him. I decided to stay in the land of the *Nakai-yes* with Geronimo, continue raiding, and also wait to learn from Chappo what San Carlos was like from an Apache viewpoint before I risked moving to San Carlos.

While we waited on Chappo, we learned that Juh had ridden the ghost pony. He had been trading and drinking mescal at Casas Grandes, still expecting the *Nakai-yes* to give him land and rations in the Carcay Mountains. Since the *Rarámuri* had wiped out his camp last Season of Ghost Face, Juh was rarely sober. I could have wound up the same way, but I knew the only way I could ever get my wife and children out of *Nakai-yi* slavery was to stay away from the mescal and *tulapai* and keep my mind clear. I often told myself that if I had not been sleeping off a drunk when the *Rarámuri* attacked, I could have kept Ishchos and the children safe.

The stories Geronimo and I heard about the death of Juh said he had been drinking all day, and, as he returned to his camp, his horse somehow slipped and fell into a little stream running about two rifle lengths below the trail. The fall left Juh stunned and face down in the stream, wandering in the lands of visions and dreams, from where he never returned. Other stories said he tested *Ussen* and rode his pony off a cliff to prove his medicine would make him fly. Years later, his youngest son, Daklugie, claimed Juh had a heart attack and hadn't drunk any mescal or *tulapai* at all that day because he still didn't trust the *Nakai-yes* when the People went into the village to trade. According to his rule, half the People had to stay sober while the others drank, and he fell in the stream on his day to stay sober. Regardless of how he died, the Apache had lost their greatest war leader. Although he didn't say much, Geronimo knew this was true, and the loss of Juh would greatly lessen our strength in the Land of the *Nakai-yes*. Since *Nant'an Lpah* had come, we had been through a cycle of bad seasons.

BY THE SEASON of Ghost Face, my band and I camped in the Teras Mountains with nearly ninety horses and mules we had taken in raids. Geronimo was camped farther south, near Bugatseka, and had been collecting the start of a good herd of prime cattle he wanted to take north if Chappo came with a good report.

Nakai-yi soldiers surprised my camp one dark night and took most of our horses and mules. It was our good fortune that the mules smelled or heard them coming and awakened us in time to drive off the soldiers attacking the camp just as the dawn was fleeing from sunlight. We found where the soldiers were holding our livestock and waited ten days to let the *Nakai-yes* grow careless. In the meantime, Chappo returned to his father with Chihuahua, Ahnandia, and Tuzzone, now scouts for *Capitán* Crawford. Chappo told Geronimo that all was good at San Carlos, as *Nant'an Lpah* had said it would be, and that he would be safe when he returned. Geronimo told them where I had camped and why I was waiting and asked Tuzzone to go to my camp and let us know that he would be leaving within a few suns for the border.

Ten suns passed after *Nakai-yes* attacked our camp. My band left, heading up the Río San Bernardino valley as soon as we stole our horses and mules back. There were *Nakai-yi* farms along the way, many abandoned because the farmers feared attacks from us, and they did well to do so. We wanted to get to the border in a day after we left the big turn where the Río Bavispe turned from flowing north to flow south.

Horses, unlike cattle, are fast to move, and near the time the sun was painting the clouds in the west, we saw Blue Coat tents at the border where the soldiers waited for us. *Teniente* Davis and his *capitán*, Rafferty, were happy to welcome us. Rafferty and Davis said they would accompany us to San Carlos to ensure White Eyes on the way didn't try to attack us. *Teniente* Davis and I got along well. We both spoke the tongue of the *Nakai-yes* well enough to easily understand each other.

That night, I slaughtered a good-looking *Nakai-yi* mare for a meal with *Teniente* Davis. I could tell he was not happy I had killed the mare for him, but he ate some of the meat just the same because I honored him with it. I liked *Teniente* Davis. He spoke straight with us and expected us to do the same with him. That night was the first time we had rested easy in over two harvests.

We waited twelve suns at San Bernardino Springs while *Capitán* Rafferty waited for Geronimo. During that time, I spoke with him about freeing my family from Mexican slavery and how that was what I most wanted. He listened closely to my story but said he had no power to speak with the *Nakai-yi* chiefs about releasing my family. He told me to talk with *Capitán* Crawford at San Carlos since he had direct access to *Nant'an Lpah*, who knew *Nakai-yi* commanders and big chiefs in Chihuahua who could free my family.

When Geronimo didn't come after twelve suns, *Capitán* Rafferty decided to send *Teniente* Davis east to wait for Geronimo near the place called "Cloverdale" in the Animas Valley, while Rafferty himself would escort us back to San Carlos.

AFTER SEVERAL DAYS of easy riding with *Capitán* Rafferty, we crossed the Río Gila and soon arrived at the San Carlos camp of *Capitán* Crawford, the man *Nant'an Lpah* had chosen to lead San Carlos. *Capitán* Crawford welcomed us and said we should camp where we wanted nearby and, if we had any problems with our rations or what was happening on the reservation, to come see him. I was glad to hear this and asked to see him privately. He said to come in four suns, and I agreed. We left our horses and mules in a corral where *Capitán* Crawford said feed would be provided for them.

I sat my pony, watching the men close the corral fence, when Naiche and Bonito rode up beside me. Naiche grinned and, making the all-is-well sign, said, "Ho, Chato! You decide to come to San Carlos. We have not seen you in three or four moons. I see all the pretty horses you bring. Is Geronimo with you?"

"Ho, Naiche and Bonito. Seeing you makes my eyes glad. These horses and mules I had to take from the *Nakai-yes* two times. Now they are here and I think safe. Geronimo comes behind me. He moves slow because he brings many cattle."

Naiche stuck out his lower lip and nodded. "Geronimo always thinks ahead. Has his Power shown him anything?"

I shrugged my shoulders. "I haven't seen him in over a moon, but I think not. He would have told me if it had."

Bonito studied my horses, saying nothing, and Naiche nodded. "Come camp with us. Bonito, Loco, Mangas, Zele, and I all camp together. The women are happy, and the children play without fear others come to steal them. Kaytennae and Nana camp by themselves. The way Kaytennae acts around *Capitán* Crawford, I think maybe he wants to start trouble."

I knew my People would be happy in the same camp with the families and followers of these men. I nodded. "Naiche is a good chief. My People and I will stay in your camp. Show us the way. We come."

Naiche nose pointed toward a hill where I remembered Loco had his camp before we forced him to leave. "There. Loco is happy to return to his old camp. It's close to the Río, and there is plenty of wood, and the no-see-ems aren't so bad there. Come!"

My warriors mounted their horses and went to collect our women and children. I was glad to stay with Naiche but hoped and expected we would get much better land around Eagle Creek, which Geronimo often said was his choice, than anything Loco had accepted in the past.

FOUR SUNS PASSED, and I went to speak with *Capitán* Crawford. His man who guarded his door knew me and knew I was coming. When I appeared, the man smiled and held up his hand, palm out, for me to wait while he went to speak with Crawford. I heard Crawford say, "Ah, good. Bring him in." The man appeared at the door and waved me in. Crawford nodded as I walked through the door and saw Mickey Free sitting in a chair near Crawford's table covered with papers carrying many tracks made by the points of little spears dipped in black water.

Crawford motioned toward a chair beside Mickey Free and said, "Since my Spanish is not so good, I've asked Mickey to interpret in your tongue for us, so I clearly understand your words." I knew enough of the White Eye tongue to understand what Crawford said, but I was glad he decided to use an interpreter to understand clearly my words. I made the all-is-well sign to Mickey Free, who smiled and nodded as I sat down in the chair beside him and looked at Crawford.

Crawford said, "Speak. I will listen."

"I want you to know that I told *Nant'an Lpah* in the mountains that his arrival made me understand that the People could not overcome the unending flood of White Eyes and their weapons filling our country. We could no longer hide even in the Blue Mountains. Our own People come after us and help the Blue Coats. The Blue Coats are working also with *Nakai-yi* soldiers to wipe us out. I understand now that we have to stay on the land the White Eyes give us."

Crawford raised his brows. "You, Chato, have seen a bright light. I'm glad."

"Knowing this, with the other chiefs and leaders, I looked hard for my People and tried to find them all to bring here to your care at San Carlos. The Blue Mountains are a big place, and it took longer than I thought to find my People."

I grinned. "They hide good. After most of the missing People were found, Geronimo called a council. We talked. Since we were still at war with the *Nakai-yes*, we decided to take as much of their livestock as we could handle to help us farm here and always have enough to eat. When we had what we wanted, then we came back. Geronimo, sly fox Geronimo, didn't want to be outfoxed by anything the Blue Coats told us and sent his son Chappo back with Naiche to see for himself if life at San Carlos was better. I thought that was wise, so I waited for Chappo to return too. I had only horses and mules to bring back, and just before Chappo returned, *Nakai-yi* soldiers attacked my camp and took them all. We learned where they were being kept and waited for the soldiers to relax before we took them back. In that time, Chappo returned and told Geronimo all was good at San Carlos. Soon we took back our horses and mules and headed for the border. Geronimo has four times the People I do, and he drives cattle. He comes slow."

Crawford nodded but held up his hand, palm out, to stop me and say, "Before you go on, I want you to understand that, while you are at war with the Mexicans, the United States is not. You are under the protection of, and part of, the United States. The army can't deal in stolen goods. Your horses and mules are stolen livestock, but *Nant'an Lpah* says the way the Mexicans swap and steal horses and mules, there is no way to tell who owned them in the first place, so you can keep your livestock. Geronimo, with cattle having brands and being near the border, is another question. *Nant'an Lpah* considers that now, since it's much more likely that the true owner of the cattle can be found. We'll see. But please, go on."

If the army took Geronimo's cattle from him, he would be very angry. I knew, if it was me, I would be very angry. But I had given my word to return and be at peace. I would keep the peace no matter the threat. Who knew what would happen with Geronimo? He might go back to the land of the *Nakai-yes* despite what he had promised *Nant'an Lpah*.

I said, "Yes, we'll see. I want you to know that gathering livestock was not my primary reason for staying in the land of the *Nakai-yes*."

Capitán Crawford frowned. "What do you mean?"

"A harvest ago, my family—my wife Ishchos and three children all under ten harvests—and I camped with Juh in the Season of Ghost Face. One night, *Rarámuri* led by *Nakai-yi* soldier chiefs attacked the camp, killed many, and took many women and children to be sold in the slave market in Chihuahua. Among them were my wife Ishchos and my two youngest children. I have done everything I can to find them and get them back. Losing them made my heart sick. I have cried bitter tears as I look for them. I would do anything for them. I even asked *Nant'an Lpah* to help me find them and get them back. I swore to him that I would always be loyal and not betray the Americans if I could get them back. He told me he would do his best to help me find them. I believe him. I will do any work I can for you if you help me do this."

Capitán Crawford studied me with sad, serious eyes. I knew he understood how I felt.

"I want you to know, *Capitán*, that I have not been the best of men. I know that, once, I was on a crooked trail. I killed many, but for us it was war. Now I see that trail leads nowhere for the People and must eventually lead to an early trip to the Happy Land. This I do not want. I want this pledge between us to last as long as the sun. All the chiefs are friends, but we fight sometimes. There are also some bad men among us who will quarrel and make trouble. Give us time. We will straighten them out.

"I hope the Great Father in the east will give us our old land back."

Capitán Crawford, scratching his chin, said, "Where do you think your land lies?"

"I think it should be from Fort Huachuca to up above Fort Bowie and east to the Río Grande."

Capitán Crawford smiled and shook his head. "That is much land, Chato. You know the Americans will never give up that much land for your People. Some of your chiefs have already said they thought Turkey Creek near Fort Apache north of San Carlos will be a good place for your People."

I nodded. "I will accept any place for my camp if I can have my family back. I will work hard for you, *Capitán* Crawford. I beg for my wife and children back from the *Nakai-yes.*"

Capitán Crawford stood and extended his hand for a White Eye handshake.

He said, "We will do all in our power to help you get your wife and children out of Mexico. I look forward to using your help for your People."

I grabbed his hand and gave it two good pumps. I looked in his eyes and he in mine. I knew he would do the best he could for me. I hoped he understood I would do all I could to help him. The Americans were my last hope for getting Ishchos and the children back.

TWENTY-SEVEN

NALTHCHEDAH

IT WAS GOOD to camp with Naiche and the other leaders. We all wanted the peace that *Nant'an Lpah* offered, and we respected each other. My daughter Maud and I lived with my sister Banatsi in Naiche's camp. My sister, a widow, was a plump, pretty woman who wore her hair just above her shoulders and smiled often. Of course, Maud helped Banatsi with camp chores, and together they looked after my needs. Maud, fast becoming a beautiful young woman, had yet to have her womanhood ceremony. Banatsi, Maud, and I spoke together often by my sister's meal fires.

The evening after I spoke with *Capitán* Crawford, I ate with Banatsi and Maud. Our meal was a collection of good *llano* foods, like steamed slices of dried mescal from agave hearts baked three days in a hot rock pit, steamed yucca tips, dried juniper berries, preserved tuna from prickly pear she and Maud had collected in the land of the *Nakai-yes*, mesquite bread, and beans with chiles made from short rations given us when we first arrived at San Carlos.

I told Maud and Banatsi about my talk with *Capitán* Crawford. They listened with interest, and then Maud, her sad eyes staring into the fire, said, "I pray to *Ussen* many times that my mother, Bediscloye, and Naboka return to us. They have not come. I think maybe *Ussen* decides to keep them in the land of the *Nakai-yes*."

I looked closely at her and shook my head. "Maybe so, what you think is true, but I'll do everything in my power to get them back. I'll talk again with *Nant'an Lpah* and make certain I heard his words as he meant them. If not, then I'll leave again into the land of the *Nakai-yes* to search for them."

My daughter nodded, and Banatsi poured and handed me a cup of coffee.

Maud said, "When Banatsi and I went to get our full rations this sun, we saw and spoke with Nalthchedah and my little brother, Horace. Horace was just off his *tsach* and walking when we left for the Blue Mountains two harvests ago. Now he runs like a true Apache. I think when he is grown, he will be a fast runner and win many races. It was good to see them again. Nalthchedah asked about our lives now that we had returned from the Blue Mountains, and we said much better than running up and down mountain trails following our warriors. My little brother asked in his child's way why his 'big brother' and sister were held by the *Nakai-yes*. I told him they were still slaves taken in war, but he doesn't understand what 'slave' or 'war' means, and we couldn't tell him so he understood."

There was a hint of a smile on Banatsi's lips. "Nalthchedah asked about you too. She says she was glad she was not caught when Geronimo took Loco's People and has been able to live in peace. She has not taken another man since you left. Now that you say you will stay at San Carlos and are pledged to support the Blue Coats, maybe you should speak to her about being one of your women again."

I stared open-mouthed at my sister and daughter. Apache women often advised their men in private. Many times, men followed their women's advice. But this advice I needed to let settle in the deep well of my mind.

"Hmmph. I think about it. That is all I have to say."

Banatsi and Maud smiled at each other across the fire's little flames casting dancing shadows framed by orange and yellow light on their faces.

LITTLE HAPPENED At San Carlos while we waited for Geronimo and his People to cross the border with their cattle. I met in council a few times with the other chiefs to talk about the best place on the reservation for us to settle. We knew Geronimo wanted land outside the reservation on Eagle Creek. His argument was that, since we were no longer at war, the reservation boundaries didn't need to exist. I think he failed to understand that the boundaries were meant as much to keep the White Eyes out as to keep us in. We also knew *Nant'an Lpah* would never agree to letting us live outside the existing reservation boundary or drive away White Eyes on Eagle Creek so we could have the land without fighting White Eyes all the time. Several of the chiefs and leaders looked at the land around Fort Apache and thought Turkey Creek was our best choice. It had meadows we could use for cattle and horses, good fast-flowing water without no-see-ems waiting to attack, easy-to-take wood, and land along the creek where we could grow crops and gardens. We ought to do well there. *Capitán* Crawford had already promised us tools for farming and seeds for planting crops. Maybe, I thought, peace is finally ours.

In those days, I thought often about asking Nalthchedah to be my woman again. If I did ask her, I knew it would be a marriage of convenience—for both of us. Despite the help of my daughter and sister, I needed another woman for my *wickiup*. The woman I truly wanted was Ishchos. If I ever got Ishchos back, she would be first wife, and if Nalthchedah chose me again, she would be second wife. Nalthchedah wouldn't be happy. Not only did she give advice, but she also expected it to be followed—that was one reason I had left her and Horace at San Carlos and taken Ishchos and her children when I rode to the Blue Mountains with Geronimo. Still, she had not taken another man, and she had lived by herself with Horace under the protection of the Bylas family, the White Mountains, whom Geronimo nearly killed on the way to take Loco. She now lived under the protection of Loco since he had returned. She had not gone into the land of the *Nakai-yes* when we took Loco. She had been visiting a White Mountain cousin on the north end of San Carlos, and we missed her when we took Loco's camp.

GERONIMO ARRIVED AT San Carlos about a moon after me. *Capitán* Crawford was right. *Nant'an Lpah* made Geronimo turn over his cattle for sale or return to the *Nakai-yes* he had taken them from. This made Geronimo very angry. I had to smile when I learned this. At least I had been allowed to keep the horses and mules I had taken—twice—from the *Nakai-yes*. I thought, *Maybe Geronimo isn't so all-powerful after all.* Nevertheless, he spoke in council as though he could demand and get what he wanted from *Nant'an Lpah* about where we lived, and he wanted Eagle Creek land. When other chiefs said they liked Turkey Creek, he waved them off and said, "Live where you want. I want Eagle Creek." I grew to dislike Geronimo more and more as he spoke in these councils, but he was a man of great Power, and no one, including me, wanted to argue with him. Again, I smiled to myself when *Capitán* Crawford told us *Nant'an Lpah* said we could have Turkey Creek, but Geronimo had to forget about living on Eagle Creek.

While we waited on *Nant'an Lpah*'s answer for our place on the reservation, we had four suns of high winds with heavy dust blowing through the camps near the Gila. Nearly all of us huddled in our wickiups while the wind and dust pounded their canvas covers. During the wind and dust, women worked on moccasins and baskets, and the men cleaned their weapons, oiled their saddle leather, and repaired pack frames. By the middle of the fourth sun, the wind and dust had left us, and the air was cold and clear with little or no breeze as the sun began its downward arc in a pale-blue sky toward the western mountains.

I RODE MY pony down to the Río Gila and let it drink. After four days of howling wind, it was a time that felt of great peace, and I was happy in the moment. I dismounted to sit in the dry brown grass filling with new green shoots and to watch and listen to the *río* flow.

I heard voices crunching through the grass in my direction. It was Nalthchedah and Horace, followed by a few other women and children, carrying bags and pots filled with water for their evening chores. They had seen my pony but not me and looked surprised and stopped ten paces away as I rose out of the tall brown grass to greet them. The other women and children looked at us and passed on.

Horace stared. Nalthchedah smiled. Horace wasn't sure who I was until Nalthchedah leaned down and whispered in his ear. His eyes grew round, and, dropping his little water bag, he threw his arms up and ran for me, yelling, "Father! Father!"

I swooped him up in my arms and whirled him around. "I have returned from the land of the *Nakai-yes*, my son. You have grown much since I left nearly two harvests ago. *Ussen* blesses me to see you happy."

He was suddenly shy and looked at the ground. Nalthchedah watched us, a thin smile on her lips, her chin tilted up to show her pride.

"I plan to come talk privately with you. Will you allow me this visit?"

She lowered her chin, looked in my eyes, then, with a big smile, said, "Of course. We have much to talk about. Come to my fire when the moon is above the mountains. Horace will be asleep then."

I put Horace down and said, "Go help your mother, my son," and to her I said, "When the moon is above the mountains?" She nodded.

Horace picked up his water bag and, taking his mother's hand, walked off behind my horse toward the camp.

A WOLF UP in the hills behind our camp called his brothers under the soft black robe of night filled with points of light and the bright golden glow of a rising, nearly full moon. With the passing of the blowing dust, the air was crisp and cold even without a breeze. The camp wickiups for the big camp of Loco, Naiche, and the others were scattered over a large, flat bench between the Ríos San Carlos and Gila. I left the *wickiup* of Banatsi and, with a good, heavy wool blanket over my shoulders, walked toward the other side of the camp, where Loco and his People had their wickiups. I didn't want to start a gossip fire by asking directions to Nalthchedah's *wickiup*, and it took me a little while wandering among the wickiups to find her fire.

She had a pot of coffee warming by the fire and was weaving a large, shallow basket, with her own blanket thrown over her shoulders. Through a crack in the door blanket, I saw Horace peacefully sleeping in her *wickiup*. I was three or four paces away when she looked up from her work, saw me, then smiled. My heart thumped in excitement to see her. She smelled of yucca flowers, and her hair, falling below her shoulders outside her blanket, was shiny in the yellow firelight.

"Ho, Chato. You come. I have a happy heart. Will you drink my coffee?"

"Ho, woman. My heart, too, is glad. I come. Yes, your coffee is always good."

She motioned for me to sit at her left side and, setting her basket work aside, reached to take the coffeepot and pour a steaming cup that she handed me. I sat where she had motioned.

"You make a new basket. You always did fine work with them, and they are always in demand."

"The value of my work lets Horace and me have a few good things the White Eyes won't give us." She studied me for a moment as I sipped at the steaming coffee. "You are happy to return from the Blue Mountains?"

We talked as Apache do, opening a conversation about everything except what we wanted to discuss until a proper time had passed. After talking about what was happening on the reservation and what might happen now that Geronimo had returned, there was a long pause between our words.

Nalthchedah said, "You said when Horace and I found you sitting by the river that you planned to come speak with me. Speak. I will listen."

I held out my cup, and she poured more coffee. I blew the steam across the top to cool it, took a sip, then said, "You, a beautiful woman, were my first wife and have given me a fine son. When I decided to follow Geronimo into the Blue Mountains and leave the reservation, you refused to follow me, but Ishchos and my three children with her followed me. I told you to stay on the reservation and that we were divorced."

Nalthchedah followed my face with her eyes and nodded at the truth of what I said.

"Ishchos and two of our children were taken into slavery nearly a harvest ago. I have, with Geronimo, Naiche, Kaytennae, and others, struggled without success to get them back. We had taken captives for trading them back when *Nant'an Lpah* came to our camp in the Blue Mountains. He made us let them go but promised to help us get our families out of *Nakai-yi* slavery. I know he has spoken with the big chiefs of the White Eyes and *Nakai-yes* in Chihuahua. Our families are still hidden from us. Maybe we never see them again. I will ask *Nant'an Lpah* when he comes to San Carlos if he still tries to get them. I think he does. He is a man of his word. If not, then I will return to the land of the *Nakai-yes* and search for them until I take them back.

"Regardless of what happens with Ishchos and our children, I need another wife. Before we divorced and I went to the Blue Mountains, you were a good wife. I liked and wanted you. But you chose to stay at San Carlos. Now I have returned. You know how I feel about Ishchos. You know that I have my widowed sister and my daughter Maud with me. I won't be running off to the land of *Nakai-yes* again unless I serve as a scout for *Nant'an Lpah*. I ask that you consider becoming my woman again."

Nalthchedah studied me with narrowed eyes for a long time as the moon rose higher and the fire crackled into orange and red glowing coals. At last, she said, "Yes, I will be your wife again. Loco is responsible for me. He will want a bride price."

I nodded and smiled. I was happy she had accepted me again. "I will speak with Loco tomorrow. When should I join you?"

"After you speak with Loco, come in two suns, and I will make you a fine dinner. Bring Maud and Banatsi with you. I have a big *wickiup*, and they are family."

"*Ch'ik'eh doleel*. You are a wise woman."

She stood and, with a big smile, took my hand. "Come. Let's take our blankets into the *wickiup*. Our son can sleep through a stampede. I'll show you how a good woman pleases her husband."

I stood and, looking into the black pools of her eyes, pulled her to me and wrapped my blanket over her shoulders. She reached and pulled back the *wickiup* door blanket, whispering, "Come, lie with me, husband. I am your woman again. I want you."

TWENTY-EIGHT

TURKEY CREEK

IN THE SEASON of Many Leaves, at the beginning of the moon the White Eyes call "May," *Teniente* Davis led the People southeast down the wagon road from San Carlos toward Fort Thomas. Near Fort Thomas, he turned north. His trail was nearly the same path through the Gila Mountains to Ash Flats that we had taken when Geronimo and his warriors had forced Loco and his People to run from San Carlos for Juh's camp in the Blue Mountains. Now we were finally leaving the sorry land and western Apache enemies at San Carlos for our own land high in the mountains along Turkey Creek.

Teniente Davis led a troop of mounted soldiers, Chiricahua scouts he had hired to help maintain order among us, a mule packtrain, and a few wagons carrying supplies and bundles of our belongings. Five hundred and twelve men, women, and children walked or rode in the long line trailing behind him. Our three hundred horses and mules were kept in one big herd behind us.

The rising sun was just a glow behind the mountains when we started down the wagon trail to Fort Thomas, and it was a hard climb up the Gila Mountains to Ash Flat, but the People were much stronger than Loco's People had been two harvests earlier and were able to keep up a good pace. The next day, we crossed Ash Flat to the narrow road up the Nantane Cliffs. The road was so steep in places our men had to push the wagons to help the mules make it up the long grade.

My family rode their horses in their own little group. Banatsi and Nalthchedah had known each other for many harvests and worked well together. It didn't take me long to understand that they had talked often about Nalthchedah becoming my woman again before Banatsi and Maud nudged me into talking to her. Maud and Horace liked each other and worked to help Banatsi and Nal-thchedah by gathering firewood and carrying water. Before we left for Turkey Creek, they played every day, running, practicing with bows and slings, and playing a hiding game, but Maud was fast growing out of the days when she could play with boys even if one was her brother.

By the middle of the third day after leaving San Carlos, we reached the Río Black. We heard the rush of water in the *bosque* before we saw its edges well beyond its normal banks. *Teniente* Davis decided to make camp a few days and let the water go down before we tried to cross. Our People were anxious to cross and begin their new homes on Turkey Creek but knew the teniente was wise to wait.

Two days passed, but the *río* was still high. Some Blue Coats thought it might be ten days before we could cross. *Teniente* Davis decided to cross using a trick he had seen his People use to float in rivers to hunt ducks when he was a child. He wetted canvas and wrapped each wagon so it floated and sent men swimming with ropes and tackle across to trees on the far bank. The wagon ends were tied with guide ropes from each bank and one pull rope for all the way across. The floating wagons were loaded with the People and supplies and pulled across, while swimmers helped guide the wagons, and the men on the far side pulled it across. The boys and men in charge of the horses and mules found a ford downstream where our herd could swim across without being swept away. It took two days filled with hard, sometimes-dangerous work, but we all got across without anyone hurt. Those were good days.

WITHIN A DAY after we crossed the Río Black, a small band of Blue Coats rode into our camp. Its leader rode a mule and wore an odd-looking white pot on his head. On his face was a great growth of hair shaped into two pointed bundles that rested on his chest. It had been nearly a harvest since any of us had seen him. *Nant'an Lpah!* The great Blue Coat chief who had dared go into the Blue Mountains to call us back to San Carlos and promised us our own piece of land in a good place—the place where we were headed.

We were all very happy to see him, and he and his subchiefs were happy to see *Teniente* Davis and the People nearing Turkey Creek. The Blue Coats com-plimented Davis for getting us over the Río Black and laughed at his clever trick to get us across without waiting for the water to go down. *Nant'an Lpah* held a council with the chiefs and leaders the next day after meeting with *Teniente* Davis and his subchiefs and drawing many lines in the dirt with a stick about where we could best put our lodges on Turkey Creek and what additional supplies we would need.

At our council, *Nant'an Lpah* asked each chief if he had anything to tell him. Most said something like Naiche, who said, "We are all happy and contented now that we have good land and tools to help us farm."

Bonito, tall and straight but with eyes that spoke of great sorrow, said, "Yes, we are in fine land. I thank *Nant'an Lpah* for this. I wish he had come sooner. I wish he had come before the Indios with sandals on their feet. The *Rarámuri* came to Juh's camp in the time of the Ghost Face over a harvest ago, looking for scalps and our deaths. They killed or took many of our women and children as slaves, including my wife and children. Now I am alone in this world without brothers—no relatives at all—and it brings sorrow to my heart. I pray to *Ussen* that this land *Nant'an Lpah* gives us will let me bring a new family to life. I will work hard to make it so."

With sad eyes, *Nant'an Lpah* looked at Bonito and, nodding, made the all-is-well hand wave parallel to the ground.

When it was my turn to speak, I said, "Giving us land in these mountains is a good thing *Nant'an Lpah* does for the People. I have spoken with you before about my need, like Bonito and others, to get my wife and children out of Mexican slavery. You said you would do what you could to help us get them back. I know the great faraway chiefs move slow, but it's been a harvest, and we still don't have those we want and need. I ask if you meant what you said about recovering our families and beg you as our friend and great warrior whose strength comes from *Ussen* to help us. I ask for my wife Ishchos, little son Bediscloye, little daughter Naboka, a niece, and two others, Bonito's family, as he says, and I know Geronimo has lost a wife and child, as he will no doubt tell you. Please help us all you can. I have spoken."

Nant'an Lpah never took his eyes off me as I spoke. He leaned forward and rested an elbow on his knee and pulled the left strand of his face hair with his free hand. When I finished, he stood and, looking at us all, said, "Yes, I told Chato when we spoke in the Blue Mountains that I would do all I could to get your families back. The great chiefs far to the east have made tracks on paper about this, and the *Nakai-yes* have answered, saying they know where your People are and will request that those who hold them give them their freedom. The *Nakai-yes* now claim they don't keep slaves, but we know this is a lie. I'll continue to work with the great chiefs in the east to push the *Nakai-yes* harder to let your People go. We can only try. There is no way our chiefs can force the *Nakai-yes* to let your People go. Only *Ussen* can do this. I believe He will. Now it is up to you. When you come to your land, build your lodges by the waters of Turkey Creek, sow your seeds, harvest your crops, raise your families, and forget the ways of war."

Nant'an Lpah's words made my heart soar and gave me hope I had not known before. I felt forever indebted to him and to *Teniente* Davis for bringing us to this land where we could have our lives back.

TENIENTE SET UP his camp under some tall trees by Turkey Creek. He had a big medicine tent where he stored a month's worth of rations and supplies and a separate tent where he slept. Sam Bowman cooked and did camp work for him, Mickey Free interpreted Apache to Spanish, and José Montoya interpreted Spanish to English. I spoke and understood Spanish well enough that I used only Mickey Free to talk with *Teniente* Davis.

The chiefs scattered their wickiups and lodges up and down Turkey Creek. Geronimo, Naiche, and the People in their bands along with some of Kaytennae's families made their camp about a hand's walk up the creek from Davis. Kaytennae and Nana made their camp on top of a high ridge above *Teniente* Davis's camp where he could watch who visited with Davis and who he sent out on errands. The camps of Chihuahua, Mangas, Loco, Bonito, and Gil-lee were but a short walk from Davis, as was mine. The chiefs each took a wagon and, where their women built their canvas-covered wickiups, laid the wagons on their sides to make a nice windbreak for their wickiups.

Our men worked a few suns clearing brush near the creek so our women had places to open the earth and plant seeds for their gardens and didn't have far to carry water for their plants. Out in the meadows, the men managed to break enough ground with the horse-drawn tools *Capitán* Crawford gave us to sow some fields of barley and wheat. After this work—which no man wanted to do since farming was woman's work—our men relaxed, looked after their horses and mules, played hoop and pole, and told stories about our days in the Blue Mountains and raiding and war before *Nant'an Lpah* came.

I visited and spoke nearly every day to *Teniente* Davis, telling him what I heard being said about living on Turkey Creek, how the crops were doing, and from where trouble might come. Already, one of Mangas's wives, Huera, had grown enough corn sprouts to make a good pot of *tulapai*—or *tizwin*, as the White Eyes called it—and she promised to make more as soon as the sprouts were ready. Now that we were out away from the Agent Crawford, we believed we could drink all we wanted as long as we caused no trouble. I tasted Huera's *tulapai* and thought it was very good. A slave in a *Nakai-yi hacienda* near Ciudad Mexico who farmed and made much mescal, Huera had learned just the right times and tricks to making good *tulapai* that we all liked. I didn't take more than a taste of her *tulapai* even though there were times I wanted to get drunk and forget my losses for a little while. I wanted to stay alert and ready for the time word came that my family in slavery was free and wanted me to come for them.

Zele had beaten his wife "for no reason" soon after we arrived on Turkey Creek. *Capitán* Crawford warned him that wife beating was not allowed. It was against *Nant'an Lpah* reservation rules, and if he did it again, he would go to the calaboose. Zele said that *Nant'an Lpah* couldn't tell him how to manage his family affairs and that he would do it again if he thought she deserved it.

Kaytennae, from his ridgetop camp, watched with his soldier glasses every time I visited *Teniente* Davis's tent. Kaytennae was a great warrior, but I disliked him for many reasons—chief among them, he was a troublemaker, his tongue was too quick and too fast to anger, he drank too much, and he was trying to talk the young men into following him back to the Blue Mountains. During nearly every talk I had with *Teniente* Davis in the cool privacy of his tent, I couldn't resist pointing to the top of the ridge where Kaytennae must be watching us and telling *Teniente* Davis how Kaytennae spent most of his time training the young boys in camp to become warriors and was also talking to the young men to get a large-enough group to break out with him. In many ways, he reminded me of Geronimo not long before he left San Carlos the first time.

Teniente Davis listened to my reports and nodded. I knew he must have his own spies telling him all they heard. Some had even accused me of being a spy, but I wouldn't do that to my People. I didn't know who any of his spies were until Geronimo broke out the next harvest.

TENIENTE DAVIS KNEW of several *tulapai* drinking times and wife beatings that had taken place in the first moon after we had arrived. Before the second moon, he called all the chiefs to the big tent, where he smoked a cigarette with us as we sat in the grass in the shade of a great cottonwood tree.

He said, "You are all chiefs and leaders of your People. You have been on the reservation before. Now I probably tell you nothing you don't already know, but just so we all understand each other, I tell you again the rules *Nant'an Lpah* has for living on the reservation."

He was right. We had all heard these rules before. As he touched the fingers of his left hand with the forefinger of his right hand for emphasis, the chiefs and leaders were looking at each other and nodding or shrugging they agreed as he went through the list. But then he got to the last two rules, and there were many scowls on faces gathered around him.

"*Nant'an Lpah* says there will be no *tulapai* making or drinking. If you are caught doing either, it's half a moon in the calaboose. Making and drinking *tulapai* always leads to fights and all kinds of trouble. Don't make it or drink it.

"*Nant'an Lpah* says you cannot beat your wives or punish them for adultery by cutting off the ends of their nose to make them ugly. If this happens, you will spend half a moon in the calaboose."

Chihuahua was on his feet, his teeth clenched under a thundercloud frown, before *Teniente* Davis finished. "When we told *Nant'an Lpah* we would return and behave ourselves—no more raids, no more war, no killing White Eyes—we never agreed to the Blue Coats telling us how to live our lives. You Blue Coats have your whiskey. Why can't we have our *tulapai*? It is our custom, part of the way we live.

"What happens in our families is our business, not *Nant'an Lpah*'s. When a woman isn't a good wife, her man has a right to straighten her out, even if it takes a stick. No, *Teniente*, this is no good. We will not obey these foolish rules."

Teniente Davis shook his head. "No. *Nant'an Lpah* makes these rules for your own good. He has seen that bad things like fights and killings and beating women follow when your men drink too much *tulapai*. Beating your wives half to death is bad, and you know it."

The leaders and chiefs had had enough of this talk. I agreed with them. Although I didn't drink *tulapai*, I believed the People ought to make it and drink it if they wanted. And keeping his wife in line, even if it took a stick of firewood, was a family man's duty. I decided to keep my opinions to myself and not endanger the search for Ishchos, the children, and the others in slavery.

As I came out of the tent, I heard Kaytennae saying to a group, "We never agreed to any of these rules about how we live when we surrendered. All rules about the way we live ought to be ignored. If the Blue Coats don't let us live the way we want, we ought to go back to the Blue Mountains. We don't have to accept any of this."

I saw several heads slowly nodding. This kind of talk was not good. It only brought trouble. Kaytennae saw me looking in his direction. He grinned and yelled in that smart-mouth voice of his, "Isn't that true, Chief Chato?" I looked away and kept on walking. Trouble was coming. I thought, *If Kaytennae's attempt to stir up the warriors for a run to the Blue Mountains causes the White Eye chiefs to stop talking to the* Nakai-yes *and leaves me without my wife and children, I'll kill him.*

TWENTY-NINE

KAYTENNAE ARRESTED

HUERA, A FEW suns after *Teniente* Davis had his meeting with the chiefs, made Kaytennae a big pot of *tulapai* for drinking up on the ridge where he and Nana had their little village. Kaytennae invited his young men to come for a drink the evening it was ready. All the chiefs and Geronimo knew if Kaytennae's *tulapai* drink led to fighting or wild partying among his fiery young men, it could get us all in trouble with *Nant'an Lpah*. They decided they wouldn't interfere with the drink since it was Kaytennae's choice to make. I disagreed. I thought it might ruin any chances with the big chiefs in the east for getting our families out of slavery, and I decided to watch the *tulapai* drink. If things started to go wrong, I would stop the disaster.

I watched Kaytennae's camp all through the night, and it was peaceful. After the sun rose a couple of hands against the horizon, most of the drinkers were drunk and looking for a place to lie down under the trees to sleep. I left off watching and worked my way down the ridge toward the creek. I froze in place when I saw *Teniente* Davis come riding down the trail through the creek *bosque* with his big-barrel gun he used to hunt turkeys. I hid without moving in the brush, and he didn't see me. He rode by slowly, watching and listening, but he had found no turkeys and passed on by. I was ready to go on to my camp when he found the little trail leading up the ridge to Kaytennae's camp and turned his horse up the ridge.

My heart was pounding. If he found Kaytennae's *tulapai* drink, it meant big trouble. He would put Kaytennae and his warriors in the calaboose, or, when they saw his gun, they might fight. I ran as fast as I could through the brush along the creek to the trail he followed, but I soon realized I couldn't reach him in time. I was afraid that if I called out to him, those drinking *tulapai* might hear me and be so drunk they would attack him. He was nearly halfway up the ridge trail when I reached the trail's beginning near the creek. *Ussen* told me how to call him. I made the gobble sound of a big turkey. *Teniente* Davis stopped and turned his head to listen. I gobbled again and waited. *Ussen* saved us. *Teniente* Davis turned his horse back down the trail to look for the turkey on the creek. I ran off down the creek toward my family's garden and nearby camp. Soon I heard the sound of his big gun in the *bosque* and knew he must have found his turkey.

BEFORE DAWN THE next morning, a scout came to my *wickiup*, coughed outside its blanket door, then waited. I grabbed my rifle and crawled out of my blankets, telling Nalthchedah and Banatsi to be still unless they had to run. I pulled back the door blanket and stepped outside into the cold darkness of the coming dawn. *Teniente* Davis's Scout, Dutchy, stood there, his breath looking like it came from a boiling water kettle.

"Ho, Dutchy! You stand at my door early. What happens?"

He said in a low voice, "Ho, Chato! *Teniente* Davis asks that you come to his tent, pronto. Now I must go on and call the other chiefs and leaders near here."

"Hmmph. You go. I come."

Dutchy disappeared down the path toward Loco's village.

ABOUT TWENTY CHIEFS and leaders waited seated in a semicircle around *Teniente* Davis's chair at his big tent. About twice that many of their warriors and followers waited quietly around them. We had no idea why we had been called to this meeting, and we had all come armed after the word spread like a hot woods fire that soldiers had come from Fort Apache and waited in a line behind the tent. The teniente sat quietly sipping coffee, waiting for what we didn't know.

Chihuahua said, "Why are we here, *Teniente?*"

"I'll tell you all as soon as Kaytennae comes. He should have been here by now. I sent for him first."

He motioned his scout Charley over. "Charley, go tell Kaytennae that *Teniente* Davis is waiting." The scout was out the door on fast feet. We waited.

Soon there was enough light to see Kaytennae leading his warriors on the trail down the ridge. They came up the trail through the *bosque* and stopped near a pine tree a long bowshot from the tent door. Kaytennae spoke a few words to them and then came on by himself, armed with a cartridge belt and revolver. *Teniente* Davis stood, put down his cup, crossed his arms, and waited.

Kaytennae strutted up to *Teniente* Davis, stood with crossed arms within an arm's length of him with a frown and a lip-curling snarl, no doubt aided by a head aching from drinking *tulapai*, said, "Why you call me here?"

Teniente Davis, staring at his face, challenged Kaytennae and said, "Since you've come to San Carlos, you've never been satisfied. You've been trying to stir up trouble among the People. Captain Crawford warned you about this before you came to Turkey Creek. You didn't listen. The warning did no good. I'm sending you back to San Carlos for Captain Crawford to deal with you."

The scowl on Kaytennae's face deepened, and he barked, "Who say I make trouble? Who tell you this? I see you talk to Chato many times with Mickey Free. Chato your spy? Chato and Mickey Free tell you this? They lie! Did the traitor Tzoe say this? Who?"

I had to bite the inside of my lip to keep from laughing. *Teniente* Davis was taking away the man most likely to start trouble and keep the White Eyes from helping us. Somehow, he must have found out about Kaytennae's *tulapai* drink, but I didn't tell him. I kept my stare focused directly on Kaytennae. The others glanced toward me and then back to Kaytennae.

"You'll learn who is accusing you and what you're accused of when you reach San Carlos. These are the orders of Captain Crawford. I follow them."

Kaytennae stared at *Teniente* Davis for a long breath and then whipped around and started walking back toward his men under the pine tree. As soon as they saw him, they spread out in a line and walked toward him, making the hammers on their leveled breech lock rifles click as they pulled them back to full cock. The two scouts who had been standing behind *Teniente* Davis, Dutchy and Charley, cocked their rifles and followed close behind Kaytennae. I slid my thumb down to the hammer on my rifle, and I saw a few other hands among the chiefs and leaders move in the same direction. If Kaytennae started anything, I planned to make sure he would be the first to die.

Kaytennae met his men halfway, turned, then walked with them toward *Teniente* Davis. Dutchy and Charley walked backward, facing them, and moved back to the sides of *Teniente* Davis. When his men were three paces from *Teniente* Davis, they stopped, and Kaytennae approached him to within an arm's length. He was so angry his face was a dark thundercloud, and his jaw trembled. "You show me, point to him, which of my men accuse me." He leaned a little forward and yelled, "Show me!"

Teniente Davis, very calm and undisturbed by Kaytennae's in-his-face anger, repeated what he had said before. He reached out, grabbed and unbuckled Kaytennae's cartridge belt with the revolver, then draped it over his arm.

"Kaytennae, you are under arrest. Soldiers will take you today to San Carlos."

Kaytennae's shoulders slumped, and he bowed his head with a deep sigh. Bonito stepped forward and said, "Charley and me, we take him and be hostages for his safe delivery if you will let him ride as a warrior with his rifle and pistol and without soldiers following."

Teniente Davis looked at both men and slowly nodded before handing over Kaytennae's cartridge belt and revolver to Bonito. Then he walked around to the back of the big tent where Blue Coat soldiers waited in case there was trouble. Soon we heard the command for the soldiers to mount, and they were on the trail in three columns down the mountain toward Fort Apache. In less than a hand against the sun, Bonito and Charley rode down the trail toward San Carlos, accompanying the armed warrior, Kaytennae, to meet his commander, *Capitán* Crawford.

Teniente Davis showed great courage that day, and my admiration for him grew from a sapling to a big tree. He had kept the chances alive that the big chiefs in the east would one day get my family out of *Nakai-yi* slavery. As I watched Bonito, Charley, and Kaytennae disappear down the trail, Geronimo stepped up beside me, his long-shot rifle in the cradle of his left arm, and said, " *Teniente* Davis showed courage today. Now that the young hothead Kaytennae is gone, we will have a better chance to have a good peace here. Maybe big chiefs in the east take our families back from the *Nakai-yes*."

SIX SUNS PASSED, and all was quiet along Turkey Creek. Kaytennae's warriors, without their leader, were peaceful and waited quietly with the rest of us to learn what *Capitán* Crawford had done with him. Near the end of the sixth day, as the setting sun was stretching the mountain shadows into darkness, Tzoe, who often did messenger rides between Fort Apache and San Carlos, rode up the trail to the teniente's tent. I saw him pass our camp and knew he must carry word of what *Capitán* Crawford had done with Kaytennae.

I yelled at Horace, "Tell your mother I am back soon," and ran through the *bosque* for *Teniente* Davis's camp. Tzoe and I came to the camp at nearly the same time. *Teniente* Davis was sitting near his fire, drinking a cup of coffee while talking with Sam Bowman, who cooked his evening meal. His scouts and Mickey Free had already gone to their families. He saw us coming, tossed the last coffee from his cup, then, smiling, approached Tzoe, who was tying his horse's reins to a hitching post as I came running up puffing and blowing.

Teniente Davis nodded at me and turned to Tzoe. "Ho, Tzoe. You come from San Carlos?"

Tzoe puffed his cheeks and blew as Sam Bowman stepped up to translate as needed, but Tzoe had already learned enough White Eye tongue to make himself understood.

Teniente Davis said, "You're in time to eat with us. Have you any word on Kaytennae from Captain Crawford?"

Tzoe nodded. "*Capitán* Crawford send word on Kaytennae. *Capitán* Crawford hold trial for Kaytennae. Jury Indians. Eskiminzin jury chief. *Capitán* Crawford judge. Jury say Kaytennae guilty of making trouble, planning breakout. *Capitán* Crawford, he say Kaytennae spend five years in leg irons on little land Blue Coats call Alcatraz in big water. *Capitán* Crawford send decision to *Nant'an Lpah* for approval. We know for sure what happen to Kaytennae by middle of next moon. That is all I have to say."

I had to work to keep from yelling in joy at the news. At least now Kaytennae couldn't lead a reservation escape, and if Geronimo avoided stirring up trouble, I thought we had a good chance that the big chiefs in the east could get the release of our families held in *Nakai-yi* slavery.

I turned to go back up the trail and return to my *wickiup*, where Nalthchedah, Banatsi, Horace, and Maud waited for our evening meal.

Teniente Davis said, "Chato! Come to my tent in the morning. I have something I want to discuss with you."

I wondered why he wanted to talk with me but raised my hand to acknowledge I had heard him. "I come *mañana*, *Teniente*. Two hands before time of shortest shadows, I come."

He waved he understood as Bowman, Tzoe, and he approached the fire. It was a good day.

THIRTY

AN ARMY SCOUT
WARNS GERONIMO

I TOSSED AND turned in my blankets the night before I went to talk with *Teniente* Davis. I was so filled with curiosity, my thoughts about what he wanted to talk about ricocheted around in my head like bullets in a stone cave. Near dawn, after little sleep, I went to the creek and washed in its icy water and then made a small fire in front of the *wickiup* and bathed in sage smoke. I heard my family stir behind the *wickiup* blanket door and knew the air would soon be filled with sleepy talk and the smells of good food cooking.

As I sat by Nalthchedah's fire, drinking her coffee, the sun glowed behind the mountains, painting the sky a soft turquoise blue, and crows flew down the creek, squawking above the trees. She said, "You rolled from one side to the other many times last night. I should have given you a wife's comfort. Maybe then you sleep better."

I smiled and raised my brows. "Maybe so, but too many thoughts about what *Teniente* might want filled my mind. Tonight, I ask you make me sleep better."

She smiled. "Husband, it will be so. We will both sleep better."

Banatsi came from the creek, where she had just bathed, her hair still damp and her skin red from fast rubbing to stay warm against the cold creek water. She awoke the children and told them to hurry to the creek, and then she helped Nalthchedah with the morning meal.

That harvest time was a great blessing. We had all we wanted to eat. There was good, productive work to do. We weren't always running from soldiers or making war or raids on other people. Our crops were growing well in the gardens and fields. With the exception of a few warriors who wanted only to drink, play pole and hoop, or lie around, the People were content.

I WENT EARLY to *Teniente* Davis's camp, expecting to wait while he spoke with others, but Loco and Chihuahua had finished a morning talk with him and passed me on the trail. We stopped to speak, and they told me no one else was there except Mickey Free and Sam Bowman.

When I looked through the big tent's door, the teniente was discussing how to better organize the rations and other supplies with Sam. *Teniente* held up a forefinger, the White Eye signal for me to wait until he finished talking with Sam. I waited, expecting him to take a while, but he soon came to the door.

"Ho, Chato. Let's go sit under the trees by the creek, where it's cool. The air in that tent gets hot and humid quick on days like this."

I nodded and followed him to a shady spot down by the creek. He rolled a cigarette, and we smoked as the water murmured past us and a soft breeze flowed through the *bosque* brush while insects skated on the water's surface, tempting targets for lurking trout. Finished with the smoke and grinding away the last bit of cigarette under his boot heel, *Teniente* looked up and down the creek as he said, "Chato, you're a true leader. Since I've been here, you've kept me informed of what your People think, how well they're living, and likely sources of trouble. From what I see as a Blue Coat, your People seem content. Is that how you see them?"

"Our People work hard, see crops, gardens grow. No shaking sickness comes here. Good water. Cool air. People happy here. Mo' betta than San Carlos."

The teniente nodded, spit a bit of *tobaho* off his lip, and said, "That's what we want, and I don't want to lose what we've gained by someone, like Kaytennae, doing something foolish and losing it for all of us. I've decided to bring my Company B scouts up to full strength. I want to use them as policemen like Crawford does at San Carlos to stop and prevent any bad things from happening. I think you would be a fine leader for my scouts. I'd like you to join them. I'll make you first sergeant. Geronimo says his brother, Perico, would make a good officer. Maybe I'll make him second sergeant. Geronimo's son Chappo wants to serve as my personal helper. The army calls those men strikers. The army will pay you a dollar a sun for your scout time, give you a blue coat—they're hot, but you don't have to wear it—a horse and saddle gear, and a rifle, cartridges, and a cartridge belt with a revolver and holster."

I raised my brows at him. Chihuahua, Naiche, and even Kaytennae had been scouts at one time, but it was not something I had thought about doing. "Hmmph. Good pay and equipment without raiding for cartridges. What I do?"

"You'll be my chief for all the men who're my scouts. I'll tell you what I need done. You'll tell the other scouts how to it. You'll lead command drills. By these commands, the unit understands what to do with one command or the right thing to do when other soldiers and officers come. There'll be bad Indians to put in the calaboose, White Eyes to catch if they're on the reservation, fights to stop, and *tizwin* making and drinking to stop. You'll report to me every day on how the scouts under your command are performing and how the People in the villages are doing. That's something you've already been doing."

"I don't know command drills or the right thing to do when other officers and soldiers come. I make you ashamed of own men."

"I'll train you and all the scouts together, so everyone knows what to do. You just have to remember the commands and procedures and how I deliver them. You'll learn all that by watching me. What do you say? Will you be my first sergeant?"

"You honest Blue Coat, *Teniente* Davis. In my eyes, you have much honor. I be your first sergeant. I tell you true. You use Perico and Chappo, Geronimo knows everything you do."

The teniente laughed. "You're right. I know that. I want Geronimo to think he knows what's going on. That will help keep the peace. When we have private army business to discuss, you come to me at night after all the others are gone. You know what I mean?"

"I know. We speak in secret like you and your spies."

He frowned. "How do you know I have spies?'

"My People see much, say little."

Laughing again, he said, "Yes, you're right. Come to my tent, morning sun after next. I'll have the paper for you to make your mark on—the White Eyes call it your signature. The paper tracks say you are in my scouts for six moons, and your signature says you agree. If I need you to stay longer, you mark a paper again and stay another six moons. Nothing changes otherwise. After you sign the paper, I'll give you your equipment, and that afternoon, I'll start teaching Company B scouts how to act like soldiers. Is this good for you?"

"Hmmph. Good. I come early in two suns and make mark on paper."

We shook hands like the White Eyes do.

TWO SUNS LATER, thirty scouts gathered at the big tent of *Teniente* Davis and made their mark on paper. He approved what was on the paper, made his mark, and then passed out our scout supplies. He made me first sergeant and said I was his chief and for the scouts to follow my orders. He had agreed to take Perico as second sergeant and Chappo as his striker. That same afternoon, he began teaching us basic army commands, formations, orders of march. The training was easy for us compared to what we went through for our training as novitiate warriors. In addition to Perico and Chappo, Geronimo had several other relatives and other men known to be loyal to him, including the brothers Fun and Tisnah and the warrior Atelnietze, in *Teniente*'s scouts.

Teniente Davis told me after our first training day was over that he believed about eleven out of the thirty scouts would be loyal to Geronimo if he decided to escape. I asked him why he thought Geronimo might try to escape. He shrugged his shoulders. "No reason now, but have you ever known him to keep his word?" I could only slowly shake my head and knew a time must come when Geronimo would decide if he had to leave the reservation. If he does go, few will follow him. Maybe then I'll have a chance to bring him back a prisoner despite his Power.

That evening as we ate the beef, mesquite bread, steamed mescal, White Eye potatoes, and berries and nuts Nalthchedah had fixed for us, I told my family about how I had joined the Blue Coats as a scout and would be the first sergeant, the lead scout, and chief policeman for *Teniente* Davis.

Horace gave voice to what the women were thinking. "What does a first sergeant do, Father?"

"Since we still learn Blue Coat ways, I don't know all I'm supposed to do. I do know it's my job to make sure that every scout knows his job and does it well, that the scouts learn to act together on a short command, to see signs of trouble and who does well and who does not, and to tell the teniente those things. He wants to help before there is harm and to stop trouble before it begins."

Horace nodded he understood. Nalthchedah smiled and said, "Then my husband does a good thing. The People will be grateful." The cool night air wrapped around us as the stars showed their faces. On a nearby ridge, a coyote yipped his greeting to his brothers. Coyote waits.

The fire's coals were burning low, and the moon was not far from the top of its night's arc. The deep breathing of Horace and Maud spoke of their sleep. Banatsi was always a quiet sleeper, and I could hear her easy breathing too. Nalthchedah's hand landed lightly on my chest, and, near my ear, she whispered, "Shall I comfort my husband and he me?"

I grinned. "Yes, wife. I much desire your comfort and to give you mine." She buried her deep-throaty laugh deep in our blankets. We were careful to wake no one.

I SAT MY pony as it grazed on the lush green grass not far from a great gate in a high wall that stretched east and west as far as I could see. The gate doors creaked open on ancient hinges to reveal the shining figure of Ishchos, small in the distance, standing in the middle of the gateway under its giant lintel. She held our children's hands, one on the left and one on the right. I whooped with joy and dug my spurs deep into the sides of my pony to race for them. Surprised, he sprang forward and ran for the gate like demons were after him. Within a hundred paces of the gate, a horse and rider flashed across my path to Ishchos and the children. Geronimo on his fast paint pony, like the flash of a lightning arrow, was there and gone. When I looked at the gate after he had passed, Ishchos and the children were gone. I tried to yell from the bottom of my gut in rage and sorrow, but no sound came from my mouth as my whole body shook.

My eyes jerked open as Nalthchedah shook me awake, whispering, "Chato! Chato! You shake and groan. Are demons in your dreams?"

I sat up feeling face water sliding down my forehead and cheeks in the cold night air and answered my woman. "No, not demons, only Geronimo. Because of him, I see Ishchos and our children no more." I listened, but no one else stirred in our *wickiup,* and I was glad they did not know the power of my dream.

I felt my woman's hand on my shoulder, and she whispered, "Sometimes dreams show the opposite of what happens. Lie back down, husband. The dream comes no more."

"Hmmph. Nalthchedah is a good woman."

THE SUNS FLASHED like galloping ponies through the moons. When I was not on scout duty, I worked with my family to develop the land we had to farm. I kept *Teniente* Davis informed of how the People did with their fields and animals and learned with the other scouts how the Blue Coats wanted us to act when the leader gave a command or their chiefs came to see how well we did as

Blue Coats. We were quick to learn, and I was glad I was chief of the scouts and had no other telling me what to do for *Teniente* Davis.

I thought of my Geronimo dream often and what it could be telling me, and always the answer was the same: Geronimo would block my family from coming to me. Perhaps that was why I always found a reason to visit Geronimo's camp every day while skipping others and keeping the teniente advised about all I saw him doing, which was truly very little other than watching his wives work in their garden or fields or talking with Mangas's wife Huera, the *tulapai* maker, or old warrior friends.

One sun at the time of shortest shadows late in the Season of Large Fruit, I rode down the wagon trail from the villages to teniente's big supply tent. The air was cool, drifting through the colored leaves ready to fall. We neared the time when we moved down close to Fort Apache to leave the deep snows sure to come. Again, I had seen very little to report to the teniente. I knew *tulapai* was being made often, and sometimes there were drinks with many warriors, but the People stayed out of teniente's sight when making and drinking *tulapai*. The scouts didn't care, and most managed to drift by for a little taste themselves. Our lives were stable and steady.

Around a shady curve in the wagon trail, I found Geronimo waiting for me, sitting on the same paint pony as in my dream. I reined in my pony and, stopping a few paces from him, nodded. We could hear the murmur of Turkey Creek now in good flow, and an eagle circled high above us.

He said, "Ho, Chato. I want to speak with you in private."

I saw no anger in his face. "Speak. I will listen."

"You are first sergeant, leader of teniente's scouts. My brothers and sons say you speak with the teniente every day about the People and how we do. You say nothing about me, yet I see you nearly every day when you speak with Loco, Chihuahua, or Naiche, but I know you watch me. I give my word to *Nant'an Lpah* in the Blue Mountains that I want peace. I have done nothing to signal anything different since we have moved to Turkey Creek. I haven't killed a horse or a man. I live in peace with my family, take care of my People, and stay contented." He smiled. "Like the rest, I sometimes have a good long drink of *tulapai* but do no harm. Why you watch me so much, Chato?"

I said, "We have family members who were taken away from us by the *Rarámuri* and sold into slavery. We tried to get them back from the *Nakai-yes*, but time and chance stopped us. Our only real chance for getting them back now is for the great White Eye chiefs in the east to talk the *Nakai-yi* chiefs in Chihuahua into freeing our families. I think that can happen, but the great chiefs in the east will never do this if we don't stay on the land that they give us and stop killing White Eyes and *Nakai-yes* wherever we go."

Geronimo shook his head. "I have told you I have given my word to *Nant'an Lpah* to live here in peace. You saw I was glad to see Kaytennae go because he was a troublemaker."

"Yes, I remember. You surprised me, but I had a dream. The dream told me you would block getting our families back. I watch you so this doesn't happen by you stirring up trouble or leading the People off the land we have."

He rested his hand on his revolver belt next to his holster, his eye slits becoming even narrower as he squinted at me. My hand hung at my side, ready to pull my own revolver if he tried anything. He said, "I say again, I have given my word to keep the peace."

I smiled and shook my head. "When have you ever kept your word to a White Eye or *Nakai-yi*? You stay peaceful, maybe we get our families back. I think, no matter how good things are here, you'll find a reason to leave within the next harvest. If you leave, our family members will be slaves until they die. If you leave, I'll come after you. I'll bring you back here in chains and watch you rot in that stinking San Carlos guardhouse before the Blue Coats either hang you or take you to live the rest of your life on the little land with Kaytennae in the big water."

Geronimo's eyes widened, and I could see them turning red in his anger. The fingers on the hand closest to his revolver coiled and straightened like snakes preparing to strike. He said through clenched teeth, "Then you are a traitor. A bullet will find you, or a witch's song will kill you. Either way, you receive what you deserve and die a traitor. Tell no tales about me or the People, and you might live a little longer. I have said all I have to say."

"Keep your word, Geronimo, and you will never know the guardhouse. I have said all I have to say."

He spurred his horse and rode past me, looking straight ahead as though I wasn't there. I watched him disappear in the shadows up the trail. I smiled a little and shrugged my shoulders, glad he was out of sight.

THIRTY-ONE

NEWS FROM MEXICO

IN THE SEASON of Earth Is Reddish Brown, we moved down out of the high country along Turkey Creek to the Río Blanco valley near Fort Apache. It wasn't nearly as cold along Río Blanco as in the mountains, and there was much less snow. *Teniente* Davis set up his big supply tent a hand against the horizon's walk to the fort down the *río*, and we camped along the *río* and the little streams running to it or in the surrounding hills out of the wind. It was a good time to hunt, and the men and boys took many deer and other game to add to the meat supply we were given by the Blue Coats.

One bright, cold day, I went to give my daily report to *Teniente* Davis. He met me at the tent flaps, grinning, with papers in his hand. "I have news from Mexico about your People."

My heart missed a beat. "Tell me!"

"The great chiefs in the east have an answer from the *Nakai-yi* chiefs. They say the *Nakai-yes* no longer keep slaves, and that your People are well and happy, that they can leave anytime they want. They send pictures made with an image catcher to show us how well and happy they look. I think your family must be in one of these. Look at them and tell me if you see anyone you recognize."

In the low yellow light of the tent, with a dry mouth and a pounding heart, I took the image-catcher pictures on paper, pictures of groups of women and children who had been taken by the *Rarámuri* two harvests earlier. As my eyes adjusted to the light, I saw the pictures must have been made in bright light. The women looked toward the ground, and the children were all squinting toward the camera. I recognized them all—there was even Geronimo's wife and child— but none of my People were in the first picture. I was quick to look at the second picture, my eyes skimming over it like insects zipping across a pool of creek water in warm spring air. In this picture, I saw in the blink of an eye, unlike the rest of the women, Ishchos standing proudly, her chin raised and mouth in a firm, straight line, staring directly at me from behind squinting Bediscloye and Naboka. The children had grown much since I had last seen them. Despite their captivity, they seemed to be in good health. I puffed my cheeks and breathed a sigh of relief, and in my thoughts thanked *Ussen* that they still lived and seemed to be well.

I pointed to them, water ready to run down my cheeks from the full springs of my eyes and my throat feeling like I had swallowed a ball of thorns, and croaked to *Teniente* Davis, "There is my family. When will they come? I see others I know too, including the woman and child of Geronimo."

"I don't know. The *Nakai-yes* tell our great chiefs, your People can leave anytime they want, but in fact, they have been bought and sold, and are being kept and used. Their owners will be slow to let them go, if at all. The *Nakai-yes* take pleasure in lying to our great chiefs and getting away with it. The great chiefs will continue trying, but I think this is what the White Eyes call a 'Mexican' standoff. I'll tell you as soon as we learn more."

I didn't know whether to laugh or cry. My family was safe and healthy. I had seen them, but I might never hold them or see them again. "Did the great chiefs learn where they were in the land of the *Nakai-yes?* Maybe I slip down there and get them."

"No, they didn't. You know Mangas's wife, Huera, worked on a mescal plantation outside of Mexico City, before she and others escaped. But she was there for nearly five years before she and others got away, and they were led by a grandmother who knew how to survive in the desert country." I nodded. I knew her story—so did the rest of the People. She was widely admired for her skill in making *tulapai.* She had learned to make her *tulapai* in the land of the *Nakai-yes.*

"They could be anywhere south of the border. At least you know they're alive and seem to be healthy if the pictures are recent, and we think they are. Even if we knew where they were down there, I couldn't let you slip away to get them. If you were caught, the *Nakai-yes* would murder you, and the great chiefs would have to make much noise about fighting. Take these pictures and show them to the families you know who have lost their People to slavery so they, too, know, as you do, that their family members still live."

I put the pictures in the sheath that had held them. "This I do. I owe you much, *Teniente* Davis. I go now."

He shook his head as he waved me out the door.

LOOKING UP FROM the fire next to his *wickiup*, Geronimo waved his women off to their garden and fixed me with a hard eye like one you might see from the wrong end of a rifle sighting down the gun barrel. I showed him the pictures. On seeing them, he relaxed. Like me seeing them for the first time, he sighed with puffed cheeks when he saw his wife and child were alive. He studied the image for a long time before looking up at me and shook his head. "I don't think I ever see them again. *Ussen* tells me this."

"Maybe so, but I keep hoping. You should too."

"Only *Ussen* knows, Chato. We can go on hoping. That's really all we can continue to do now."

"Then let us hope."

"Yes, let us hope and pray to *Ussen*."

"If you want to see the pictures again, *Teniente* Davis will have them in his tent."

He nodded and said nothing more about me being a traitor, but I knew he held a hot stone in his gut for me, even if he thought I had done well showing him the pictures.

IT WAS A PEACEFUL Season of Ghost Face but very cold and with much snow, even down from the mountains and close to Fort Apache. There were visits many times to the trading post, women making and selling baskets and sewing their dresses and men's shirts, and men gambling and hunting and playing games. Among our rations was shelled corn, and Huera and other good *tulapai* makers made much *tulapai* and much was drunk. *Teniente* filled the calaboose with those he caught drinking or making *tulapai*, but many more were missed and almost none of the scouts reported drink fiestas, even though some got an occasional drink themselves.

The fighting that winter was among the White Eye and Blue Coat chiefs over who was in charge of us. *Teniente* Davis told me *Capitán* Crawford, disgusted by the White Eye he was supposed to share command responsibility with, had asked to return to commanding soldiers rather than Apache at San Carlos or Fort Apache, and *Nant'an Lpah* let him go. Some Chiricahua chiefs thought this meant *Nant'an Lpah* had left too, but this was not so.

In the Season of Little Eagles, when warm winds began blowing up the canyons and melting deep snow and the ice on the little streams, and the Río Blanco had little more than a thin skim of surface ice in the mornings, great flocks of noisy birds flew north, and we were ready to pack our things and head back up the mountains to our camps on Turkey Creek. The night before we left, we held a big dance and invited the White Mountains, our neighbors, to join us in the celebration.

Teniente Gatewood, commander of the White Mountain scouts, told *Teniente* Davis that a White Mountain outlaw named Gar, young, fast, and slippery, probably wouldn't be able to resist coming to the dance, and Gatewood hoped to catch him. I was with *Teniente* Davis the night of the dance, and when the moon was at the top of its arc, I spotted Gar dancing with a hard-to-see group in the shadows of some tall pine trees.

I told *Teniente* Davis where Gar was, and with another scout, we edged through the dark shadows beyond the fires and got close to Gar's dancing group. As soon as the drums and singing stopped and the dancers began to leave, Gar walked just past us. I sprang on him like Cougar and threw him to the ground, the blood left from past fighting days coursing through me and filling me with the excitement of battle. The other scout handed me a piece of rawhide rope, and I tied his hands behind his back while keeping my weight on his back. He knew a little of the White Eye tongue and was begging, "No kill me, *Teniente*! No kill me! I be good Injin! I be good!" *Teniente* Davis gave him to *Teniente* Gatewood, who took him to the Fort Apache calaboose.

Gar's pleading drew a crowd watching with curious eyes. I stood, hauled Gar to his feet, then handed him over to Gatewood's scouts. As they took him away, I glanced at the crowd, and there stood Geronimo, his arms crossed, teeth clenched, and eyes staring at me, the whites looking red in the torch light others had brought. He said, so all could hear, "Traitor!" turned on his heel, then stalked away. At least now he knew I meant business when I told him I'd catch him, even in Mexico, if he did anything to stop the great chiefs in the east from getting our families back.

NOT LONG AFTER our mountain camps were up again, the women, with the help of a few men and older boys, planted their gardens and fields of barley. Some of the shelled corn we had collected during the winter were usually planted first, watched carefully, and much of it harvested soon after it sprouted, to make *tulapai*. I reported this to *Teniente* Davis, but the *tulapai* makers kept well hidden. It was only when big *tulapai* drinking parties were held and fights and wife beating happened often that we were able to catch a few who were breaking *Nant'an Lpah*'s rules.

Not long after one sun had passed the time of shortest shadows, *Teniente* Davis and I sat near his big supply tent drinking the last of the strong, bitter coffee Sam Bowman had made for the morning meal. The air was warm and still. Turkey Creek continued to run very cold from the snow melt, and the insects were emerging from the cold days of spring. *Teniente* Davis and I talked about how we could get the *tulapai* making and wife beating under control.

I glanced up the wagon road and saw a woman staggering down a wheel rut, supporting her left arm with her right. There were wet splotches on her hair, and it looked like the back of her dress around her shoulders had wet places too. She stared at the rut she staggered toward us in, so I couldn't see her face. I heard her mumbling, " *Teniente*, help me… *Teniente*, help me."

Teniente Davis was sitting with his back to the road. He saw my face when I saw her, and then he heard her too, turned, saw her, then jumped up to run to her. He was several steps ahead of me, and when he reached her, I heard him say in an angry voice, "Great God Almighty!"

Her hair was matted in blood. The back of her dress showed straight lines of drying blood, black and breaking into flakes like bark on an oak tree. Her face was bruised, one side so swollen she couldn't see out of that eye. The arm she carried had two swollen lumps and likely had been broken twice. *Teniente* Davis supported her around her waist and told me to go spread a blanket for her to rest on where we had been sitting and to get Mickey Free and Chappo, who were in the tent, arranging rations for the coming week. She recognized who was supporting her and said in Apache, " *Teniente*, help me. Give me medicine to ease my wounds?"

He knew enough Apache to understand what she had asked and said, "Yes. Yes, we get you medicine pronto." He helped her sit on the blanket, where she sat leaning forward, holding the arm, and rocking back and forth to ease the pain.

Mickey and Chappo frowned when they saw her. They knew without asking what had happened.

Teniente Davis said, "Chappo, harness the horses for the wagon. I want you to take this woman to the post surgeon at Fort Apache. He'll probably keep her overnight, maybe even a day or two. You wait to bring her back." Surprise and shock showing in his face, Chappo nodded he understood and went to harness the horses.

Teniente Davis said to Mickey Free, "Tell her we're taking her to our most powerful *di-yen*. Ask her name and tell her I want to know what happened." Mickey sat down beside her and leaned into her and began asking in a low, soft voice the questions the teniente wanted answered. Soon Mickey was back on his feet, giving his report.

"She say her name Sons-nah (corn tassel). She wife of older warrior Was-i-tona (Washington). She say beating all her fault. Leave husband alone. Was-i-tona come home from all-night *tulapai* drink. Can hardly stand, he so drunk. Tell her pull up dress, get on knees. She laugh and say even if she did, he couldn't do what he wanted. He get plenty mad. Use stick of firewood. Teach her do what he say. After he teach her to obey, he go to sleep in *wickiup*. She come here for medicine before he wake up, maybe use stick again. That is all she has to say."

Teniente Davis's face was a thundercloud filled with fury. He turned to me. "Sergeant Chato, get two more scouts and my horse. Mickey Free, you come with us." Mickey and I nodded, and I went for the horses and to find a couple of scouts.

Chappo brought the wagon around. *Teniente* had made Sons-nah a sling to support her arm, and we helped her up on the seat beside Chappo. He instructed Chappo to drive easy over the rough places and fast over the smooth ones. The boy nodded and headed off down the wagon road at a smart clip.

I came with the other two scouts and the horses for Mickey Free and the teniente. We rode less than half a hand up the road and found Sons-nah's *wickiup*. Was-i-tona was sleeping in his breechcloth, his other clothes in a pile nearby. A blood-covered stick lay nearby, and blood was splattered on his face and arms. I pushed the toe of a moccasin against his ribs and woke him up. His eyes snapped open, and he stared red-eyed and still drunk up into the gloom at the sticks covered with canvas forming the top of the *wickiup*. He remembered nothing from the *tulapai* party or his time with Sons-nah. We held him under his arms while he waved back and forth, attempting to steady and find his balance.

Teniente Davis spoke to him. "Was-i-tona, you broke two of *Nant'an Lpah's* rules, one for drinking *tulapai* and one for beating your wife. I'm having the Blue Coat *di-yen* fix her up after you beat her. You're going to the calaboose at Fort Apache for the next half-moon. Don't ever do that again, or you might wind up for a very long time on the little land in the big water where Kayten-nae stays now."

Was-i-tona stared at *Teniente* Davis and shook his head. "When I beat Sons-nah? No remember."

Teniente Davis stared at him, started to say something, closed his mouth, and then said, "I'll talk to you in seven suns." He turned to the two scouts, "Get his pony and take him to Fort Apache. Stop at my tent on the way down the trail, and I'll send instructions for the commander at Fort Apache about what to do with him. Chato, you and Mickey come with me. We have much work and planning to do."

THIRTY-TWO

WHAT SAYS NANT'AN LPAH?

CHAPPO BROUGHT THE beaten woman back to the Turkey Creek camp in two days and stopped at the ration tent for further instructions. The Fort Apache *di-yen* sent *Teniente* Davis black tracks on paper describing Sons-nah's injuries and explaining that he had given her a healing salve to rub on the places on her head and back and a splint on her arm so it would grow back as straight as it should. The swelling in her face had gone down enough that she could see out of the eye on that side. She was anxious to get back to her *wickiup* and cook for Was-i-tona. I watched *Teniente* Davis, through Mickey Free, explain to her that Was-i-tona was in the calaboose for beating her and would be there another ten suns. She begged *Teniente* Davis to free Was-i-tona that day, saying the beating was all her fault, but he shook his head.

He said, "If Was-i-tona beats you again, I want to know about it. You come to me. Do you understand my words?" She stared at the wagon bed floor and slowly nodded. "Take her back to her *wickiup*, Chappo." Chappo snapped the lines and headed the horses for her *wickiup*.

No sooner were they out of sight than Naiche appeared riding down the road. He stopped his pony in the shade and, throwing a leg to one side, slid off his pony and walked tall and proud over to speak with *Teniente* Davis.

"You put Was-i-tona in calaboose, *Teniente*?"

"I did. He'll stay there half a moon for beating his wife, the woman Chappo was driving as you just passed. He broke her arm in two places and beat her with a stout stick so bad that the *di-yen* at Fort Apache kept her for two days to ensure she was all right."

"Let him go, *Teniente*. This not Blue Coat business. This family business.

Family take care of him if he bad with woman. We tell *Nant'an Lpah* we fight no more. Come to San Carlos for peace and for work on good land. We no agree that Blue Coats tell us how to do private family business. Let Was-i-tona go, *Teniente*."

"No, I won't let him go. He must live by *Nant'an Lpah's* reservation rules, and I have orders to keep them. Was-i-tona beat his wife, beat her bad because he drank *tulapai* all night and was so drunk he could barely stand, much less do with her what he wanted when he got home. For what he did, I'm being very easy. He ought to be in the calaboose a full moon."

Naiche crossed his arms and stared at him. "This not right, *Teniente*." He turned away, stalked to his horse, jumped in the saddle, then charged up the road.

I said as we watched him, "More chiefs come, *Teniente*."

He shrugged his shoulders. "Rules are rules, Chato. They have to be enforced. That's my job. In a couple of suns, we go visit Was-i-tona. I want to know who had the *tulapai* party where he got drunk. Soon he has company in the calaboose."

I knew that was his job, but it was fast stirring up trouble to do this. I thought he ought to leave the Chiricahua personal business alone, but it was not my business to tell him so.

Chihuahua, angrier than Naiche, came with Mangas (man of Huera, who made the good *tulapai* and was getting presents and money for her brews) the next sun. They, too, demanded the release of Was-i-tona. Again, the teniente said no, and they stormed off.

The third sun after Naiche came demanding Was-i-tona's release, I rode down to the Fort Apache calaboose with *Teniente* Davis and Mickey Free. We learned from Was-i-tona where he had his *tulapai* drink. When we returned to the Turkey Creek camp that night, the teniente wrote out a paper, gave it to me, then told me to take care of the arrest and jailing of the man who had the *tulapai* drink.

The next morning, I gave the paper for the comandante to Perico and sent him and a couple of scouts to collect the man for the Fort Apache calaboose. When I saw Perico and the scouts pass down the road to Fort Apache with the man under arrest, I knew trouble was not far behind.

I HEARD RUMORS that Huera was making a big pot of *tulapai*, enough to make every man, woman, and half-grown boy among us drunk. I thought, That's strange. That much *tulapai*, and that many drunk, will get them all found out and in trouble. I decided my best scout, the Blue Coats called him "Dutchy," and I should stay close by *Teniente* Davis day and night until things had cooled down, and I told my scouts to come to the supply tent at dawn and I'd give them work orders for the day. Dutchy and I put our bedrolls in Sam Bowman's tent during the day and slept near *Teniente*'s tent, taking turns to look around the camp during the night. We were up about the time Sam Bowman got up to start his fire in his stove for cooking. I thought that time of morning was the best—there was no hint of sunlight on the horizon, and the air was cold, the frogs in good voice, and the points of light, in the obsidian-black sky, brilliant.

A few suns after Perico had arrested Was-i-tona's *tulapai* maker, Dutchy and I sat warming my Bowman's stove, drinking our first cups of coffee for the day, when shadows, dark stealthy forms coming from all directions, began appearing in the gray dawn light. I checked to be sure I knew my rifle was loaded as the beating of my heart began to pick up.

I counted and noted the shadowy men as they appeared. Naiche, Loco, Chihuahua and his brother Ulzana, Geronimo, Nana—at least thirty, including all the chiefs and subchiefs, were standing quietly in front of *Teniente*'s tent, waiting for him to leave his bed. A few of the chiefs had revolvers, and they were all carrying their long knives. Others in the crowd had their rifles in the crooks of their arms. No women and children were with them, and up the hill by the camp, I could barely make out armed sentinels watching for anyone coming from Fort Apache. The way some of them, including three or four chiefs, swayed like grass in a breeze told me they were drunk or wishing they had not been drinking earlier. This was serious. I eased my rifle up between my knees and felt the comfort of its hammer under my thumb. Dutchy already had his rifle ready, and I saw my scouts wandering into camp, fortunately all armed.

I heard the teniente's feet hit the floor and him grunt a little as he pulled his boots on and stomped them tight. He came out of his tent to do his morning business and wash at the creek. His brows went up in surprise.

Loco stepped out from the crowd. *"Teniente* Davis, we come for talk."

Teniente smiled and nodded. *"Enjuh.* Let me do my morning business and wash my face, and I'll join you in the ration tent. Go on inside. I'll be along shortly," he said through Mickey Free.

He headed for the brush while all the chiefs and subchiefs except for me went in the big tent and squatted in a semicircle around the teniente's chair to wait for him. I stood to one side of the tent flaps with my rifle and Dutchy on the other. Soon the teniente returned from the creek. Bowman handed him a hot cup of coffee, and he went in and sat down in his chair. He took a slurp of his coffee, and I heard him say through Mickey Free, "Now, gentlemen, what can I do for you?"

Loco began to speak. He was slow and began by talking about when Clum first forced the Chihenne to come to San Carlos. He didn't speak more than four or five breaths before Chihuahua, his voice loud and angry—I could tell he was drunk—broke in.

"What I have to say can be said in a few words. Then Loco can take the rest of the day to talk all he wants. When we talk with *Nant'an Lpah* in the Blue Mountains, we agree on peace. We agree no more fight the *Nakai-yes* and White Eyes and keep peace at San Carlos. This we do. We found all our People and came to San Carlos. We harm no one. *Nant'an Lpah* say nothing about conduct among us. We never agree to White Eyes and Blue Coats managing our private family affairs. We not children you teach how to live with our women and what to eat and drink. We do all we promise to *Nant'an Lpah* in the Blue Mountains. Now you punish us for what we have right to do so long as we do no harm to others."

There was a short pause, and then *Teniente* Davis said, "When *Nant'an Lpah* became chief of all reservations nearly ten harvests ago, he learned *tulapai* making and drinking made Apache drunk. They fight, say their women take other men, cut off end of their nose when women do nothing. To stop this, he says no more *tulapai* making or drinking and no longer make wives ugly by cutting off end of noses. Apache still make *tulapai*. Blue Coats can't catch 'em all. Now Apache beat wives, not cut off end of nose. This not good. It must stop."

I heard a walking stick thump on the floor and a groan from an old man standing up. A dry, rumbling voice said a few words in Apache that made me smile, and then Nana with a thundercloud frown appeared at the tent flaps and walked down to the group waiting in the growing light.

Teniente Davis asked Mickey Free what Nana had said.

Mickey said, "Just an old man needing to leave a meeting, *Teniente*. Nothing important."

Teniente Davis snorted. "I know that's not so. Tell me exactly what he said."

Mickey cleared his throat and sighed. "Nana say, 'Tell the Nantan Enchau (stout chief) that he can't advise me how to treat women. He only a boy. I killed men before he was born.'"

Again, a long pause, and then Chihuahua said in a loud accusing voice, "We all drink *tulapai* last night. All of us in this tent and out, except for the scouts. Everybody drinks *tulapai*. What are you going to do about it? Your calaboose not big enough to hold us all even if you tried. Who goes to calaboose?"

There was dead silence inside the tent and out. I saw faces in the crowd frowning and tightening with resolve and my scouts' thumbs creep up to their rifles' hammers.

Teniente Davis said, "This is serious business. Too much for me to decide. I'll use the talking wire to ask *Nant'an Lpah* at Fort Grant what should be done, and I'll call another meeting to tell you his answer. He's prompt answering my questions. We should know by this afternoon."

I heard the voices of Bonito and Zele call to the teniente, but Chihuahua said, "No more talk. We wait."

The council was over. As the chiefs filed out of the tent, I realized Chihuahua was the only one who had spoken. None of the other chiefs or Geronimo had said anything. I knew *Nant'an Lpah* would straighten this dispute out pronto.

Teniente Davis made tracks on paper what he wanted the talking wire to say to *Nant'an Lpah*. He folded up the message, put it in a message sheath, then asked that I have a scout take it pronto to Fort Apache for sending on the talking wire. I was to tell the scout to wait there for an answer, and he was to bring it back to the teniente as soon as it came.

THE SCOUT DIDN'T return from Fort Apache with *Nant'an Lpah*'s answer all that sun. As the sun was falling behind the mountains, sending bright shafts of light through the trees and painting the western clouds purples, reds, and oranges, Naiche and Chihuahua rode up to the teniente's fire, where he sat cleaning his revolver.

The men stayed mounted and nodded. Naiche said, "Ho, *Teniente*. What says *Nant'an Lpah*?"

Teniente shook his head. "His words from the talking wire have not come. I have a scout waiting for them. *Nant'an Lpah* must be busy. He'll answer soon. As soon as I know, we'll have a council."

Naiche said, "Hmmph. He send answer, you tell us?"

"Yes. I'll tell you as soon as I have his answer."

"*Ch'ik'eh doleel.*"

They turned their ponies toward the wagon road and headed for their camps in the growing darkness.

OTHER CHIEFS APPEARED at different times during the next sun, always with the same question, "What says *Nant'an Lpah*?" They all got the same answer, "*Nant'an Lpah* hasn't answered. We tell you when we know." I saw frowns of curiosity and concern in their faces. Why hadn't *Nant'an Lpah* answered? I knew they must be thinking new rumors were true. Maybe he was coming with many soldiers to take them far away to exile like he had the Sioux and Cheyenne. Maybe he was going to send the chiefs to the little land in the great water where they kept Kaytennae. Maybe all drinking *tulapai* and getting drunk was a bad idea.

Perico and Chappo disappeared for a while during the time of shortest shadows. I would have bet my best pony they were telling Geronimo that still no word had come. He also was getting worried about what *Nant'an Lpah* would do.

Late in the afternoon, one of my scouts told me the chiefs had held a council to decide what to do. Geronimo wanted to leave, certain *Nant'an Lpah* was coming after them. Naiche and Chihuahua counseled patience. They said *Nant'an Lpah* was a reasonable man. He wouldn't drive them away because of some foolish rule. There was much agreement on this point of view when the council broke up. I told all this to *Teniente* Davis, who thought the chiefs were thinking straight and the concerns would be straightened out. Even so, I had a bad feeling about all this.

THIRTY-THREE

ESCAPE!

I SAW SAM Bowman running toward me across the field where I worked at making a big pen for sheep I planned to get from the White Eyes. It was about two hands past the time of shortest shadows during a sun the White Eyes say their god rested, some god if it rests, and so they did too. *Teniente* had gone to Fort Apache to wait on *Nant'an Lpah*'s talking-wire message and had given the scouts a rest day.

Bowman was gasping and wheezing, with water rolling off his face from running, when he came up to me. I felt a tremor in my right arm, an *Ussen* warning, and knew Bowman must have bad news.

He puffed, "Chato... Chato... a man tells me a band of Chiricahua... are leaving the reservation. He doesn't know who or how many, only that he's not going."

I stabbed my spade in the earth, grabbed my rifle and bullet bandolier, then said as I ran for my pony, "I feared this. Geronimo just couldn't stand the peace. Mangas is so anxious for Huera to make *tulapai*, he must be in on it, too. Come on! I'll get you a pony and saddle, and we'll ride to Fort Apache pronto."

RACING TO FORT Apache, I tried to reason out what Geronimo would probably do while the excitement of the chase filled my blood. I knew if Geronimo was leading, then he would run for Ash Flat and then turn southeast for Eagle Creek and use one of the corridors we had used before to get into Mexico. If Mangas was in the lead, being a Chihenne, he would run east and into the Mimbreño Mountains, what the White Eyes called the "Black Range."

We reached Fort Apache about four hands from the time of shortest shadows. We found *Teniente* Davis judging a game the soldiers played where they hit a thrown ball and then tried to run around the points of a square before being touched with the ball. They called it "baseball." *Teniente* Davis saw us racing for him, motioned for another soldier chief to take his place, then ran to meet us.

I slid off my pony and met him. " *Teniente*! Geronimo and Mangas have left the reservation."

He frowned. "I was afraid this might happen. How many do you think have left?"

"They have at least twenty men, maybe more."

"Come on. We'll tell Captain Allen and then return to Turkey Creek to round up scouts and give out extra ammunition."

BY THE TIME we returned to Turkey Creek, the sun was nearing the mountaintops. Sam Bowman, Mickey Free, and I had found eleven scouts and told them to assemble at the teniente's supply tent. I rode to Geronimo's and Mangas's camps and found them empty. I met a man who lived near their camps, who told me that Naiche's and Chihuahua's camps were empty too. If they had gone out with Geronimo, then there must be forty or fifty men out and maybe twice that many women and children, nearly half of the Apache at Fort Apache. This was going to be a long campaign, probably fought in Mexico.

The sun cast the sky in purples, reds, and long, quiet streaks of orange and yellow. Frogs were beginning their chorus in the dimming light as the scouts assembled at the supply tent. *Teniente* needed to pass out their extra cartridges and tell them his intent. The only scouts he was certain were loyal to him were Dutchy, Charley, and me. He thought as many as half his scouts might desert if there was a breakout. He had the scouts assemble in a line in front of the tent and told me to have them ground their weapons—put the butts of their rifles on the ground and hold them by the ends of their barrels. He ordered Dutchy and me to stand on either side of the tent door with rifles ready and to shoot any man who raised his rifle off the ground. By then, it was nearly dark, and Bowman brought him lighted lanterns to issue cartridges.

I glanced inside the tent, and when I looked back at the line of scouts, three were gone—Atelnietze, Fun, and Tisnah. The latter two were Geronimo's half-brothers and Atelnietze a powerful warrior close to Naiche. Knowing Geronimo, I suspected he'd told his brothers to kill *Teniente* and probably me.

The teniente's orders to ground rifles had probably saved us. I remembered my family in *Nakai-yi* slavery and what I had told Geronimo about destroying our chances of getting them back. One way or the other, I would catch him and give him to the White Eyes. I hoped they hung him. I knew now I would never see my wife and children again. I didn't understand Geronimo. He had two wives and daughters in Mexican slavery. Why would he endanger their chances of getting free?

The teniente gave ammunition to the scouts, and they made their mounts ready. Soon Captain Allen, with a hundred mounted soldiers and *Teniente* Gatewood with ten White Mountain scouts and a mule packtrain, met us. My scouts had already found Geronimo's trail outside his camp. We followed it across the rough country canyons, mesas, creek beds, and ridges Geronimo knew would slow us down. We didn't have much light, less than that from a quarter moon. The country was so rough a few horses were hurt, and one soldier broke a leg when his horse slipped and rolled on him. A couple of hands before dawn, we came to the Black River and rested until daylight.

At dawn, we began crossing the *río* and, with good light and soldier glasses, saw a distant dust cloud toward the east and knew we were closing in on them. So Mangas was leading them toward the Black Range and not Geronimo, headed for the land of the *Nakai-yes*.

We begged and urged the *capitán* to hurry, but he was new to the country and to fighting Apache and was too cautious. The escapees soon left us far behind. Two hands past the time of shortest shadows, we came to a ranch on Eagle Creek and stopped to rest the horses and wait for the packtrain, which came in after dark.

The People were now a full day ahead of the soldiers and would never be caught on this trek. The *capitán* intended to follow the trail, but *Teniente* Davis left his scouts with *Teniente* Gatewood. I returned with him to Fort Apache, where he could use the talking wire to inform *Nant'an Lpah* information he would need to organize his soldiers to stop the escapees on the way to the land of the *Nakai-yes*. I wanted to recruit and organize enough scouts to run the escapees to ground and make them return to Turkey Creek or wherever *Nant'an Lpah* thought they deserved after breaking their word to him.

TENIENTE DAVIS LEFT me at Turkey Creek and went on to the talking wire at Fort Apache. The sun was two hands above the horizon, but the western side of the mesas was already turning dark in shadows when I found Bonito near his *wickiup*, sitting on a blanket under a tall, straight pine. He sat with his rifle, gleaming with a coat of fresh of oil, across his folded knees as he studied the growth of the distant shadows on the mesa across the creek. A blackened coffee pot sat on the edge of his fire. He had not yet taken a new woman since he had lost his entire family to the *Rarámuri* attack against Juh, where I had lost Ishchos and two of our children. I walked openly up the hill toward him so he could see who was coming.

I called to him, "Ho! Bonito! Don't shoot. I am Chato, your *amigo*."

"Ho, Chato. *Nish'ii*. Come, tell me of your chase with the scouts. Have you caught that crazy Geronimo already? I have coffee on the fire and cups nearby."

I was glad for the coffee. *Teniente* and I had ridden all day without stopping, and I was tired. I poured a cup and raised the pot to Bonito, but he shook his head and stared at the mesa darkening in the falling shadows. He motioned with his head for me to sit to his left, a place of honor. I sat down, placed my cup between my knees, then pulled *tobaho* out of my vest pocket and made a cigarette. I lit it with a red-head match and smoked to the four directions while Bonito watched, curiosity filling his eyes. I passed it to him, he smoked and gave it back, and I finished the last bit before crushing the tiny coal under my moccasin.

"When *Teniente* and I left *Capitán* Allen leading the Blue Coats and *Teniente* Gatewood leading the scouts, they were still tracking Geronimo, but he was headed east, and *Capitán* Allen had let them get about a sun ahead. From this, I know two things. *Capitán* Allen will never catch up with them, and Mangas is leading. Mangas heads for the Mimbreño Mountains, the ones the White Eyes call the Black Range. If Geronimo led, he'd be going south. I pray to *Ussen* that Geronimo has not destroyed the chance *Nant'an Lpah* has of getting my woman and children out of *Nakai-yi* slavery. If I had him in my sights now, I'd kill him. Such a fool. He goes crazy thinking of himself in the guardhouse, and this breakout probably keeps his wives and children as well as mine and many others in slavery. Mangas listens to his woman, Huera, who makes much in trade for her *tulapai*. He also thinks *Nant'an Lpah* puts him on the little land in the big water with Kaytennae. He and Geronimo ruin our lives to come."

Bonito cocked his ear to hear a coyote yip as the shadows on the mesa grew longer. "Hmmph. Coyote waits, Chato. Either one comes back, I help you kill them. What you do now?"

"I want to get the best men I can into *Teniente*'s scouts. Then we lead them to camps like Bugatseka, where those who run will surely go. If not Bugatseka, then we look other places we know they will camp. We catch 'em. I want to bring Geronimo back in chains. Make him suffer in stinking guardhouse at San Carlos he so fears or maybe chained to a rock on the place the Blue Coats sent Kaytennae, the place they call Alcatraz."

Bonito made a fist and shook it. "I go with you, Chato."

"Bonito *es mi gran amigo. Sí*, come with me."

I ASKED BONITO to come with me to my wickiups, where my women would have good food hot on the fire, but he said I should go and be alone with them, that we might be leaving soon and that it could be moons before I saw them again. I left Bonito's fire and rode alone to my family.

It was dusk, but still with enough light from the blood-red clouds catching the sun's last light to see, when I rode into my camp and saw my wife, sister, and two children eating by the fire. Their smiles lit up the evening as they welcomed me. I was happy to sit among them, a pleasure I had not expected the night before for a long time. As I ate, I told them all that had happened during the breakout and trailing Geronimo. The women listened with tight, solemn faces. They knew what it meant to be on the run with the Blue Coats, scouts, and *Nakai-yes* after us. But the children, Maud and Horace, listened wide-eyed, eager for every detail.

Later in the evening, when the children slept and my sister, Banatsi, was in her *wickiup*, my wife, Nalthchedah, came to my blankets and made me happy we were together even as I saw Ishchos's face in hers and yearned to feel her warmth and know the smell of her hair.

I SAT BY Nalthchedah's morning fire, bathing in the smoke of sage after praying to *Ussen* that Geronimo's escape wouldn't bring disaster to my family in captivity. I watched the sun rising, squashed into a red egg through patches of low clouds, and heard the crows squawking to each other as they flew up Turkey Creek canyon toward the high places and the thump and shake of brush by axes as the children and Banatsi gathered wood for the day. The coffee pot Nalthchedah had fixed bubbled, and, raising her brows, she silently asked if I wanted some. I nodded, and she poured some in a cup she carried for me to use. It was steaming hot and burned from my mouth to my belly but left me wanting more. Soon Banatsi and the children brought their wood, and we gathered for a morning meal of mesquite bread fresh and hot out of Nalthchedah's covered iron cooking pot and steamed dried mescal slices.

After eating and telling my family what I thought would happen in the chase for Geronimo and the others, I took my rifle and walked the short distance to *Teniente*'s camp to learn if he had returned from Fort Apache with news of what *Nant'an Lpah* wanted us to do. I found him sitting by his fire, eating a morning meal Sam Bowman had made for him. Mickey Free was drinking coffee nearby. The teniente saw me on the road and waved me over to join them. Sam Bowman, grinning and nodding a morning greeting, poured me a cup of coffee I was glad to take.

I said, "Ho! *Teniente*. *Nant'an Lpah* speaks to you on the talking wire? Says what we must do?"

Teniente nodded, scooped a last spoonful of beans from his tin plate, took a swallow of coffee, then said, "He did. We spoke several times on the talking wire as soon as I got back last evening. He thought about the situation and then sent his instructions that came a little while ago."

Teniente took another swallow of coffee and said, "*Nant'an Lpah* says he has been trying to get your People out of Mexican slavery for more than a harvest. A few had even come back when Geronimo left. Unless those who left are returned and peace times come again, the business of getting your People back will have to be stopped. The Mexicans will be too angry about the raids and war on their People. They'll never listen to *Nant'an Lpah*, and he won't waste his time trying."

My gut tensed as I heard what I had feared Geronimo would cause to happen. Never again would I see Ishchos and my children. I was ready to kill Geronimo, cut his throat with my knife if I only could. But then the teniente said, "*Nant'an Lpah* knows the only way to bring Geronimo and those with him back from Mexico is for those men who stayed on the reservation to go after them under the leadership of our scouts. *Nant'an Lpah* says if they want to go, then they should go. The army will supply them with bullets and rifles and anything else they need. You're their leader. You know where those who left will go in Mexico. *Nant'an Lpah* says show the way. We'll follow you."

I was astonished. My worst fears and greatest hope had been fulfilled in one talk with *Teniente* Davis. I might yet save our People and see my sweet wife and children again despite what Geronimo had done. I knew what had to be done.

"I happy to help *Nant'an Lpah* bring the People back from Mexico. I know how to do. First, make whole scout company with the best men. Then ask all the rest help us and they be scouts under your orders too. Most help us for a while until their crops are ready. *Capitán* Allen no catch those running with Geronimo now. Too far ahead. Geronimo follows Mangas for the Mimbreño Mountains, but soon I think he turns for land of *Nakai-yes*. He thinks safe in land of *Nakai-yes*. Now I talk with Bonito, and then we find men for scouts and others to follow. I see you at the end of this sun with scouts I've picked for you to sign on the tracked paper."

Teniente Davis made the sign of all-is-good and grinned. *"Ch'ik'eh doleel.* I'll be here at the end of this sun, and the next one or two if it takes it, to see and sign scouts you have chosen."

THIRTY-FOUR

SCOUTS INTO MEXICO

I WALKED FROM *Teniente*'s supply tent up the wagon road toward Bonito's camp. I found him making a fence for sheep the agent said he would give him if he kept them fenced in and wolves and coyotes away. He motioned for me to come sit by his fire as we smoked. I told Bonito what *Nant'an Lpah* had said to *Teniente* Davis on the talking wire about how the work he had done to free our People was in danger if we couldn't find and bring the others back pronto. *Nant'an Lpah* wanted as many men recruited as scouts as possible and for me to lead them to catch Geronimo.

Bonito, still very angry with Geronimo for endangering the chances of getting our families out of *Nakai-yi* slavery, sat staring at me with his arms crossed as I talked. When I finished, he said, "Hmmph. *Nant'an Lpah* sees things with a clear eye. He's wise to make you leader of scouts after Geronimo. You catch 'em. We find many who sign scout paper, not afraid to fight, even if against own People. I go with you." He grinned. "I sign first."

Ever since our raid north of the border two moons before *Nant'an Lpah* came to our camp at Bugatseka, Bonito and I had been good *amigos*. It didn't surprise me that he was anxious to go after Geronimo. I laughed and said, *"Enjuh."* We started recruiting men that morning.

It was easy to recruit Chihenne—there weren't many left. They blamed Geronimo for the disaster and losses at Aliso Creek, and they realized that he and the others leaving the reservation endangered their chances of getting back women and children taken at Aliso Creek and other places and their own chance for a new life on Turkey Creek. Chokonens were not as anxious to go after their friends and relatives like Naiche and Chihuahua but believed they had to if they were to see their women and children brought out of *Nakai-yi* slavery. Their anger focused on Geronimo as the leader. He was the one who made Apache fight Apache.

By the end of the second day, there were twenty-six Chiricahua scouts signed in Company B loyal to *Teniente* Davis who would follow me into Mexico. *Teniente* Davis decided to leave four scouts led by Bonito to watch over Turkey Creek. My good friends Cooney, Charley, Tuzzone, Dutchy, Kayitah, and Martine (who together in the next harvest with *Teniente* Gatewood helped talk Geronimo's men into surrender), José First, and my brother Gon-altsis were going with me into Mexico. Most of *Teniente* Davis's Company B scouts were from Naiche's Chokonens; about half as many were Chihenne. Most of the scouts had been warriors with Geronimo in the Sierra Madre before *Nant'an Lpah* had gone there.

On the night before I left with the scouts, we held a big war dance. There was a great roaring fire, and close to four hundred of the People surrounded it. The *di-yen* who led the singing called to me by name, "Chato! You are a man. You are known to be a great warrior. You have fought your enemies in close battle. We are calling on you to dance."

I was eager to dance. I had warned Geronimo I would bring him back to the guardhouse in chains. Now I saw and heard my warning coming true. I jumped into the firelight, yelling in my pleasure and firing my rifle in the air as I mimicked the way I would hunt Geronimo. After I made four trips around the fire, the *di-yen* called others to dance while I kept on. Before we quit, all the Chiricahua scouts had been called on to dance.

It was a fine night, full of Power from the singing and dancing. When the moon began falling into the southwestern sky beyond the river of stars and I lay down to rest that night, Nalthchedah made sure I remembered her.

I LED *TENIENTE* Davis with thirty-two White Mountain scouts, twenty-two Chiricahua, and four San Carlos Apache toward the Mogollon country in New Mexico territory, where *Capitán* Allen was following a band of the breakout Chiricahua. The country was roaring angry at the Chiricahua for all the killing and stealing the Apache had done in the two days before we arrived, but they were ready to hang *Nant'an Lpah* because the army let Geronimo get away from Fort Apache. After ambushing *Capitán* Allen, the day *Teniente* Davis and I left

Fort Apache with our scouts, the Chiricahua had split into at least four groups and seemed to be all over southern Arizona and around what the White Eyes called the boot heel and Black Range of New Mexico.

Six suns after leaving Fort Apache with *Teniente* Davis, our scouts found the trail of who I believed must be Chihuahua and his band and followed it to the Río Gila. The next morning, we found no one in his rancheria where Sapillo Creek runs into the Gila. We tracked north along Sheep Spring Canyon. On the trail, our men found the bodies of two newborn babies and buried them.

My scouts and Chihuahua's men saw each other at about the same time and traded gunfire until Chihuahua abandoned that camp and went for higher ground. We took the seventeen horses, two mules, and six saddles they left behind.

I took a few of my scouts who had relatives in Naiche's band and rode up toward Chihuahua's higher ground. We tried to get them to talk, but all we got in return for our attempts to begin reconciliation was a lot of smart-mouth talk. Naiche was my friend. We had known each other a long time and lived side by side in our San Carlos villages before our breakout in the harvest year the White Eyes called 1881. It is a sad thing that Naiche was not with the group up the mountain but out trying to take horses for others. If he had been there to talk to us, he and Chihuahua would have learned that *Nant'an Lpah* would have let them go back to Turkey Creek with only a little punishment. Now he and Chihuahua were on the run to stay out with Geronimo.

Moving about the countryside, Naiche and Chihuahua were like insects on a quiet pool of water, flitting from place to place. We followed but couldn't seem to gain on them because their path was unpredictable. It was evident they were moving south and west, but which of our old camps they might use, I couldn't guess unless I knew where they planned to cross the border.

Teniente Davis decided to make a report to *Nant'an Lpah* at Fort Bowie using the talking wire, tell him what we had learned, and ask for further instructions on how best to use his scouts. The *Nant'an* told *Teniente* Davis that from all the reports he had, he was sure that the Apache were heading for Mexico and that it appeared they were in four separate groups. He said he had decided to use two field commanders to go after them. He had recalled *Capitán* Crawford from his Texas regiment, and he would be our commander. The other was *Capitán* Wirt Davis. He would come to Mexico after *Teniente* Gatewood and his scouts had swept the Black Range to ensure all the Apache had left. *Teniente* Davis was happy to serve with *Capitán* Crawford. He admired him and had worked with him at San Carlos. I was glad to lead the scouts under him. He was always a fair man with us when he was our agent at San Carlos. *Nant'an Lpah* told *Teniente* Davis to refit for a long trail and to meet *Capitán* Crawford and Chief of Scouts Al Sieber, with more scouts and a fifty-mule packtrain, who were expected to make Skeleton Canyon during the sun the White Eyes called June 9.

ABOUT TWO HANDS past the time of shortest shadows, we rode up Skeleton Canyon and found *Capitán* Crawford and his detachment camped expecting us. His men included fifty Blue Coat soldiers, their chiefs, a packtrain of mules with their packers, and twelve Mescalero scouts under their old but very capable chief, San Juan.

Crawford and Davis wore big smiles as they gave the Blue Coat arm-wave greeting, each touching his forehead with the edge of his hand and swinging it down to his side. They shook hands, talking with strong pumps as the White Eyes do, and spoke in loud, happy voices like brothers who have not seen each other for a long time. The *capitán* squinted to see my face against the sky, grinned, then said, "Chato! Leader of my scouts, I'm glad to see you. With your help, we're gonna get those renegades, but I know it ain't gonna be easy."

I swung my arm parallel to the ground in the all-is-good sign and said, "*Sí, Capitán*. We catch 'em by and by. The trail long and hard. Maybe some die, maybe not. We work until they return to reservation to stay."

He grinned and nodded, made the Blue Coat arm wave to me, and then turned back to *Teniente* Davis, who followed him under the shade cover in front of his tent.

Crawford's first sergeant of soldiers showed my scouts and me where to camp and where to corral our horses and mules. Not long after we had made camp, Al Sieber, the White Eye chief of scouts who was located at San Carlos, came with a fifty-mule packtrain and thirty-four scouts, most White Mountains. I liked Al Sieber. I always knew where I stood with him, he respected the Apache as men, and he knew the desert and mountains and how to survive in them.

Late that afternoon, when the shadows were long, Crawford and Davis asked Sieber and me to walk with them around camp, look over who and what we had, then help him determine if we had all we needed and wanted on the long trail in Mexico. We talked for a while with Chief San Juan and learned the Mescaleros had little experience in the Sierra Madre. We already had ninety-two scouts, including twenty-two Chiricahua who *Teniente* and I brought from Fort

Apache and Al Sieber's scouts. Crawford thought we had enough scouts without the Mescaleros. He sent them back to Mescalero to ensure the bands we
chased didn't sneak into their reservation. San Juan looked more relieved than
disappointed and promised he would make sure the reservation boundary was
closely watched.

Crawford talked with the commander of the Blue Coat soldiers and was
thinking about sending them back, too, but Sieber thought it would be wise to
keep them and use them to provide protection for the two packtrains while the
scouts ranged ahead. I agreed with Sieber. Crawford nodded he understood and
said he would keep the soldiers to protect the packtrains.

AFTER THE EVENING meal, as shadows from the setting sun turned the long
light dusk into cool darkness, *Capitán* Crawford asked that I come to his tent for
a council. He offered me coffee when I arrived and introduced me to the Blue
Coat officers I didn't know. After his cook gave me a good strong cup, he looked
around the circle of officers in the flickering gold and orange firelight and said,
"Gentleman, Chato is first sergeant of scouts in Lieutenant Davis's Company B.
He's also a Chiricahua chief and, in past fights and raids, has killed many of our
People even as we've killed his. That's all in the past. He knows and has been
brothers and friends to most of the men who left Fort Apache. He's lived a long
time in camps all over northern Mexico. For his own reasons, he's anxious to
get his People back to Fort Apache. General Crook thinks Chato is the man
who can best guide us in our search to find the renegades. I couldn't agree more.
Davis says he's totally reliable and the best of men. I hope you'll get to know him
as well as Davis and I do. Tonight, I asked him to join us and tell how he thinks
we should go after the renegades. Speak, Chato. We will listen."

I took a swallow of my good White Eye coffee and stood to look at the men
around fire. It was strange. I felt like I was speaking to my own People. I said,
"*Nant'an Lpah* say from what his patrols along the border see that there must
be four groups of Chiricahua in camps across Chihuahua and Sonora. Geronimo, dislike Sonora people, he wants camp somewhere in Chihuahua. He likes
the place we Chiricahua call 'Bugatseka,' close to Sonora/Chihuahua border the
place the *Nakai-yes* call "Mesa Tres Ríos". Same place *Nant'an Lpah* found my
camp two harvests ago. Naiche, Chihuahua, and Mangas will be in Sonora and
not far from the border. Not far up Río Bavispe from Oputo my People often

use a place when they come together after splitting for a while. I think either Naiche or Chihuahua or maybe both camp there. Maybe all come at same time. Good place to start."

Capitán Crawford nodded. "I think you have the right idea, Chato. If it's not far from Oputo, then it's on the south-flowing leg of the Bavispe, where we can ride down the San Bernardino Valley and follow the river from its big turn south at the village named Batepito and probably have a good trail all the way to Oputo."

I shook my head. "No good, *Capitán*. The Chiricahua will be watching north up the *río* for us coming after them. Maybe ambush us if time and place is right."

Crawford frowned. "All right. What do you suggest?"

The officers leaned in from their chairs and turned an ear toward me to hear what I had to say. Coyotes began to yip, and a fingernail moon showed in the eastern sky, making the blanket of stars above us shine bright in the cold, black canyon air. I looked around at all who now depended on me to make good decisions.

"We use Skeleton Canyon to go east across border mountains, then south down Animas Valley to the place *Nakai-yes* call 'San Luis,' and go down the eastern side of the Sierra Madre. Good water at Sierra Enmedio. Good place to camp. Sieber knows this." Sieber was grinning and made a finger pistol to point at me. "We cross sierras west using paso Carretas to Bavispe. Go upriver to Huachinera. Cross Sierra del Tigre—I know good trail there—come out of sierras at Oputo. Then we south of Chiricahua camp. They not know we there. Then scouts and me find 'em. Maybe take many captives. That is all I have to say."

Capitán Crawford was grinning and nodding. "Chato is a great warrior. Has much light behind his eyes. Gentlemen, we're heading east in the morning."

THIRTY-FIVE

CHIHUAHUA'S CAMP

WE WERE UP before the gray light of dawn began driving away the night shadows and rode toward the sun through Skeleton Canyon, over to the Animas Valley, then crossed the border through San Luis Pass and down to where the little Sierra Enmedio stuck up out of the *llano* like a bent thumb knuckle on a giant's hand. I remembered this place well. It was where Sieber and the Blue Coats had attacked Loco's People three harvests before. We fought well there, but our losses were heavy. Two of the younger men, Fun, Kaytennae, and I, had enjoyed getting behind some scouts who were pinning us down and making them run when we opened fire.

Our command left the Sierra Enmedio camp before dawn and passed Aliso Creek, a place I didn't want to see, still filled with white bones, beads, and pieces of cloth, just as the morning light was filling the *llano* and making the day golden and bright. The night water that had collected on some plants in the low places made the ground look like it was covered by glints from scattered pieces of silver.

We rode suns filled with dawn-to-dark rides over the sierras using El Paso Carretas, south down the north-flowing Bavispe, and then west across the Sierra Tigre until we came to Huasába, a small village below Oputo on the south-flowing Bavispe. We followed the south-flowing Bavispe north toward Oputo, the scouts looking for trail signs on both sides of the *río*. The land along the river became wider and flatter as we passed Oputo, and the scouts having to cover more land area to look for Apache trail signs slowed us down.

In a couple of suns, *Capitán* Crawford said we were about twelve miles up the *río* from Oputo. We had just camped for the night, scouts on one side of the *río*, soldiers and packers on the other. A scout came galloping from upriver with news that Mexicans had mistakenly shot two of the scouts, wounding one and killing the other. Those scouts who had come in began stripping for battle and saying they would ride back toward Oputo and kill any Mexicans they found. As much as I would have liked to have joined them, I knew they had to be stopped before the whole country went up in flames and Geronimo and the others slipped away laughing. *Teniente* Davis, Al Sieber, older White Mountain scouts, and I talked the angry men out of their revenge. I argued that the men the Mexicans shot wouldn't have been there anyway if it hadn't been for those leaving Fort Apache. The renegades were the ones who had to be caught. The next sun, a few of us went with *Teniente* Davis upriver a short distance and buried the scout.

The scouts continued looking for trail signs on both sides of the river for the next two or three suns. They finally found a trail of eight to ten warriors mixed in with the tracks of cattle and followed them for a time before returning to *Capitán* Crawford's camp.

Under the shade of his tent, I told the *capitán*, the teniente, and Al Sieber what the scouts had found.

Crawford nodded with the others. "That's good news, Chato. Looks like you led us to the right place. How long do you think it'll take us to reach their camp?"

I shook my head. "It's not far if it's the place where I think they must be, but if you go charging up the river, they know you come and will leave in a hurry. You never see them."

Crawford glanced at Davis and Sieber, who were both nodding I was right. "So what we should do?"

"Big Dave, first sergeant of the White Mountains, thirty scouts we choose and me take a couple of days' rations and a hundred cartridges for each man. We move fast, find the camp, and cover it. Send a scout back to lead you to us. Then we catch 'em all."

Teniente Davis said, "I think Al Sieber and I ought to go with you and at least be recorders and witnesses for what happens."

Crawford thought for a short time and then said, "No. I think you'd just slow Chato and his scouts down. You need to stay with me and help control the rest of the scouts."

Davis and Sieber looked at each other and made faces before Sieber said, "You're calling the shots, Captain. We'll be certain the men are ready to go when you're ready to ride."

Crawford smiled and turned to me. "Choose your scouts, and I'll have a packer provision some mules with what you'll need. Leave when you're ready. We'll be waiting for your signal. Good luck."

I made the all-is-well sign and left Crawford's tent to find Big Dave, who was with the White Mountain scouts across the river. After I found him and told him what I planned, he whooped and shook his fist in the air. I left him to choose his fifteen scouts while I went over to the Chiricahua side of camp to choose mine. Most of the ones I chose were friends or men I knew were always cool and able to think in battle.

A packer brought three mules loaded with provisions and ammunition from *Capitán* Crawford's camp. We left camp as a three-quarter moon spread its cold white light from just above the horizon, forming long black shadows. Riding the east side of the *río bosque* with our best trackers in the lead, we soon picked up the trail of the warrior-driven cattle north. It was easy to follow if the moon was with us, but after a couple of hands, the moonlight dimmed as clouds began rolling in from the west, and it began to rain, wiping out the trail of tracks. I spoke with Big Dave. We decided to camp and let the men make fires, boil a little coffee, and dry off. Even without tracks, I had a good idea where the warriors and cattle were headed. It was a place up on a ridge where it was easy to watch the river and wagon road below, and raiding parties camped there often. With some rest, I thought I could find the place in the morning light.

THE GRAY LIGHT of dawn came, but still the rain fell. Our blankets were damp. I was glad we had stripped down to go on this hunt, so the only wet clothes were our moccasins and breechcloths. I stood on the edge of the *bosque*, with the rain still falling through mists, looked in the direction of the trail we had followed, and saw no signs of men or cattle. The ground was soaked, making it impossible to tell if a rock had been moved by foot or by hoof, and the brush that might be broken by passing cattle was already bent over, heavy with water dripping off the leaves, and the distance I could see through the rain and mists wasn't more than half a bowshot. It would have been nice to see that trail, but I was already betting I knew where the camp was for at least one group of escapees—I smiled to myself—or renegades, as *Teniente* Davis called them. I liked the word "renegades" better than "escapees" because it better described the thinking of the men who had run.

We broke camp, and I led the men through the mists and rain in the direction toward the mountain ridge where I believed the "renegades" were camped. I heard some of the White Mountains complaining about slogging through the mists where they couldn't see, nor could their horses run fast if we had to run for cover. We hadn't ridden for more than about two hands when we found the remains of eight cows that had been butchered for meat. I was more certain than ever we were headed for the right place.

Halfway between sunrise and the time of shortest shadows, we rode up into the brush and trees on a ridge a short run down a valley side to the mountain ridge where I believed the renegades were. It had stopped raining, and the sun was struggling to appear. I was glad I had a case to keep my soldier glasses dry, or we would have been blind until our cloth dried out to wipe the glasses clear. The clouds were fast moving away. I had my glasses out, scanning the next ridge, when the sun finally burst through the clouds. I could hear sighs of delight from the scouts as the light and warmth from the sun lifted their spirits. At nearly the same time, I saw wickiups under the big trees and women moving about their fires, drying clothes, and minding children maybe two long bowshots away. I saw warriors nearby as they smoked and dried their rifles and pistols. I recognized these People. I had lived among them since I was a young boy. They were part of Chihuahua's band. I hoped we could take them without any killing.

I turned to Big Dave, who stood beside me, looking through his soldier glasses in the same direction. "You see the People?"

"Hmmph. I see. You find 'em pretty good, I think."

"Yes, I think we did. Here's what I want to do. I'm going to take five men and work our way around the far side of that rise just above the back of the camp. See the edge where we'll come up?"

"Hmmph. I see."

"I want you and the rest of the men to get over to the near side of the ridge below their camp. Wait for my shot and those from the five men with me. We don't want to kill anyone we don't have to. A volley of shots from your men should make them think they're surrounded and want to surrender. If they don't surrender, they'll scatter and try to hide the women and children before they run. We'll get the women and children first and all the supplies they run off and leave. Then we'll talk about following them. *Comprende?*"

"Hmmph. *Comprendo.*"

I PICKED OUT my five best men, told them what I planned to do, left the rest with Dave, then led off through the still-dripping brush. We worked our way down our ridge and up the far side of the ridge where the People camped. The rise behind the camp was covered with large boulders and offered many places for cover. I had my men spread out so they fully covered the camp and told them to wait for my shot before they fired and not to shoot anyone if they could avoid it.

I crawled out on a boulder and sat down so I could steady my rifle with my elbows on my knees. I had an easy view of the camp maybe two hundred paces away and saw Chihuahua come walking out of the brush, probably after finishing some personal business, and step up on a long slab of white rock, waving his arms for balance as he approached the camps. I could have killed him easily at that range but almost didn't fire at all. I didn't want to risk killing him. Then, looking down my rifle sights, I saw a vision of the faces of Ishchos and the children following behind him. It was Chihuahua standing between them and me.

My first shot ricocheted off the white stone on the right side of Chihuahua's right foot, sending dust and bits of gravel into his bare leg. He clenched his teeth, drawing his lips over them in pain, and dove out of sight into the brush. Rifles from the five scouts with me roared, and there was instant pandemonium everywhere in the camp. A sentinel on the far side of the camp jumped up and, throwing his rifle to his shoulder, scanned the brush for a target. The sentinel was young and didn't know what he was doing standing exposed like that. I hated to shoot the young fool, but I did. He staggered backward, bleeding from the chest, and fell off the boulder into the brush below. I learned later the sentinel was Ulzana's son. Ulzana was Chihuahua's brother. Even if I had not pulled the trigger that killed the boy, because I led the attack, Ulzana would blame me for the boy's death and come after me when he could. Hmmph. Let him come. My Power will warn me, and I'm as strong as or stronger than he is.

The women and children disappeared just as the volley from Big Dave's scouts started zipping through the wickiups and tall trees. Men and boys had run in all directions at the first shots. My men sprinted up the hill to catch the running Chiricahua. Besides Ulzana's son, an old woman—perhaps a mother-in-law of Chihuahua, for her cooking fire was next to Chihuahua's—had also been killed. We learned later that Colle had been wounded in the hip, but the men had carried him off, and Ulzana's wife had been shot through both hips. Our only casualty had been Big Dave, who had been hit in the elbow.

We entered the camp slowly and quietly from all sides but found only the two bodies. I sent three of the scouts to track the women and children. Chihuahua's men, then down by the river, called for us to come fight them man-to-man. They said if we didn't come, our wives would think we had lost our manhood to them and no longer stay with us. "Come out and fight," they called repeatedly. Some scouts wanted to engage them, but I said, "No, it's just a trick to get us away from their camp."

We bandaged Big Dave's elbow and put it in a sling until we could get back to *Capitán* Crawford's White Eye *di-yen*. I had the scouts collect everything the renegades might use, which included five army horses, a mule, two revolvers, cartridge belts, three saddles, and food supplies. It wasn't too long before the scouts found fifteen women and children; among them were Chihuahua's entire family and Ulzana's wife and two children, hidden in a cave. They were brought back to camp. I talked to them and learned that eight men, including Chihuahua, four boys, and three women and children had escaped. I thought, If we have all of Chihuahua's family and a wife and two children of Ulzana's, they might be so low in spirits that they would surrender. I might be able to do some good here.

I called a grandmother out of the group of women and children and asked, "Grandmother, will you take a message to Chihuahua and Ulzana down in the *bosque* below us? You can stay with them if you want."

She looked at me with rheumy, hate-filled eyes for a moment and then softened and said, "Yes, I take message. I speak true."

"*Ch'ik'eh doleel.* Say to Chihuahua, kill Geronimo or surrender. Do you understand what to say, Grandmother?"

She nodded and passed silently out of sight, down through the trees, toward the *bosque* where I knew Chihuahua must be watching. It wasn't long before I heard screams of anger and a few rifle shots. Chihuahua and Ulzana were so angry and filled with hate for me that they would all rather die than surrender. From what I had heard about Geronimo's tricking Chihuahua to follow him out, if Geronimo had been there, Chihuahua probably would have killed him.

The old woman returned up the ridge, walked up to me, then crossed her arms, and with a smile playing at the corners of her ancient, wrinkled mouth, she looked me square in the face and happily said, "No! Chihuahua and Ulzana both say no. No kill Geronimo. No surrender. Both very angry. Both say you led the attack against their village. Chihuahua's nephew and Ulzana's son killed. One day, they kill you no matter how long it takes." She tilted up her chin in defiance. "You walking dead man, Chato." She turned away and went back to the women and children who were waiting to follow us down the ridge. I knew the words she spoke were true.

THIRTY-SIX

HARD DAYS IN MEXICO

WE RETURNED TO *Capitán* Crawford's camp on the Bavispe with our Chi-huahua camp prisoners and booty late that evening and next morning. Craw-ford, Davis, and Sieber all had big smiles when they watched us ride in. We had caught the first renegades, and even if they were only women and children, it had been a good victory that would help pull most warriors back to Fort Apache. I spoke with *Capitán* Crawford about how we took Chihuahua's camp. He made a paper with tracks telling *Nant'an Lpah* what had happened and the booty that had been recovered. He sent the paper with tracks by one of his tenientes and a guide, both riding mules north to Fort Bowie. The prisoners and booty were sent to Fort Bowie with another teniente and ten soldiers and ten scouts as guards and protection if renegade warriors attacked.

Capitán Crawford, happy with the attack on Chihuahua's camp, believed that if he could take or kill Geronimo, then the other leaders would surrender. He asked where I thought Geronimo might be hiding. I told him I believed there was a good chance Geronimo was somewhere near the headwaters of Río Aros or on the southern edge of Bugatseka. *Capitán* Crawford decided he would send *Teniente* Davis and some scouts to look for Chiricahua camps in the vicinity of Río Aros headwaters while he took the rest with me south below Nácori and then up toward Bugatseka.

Driving away the early-morning chill, the sun became very hot by the time of shortest shadows. The dawn-to-dusk rides in the high heat were hard on men and animals. For a moon, we covered most of the trails south below Nácori but found no trace of any Chiricahua. We turned back east toward our supply camp and were passing south of Bugatseka when we found *Capitán* Wirt Davis's camp while he awaited his scouts led by White Mountain First Sergeant Bylas, looking over a camp that might be Geronimo's. At last, maybe we would find some information on the Chiricahua. *Capitán* Crawford made camp and visited with *Capitán* Wirt Davis to talk strategy and study maps while we waited for the scouts to return.

As the sun floated to the edge of the mountains before disappearing, *Teniente* Day and Chief of Scouts Roberts for *Capitán* Davis's eighty-six scouts returned to camp with their scouts. They had found and attacked Geronimo's camp at Bugatseka and captured fifteen women and children, including Geronimo's three wives and five children and the wives of Perico, Beshe, Dahkeya, and Mangas. Geronimo's beautiful daughter, Dohn-say, had been wounded, and two women and a child had been killed.

Capitán Crawford, anxious to get good information that would allow him to follow and capture or kill Geronimo, asked *Capitán* Davis if we could talk to the women to see what we could learn. *Capitán* Davis agreed, and after the prisoners had been fed, *Capitán* Crawford asked me to question Geronimo's two ranking wives, Zi-yeh and She-gha, to learn what they knew while he sat listening, smoking his pipe, and making tracks on paper.

I was gentle with the women. I didn't want to frighten them into shutting up. I asked them together and apart and from several different angles what Geronimo's plans were, but they kept saying, "We don't know. He never tells us where we go or when except when he's ready to leave." They did tell us that Naiche and his band were in the mountains to the west, but they didn't know anything about Chihuahua. They hadn't seen or heard from him since the first two days after they left the reservation. Chihuahua was coming to kill Geronimo for lying about *Teniente* Davis and me being killed. Geronimo learned of Chihuahua's rage and headed east, barely escaping, with no time to spare.

After I told *Capitán* Crawford they knew nothing more, he decided to question them himself and stepped inside his tent alone with them. I stood next to the tent door, listening, worried that the stress of the last moon might make him do something to get information from the women we would all regret later. Looking weary and with little energy, but knowing *Nant'an Lpah* was desperate for information, *Capitán* asked the same questions I had and got the same answers.

The cooking fires around the camp burned down to orange, glowing coals, coyotes yipped, and most of the camp slept. Still not knowing much more than when he started and losing his patience, *Capitán* Crawford clenched his teeth, eased his revolver out of its holster, held it against She-gha's chest, then cocked it. Like Zi-yeh, her wide eyes looked like they were holding back water, and her lower lip trembled.

Capitán Crawford snarled, "I'm telling you, I want to know everything you know about Geronimo's whereabouts. If you don't tell me, I'll blow a hole in your chest big enough to ride a pony through. Now! Where is he?"

Both women, water leaking from their eyes and running down their cheeks, said, "We tell Chato, and we tell you, we not know where Geronimo is or where he goes. Kill us if you must. Be quick. But we know nothing of Geronimo."

Capitán Crawford sighed in defeat and weariness, shook his head, then looked at his cocked revolver. He pointed it at the ground and let its hammer down. He called, "Chato."

I was inside the tent in less than a breath. *Capitán* Crawford sat on his tent stool, his hand limp as it held his revolver. He said, "Chato, please tell these ladies I'm sorry to threaten them this way. It was uncalled for, but somehow we must stop Geronimo even to the point of daring to cross the line of fairness. Please take them back to the other prisoners."

"*Sí, Capitán.*"

CAPITÁN CRAWFORD SENT his cavalry soldiers back to Fort Bowie along with the prisoners they guarded. He had known from the beginning of our long ride that cavalry was of little use in the mountains.

After a long talk with *Capitán* Wirt Davis, he sent him and his scouts to the west side of the Sierra Madre to look for Naiche and Chihuahua. *Capitán* Crawford, now only with his scouts, mule packers, *Teniente* Davis, Al Sieber, and me, decided to get on Geronimo's trail and stay there until we either caught him or killed him. Our scouts found Geronimo's trail four suns after leaving *Capitán* Davis's camp and estimated he and twenty-five to thirty Chiricahua were about a day and a half ahead of us.

The evening when we found his trail, *Teniente* Davis, Sieber, and I met with *Capitán* Crawford in front of his tent. As we drank some good strong coffee while the cooks filled the evening air with the smells of good food, I told them Geronimo's trail was predictable. It would go east over the roughest terrain he could find to slow us down, even to the point of making us give up trying to follow him. I put my hand over my heart and said, "But I will not stop." The others grinned and nodded. *Capitán* Crawford decided to send *Teniente* Davis, Al Sieber, me, and forty-two scouts with seven mules carrying three days of rations and extra ammunition to move as fast as we could to try to catch him while the *capitán* followed with the rest of the scouts and pack mules.

We left camp the next morning under a steady female rain that poured for five days and made finding and following Geronimo's trail much harder and slower than it might have been. Even so, one of the mules with Geronimo's band wore iron shoes, and its tracks marked the trail well for us.

After the rain stopped and the land dried, those of us in the lead made progress catching up with Geronimo. But we learned later that his scouts had heard us shoot three range cows for food, and when Geronimo learned we were near enough for them to hear our rifles, he turned and pushed hard south. It was also then that our Blue Coat chiefs became entangled in a misunderstanding with the *Nakai-yi* chiefs in San Buenaventura that cost us several suns because some scouts had to spend time in the San Buenaventura calaboose until *Teniente* Davis could get the misunderstanding straightened out.

Capitán Crawford, angry at the *Nakai-yi* soldiers for the way they treated us, passed through San Buenaventura with his scouts holding the butts of their rifles against their thighs, daring the *Nakai-yes* to do anything else to us. After he was out of the town, a *Nakai-yi coronel* told the *capitán* that the *Nakai-yes* had the Apache under control and that the *capitán* needed to return north of the border. Crawford told him no, that he wasn't ready to leave, but led his men past Casas Grandes and stopped at the Carretas *Hacienda* to refit from this packtrain supplies.

Farther east, the same *Nakai-yi coronel* found *Teniente* Davis. We were then about three days across the Chihuahuan desert from El Paso del Norte. The *coronel* said he had the Apache under control, and we needed to leave. He was on a chase south after Geronimo while our scouts believed that Nana was the leader and, with Geronimo, was headed north across the border for Mescalero. *Teniente* Davis, although not showing it, was glad to leave the land of *Nakai-yes*. He told me that we were about a hundred miles from El Paso del Norte and that he needed to get to Fort Bliss and send his information on the talking wire to *Nant'an Lpah.*

The next three days were as hard as any I'd ever had. We had already been heading north in the desert for four days and were running low on supplies and water. On my recommendation, we walked at night and rested in the heat of the day. On the way to El Paso, we ran out of rations, our animals died, and we had to ration our water. We were lucky I knew where a spring or two dribbled out a little water for our canteens, and we didn't have to fight *Nakai-yes* or Apache. Our legs ached from walking, and the bandoliers of bullets I wore rubbed my back and sides raw. Our moccasins were cut to nothing but strings that forced us to walk a long way nearly barefoot. When our animals were gone, there was nothing left to eat except what we found in desert plants.

At last, we came to the Río Grande running through the big village *Teniente* Davis called "El Paso" on one side and Ciudad Juarez on the other. We drank until our thirst went away and then crossed the *río* to hobble along on a trail that took us to Fort Bliss, where the jaw on the commander dropped when *Teniente* Davis told him what he had just done. The commander said he didn't doubt us but thought what we had done was unbelievable.

Teniente Davis used the talking wire to tell *Nant'an Lpah* that our scouts thought Geronimo was probably headed north and would lie up in the Sierra San Mateo. *Teniente* Davis's report complete, we all took some rest, awaiting further instructions. *Teniente* Davis looked particularly weary and told me privately that the two years of being the Chiricahua commander at Fort Apache and now having chased the renegades across great sweeping deserts and high, steep mountains in Mexico had him nearly to the limit of his mind and body strength.

The night after he told me this, he rode into El Paso with some of his soldier friends from Fort Bliss for an evening meal and drinks. While they were eating, he saw an old friend of his father's. His father's friend oversaw a big company's businesses, everything from mines and stamp mills to big ranches in the north land of the *Nakai-yes*. He didn't hesitate to offer *Teniente* Davis work as chief at the big ranch of the Corralitos *Hacienda*. It didn't take *Teniente* Davis long to think over the offer, take it, then leave army work. He was the happiest I had seen him in a long time when he came to our tents, sat with me drinking coffee, then told me his plans. He expected to escort my scouts and me to Fort Bowie, where he would talk over his decision with *Nant'an Lpah* face-to-face before leaving the Blue Coats.

AFTER *TENIENTE* DAVIS, our scouts, and I reached Fort Bowie, we waited to learn what *Nant'an Lpah* wanted to do and prayed to *Ussen* that he would change *Teniente* Davis's mind about leaving us. The teniente didn't change his mind, and *Nant'an Lpah*'s heart was heavy to lose him. While we were at Fort Bowie, word came from *Capitáns* Crawford and Davis that it appeared Geronimo was moving north, likely to cross the border soon if he hadn't already. *Nant'an Lpah*, happy to get this unexpected confirmation of what we thought the trail was telling us, began issuing orders and moving his soldiers to stop Geronimo from leaving the land of the *Nakai-yes*.

My scouts and I were fearful that if Geronimo or the others could get past the Blue Coat lines to stop him, they would head for Fort Apache and Turkey Creek to look for revenge against us by attacking our families. I knew that if Chihuahua was with Geronimo coming north, he would especially look for my family because I had led the raid on this camp two months earlier. *Nant'an Lpah* sent three scouts to Turkey Creek to help look after and guard our families.

We learned that Naiche and Chihuahua had crossed the border along with Geronimo and Nana. We learned much later that the purpose of riding north was an attempt to get back family members we had taken during raids on the camps of Chihuahua and Geronimo. But seeing all the two hundred scouts, including me and thirty-five Chiricahua, they decided it was too risky to try to get family members or take revenge.

Nant'an Lpah had patrols covering southern Arizona, but they always seemed to be about a sun behind the Apache. He sent a patrol to the west side of the Chiricahua Mountains under the leadership of *Capitán* Crawford and me. When the sun was halfway to the western horizon, we found a trail headed south toward Mud Springs. We tried to catch those making the tracks but had to give up after making no progress against the renegades as they headed for Sonora.

A few suns after we returned to Fort Bowie, *Capitán* Crawford, the Chiricahua scouts, and I had a long council with *Nant'an Lpah*. Four months in the Sierra Madre had worn out officers, scouts, and mules. We needed to rest for a while, and *Nant'an Lpah* agreed. He let all the scouts and me end our terms of work with the army and go back to our families and farms.

Before we left, *Nant'an Lpah* spoke with me privately and told me he had learned from captives who had gotten out of Chihuahua that my wife and children were in the custody of a Mexican in Ciudad Chihuahua and that he had begged the big chiefs in Washington to do what was needed to get them out of *Nakai-yi* slavery. They had said they would try. I told *Nant'an Lpah* there was nothing for which I would be more grateful. I prayed to *Ussen* to let it be so.

THIRTY-SEVEN

RETURN TO TURKEY CREEK

IT WAS NEARLY dark when the council with *Nant'an Lpah* and *Capitán* Crawford ended. The Chiricahua scouts decided to ride back to Fort Apache when I went. We decided to wait until near first light before leaving Fort Bowie with a couple of pack animals carrying ammunition, trail supplies, and presents for our family. I had a cup of coffee with *Teniente* Davis, who himself would be leaving the Blue Coats in a few days.

Blowing the steam away from across the top of my cup, I said, " *Teniente* Davis, I'm proud I was your first sergeant of scouts. You're an honest and brave man, and I know you hold the best interests of the People close to your heart. We scouts are ready to fight anyone, anytime when you point the way. I pray *Ussen* protects you in the suns to come. Call on me if you need help."

Smiling, he said, "Chato, you're one of the best. I was lucky to have you as my first sergeant, and I hope the Power *Ussen* has given you remains strong. Good luck in the suns to come."

We shook hands, good solid pumps, and then he walked off into the darkness. I don't remember ever seeing him again.

THE SUN'S EDGE was just showing at the top of the distant mountains, pouring gold along its seam between earth and a sky still filled with stars in its upper reaches, when we rode down from Fort Bowie onto the barely lighted *llano* filled with long dark shadows from yucca and mesquite. I sat a walk, jog, gallop pace for the horses that ate up the miles without wearing them down as we rode for where Bonito Creek enters the Río Gila and then up the creek to Solomon Pass. We made Ash Flat, the high grass-covered *llano*, before nightfall, and camped near a spring by the trail up into the Nantane Mountains. It was the same place we'd had Loco, and his People, stop for rest and food three harvests earlier.

On trips like this, warriors often took acolytes to cook for them and look after the camp chores, but we were scouts and had no acolytes. Since we weren't working for the Blue Coats anymore, there wasn't even a White Eye cook for us. The scouts managed to take a couple of antelopes before we camped. Others prepared the meat to cook on sticks angled over low hot fires, where we made coffee.

The night was getting cold under the black sky sprinkled with stars as we drank our coffee and waited on the meat to roast. My friend Cooney and my brother Gon-altsis had spread their blankets near my fire and were cooking their meat there too.

Cooney took a swallow of the boiling-hot coffee and said, "Ho, Chato! Do you think *Nant'an Lpah* catches Geronimo?"

Off in the distance, coyotes yipped, and I smiled. Coyote waits.

I said, "If *Capitán* Crawford with White Mountain scouts keeps after Geronimo as we talked in council with him last sun, I doubt Geronimo will continue to run any longer than next Season of Many Leaves. The warriors with him still have family at Fort Apache, and I know they want them back. *Nant'an Lpah* thought Geronimo might come to take his family back and moved them to Fort Bowie. But She-gha and another woman, Bi-yah-neta, had just been returned from the Mescalero calaboose and were still in camp at Fort Apache when he crept to She-gha's *wickiup* with five or six others and took them and his little daughter not more than half a moon ago. Family is a powerful pull. They'll be ready to end their raid soon and return to Mexico. When they do, the nant'an will make sure they won't do it again."

Cooney frowned. "What do you mean? Will he catch and send them all away like they did Kaytennae?"

" *Teniente* Davis told me that after the plains people, the Sioux and Cheyenne, surrendered, *Nant'an Lpah* sent their warriors to the place called 'Florida' for two harvests, and when they came back, they wanted war no more. I think he does the same thing with these warriors."

With big eyes, Cooney said, "Will he do that to us too?"

I took another slurp of coffee and shook my head. "No. The nant'an is a fair man. We didn't break out of Fort Apache. We helped him bring the renegades back. Why would he send us away? I think we'll have time to make ourselves very good farms while they're in this place called Florida. Hah! We'll be rich, and they'll be poor when they come back. I hope by then he'll have Ishchos and the children out of Mexican slavery and with me. Times will be good."

Cooney grinned and shook his fist. "Yeh, Ho."

THE FALLING SUN was filling the canyons and valleys below the streaming shafts of light still lighting the tops of the eastern mountains along the east fork of the Río Blanco. We were about half a hand easy ride from Fort Apache. *Googés* (whippoorwills) were just beginning their calls. The day had been hot but not uncomfortable. When we passed down Turkey Creek on the way to Fort Apache, it was strange to see all the empty wickiups near the clean, weed-less gardens our wives had planted. Now close to Fort Apache, the fields were much larger next to Río Blanco, where our families now lived. The air was still in the *río's* canyon, and myriad thin smoke columns rose from wickiups among the fields. The scouts scattered toward smoke columns marking their family farms, and I rode for mine.

Like several others, I had started a cabin for my family but only had the wall about chest high when the breakout came. I didn't have a chance to finish it. Even in the gloom, I could see the wickiups of Nalthchedah and Banatsi and shadow-like figures blocking the light passing in front of their fire. I pulled my saddle and tied my pony with a reata in the trees by the river so he could drink and nibble at the brush while I crept up close to the fire.

My daughter Maud sat stirring a pot of stew. Its good smell of meat, pota-toes, onions, and chilies was overpowering. Nearby, another pot was steaming slices of cooked and dried mescal and yucca tips. My mouth ran water like a little spring. Nalthchedah appeared to be grinding mesquite pods, and Banatsi and Horace were cracking walnuts and acorns and digging out their bits of meat. It was a scene I had dreamed of often when I was with the scouts in Mexico.

I walked into the light. "Is there any food in that pot for a hungry man?"

Maud's head jerked up, and her jaw dropped. She yelled, "Father!" dropped her stirring spoon to clang against the side of the black *pesh* pot, then ran for me to throw her arms around my waist just before her brother arrived and did the same.

Nalthchedah, a big smile spreading across her face, stood, folded her arms across her waist, then said, "My husband is home from a long ride. Your meal waits for you. Come, sit by the fire, and let us serve you."

Banatsi stood and smiled. "*Nish'ii*," brother. Your family is filled with joy on your return."

The children gave me a gourd filled with stew and a piece of mesquite bread and then, at my urging, served themselves. We stuffed ourselves while they asked me about my life as a scout with *Teniente* Davis chasing Geronimo. I told them a little about my trials in the land of *Nakai-yes* but would wait to tell the best stories until we had a big feast for everyone so all the scouts could tell their stories.

They told me of the work they had done on the farm field and garden and how well provisioned we were now. I was very proud of them all. They had worked hard. Our life was getting better. We stayed up long into the night until Maud and Horace finally went to their blankets in the *wickiup*. Banatsi soon passed to her *wickiup* after telling me how happy she was that I had safely returned. I sat a while longer with Nalthchedah and then went to rub down and move my pony out in the good grass so he could graze.

When I returned to the trees for my saddle, Nalthchedah was there with a blanket in her arms. She said, "My man returns to our *wickiup*. I have hungered for his closeness. Come, husband, let us lie here together and listen to each other and the murmuring water." I took and held her in my arms. My dreams in Mexico had spoken true.

SINCE NALTHCHEDAH, BANATSI, and the children had the crops in good shape near their harvest time, I decided to first finish our cabin and then build a pasture fence for our sheep and horses. I worked for half a moon cutting and trimming logs for the cabin, and then Cooney and Gon-altsis helped me lift them into place. I knew about the hogans Navajo built and used their idea with a few changes to build our place. The hardest part was getting the roof beams to fit together nice and tight around the hole that let the smoke out. Then I had to cut many thin branches to help form the roof. The women and children worked hard several days plastering the walls and using tent cloth and mud to make the roof leakproof. When we finished, ours was the only cabin completed among all the other families. Most of the scouts who had been with me decided to winter in big tents the army gave them as they had done the harvest before.

I made big corrals for the sheep and horses, letting them out into the fields to graze all day before we penned them up in the evening. I found a wagon with a good team of mules and their harness for sale. With what I had earned as first sergeant leading scouts, I was able to buy it and still have money left over. I was soon making a little money from the other scouts using my wagon and team to haul things they needed as the days grew shorter and the nights colder.

Nalthchedah moved our things into our cabin. We slept there, and she and Banatsi began cooking using the center firepit. We labored hard during the day, but we were able to find rest and comfort in our cabin in the evenings. When the first frost came, we were glad we had a warm building around us.

Near the end of the moon the White Eyes call "November," word came that Chihuahua's brother, Ulzana, was raiding closer and closer to Fort Apache and then had suddenly stopped and disappeared. The rumors flew like clouds of long arrows that Ulzana wanted revenge against Bylas and me for leading the attacks on the Chihuahua and Geronimo camps in Mexico. I regretted, and it saddened me to know, that Ulzana's sixteen-year-old son, who was supposed to be the Chihuahua camp's sentinel, had been killed in the first exchanges of gunfire. He'd shot wildly at nearly anything on the fringes of the camp while he stood exposed on a tall rock pillar. I killed him. Live like a man, die like a man. It had been a natural choice for a boy, but a foolish one.

I paid little attention to the rumors about Ulzana until one sun, a hand or two after the time of shortest shadows, Nalthchedah and I were cutting brush and weeds, clearing a field to increase the grazing area for our horses and sheep. I stopped to relax a little after chopping down several thickets of thorny brush that Nalthchedah had been trying to clear a little at a time by herself. She had just returned to me, after moving some of the cut brush over to a big pile she was making that we planned to burn. I felt the muscles in the right side of my arm start to tremble and twitch. It was my Power's way of warning me of danger.

I grabbed Nalthchedah by the arm and motioned toward my horse grazing in the soft, golden grass near the field fence line. "Run! Get on that horse with me. We must get out of here in a hurry and ride fast for the fort."

We rode for the fort's safety solely on that muscle-tremor warning *Ussen* had sent me. Banatsi and the children had taken the wagon and were buying supplies to get us through the Season of Ghost Face. I thanked *Ussen* we didn't have to worry about them.

I learned years later from a man who had ridden with Ulzana that they were on a high ridge above Río Blanco when he saw with his soldier glasses Nalthchedah and me working in the field. He dismounted, grinning, and sat down to watch us while he decided how best to kill us. When he and the other warriors saw me suddenly drop what I was doing and run to my pony with Nalthchedah, they thought someone had warned us and decided to get away themselves.

The next day, after learning Ulzana was nearby, I gathered ten White Mountain and seven Chiricahua scouts to ride with a new teniente, Nordstrom, who with us and ten soldiers followed the trail of the raiders but couldn't catch him by dark and returned to Fort Apache. While we were gone, the fort commander had moved the Chiricahua to camps closer to the fort so troopers could ride to protect us faster.

That night, near the glow of coming dawn, Ulzana and his men—by tracking them that sun, we had decided there were nine or ten in his war party—attacked some White Mountain *rancherias* and killed eleven women, six children, and four men. An old man who was returning from hunting had seen part of the raid and the Chiricahua smashing out the brains of his grandson. He used his big buffalo rifle to send a thundering, angry bullet into Ulzana's warriors and thought he wounded one standing by a fire, but we could find no blood around the spot.

There were rumors that Ulzana had vowed to stay around Fort Apache until he killed me. He stirred up trouble between the Chiricahua and White Mountains for the next five days before he began drifting back to the land of the *Nakai-yes* without his family.

*Capitán*s Crawford and Wirt Davis had reorganized and refitted their commands and were ready to leave Fort Bowie when *Nant'an Lpah* met with them and urged them to capture, kill, or drive back to Fort Apache all the renegades. I spoke with the Chiricahua scouts.

I said, "Don't hesitate to shoot at a Chiricahua—it's his life or yours. The renegades are putting your families in danger. They care nothing about us here, only that they can raid and make war with Geronimo. They are traitors. They deserve to die. Don't be afraid to wipe out the entire band if you can. I and the other men who stay here with our families to prepare the land will work on your behalf, too. You are doing good to support *Teniente* Nordstrom. When this war is over, the People will thank you for what you've done, and the greatest threat to our lifeways will be gone. Go! Take many prisoners. Be strong. Return in Power. We're eager for your return. Your fields will be showing the fruits of your labor. That is all I have to say."

THIRTY-EIGHT

DARK HORIZON

CAPITÁN CRAWFORD LED his scouts, including the Chiricahua I had encouraged to wipe out the renegades, into Sonora. After the last of their dust disappeared down the trail, my family and I began working from dawn to dark to make our farm produce more and support more livestock. It was the first time I had with my family establishing a place where we could live and support ourselves without warfare and raiding. It was the first time I wasn't spending most of my time thinking about hunting and killing men. It was a good time.

Our cabin with smooth plastered walls and a place of fire at its middle and a horse blanket to cover the doorway kept us warm in the nights of the Season of Earth Is Reddish Brown and into the Season of Ghost Face. I was proud of our cabin, and the women and children were happy in it.

Nalthchedah and I finished pulling the brush out of the pasture where we had dropped everything and ran after *Ussen* warned me of danger. The more I worked with Nalthchedah, the more I respected her willingness to work hard and look after our family. Still, she had a mind of her own, and when I told her to do something she didn't agree with, she was disrespectful. Sometimes I felt like taking a piece of firewood to her, but I never did. She made us good meals, kept the cabin neat, was slow to complain, and kept me warm in her blankets as she begged *Ussen* to give her another child.

After the renegades disappeared south, I made sheds for the sheep and horses to huddle in out of the weather and, with Horace helping me, hauled hay for them with my wagon to a shed I had built to hold our feed supplies. The sheep we were given did well growing thick white and brown coats. Several ewes looked as if they would have lambs in the Season of Little Eagles. Our ram thought he was the big chief on our farm and tried to butt us a time or two when we weren't looking. I managed to whack him with a good stick the last time he tried using his hard head against us, and he gave us no more trouble. Nalth-chedah didn't like sheep and their smell. She called them "wolf bait." It was true the wolves were often after them until I killed enough of them near our fence that they remembered to stay away from our pastures.

I checked often with *Nant'an Lpah* on the big chief progress getting Ishchos and the children out of Chihuahua. Progress was slow, but he claimed the big chiefs far to the east were doing all they could. I always expressed my gratitude to *Nant'an Lpah,* only to go away, return, and ask again. Perhaps I was too anxious to see my woman and children, but I didn't care. I wanted them back and had waited a long time for them.

Several men came to our cabin to visit my widowed sister, Banatsi, and to eat a meal she prepared. Most who visited her sat with me by the fire to drink their coffee while the women cleaned up the cook pots, eating boards, and gourds. During these visits, I often smiled to myself. They all said the same things but in different ways. They said they liked her and asked if they should offer me a bride gift for her. Of course, she was a widow and therefore used property that should have a low bride-gift value, but she was sweet tempered, made anything she cooked taste good, kept a clean *wickiup,* and never complained. So they didn't lower the bride-gift value much and seemed anxious that she be their woman. She didn't like any of them and said no. Some made me an offer anyway, hoping she would change her mind, but I said no, and she continued living with me and my family.

I made Horace a good bow from mulberry wood with straight arrows made from arrowwood stems and gave him advice and guidance for him to become a good shot. I also taught him to load and shoot my rifle and revolver. Since I had been a scout chief, I knew where and how to get the ammunition we needed to practice shooting, and I wanted him a good-enough shot and handler of firearms that he and the women could help protect the farm when I was gone. He made much better progress using the bow I made him than with the rifle and revolver. I couldn't get him to breathe half out, pause, and squeeze the trigger when he fired. He tended to jerk rather than squeeze the trigger, anticipating the noise and recoil. His shots always kicked up and to the right from his aim point. Practice, I knew, would make problems such as these go away.

I asked some White Mountain men to teach us how best to shear our sheep, how to care for them when the snow was deep and the wind howled up the *río* canyons, and how to help the ewes when lambing time came. There was still resentment among the White Mountains for the way Geronimo had treated Bylas and the Stevens's sheep chief at Ash Flat when the Chiricahua came to force Loco to move his People off the reservation and down into Mexico. I had been Geronimo's *segundo* then, but now after I had told the Chiricahua scouts to wipe out the renegades, other Chiricahua and I were no longer their enemies, and they said they would come in the Season of Little Eagles, when the sheep could do without their wool because of the warm weather. I also wanted to talk with them about where to find a good well-trained dog to herd the sheep if we took them out of our pasture and up Turkey Creek. Every day, I looked over my farm and the labor my family and I put into it and thought, *These are good days.*

ONE DAY, DEEP in the Season of Ghost Face, I took the wagon to Fort Apache to get rations due our family. It was a bright, sunny day, the sky so brilliant blue it seemed shiny. I stepped down from my wagon and had just anchored my team when *Teniente* James Lockett, who had replaced *Teniente* Gatewood, saw me and waved a hand for me to wait as he came crunching toward me on the frozen ground. He had a sour face, and I wondered what had happened. As he approached, he said, "Chato! Have you heard the news?"

I didn't know what news he was talking about and shook my head. "No, *Teniente* Lockett, I hear nothing."

"A talking-wire message has come from *Nant'an Lpah.* A few suns ago, Captain Crawford attacked and overran Geronimo's camp in the Espinosa del Diablo (Devil's Backbone) Range in Sonora. The Chiricahua took off to the other side of the river and then decided they wanted to talk peace with him, but before they could meet the next day, *Rarámuri* Indians, Mexican militia under Mauricio Corredor, attacked the scouts looking for scalps."

I clenched my teeth in fury. "Corredor! He's the snake the *Nakai-yes* say killed Victorio. He's a lying thief. Victorio killed himself after he ran out of bullets. I hope Corredor was killed."

The teniente nodded. "He was killed, but there's bad news. At the beginning of the fight, Crawford thought the attack was a mistake. He crawled up on a rock in plain view, waving a white flag, and they killed him. Shot him in the head. The scouts poured the lead to them. Killed all the Mexican officers, including Corredor. Lieutenant Maus is leading the troops and scouts on their way back. They had to bury Crawford's body at Nácori Chico until they can send someone to retrieve it for a proper military burial. Maus had a parley with Geronimo and Naiche. They gave him nine Chiricahua hostages, including Nana, two wives and a child belonging to Geronimo, and some of Naiche's family, to guarantee that they wanted to talk to *Nant'an Lpah* about full surrender near San Bernardino crossing in two moons."

He paused for a moment, staring at the muddy road, and shook his head. "Damn, I hate to see Crawford gone, but it looks like the war may be about over. We may have gained a peace, but we lost a great officer and a gentleman."

I stared at *Teniente* Lockett, not knowing what to say. *Capitán* Crawford was a true Chiricahua friend. Now he rode the ghost pony to the Happy Land. I hoped his journey was fast. I said what was true. "This a black day for the Chiricahua. *Capitán* Crawford fair and treat us good when he reservation agent or commander on trail after renegades. He great chief. He listen to scouts. He win many battles. I pray to *Ussen* to help him hurry to the Happy Land."

Teniente Lockett nodded and said one of the few Apache words he knew: *"Enjuh."* He left me standing there wondering if peace was at last coming. Knowing Geronimo, I doubted it.

EPILOGUE

CHATO'S DOUBTS WERE fulfilled. Geronimo and the other renegade Chiricahua surrendered to General Crook twelve miles south of the border at Canyon de los Embudos in late March 1886. Within two days, still three miles south of the border, Geronimo and Naiche with thirty-eight followers rejected the surrender terms and left the main band late in the night to remain at war and raiding in northern Mexico.

The main band of seventy-seven men, women, and children were shipped to Fort Marion *(Castillo de San Marcos)* in Saint Augustine, Florida, for their captivity as prisoners of war. The Geronimo-Naiche band raided on both sides of the border for the next five months. Immediately after the Geronimo-Naiche band broke away, the army replaced General Crook with General Nelson A. Miles. The Geronimo-Naiche band surrendered to General Miles on September 4, 1886, after he offered to take them to their families and give them their own reservation. General Sheridan, Commanding General of the Army, turned Miles's offer into a lie. The men were sent to Fort Pickens on Santa Rosa Island in Pensacola Bay, their women and children to Fort Marion.

In the summer of 1886, the Secretaries of the Interior and War recommended designating all Chiricahua as prisoners of war and sending them to Florida with the renegades. President Grover Cleveland agreed. General Miles asked Chato to lead a delegation of ten men and three women from Fort Apache to ask the president to let the scouts who hunted Geronimo for the army and those who remained peaceful stay on the reservation. After meeting with President Cleveland, the delegation believed they would stay on their farms at Fort Apache. Chato was given a big silver medal by the president in recognition of his service and a letter that said they had come to Washington. But in one of the most shameful episodes in United States history, Chato and his delegation, thinking they were returning to Arizona, were rerouted to join the exiled renegades as prisoners of war at Fort Marion. A month later, they were joined by the Chiricahua from the reservation. They were prisoners of war for the next twenty-seven years.

When the government released the Chiricahua from their captivity in 1913. Seventy percent chose to move to the Mescalero Reservation in New Mexico. The remainder moved to farms in the Fort Sill, Oklahoma, area. During the early years after their release, the vitriol grew between the old Chiricahua war and peace factions at Mescalero. Geronimo had accused Chato of being a liar and a traitor, and the war-faction Chiricahua spoke that condemnation openly. Eventually, many Mescaleros came to believe the war-faction claims and treated Chato as an outcast.

Chato became a bitter old man, betrayed by the government he had served and the People he loved. He chose to live high in the reservation mountains with his wife, separated from both the Chiricahua and Mescalero communities. He never understood why the president had given him a big silver medal for his service and then made him a prisoner of war.

In late summer 1934, Chato's T-Model ran into and overturned in an irrigation ditch, where, trapped, he spent hours in cold water before being found and carried to the Apache hospital at Mescalero. He had two broken ribs and a broken clavicle. From the long soak in cold water he developed lobar pneumonia. He died two weeks after lying in the irrigation ditch.

The second book in the Chato duology, Proud Outcast, tells the story of Chato's struggle to survive as a prisoner of war in the years after Geronimo surrendered and in the years after the Chiricahua were released from their captivity. It is a story of courage and endurance by a man, unjustly shunned by his People, who kept his honor trying to do the right thing for them.

ADDITIONAL READING

Ball, Eve, *In the Days of Victorio: Recollections of a Warm Springs Apache,* University of Arizona Press, Tucson, AZ, 1970.

Ball, Eve, Lynda A. Sánchez, and Nora Henn, *Indeh: An Apache Odyssey,* University of Oklahoma Press, Norman, OK, 1988.

Barrett, S. M., *Geronimo, His Own Story: The Autobiography of a Great Patriot Warrior,* Meridian, Penguin Books USA, New York, 1996.

Bourke, John G., *An Apache Campaign in the Sierra Madre,* University of Nebraska Press, Lincoln, NE, 1987. Reprinted from the 1886 edition published by Charles Scribner and Sons.

Bourke, John G., *On the Border With Crook,* Charles Scribner's Sons, New York, 1891.

Cozzens, Peter, *The Earth Is Weeping,* Alfred A. Knopf, New York, 2016.

Cremony, John C., *Life Among the Apaches,* University of Nebraska Press, Lincoln, NE, 1983.

de la Garza, Phyllis, *The Apache Kid,* Westernlore Press, Tucson, AZ, 1995.

Debo, Angie, *Geronimo: The Man, His Time, His Place,* University of Oklahoma Press, Norman, OK, 1976.

Delgadillo, Alicia with Miriam A. Perrett, *From Fort Marion to Fort Sill,* University of Nebraska Press, Lincoln, NE, 2013.

Farmer, W. Michael, *Apacheria: True Stories of Apache Culture 1860–1920,* Two Dot, Guilford, CT, 2017.

Farmer, W. Michael, *Geronimo, Prisoner of Lies: Twenty-Three Years as a Prisoner of War, 1886–1909,* Two Dot, Guilford, CT, 2019.

Goodwin, Grenville, *The Social Organization of the Western Apache,* Original Edition Copyright 1942 by the Department of Anthropology, University of Chicago, Century Collection edition by the University of Arizona Press, Tucson, AZ, 2016.

Haley, James L., *Apaches: A History and Culture Portrait,* University of Oklahoma Press, Norman, OK, 1981.

Hutton, Paul Andrew, *The Apache Wars,* Crown Publishing Group, New York, 2016.

Mails, Thomas E., *The People Called Apache,* BDD Illustrated Books, New York, 1993.

Opler, Morris Edward, *An Apache Life-Way, The Economic, Social, and Religious Institutions of the Chiricahua Indians,* University of Nebraska Press, Lincoln, NE, 1996.

Opler, Morris, *Apache Odyssey, A Journey Between Two Worlds,* University of Nebraska Press, Lincoln, NE, 2002.

Robinson, Sherry, *Apache Voices: Their Stories of Survival as Told to Eve Ball,* University of New Mexico Press, Albuquerque, NM, 2003.

Sánchez, Lynda A., *Apache Legends and Lore of Southern New Mexico, From the Sacred Mountain,* The History Press, Charleston, SC, 2014.

Sweeney, Edwin, *From Cochise to Geronimo: The Chiricahua Apaches, 1874–1886,* University of Oklahoma Press, Norman, OK, 2010.

Thrapp, Dan L., *Al Sieber: Chief of Scouts,* University of Oklahoma Press, Norman, OK, 1964.

Thrapp, Dan L., *The Conquest of Apacheria,* University of Oklahoma Press, Norman, OK, 1967.

Utley, Robert M., *Geronimo,* Yale University Press, New Haven, CT, 2012.

Worchester, Donald E., *The Apaches: Eagles of the Southwest,* University of Oklahoma Press, Norman, OK, 1992.

W. MICHAEL FARMER combines fifteen-plus years of research into nine-teenth-century Apache history and culture with Southwest-living experience to fill his stories with a genuine sense of time and place. A retired PhD physicist, his scientific research has included measurement of atmospheric aerosols with laser-based instruments. He has published a two-volume reference book on atmospheric effects on remote sensing as well as fiction in anthologies and award-winning essays. His novels have won numerous awards, including three Will Rogers Gold and five Silver Medallions, New Mexico-Arizona Book Awards for Literary, Adventure, Historical Fiction, a Non-Fiction New Mexico Book of the Year, and a Spur Finalist Award for Best First Novel. His book series includes *The Life and Times of Yellow Boy, Mescalero Apache* and *Legends of the Desert*. His nonfiction books include *Apacheria, True Stories of Apache Culture 1860-1920* and *Geronimo, Prisoner of Lies*. His most recent novels are the award-winning *The Odyssey of Geronimo, Twenty-Three years a Prisoner of War, The Iliad of Geronimo, A Song of Blood and Fire*, and *Trini! Come! Geronimo's Captivity of Trinidad Verdin*.